Gold Coast

Copyright © 2026 by Rylee Stagg

All rights reserved.

No part of this publication may be reproduced, distributed, or transmitted in any form or by any means, including photocopying, recording, or other electronic or mechanical methods, without the prior written permission of the author, except as permitted by U.S. copyright law.

The story, all names, characters, and incidents portrayed in this book are fictitious. Any resemblance to actual persons (living or deceased), places, buildings, or products is purely coincidental.

ISBN: 979-8-9951914-0-7

E-book ISBN: 979-8-9951914-1-4

Cover design by Lindy Blair

<u>Statement of Authenticity</u>

No part of this book was written, edited, or designed with the aid of generative artificial intelligence. All ideas are original and are a product of real human brainstorming, intellect, and creativity to ensure an authentic reader experience.

To my family,
I love you all so much. Thank you for believing in me.

Little star, little wonder
Little drop in nature's thunder
One slight slip, one little blunder
Will it throw you there asunder?
Perhaps it drags you down below
Perhaps it marks your time to go
But can you see it? Can you bear it?
Can you stand to lose your merit?
What will they do? What will they say?
Little star, fading away.

Little star, shining bright
Can you see past your own light?
Can you see the planets 'round
And can you see what's on the ground?
Do you see the rocks ahead?
Do you know who wants you dead?
You've come so far, you little star,
But far from home is what you are.

1

Warren

Kearon Romney kept the key to my life around his neck.

It wasn't flashy, but it hung from a rusty steel chain and rested against his heart. He's told me many have asked to look at it, but I specifically instructed him to wear it at all times, which is a promise he's kept well.

I did not tell him what to do if someone discovered what the key unlocked.

The oil-lit flames in the lampposts are dim as I sprint through Lexington's twisty streets, my boots slipping on the damp gravel. The crumbling cobblestone of the blacksmith's shop and rickety, moss-rotted buildings are nothing more than a blur in my vision as I pass.

Please, I silently beg. *Please tell me I haven't missed him.*

My legs tremble as I race up the hill to the Romney residence, which is nothing more than a moldy shack overlooking the town. I pound on the door with both fists as I glance out at the harbor, where a mighty galleon is moored about a hundred yards from the dock as it towers over Lexington's puny ships. A red, yellow, and blue striped flag whips atop the ship in the wind as a single dinghy cuts through the inky black water.

The gray-coated sailors aboard row under the dewy light of a lantern fixed to a wooden pole at the bow, but they don't make my stomach churn—their leader in her red coat does, crouching in the back of the boat as she stares at the dilapidated town ahead.

The shack's door creaks open, snatching my attention and staunching my anger as Rebecca Romney gasps and smiles at me. "Mr. Chadwick! What a nice surprise!"

"Where is your son?" I pant, gripping the splintered doorframe. A bead of sweat rolls off my nose. "Is he here?"

Rebecca opens her mouth as her bright green eyes flick between my red face and sweat-drenched blond hair. "He just left for the Green Sailor. Why?"

No.

I twist back just in time to see the soldiers race up the shore and into the city, led by their red-coated monster. My chest swells with hot, angry panic.

"What's going on?" Kearon's burly father storms toward the door as he buttons his grease-stained shirt.

"Call the authorities," I blurt, my shoulders rising and falling with panicked breaths as I turn the rest of my body to run down the hill. "You must—"

"Is Kearon all right?" Rebecca grabs my forearm before I can move. "He said he was—"

"It doesn't matter. Send the authorities to the bar." I break into a dead sprint down the hill. "Hurry! Go!"

I nearly slip in the mud at the bottom of the hill, but the pieces fall into place in my mind without error. Tiny, pathetic Lexington would never be useful unless its mighty northern neighbors wanted something. Padstow's Armada would be welcomed with an entourage of military personnel, and they most certainly would not drop anchor a hundred yards offshore and sneak into the city like thieves in the night.

Not thieves. Hunters.

They shouldn't have known I was here.

Who betrayed me? How did they know?

It doesn't matter, because no one is around to witness the crime that's about to take place.

A thousand questions race through my mind as I jog to a stop, snatching the pistol that's strapped to my ribs and hiding behind a sagging brick wall. I wipe the sleeve of my black coat across my forehead and peer around the wall, staring at the Green Sailor and praying to any god who will listen that I am not too late.

But the door to the bar is already open, and three armed soldiers stand underneath the building's creaky wooden sign. I turn on my heel and race around the block, and to my luck, the back of the stone structure is unguarded. I crouch as the sound of voices echoes through the open windows.

"—think you're protecting him, but you aren't," a sharp voice snaps. "Where is he?"

That voice. I can picture its owner in my mind as clear as a portrait. Gold hair, gold eyes, gold buttons, and gold embroidery on a shiny red coat.

Padstow's golden girl always looks lovely in red.

I dare to steal a glance through the window as Emery Walker storms into view, emerging from the closet that leads to the bar's basement stairs. Her knuckles are white on the hilt of her silver cutlass, and a flintlock pistol rests in the holster on her hip. Her other fist is clenched around Kearon's necklace, and the vault key dangles from her slender fingers.

I flinch as two soldiers haul Kearon up the stairs and shove him onto the dusty floor, where he tumbles into a chair. His ashy brown hair hangs limp down his face as he scrambles to his feet, and two soldiers point their rifles at his chest.

A third emerges with Kearon's leather logbook.

Dread drips between my ribs as he flips the pages, scanning through the names of my business partners and a count of the money I've exchanged with them.

My trigger finger twitches.

"I don't know where he is!" Kearon's panicked voice tugs at my heart. "P-please—"

"Do *not* play stupid with me," Emery spits, holding up the key and advancing on him with a manic sheen in her eyes, like a wolf stalking its prey. Strands of her wavy blonde hair are plastered to the sides of her face with sweat. "People who know nothing wouldn't have their hands in a criminal's vault, so don't you dare lie to me."

"I'm not!" Kearon sobs, his hands trembling as he raises them in surrender. "He just asked me to manage his money. I didn't do—"

My heart freezes as she strikes him across the jaw with the hilt of her sword, and he stumbles back into the arms of two more gray-coated soldiers.

"Fine," she snaps, sheathing the sword. "Maybe you'll change your mind after sitting in a cell for a few days and shouldering a piracy charge."

Piracy.

I stay crouched, my muscles burning as I dart behind a nearby palm tree a mere second before Emery and the other soldiers exit the Green Sailor. I frantically search the street, praying that Lexington's law enforcement will jump from the shadows, praying that someone takes aim and shoots the golden girl before she can walk away.

But neither happens. The only sounds are Kearon's hysterical pleas that echo through the empty night as he's dragged from the bar. One of the soldiers jams a thick wad of canvas into his mouth as the other retrieves a pair of shackles from his belt.

My hands tremble. *Please. Please.*

Two more soldiers emerge from the building, hauling a pair of massive leather sacks that jingle with shiny nova coins.

My body screams as I helplessly watch.

But I am not the only one.

I close my eyes as Rebecca's sobs pierce the air in the distance.

"My boy!" she wails. "Where are they taking my boy?"

2

"Shining Star! Shining Star! Today's a great day for history, ladies and gentlemen. The city of Padstow and its Armada are getting ready to induct their youngest captain in over a century, twenty-year-old Emery Walker. All are invited to the Armada command post this Friday at noon for—"

Callie yanks the missile-shaped news capsule off the spindle, and soon, the creaky rotor that spins the capsule loses its momentum and grinds to a stop. She sets it on the table and sighs, tucking her chin-length curls behind her ears.

The silence is welcome. The heels of my polished boots click against the stone floor of one of the command post's charting rooms as I pace past the parchment maps and diagrams pinned to the walls, posture stiff and jaw tight. I twist the rings on my fingers and stare ahead, my throat tightening at the thought of how many hundreds of eyes will be watching.

Some were speculating that nearly a thousand would show, cramming themselves under the shade of the massive palm trees outlining the perimeter of the courtyard.

My heart hammers in my ears. Even though we're tucked into the back corner of the building, it's as if they're standing just on the other side of the door, anxiously watching to see when I will emerge.

Callie's brow knits. "How do you feel?"

They counted nearly five hundred spectators at the last ceremony. What's to say there won't be at least double that this time?

"Emery." Callie's tone sharpens, yanking me back to the present. "Do you need to sit down?"

"Is it that obvious?" I breathe.

"Yes." She stuffs her hands into the pockets of her black uniform coat, adorned with real silver buttons and gray embroidery on the sleeves. "But everyone will be too far away to notice, so don't worry." She studies my hands, swollen and clammy underneath the gold.

I bite my cheek. Her calm, resolute presence is not enough to dismiss my nerves like it has in the past.

"How do I look?" I whirl around, facing her and the wooden door that leads to the hallway. "The stylist wouldn't let me look at myself on the way out the door."

Callie's lips pucker in dissatisfaction as she heads for the service table. "She went a little heavy on the blush." She dips a napkin into the pitcher of ice water standing near the news spindle. "You look sunburned."

"That might be the heat." I tug the collar of my white blouse. "This blasted humidity is a pain."

She dabs my cheeks and lets the wet cloth sit on my neck, underneath my blonde curls. The cold relaxes the knots in my shoulders.

"Thank you," I sigh.

Callie narrows her eyes and smooths out the wrinkles on my coat, plucking away stray balls of fuzz or strands of hair. She adjusts the neck of my blouse and straightens the coat's buttons, which match the gold adorning my hands and my ears. The two tiny gold hoops in the upper curve of my ear match the silver ones she's wearing, which were my gift to her the day she graduated from escort training two years ago. It was my turn to celebrate her then, but yesterday, she returned the favor by giving me the braided gold ring I now wear on my left little finger, matching her silver one.

While the trinkets are nice, the real jewel is the coat, redder than a cherry and hand-sewn to a T. The gold-embroidered hem sits below my waist, not too loose or too tight. It was made specifically for the ceremony and is more formal than my previous coats with its gold embroidery, but it's still functional for sailing like a typical captain's coat.

Everything has to be formal for today. Everything has to be perfect.

"Remind me why you don't want to dress me full-time." I grin at her as she straightens my collar and adjusts the gold swirls sewn next to the buttons.

"Because your protection is infinitely more important than how you look." She doesn't break her focus as a black curl of hair falls into her eyes. "Obviously."

She steps back to assess her work, then turns her attention to my hair, where half is tied up in a neat twisted bun while the rest falls past my shoulders. She pulls a few loose strands in the front so they curtain my face. "I know my way around a pistol better than a vanity, anyway. If I had to do your hair every day, I'd be out of a job."

I scoff. "Hardly. I'd keep you around and find *something* for you to do."

She smirks. "Flattering."

She crouches and dusts something off the leg of my white uniform pants, and when she stands up, she shakes her head in awe. "Wow."

"Good? Perfect?"

"I can say that nothing I've seen in all the years I've known you can beat this."

"Good." I exhale, taking the napkin off my neck and setting it on the table. "Where's your brother?"

"Late, as usual," she mutters, rolling her eyes.

"Not quite!"

We turn to the echoing voice and staccato of footsteps approaching from the hallway.

Vaughn, all business except for the half smile he aims at me, comes sweeping into the room, cradling an object wrapped in a white cloth. My posture stiffens when I see him, as if his fingers weren't buried in my hair and his lips weren't tracing my jaw just last night.

Like his twin, his hair is blacker than the night, though his is shorter and styled rigidly into soft spikes with the part down the middle. My eyes follow the angled lines of his handsome face. It's sporting a scant beard, but his mustache is more abundant in a thin line above his upper lip.

He stops, slides his heels together, and bows with unnecessary extravagance. "Captain Walker."

"Please don't," I laugh. "The air is already stuffy as is."

Callie scowls at him. "Why do you act like this in public?

"We're not *quite* in public just yet." He smiles. "You almost forgot the most beautiful part."

He unfolds the cloth to reveal a cluster of white flowers at the end of a long green stem.

The white Walker orchid is a symbol of strength and endurance, and while other flower species will be on display across the crowd from each of the families, none is quite as striking as the orchid, in my opinion.

"Your mother asked me to deliver it." Vaughn gently brushes my hair to the side and works to fasten the orchid to my lapel with a special pin that holds the flower in place without breaking the stem.

We're so close that I can hear his gentle breaths and see each sharp, handsome line of his face. He smells like the earth.

I reach up to hold the lapel in place, and our knuckles brush as he carefully presses the pin down. We both look up at the same time.

My anxieties about the ceremony seem to melt like warm oil that seeps through my chest as I look at him. My eyes briefly flick to Callie, and I hope she doesn't pick up on the subtle tension between him and me. She would throw an overprotective fit if she knew.

The peal from the town's belltower sounds in the distance, and my guard snaps right back to attention. The bell rings when something important happens in Padstow, and today it's ringing for me.

Vaughn takes a step back and grins, and I can't help but grin as well.

I have been dreaming of the moment I'd finally see my name etched into the wall of the Captains' Hall since I first set foot in the Armada Academy over six years ago. When I was cross-eyed from staring at maps and books in the wee hours of the morning, I'd lie on the desks and stare up at the ceiling, imagining a time when I could finally be at the helm of my own crew, on my own ship, diving deep into the criminal underworld to catch pirates like many before me.

And now, I can look up and say, "*Finally.*"

I glance back and forth at my protectors, my friends. They both wear the same soft expression of love and excitement.

The bell rings again, and I take a deep breath and set my jaw as we move. Callie stays at my front while Vaughn stays behind me as we walk through the winding halls of the command post, which is eerily silent without the chatter of on-duty Armada soldiers. Each click of our boots on the stone seems to pound into my head like nails, but I don't falter. I never do.

3

Warren

I *DESPISE* CROWDS.

I turn away from the masses of people in front of me to glance at the hordes behind, all of whom sandwich me in the middle like a shriveled, miserable sardine. The crowd stretches from the stage at the front of the command outpost—which is already lined with ranks from the Armada—to the mossy wooden docks of Padstow's monstrously large harbor. We are packed shoulder to shoulder, baking in the noonday sun, and I am bitterly trapped in the middle where I am less likely to be spotted. My face, underneath my bushy wig and beard disguise, is sweating an ocean, as is everyone in the crowd, so much so that the dirt beneath our feet might turn to mud. It hasn't dissuaded anyone, though. We are all eagerly searching the stage, waiting for the golden girl to take her place.

They are here because they adore her, but they don't know half of what's really going on.

My first visit to Padstow took place six years ago, but half that time had passed when I began to hear whisperings of a navigator who was building a name and a reputation for herself as she hunted the pirates in the Eastern Commonwealth. She had a sixth sense for ferreting them out and orchestrating elaborate captures that caught everyone's attention.

Little did I know that the morning I sailed away from Padstow after a night of chaos and terror, she was watching. She knew my name. And soon, I'd know hers.

Everyone's infatuation is borne from her famed uprising after that night. Nobody climbed out of the rubble of the attack and fought back as hard as she did. For the last six years, she has toiled through the Armada Academy and dove deep into the nasty criminal world to learn their behaviors and sniff out their illegal dealings. She spearheaded new hunting techniques and encouraged the other navies in the Eastern Commonwealth to do the same. Each achievement has been a stepping stone toward catching the man who orchestrated the attack on her home.

That man may or may not be glaring daggers at the stage as he hides under a hairy disguise, but I digress.

We've met multiple times as we've risen in our respective worlds, though neither has been successful in getting rid of the other. I've foiled her traps for me while she's uprooted my trade operations in this endless, pathetic game of cat and mouse where the roles are constantly flipping. If she corners me, I slip away before she can make the arrest, and if I corner her, her little crew is there to help her escape.

It was only a matter of time until one side of the conflict cracked. It was only a matter of time before either of us landed a truly devastating blow to the other, which is why I am standing here today.

Even then, everyone agrees that because of her, there hasn't been a single attack on Padstow or any island city within a twenty-mile radius. No one has dared to stand up to Padstow because of the work she's done.

I scan the crowd, checking the Riggs guards' positions at the perimeter, and making note of the city's aristocracy at the front of the crowd. The families who run this city are all dressed in their respective colors, hiding under black and white silk umbrellas while the majority of the crowd hides under the few palm trees on the grounds, or linen scraps they've draped over their heads.

On the outskirts of the crowd, the Armada sailors in their gray-and-black striped uniforms stand on the decks of their ships, and on the watchtowers that stretch into the sky around the command post. They stare through binoculars and telescopes to catch a glimpse of the ceremony.

Sailors, civilians, and snobs alike melt from the humidity, but how could anyone dare to miss history?

The sounds of the crowd turn to whispers and my attention is drawn to the stage where Admiral Yanni Van Pelt hobbles across from the left hand side, his back bent under decades of battle stories. He's only there for spectacle, though, and sits in a chair off to the side, stroking his ashy white beard with a wrinkly scowl.

Following him are his left- and right-hand co-commanders, Jonathan and Marissa Walker, and their two sons. I study them curiously as their parents take the lectern. Charles, the eldest at twenty-five, looks the most like Emery with his blond hair and tense jaw. He tucks his curls behind his ears and takes a deep breath while Miles, the roguish, bronze-haired middle child at twenty-three, keeps a narrowed eye on the crowd, his chest puffed out and shoulders tight.

They carry themselves with poise, but I wonder what they must be thinking under that shiny facade, because I know I'd be reeling with resentment if my younger sister outworked and outperformed me. Their positions in the Armada have earned them prestige and honor, but none of that matters when they're competing with their family's darling girl.

I turn my attention back to Jonathan and Marissa, who always begin these ceremonies by introducing the captain-to-be and listing their accomplishments and acts of bravery during their Armada service.

My eyes glaze over as Jonathan speaks into the horn fixed to the front of the lectern, which projects his voice over the large crowd. "Nearly a hundred pirates arrested, six captains imprisoned, and two massive smuggling operations shut down . . ."

I roll my eyes. We all *have* to know just how special his little crime bloodhound is. She seems to sniff it out wherever she goes.

I am more focused on the Walkers' perfect appearance—perfectly polished black boots, white pants for Marissa and black for the gentleman, and those bloody red coats. Marissa's orchid is strung through the knot in her hair while Jonathan's and the two sons' are pressed into their lapels.

Just below the stage, the media crew from The Shining Star News crouches in front of the stage, aiming a sleek metal horn at the co-commanders to record their speech. One of the crewmembers is twirling the flat dial on the wooden box that etches the sound waves onto a piece of paper. Later, the crew will pockmark a piece of a thin, floppy metal and roll it into the capsules which will relay the sounds back on a news spindle.

I count each black-coated Riggs sibling and cousin peppered across the crowd, and the select few of them who stand as personal guards next to the elites in the front. The security commanders, Eldon Riggs and his sister Rita, stand near the stage, watching the crowd with a keen eye for anyone who may disturb the peace.

Marissa speaks after her husband, and the two of them move to the side with their sons as Chief Judge Reese Gordon rises from beside Admiral Van Pelt and stands behind the lectern, dressed in a pressed white shirt and a gray robe. He wipes his brow with the handkerchief in his breast pocket and sighs, and a strand of graying brown hair falls into his eyes. "I apologize for this weather, ladies and gentlemen. I don't imagine anyone would happen to have an ice bucket on them, would they?"

I roll my eyes again as the crowd stirs with obligatory chuckles.

He clears his throat and grips the edges of the lectern with his knobby fingers. "These Sealing ceremonies are always an honor to lead, but this one is extra special in my heart because I've had the privilege and honor of serving beside this family and this amazing young woman for years now. I want to reiterate the significance of this particular Seal."

He smiles and takes a deep breath. "The Armada has not had a recruit like her for quite a long time. She graduated early from the Academy at the top of her class and will be the youngest recruit ever inducted into the Captain's Hall. She and her crew's work tracking down pirates and other dangerous criminals throughout the Commonwealth has been quite remarkable, including imprisoning three pirate captains in the last year alone, which no sailor, let alone captain, has ever done before. I believe it's safe to say the seas that most of us call home would not be as safe without her. It is my honor and my privilege to be standing here today to seal Miss Emery Walker as a captain in the Padstow Armada."

The crowd, aware of the solemnity of the moment, remains silent as the star of the show steps out from a curtain on the left side and crosses the stage.

Anger seethes in the pit of my stomach. If I pulled my weapon, I could shoot her right now and exterminate her like the nuisance she is, but I curl my fingers instead. The long game I want to play with her is tedious, but it will be more rewarding in the end.

She walks with the stiff, graceful posture of a veteran with years of expectation on her shoulders. She smiles at the crowd and clasps her hands together as she stands next to the judge at center stage, facing us with an aura of confidence as thick as the humidity in the air. Hundreds and hundreds of eyes are watching her every move, but she endures it well—the darling girl of the Walker family, their beacon to carry the Armada for the next generation. She's quite a beautiful spectacle. There's no denying that.

Speak to anyone on this blasted coastline and they will parrot that exact sentiment.

I glance over her head at the command post, then above it at the prison nestled against a tall, lush hill, where I imagine Kearon huddled in the corner of a cell, starved and shivering and afraid. That's what she's reduced him to. That is what she did to him.

Judge Gordon drones on about the history and significance of the Captain's Seal, but it doesn't break the crowd's trance.

"She's so beautiful," an older woman next to me whispers to her husband. "Her parents have to be so proud."

"Papa, can we go home?" a little girl in a ruffled blue dress complains. "It's hot."

"No, but look at her." Her father picks her up so she can see over the rest of the crowd. "That could be you someday."

The girl wrinkles her nose. "I don't like boats."

I purse my lips and smile as a few others chuckle around her. She covers her face and curls against her father in embarrassment.

On stage, Emery's father passes a small polished box to the judge, who produces from it a ring that he slips onto her left middle finger. Though I'm too far to see, I can guarantee it's gold to match the rest of the jewelry she wears.

Afterward, Gordon pulls out the Seal coin and places it in Emery's right hand. She takes a deep, resolute breath, and holds both hands open in front of her, palm up, with the Seal resting in her right hand.

The judge places his left hand atop her right and tells her to recite the Captain's Decree. She repeats her name and a bunch of other self-righteous garbage before the final line:

"I swear to protect the lives of my crew and make the best decisions that I can for the betterment of the Armada. All rights and responsibilities of the captain fall to me and I will fulfill my duties with honor."

I narrow my eyes. *Honor.*

Gordon speaks one final time. "On behalf of the Armada and by the power vested in me, I declare Emery Jane Walker a captain of the Padstow Armada and bestow the rights, powers, and responsibilities stated herein."

The crowd cheers as he finishes the Seal. The Shining Star crew rises from their crouched positions and pushes the horn closer to the lectern to capture the last moments of the ceremony.

Everyone is focused on her, but I duck my head as I wade through the crowd and exit the courtyard. The Commonwealth's newest golden girl can have her moment, but it isn't going to last.

Plaster this headline across every city and play the news recordings until the end of time:

"Shining Star! Shining Star! How long have we been promoting a fraud?"

4

Emery

My ears ache as the vaulted ceilings of our home echo with the chatter of partygoers. They're packed in every corner from the kitchen to the foyer, and into the sitting room, crawling through the house like ants.

It continues for hours. Our grand entryway is packed with guests from the Armada and the other ruling families, their lapels and collars adorned with their respective flowers. They mill between shiny white walls and around the pieces of antique wooden decor my mother has collected over the years.

And the orchids. The orchids are everywhere, whether they're scattered on random shelves or springing out of vases around the halls.

I've never seen the house this full, and though I've been to plenty of parties, it's interesting to be at the center of it.

"Congratulations, Captain," a sailor with a crooked nose says to me as he passes.

I love looking at the formal attire and the mishmash of neutral colors mixed with the darker blues, purples, pinks, and greens. The flowers are just as gorgeous. The Nowaks wear plumerias, the Stantons wear chrysanthemums, the Hadleys wear laceleaf . . . I could go on. The orchid and its earthy sweet scent, for me, will always stand as a beacon of comfort because it means I am home with the ones to whom I owe my life and my love.

Charles leans down to my ear, and a blond curl falls across his forehead. "My favorite part of these gatherings is watching all of them pretend they don't hate each other."

I grin. "It makes the people-watching more interesting because we actually *know* the people."

"*Exactly.* I'm glad you understand."

The black-clad Riggses mill through the crowd with keen, watchful eyes, and part of me wants to see what would happen if a criminal with lofty ambitions attempts to breach the house.

Callie and Vaughn stay relatively close to the boys and me, and throughout the afternoon, I watch as dozens of people brush past them as if they aren't there. There are hundreds of law enforcers across the city who are employed by the Riggses, but the core of Eldon, his wife Nettie, the twins, and other brothers, sisters, and cousins haven't quite recovered from the scandal where Eldon's brother Kon took money under the table to release offenders from prison. He created an entire web within the law enforcement system that involved more than twenty guards, including some of the twins' cousins.

The public and the upper class haven't looked at the Riggses the same since, and many dropped their personal escorts because of it. Callie has complained about the cold shoulders in the past, but she keeps those feelings locked behind the stony, expressionless mask she wears as she scans the crowd.

I watch Reese Gordon and his wife Penelope say hello to Eldon and the twins, and I exhale in relief. Not everyone follows the mob.

Vaughn keeps meeting my eye and smiling, and dimples appear in his cheeks each time he does. My favorite is when he flips back to what I call his "business" persona and narrows his eyes, straightens his back, and politely clasps his hands. He commands the room.

Well, he commands *my* attention at the very least.

"Distraction," I mouth to him, to which he touches his chest and looks at me with faux pain in his expression. He sticks up his nose and turns away.

My parents make their rounds with each of the other family heads, accepting their congratulations and exchanging pleasant party chatter.

"You must be so proud of the woman she's become," they mumble. "We expect great things from her."

My hand slips into my coat pocket and curls around the Captain's Seal.

How odd to think that everything I've worked for has been for the little round coin in my palm. How odd to think that I will be in charge of commanding my own crew and can do it all exactly how I want.

How *exhilarating.*

Miles plucks a drink off the tray of one of the white-coated servers, but I pass on the alcohol to keep my eyes sharp. He lazily swirls the drink in the crystal flute and looks around with twisted lips as he, Charles, and I walk through the crowd, a brother on either side of me. We are the only ones dressed in red, and their coats were custom-made for today just like mine was. The three coats are nearly identical, save for the lack of excessive embroidery on the boys'.

"How do you two stand the stuffiness?" Miles asks, tugging at the collar of his tight dress shirt. "Do you even know half of these people?"

"No." I smile. "Not personally."

"Mother's list of friends is never-ending," Charles says, his hands clasped behind his back. "Though I don't think she's talked to many of these people in years, if I'm being honest. It's diplomatic."

"Diplomatic." Miles takes a sip and rolls his eyes as he nods at the Howell family, who hover near my father's collection of rifles mounted on the wall in the massive sitting room. "It's just another part of this stupid game. The only reason *they're* here is because *we* went to one of their gatherings. I seriously doubt they or anyone else here cares about diplomacy."

A small part of me agrees with him, though I'd never tell him that he's correct. His ego is large enough.

"Emery, have you even seen any of the people we actually care about in the three hours we've been here?" Miles presses. "The Gordons? The Scotts?"

"The Scotts left, but yes, I have," I say defensively, elbowing his arm. "Don't be a bore."

"I wish the Ridgewoods hadn't moved away," Charles says glumly. "They always appreciated a good party."

I wrinkle my nose in disappointment. "That's true."

"I'd hardly call this a party." Miles downs the last of his drink and quickly snags another from a passing waiter. "Parties are supposed to be *fun.*"

Charles watches him disapprovingly and rolls his eyes. "Yes, because your version of a fun party is running around like a lunatic while music blares and drinking until you pass out."

Miles runs a hand through his slicked-back bronze curls and grins. "That sounds like a nice night at The Tab."

Charles rolls his eyes, and I resist the urge to do so. Our brother's brash disregard for structure nearly cost him a spot in the Armada Academy because of his derelict behavior, but that issue was quickly resolved after a few called-in favors to Academy officials. No blemishes are allowed, no matter how much one must bend the rules to cover them. That is the unspoken rule everyone in this room plays by.

I clear my throat and force the uncomfortable thought away.

"Maybe instead of complaining, you could try being happy and supportive of your favorite sister." I pout my lower lip. "Maybe?"

"As if you wouldn't gladly run around The Tab with me after a nice glass of whiskey." He sticks his tongue out at me. "We haven't been down there in a while, anyway. Why don't we pay Mickey and the lot of them a visit after this?"

"He says with a drink in his hand." Charles wrinkles his brow and glances at me. "I know this isn't how you like to celebrate, but really, Miles?"

I wait for Charles to turn away before whispering, "We'll go later," to Miles, and I raise my voice slightly. "Speaking of, did you two see Mickey or the others today? I invited them."

"I might've seen Jessie, but I don't know." Miles wets his lips. "There were a ton of people."

Another approaching figure catches my eye, and I gasp.

Fallon Scott returns my giddy grin as she weaves through the crowd and nearly tackles me in a hug. She's nearly fifteen years my senior, and she became somewhat of a mentor the second I declared my intent to become a captain in the Academy.

"You rascal," she laughs in my ear. "You actually did it."

"I didn't think you were going to make it!" I exclaim, taking in her disheveled sailing attire. Her striped coat is unbuttoned and wrinkled. "What are you doing here?"

"The patrol rotations switched just at the right time. We docked early this morning." She steps back and rests her hands on her hips. "You looked *gorgeous* on that stage. You look gorgeous now!"

"This morning is cutting it close." Charles smiles at her and folds his hands. "Good to see you, Captain."

"How's Thayne?" Miles asks her. "Do you know when he's coming back?"

"He was just asking about you in his last letter, actually." Fallon puffs a loose strand of hair from her eyes. "He's planning to visit at the end of the month and is still on track to graduate early."

Miles's face beams with pride for his best friend.

"Look at you three." Fallon's eyes dart between us. "I can't believe it. Your name is going to look amazing next to mine when it's carved into that wall, Emery."

The social whirlwind continues as Reese approaches us with Penelope on his arm. She reaches forward to hug me, and I grin as she kisses my cheek. "Hi, Penny."

"Congratulations, honey." Her perfume smells like honeysuckle. "You're phenomenal."

"Thank you."

"Captain Scott!" The judge smiles and squeezes her shoulder. "When did you arrive?"

"This morning, actually." She rehashes the story she gave the boys and me.

"Have you caught that one captain yet, Fallon?" Penny asks. "What is his name?"

"Dasher, wasn't it?" Charles cuts in.

"No," Fallon pokes him in the ribs with her elbow. "Well, yes. That's his name, but no to your question, Miss Gordon. Piersford had requested reinforcements in their hunt for him, but he is such a minor threat that we decided to take a short break and leave them to handle him. He's been quiet for about a month, though. We weren't really worried about him and told them they didn't have to be, either. Call it dull, but since then we've just been patrolling down south to make sure no fights break out."

"How far south?" Reese asks.

"We started in Marshland and Ely, but made it down into the

Southern Chain and had a stop in Kahu and Hana Kailea to replenish supplies.”

I nod. Beautiful islands, rampaging crime rates. The South has always been known for its rich culture and scenery, but it’s grown less peaceful as time has gone on.

“Oh, I love Kahu!” Penny touches her husband's arm. “It’s such a gorgeous little island, Reese. We need to visit sometime, and we could do a trip across the South!”

“That’s a long way to go for a vacation,” Miles mutters in my ear.

“Well, I’m glad you made it home safely.” Penny takes Fallon’s hand and smiles, and I catch sight of Fallon’s captain’s ring. It shines silver with a band of graphite gray running through the center, whereas mine is gold with a band of red. I glance down and run my finger across the ruby strip, grinning.

“Have you seen any of the other captains here yet?” Fallon asks me. “I have to make the rounds, you know.”

“I haven’t yet, but be sure to find my parents,” I reply. “They’ll be excited to see you.”

“Will do. I’m proud of you.” She gives me one last hug before disappearing into the mass.

Reese purses his lips and sighs. “First her, and now you. I can’t believe it.”

“Reese, don’t say that.” Penny gently swats his arm.

“No, I don’t mean it like that, it’s just . . .” He adjusts his wire-framed glasses and looks between my brothers and me. “You all are still so young in my mind and now the youngest has been Sealed.”

Miles smiles at me.

“When do you get to meet your crew, Emery?” Penny asks eagerly.

Reese chuckles. “That’s not going to be the case, actually.”

“My father wants to keep the crew together, so I’ll be on the *Chaplain's Heart* again,” I explain. “Captain Martinez was set to retire anyway, and I think Admiral Van Pelt signed the order this morning.”

“So when do you officially start?” Penny goes on.

“Soon, right?” Reese frowns at me. “Especially with the errand boy—”

"Yes." I grin and pop up onto my toes. "If I had my way, we'd be at the command post planning right now."

I haven't seen him since the night I arrested him, despite my incessant requests to interrogate him. Padstow's due process requires Reese and the other judges to begin the investigation and review preliminary evidence, but I've been itching to interrogate the boy myself for weeks. Preparing for the Sealing and the Armada Academy graduation didn't quell the antsiness.

The judge's eyebrows flash. "Starting off strong, are we?"

"She never sleeps." Charles wrinkles his brow. "I had to break into the Academy one morning and rescue her because the groundskeeper locked her inside."

"You never admit to a crime in front of a judge, Charles." Miles bats at his shoulder.

"Oh, hush." Penny scowls, her brown eyes flashing with suggestiveness. "Don't draw his attention to it."

"When is his trial, speaking of that?" I ask Reese.

Reese nods. "The other judges are convening about it now, but it's going to take some time. Piracy charges always do."

"Pity," Charles murmurs.

"I still haven't spoken to your parents yet," Penny says to me. "Have you seen them? Where are they?"

"They're there." Miles points at our mother and father as they maneuver toward the kitchen, and Penny leans into my ear one last time.

"Good luck," she murmurs. "If either of those boys gives you trouble, just shout. But I'm sure you could take care of them yourself."

I thank her, and Reese gives me a proud grandfatherly grin and holds me tight. Each of my parents' parents is dead, and for me, I've seen Reese and Penny in that role since I was a little girl.

"I'm proud of you, Em," he whispers in my ear. "Be great."

"Thank you for everything." I smile as my chest grows warm. "Truly."

He squeezes my hand before he walks away, and I silently promise him and everyone else that I will. I have not come this far to be anything but.

· · ·

"I did not say that," my mother chuckles.

"You did!" Miles points at her. "You did say that!"

I laugh. "I remember it like it was yesterday! I was in the kitchen listening."

My father leans back onto the sofa in my mother's study and covers his face to hide his giddy smirk

"Jonathan, don't even start," my mother scolds, pointing her finger and widening her eyes..

My stomach aches from all the giggling. My mother's cozy study provides a nice sanctuary for just the five of us, even though the party ended long ago and the watching, judging eyes have left the house. We dismissed the Riggses for the night, so, besides the servants, it's just us, tucked away and out of sight.

My father and I sit on one of the two parallel sofas while my mother sits at her massive mahogany work desk, and the room smells like old paper and orchids. A large bookshelf stretches from floor to ceiling and covers the entirety of the wall behind her. Vases of white and pink orchids decorate the empty spaces between the books.

"No no no, this is exactly what happened, Mother." Miles sits on the edge of the ottoman in the middle of the room. "I brought Sandra inside—"

"Which was the first warning sign," Charles butts in.

"No no no! Listen, listen." Miles smacks his knee. "I brought Sandra inside because it was hot and she wanted some water, and I heard you"—he points to our mother—"around the corner talking to Marianne Hadley. When she and I walked into the kitchen, Emery was sitting at the counter, and you said—"

"'I hope Miles knows Sandra Nyland was snogging Barrett Nowak in The Tab the other night before he brings her into my house.'" My father leans forward, his face turning cherry red as he laughs.

A pen suddenly flies across the room and strikes him in the chest. I have to cover my face to hide my amusement, and even Charles smiles.

"That information does not leave this room." My mother points

23

another pen at the four of us, but even her stone-cold persona falters as she breaks down into laughter. "Miles, you dimwit."

He sticks his tongue out like a clown in mockery.

"She was as white as a ghost when you said that, Mother. You should have seen it." I can't stop laughing as I pull down the collar of my blouse and touch my neck. "She was covered in lovebite bruises all the way down to her shoulders."

Miles raises his eyebrows suggestively. "Oh, you'd know a little about being covered in lovebites, Emery, wouldn't you?"

I gasp and throw one of the couch pillows at his head, but he laughs and swats it away.

Charles points at him with a wide look in his eyes. "Oh, you speak to *any* other captain like that and you'd be dishonorably discharged in an instant."

My father, a soldier who has seen battles and other horrors that would haunt any man for the rest of his life, giggles like a child as he roughly slings his arm around my shoulder and kisses my cheek. "I love you, Cap," he says jokingly in my ear, "Even if you sneak around with boys you aren't supposed to."

I scowl and playfully smack his leg.

"Leave your sister alone, Miles," scolds my mother. Using a match, she lights one of the oil lanterns sitting on her desk as the evening sunset begins to grow weak through the window.

"Yeah, Miles, leave your baby sister alone." I fold my arms.

He scoffs. "Three pirate captains in the last year. Two smuggling operations disbanded.

Why do you always jump to her aid when she's clearly capable of handling herself?"

Someone knocks on the door, and I jump up. "The ladies have to stick together."

"That's right." My mother smugly folds her arms and sits back in her desk chair.

Miles rolls his eyes, and I hold up my finger.

"Ah ah ah. I would hate to share all of your late night blunders. If the lock on the back kitchen door could talk, it'd tell some very interesting stories."

Miles turns white as my mother narrows her sharp eyes and leans forward. "Oh?"

"I was a teenager when this all happened!" He holds his hands up in surrender. "I have matured and grown into a respectable adult, thank you very much."

"Only one of those things is true," Charles says snootily, crossing his legs and thumbing through one of my mother's books. The dim lantern light casts shadows that accentuate the sharp lines of his cheek and jaw, making him look like a figure in an oil painting.

I open the door. One of our maids, dark-haired and younger than me, is holding a stack of envelopes and a news capsule. She's the newest of the staff, and she smiles when she sees me. "Just the mail. I sorted it all by—"

Her fingers slip as she hands the stack to me, and the papers go flying as the capsule clatters to the floor.

She gasps and turns pink as I kneel to help her. "I'm s-so sorry!" she stutters, her face flushing with pink as she hurriedly gathers the fallen envelopes. "My fingers—"

"Elle, it's okay." I set my hand on her shoulder, and she looks up, surprised. "Accidents happen."

She takes a deep breath. "Sorry, Miss—Captain! I meant Captain." She covers her face. "I'm so embarrassed. I'm sorry."

"Call me Emery." I squeeze her shoulder and smile. "Though, 'Miss Captain' does have a nice ring to it. Maybe I'll have people start calling me that at the harbor."

That gets her to grin, and she sighs. "Thank you, Emery. I'm sorry. I don't know why I've been so flustered."

"Don't be sorry." I grasp her hand and help her back to her feet. "You're doing great, but if you ever need a second to breathe, the door to my room is always open. I'm not in there very often during the day, which is when you're usually here, right?"

"Yes. I'll remember that." She takes a deep breath. "Is there anything else I can get you?"

"We're okay, but thank you so much."

She nods somberly and disappears around the corner.

I drop the mail on my mother's desk and sit on the stool next to her as my father and brothers converse about others they spoke with during the party.

"Letters and letters," she mutters as she flicks through the parchment. "This one's for you."

"Kobayashi?" I frown at the return address. "Who is this? Who do you know in Kyota?"

"We briefly partnered with this family for an entourage when they were passing through the Commonwealth a long time ago," she says. "This was before the attack and the drama following it. They've always stayed in contact with your father and me."

"Hm."

"Emery, do you have the capsule?" Charles asks.

I toss it to him and he works to hook it up to the news spindle. Usually, the capsules are delivered the following morning, but the news outlets hurried to release a special evening edition because of the ceremony.

Charles unscrews the capsule's wide lid and slides it onto the long metal bar that stretches the length of the wooden base.

I notice the pens on my mother's desk have fallen out of place and adjust them so the tips align. I run my finger over the glossy black metal of her fountain pen.

She touches my knee and smiles. "How are you feeling?"

My head lolls to one side as I grin at her. "I'm excited that I can finally do things I couldn't do as a navigator and can work how *I* want."

"Are you nervous?" Her brow furrows. "Even a little."

I open my mouth to scoff, but I remember that right now, she's my mother, not my commander. Commanders don't worry like mothers do.

"No. I've been planning how I want to do it for so long, and I can see it so clearly." I grab her wrist. "You always say a clear head makes a clear path, and I can see it."

I can see Warren Chadwick's head on a spike, and all the pirates of the world slowly dying out or disappearing as we catch them. The constant fear lingering in the air among the Commonwealth disappearing permanently.

I can see the fortification of dedicated pirate-hunting crews across the region so they're better prepared for trouble when it knocks. I see Chadwick's swollen, dead eyes, and when the rest of the criminal underworld sees one of their titans dead, it will be a reminder that none of them are untouchable.

She squeezes my knee and takes me back to the present. Her eyes brim with pride. "It's not too much for you? You don't feel pressured or overwhelmed?"

"You'd be the first to know if I did. I promise."

She grabs my face and kisses my forehead. "You're going to be amazing. I feel like I don't tell you that enough as your mother."

I scoff lightly. "You have told me enough to get me here."

I don't think I would have gone as far as I did without her constant support and guidance. She is my other half. Nothing could ever replace her.

She chuckles and kisses my cheek as Charles spins the capsule, and the news starts to play:

"Shining Star! Shining Star! Folks, today was a remarkable day for the city of Padstow. For only the third time in the last twenty years, the Captain's Hall had a woman's name etched into its wall. And she is the youngest to have ever done it at only twenty years old. Before her, the youngest was twenty-seven. She began training when she was fourteen, and to have completed the Armada's sailing academy and then gone through navigator and captain's training during that time is no small feat, folks. The most seasoned sailors take nine to ten years to work up to that point, but with her accomplishments as the navigator and capture-strategist aboard the Chaplain's Heart, *it was only a matter of time."*

My father smiles at me as I continue to flip through the mail, leaving the pieces not addressed to me in a neat stack on the desk.

"Emery Walker is not a name you'll soon forget, ladies and gentlemen. It might be one that sounds familiar. In the last year alone, she has captured three pirate captains and has shut down their illegal exchange businesses. These pirates stole and traded everything from fruit to people, folks. She's currently on the hunt for Warren Chadwick, the pirate that no one can seem to catch, but her ledger is already

remarkable. She earned her first capture when she was only seventeen, and—"

"I led my first boatswain team when I was seventeen." Miles sinks down into the couch beside my father and stretches out his legs. "You threw a woman in jail."

"She held six people hostage the night she aided in the attack on Padstow," Charles mutters. "You make it sound so menial."

I scowl and glance down as my mother takes one of the envelopes.

"Look!" She rips it open. "This is from the Halapua family. Do you still write to Theadora?"

"Yes. Once a month." I take the letters and shuffle through them.

Thea is the daughter of the king of Hana Kailea, the strongest and largest city in the Southern Chain, and about three years ago, my family and I were on a diplomatic trip to King Tanuvasa's royal wedding when Thea and I discovered a mutual love for literature and old books. I try to write to her at least once a month, and I usually hear from her about that often depending on the weather along the air mailing routes of the carrier shearwaters.

My mother and I skim the king and queen's congratulatory note, and I thumb open the envelope and notice there's another folded piece of paper.

Dearest Emery,

I hope you'll have already been Sealed by the time you're reading this. If that's the case, I could not be happier for you! I know I've not been there to watch you grow, but not one person deserves this more than you. I hope you'll stop by Hana Kailea one day and say hello. My parents give their congratulations as well.

I GLANCE inside the envelope again and pull out the small postcard she included, which is a beautiful painting of the beach during sunset. A girl with a red coat and blonde hair stands in the sand, watching the purple and orange swirls of the sky as they slowly begin to melt into an entrancing shade of cobalt. I smile. The bottom corner is painted with the purple and teal of Hana Kailea's flag.

"Did she do that?" My mother leans over my shoulder and squints. "It's beautiful."

"She has a talent," I reply proudly. "Last time she wrote to me, she said she was able to sell some of her bigger paintings."

She sets the stack on the desk. "We should invite their family here for a visit sometime."

"Oh, yes!" I turn to face her. "I want to tell Thea about that new Kyotic collection you just had shipped in. Have you read any of it yet?"

"A little. There's a book of poems that I think you'd really like."

"I might steal it later, then."

"Um, hello?" Charles lazily raises his arm to remind us that he's present. "I will not be a literary third wheel in my own house. Let me have it first. I'll read it faster since you're busier, Emery."

"—at least a thousand people in attendance, and—"

"There were not a thousand," my father snorts at the capsule. "That's dramatic."

"The Shining Star always dramatizes things," says Charles. "I've been saying this for years."

"They're the most unbiased, though. I can't stand listening to The Messenger, or The Shout, heaven forbid."

"Is he new?" My mother points to the spindle. "The reporter, I mean. I don't think I've ever heard his voice. Did you talk to him this afternoon, Emery?"

I shrug. "It's possible I did. There were so many of them at the command post, and Callie complained about it the entire carriage ride back here."

"It isn't like a reporter is going to try and kill any of us," Charles mumbles to himself.

"He's new," says my father. "Jessup told me they had hired a few new reporters."

"He isn't very good." Charles sighs boredly, "But at least he's getting his chance."

Miles points to the stack of mail. "Is the newspaper up there, Emery? I want to see the pictures they took today."

I glance at the stack and stand. "I can get it. Elle must have missed—"

"*—a little easier to do something like that when your parents are at the head of it all.*"

We all go silent. I turn and frown at the spindle.

"*I know there had to have been at least some number-fudging going on behind the scenes. She's done it all so quickly, and there's no way her parents didn't give her a little leeway in their decision-making or ushering her through classes.*"

Charles scowls. "See what I mean?"

"That's ridiculous!" I snap. "Why would they add that? They haven't said a bad word about us in years!"

"*—will always be an asterisk next to her name because of her parents' positions. Nobody that rich ever works that hard because they don't have to. It's impressive that she's caught pirates, but I wouldn't be surprised if this all unravels and is revealed as a hoax.*"

The spindle falls silent.

"I'll talk to Jessup in the morning," my father huffs. "That's pathetic."

My chest swells with anger.

"This is why you don't rely on what other people tell you." Charles rips the capsule free and tosses it into the trash bin between the bookshelves.

I fiddle with my collar and try to straighten it, but it stays folded. My fist tightens.

No, I tell myself. *Level head. Level head.*

I can't be angry about something as pathetic as this when I have more important things to worry about.

"Ridiculous," I mutter, beelining for the door. "Absolutely ridiculous."

"Bring the paper when you come back!" Miles calls just before the door slams shut.

5

Warren

"May I see your identification?"

I hand over a crumpled piece of parchment and slump my shoulders.

The black-coated prison guard glances back and forth between me and the fake, poor-quality photograph of Carden Ebenezer Foster, which sounds like the name of a personified sneeze. The name was my first mate Hyde's idea, not mine.

Mr. Foster is a dirty, scruffy vagrant who lives on a tiny island in the Northern Estates called Kerrisberg. He has a greasy mop of black curls tucked under a black cap, my substitutes of which conveniently cover my spiky blond hair and most of my face, as does a crusty beard that was unceremoniously strapped around my head with a band of elastic. He wears leather, a disgusting material that anyone with a brain would never wear in the sun. He also has a brown birthmark around his eye that was meticulously painted on with some cheap makeup we bought at the boutique down the road.

The guard nods. "Mr. Foster—"

"That's my father," I grunt.

He smiles. "Sure. Who are you visiting?"

"Lots." I sniffle and make a show of rubbing my finger under my nose. I hold up the sack in my left hand. "I just wanted to bring some food and whatnot to the inmates."

"Really?" His forehead wrinkles. "I've worked this post for two years and have never seen you before."

"I used to live in Kerrisberg." I clear my throat and point to the fake identification. "Just continuin' an old tradition."

"That's very noble of you . . . ." He checks the paper again.

"Carden." Spittle flies from my lip.

"I'll just have to search the bag before you go up."

I grunt again and hand it over.

He finds nothing after a long inspection of each item and flaps my identification paper. "I'll keep this here for you to collect on your way out. There are guards on every floor in case you have any problems."

I nod and move on, concealing a shudder as the gate creaks open and I walk—*limp* into Padstow's mighty prison. Carden Ebenezer Foster sustained a leg injury in his youth. Also Hyde's idea.

The prison sits atop one of the many green plateaus across the island. It has two annexes jutting out from the main building, one on each end, creating a square that's missing one of its sides. There isn't a ground floor, and stone pillars support the entire building as it seems to hover above the soil. Riggs patrol officers wander the space under the building, their rifles positioned toward the ground.

We're far up from the bustle of the city, but instead of peace, the silence brings an eerie chill to the air that follows me into the building.

I wind my way up the visitor's stairs near the back left corner of the building, and soon my footsteps echo down the gray stone hallways. The guards inside nod as I pass into the main cell block, which is just a long, decrepit hallway with barred cells on the left-hand side that stretch as far as the eye can see. Every slight movement or noise from the prisoners echoes off the jagged stone walls. My throat tightens as I reach up and touch the ceiling, just inches from the top of my hat.

The closet-like cells are separated by block walls, but the prisoners communicate with each other by sitting on their respective sides of the wall and speaking as if it weren't there. Two of them even play cards by sticking their arms through the bars to play their hand.

The prisoners' jeering grows quieter as I ascend to the upper levels, and the further I climb, the emptier the cell blocks. Every sound reverberates through the tight space with a shrill, earsplitting peal that makes my heart pound like a drum, and I wonder if these imbeciles designed this prison to drive its inhabitants insane.

It takes a moment to find him, but he is in the cell wedged in the corner on the highest floor of the prison and isolated from the others.

He flinches when he notices me standing in front of the bars, and I remember my idiotic disguise. I glance down the hall before leaning in and lowering my voice. "It's me. Hush."

His eyes go wide. "Mr. Chadwick?"

"Sh!" I press my finger to my lips.

The guard standing near the window at the end of the hall glances at me briefly.

Kearon scoots closer to the bars, and the shackles on his hands rattle. "Why do you look like that?"

"Because if they recognize me, then they'll lock me up with you." I pull the beard down slightly and gesture to the chains with a scowl. "What are those for?"

"They haven't taken them off since I got here." He rubs his nose and rapidly blinks at the floor. "They don't like pirates very much."

"You are not a pirate," I say sternly. "Have they hurt you at all?"

"I'm fine, but my parents—"

"They will be taken care of. I promise."

Kearon rubs his hollow face, and it looks like someone sucked the roundness right out of his cheeks. Every inch of his pale skin is caked with dirt, including under his fingernails, and he grips the bars and stares at me with eerily bloodshot eyes. "Padstow has always been just in their dealings. They can't convict me, can they?"

I shake my head. "Padstow is not the golden statue on the hill that you've been conditioned to believe it is. More things are going on here than you will ever understand."

His eyes shine with tears. "Can you get home to Lexington and tell my parents some things for me?"

"Well, if all goes fine here, you will be able to tell them yourself."

Two more armed guards appear at the end of the hall, and I use the hat to conceal my face.

"Will you be here for the trial?" Kearon whispers.

"You won't be going on trial." I lean closer. "I'm going to get you out before then."

"How?"

I press my finger against my lips and shake my head.

He wipes away tears before they fall onto his black prison uniform.

"I don't believe any of the things they said about you when they questioned me. It can't be true."

I chuckle despite the tension and anxiety knotted in my chest. "You should not be worrying about me."

"I owe you so much more than you could ever know." Kearon sits back against the wall. "If anything happens to me—"

"Don't even," I say quickly. "I'm going to try to resolve this and get you out. They have no evidence to link you to anything that they're claiming I've done." I reach through the bars and touch his shoulder. "Even if I have to blow up this wall and drag you out of here through the rubble, I will."

That gets him to smile.

"I'll have you out by this weekend. I promise." I glance at the guards one last time. Both of them are looking at me now, and I adjust my fake beard.

I reach into the bag I brought inside and hand him a sandwich wrapped in linen and a leather water canteen. "I don't imagine the food in here is anything fancy," I say loudly, and the guards turn their attention elsewhere.

Kearon chuckles through the tears and takes a bite of the sandwich.

"Deny anything that they accuse you of." My voice is so quiet that I can barely hear myself. "I paid you to watch my funds and that's it. Nothing else."

"They took your logbook, though." His voice trembles. "They're going to see everything I marked, and my initials, and—" His voice catches, and he shakes his head. "Mr. Chadwick, I can't do this. I didn't—"

"Do you think I'd be here if I didn't think you had a chance?" I lean closer and grab the collar of his jumpsuit. "If the girl who arrested you comes to speak with you, deny everything she accuses you of. She's going to try and break you, and you *cannot* break. Do you understand?"

His tears and trembling painfully remind me that he is just a *boy*. She did this to an innocent *boy*.

"Kearon." My grip tightens as I glance down the hall again. "I trust you to do what you've done for me for the last year, and that's use your head. Nothing can beat you if you keep it on straight."

He takes a deep breath and nods. "Okay."

I retract my arm and stand up. "You don't have to worry about a thing. I promise."

He nods.

"I'll see you soon."

I pull my hat snugly over my head and leave him alone.

. . .

"How was it?" asks Hyde.

"He's *glowing.*" I sigh, dropping my things into a heap on the floor of our inn room. "He's living in filth and looks like a hunched-over slug coated in dirt. How do you think it was, Hyde?"

He scowls and throws up his hands. "Sorry for being optimistic."

"There's no such thing as optimism in this hellhole," I mutter, wiping the sweat off my face and dropping my disguise onto one of the creaky twin beds. A splintered nightstand sits between the two beds, and I pull a match from the drawer and light the pool of oil sitting in the bottom of the lamp that sits atop it.

Hyde throws me a rag to wipe the fake birthmark off my face.

"Thank you."

He grunts and fiddles with his sack of chewing tobacco.

"Hyde, it smells bad enough in here," I complain. "Please don't."

"I'll spit it out the window and you won't smell a thing." His face twists in annoyance. "Or you could allow me to go outside."

"You can wear the wig and beard if you want." I sink into one of the rickety chairs that sit around the equally rickety wooden table. "But even those are starting to smell."

He mutters something under his breath and sinks deeper into the cushioned chair in the corner of the room, pouting like a toddler. He rubs his left leg, which is bent inward and twisted awkwardly from an old injury that never healed correctly.

"I saw a wanted sign for you while I was out." I tease him and hold out my hands like I'm sizing a painting. "It said to beware of a tall, handsome man with dark skin who smells like tobacco."

"Did it mention the new haircut?" He touches his tight-coiled black hair and waggles his eyebrows. "I think it's nice."

"No, but they specifically mentioned that he may have been dull enough to risk being seen for the sake of a quick chew."

He scowls and throws his hand at me. "The only one who'd recognize me is Emery, and even if she did, I could take her." He pounds his massive fist into his opposite hand. "I'd squash her like a roach."

"Oh, I'm sure you would." I humor him. "Where's Harrison?"

Hyde folds his brawny arms and rolls his eyes. "Probably wrestling the bird. He's been gone for almost an hour."

I glance at his twisted leg as he rubs it again and winces. "Are you in pain?"

He ignores my question. "Harrison promised he could handle getting the bird back here, but he made me repeat the directions to the mailing outpost six times before leaving because—"

As if on cue, the door clatters open and my disheveled, sweaty ship doctor stumbles inside with a covered birdcage. His circular wire-frame spectacles are knocked off the center of his face.

I raise my eyebrows and glance at Hyde. "You were saying?"

"He bit me!" Harrison clumsily sets the cage on the table and holds up his bloody pinky finger. "Lucky tied the letter too tight around his belly, and it aggravated him. Does he usually bite?"

"Only if he's spooked." I pull off the white drop cloth to reveal Chip, my beautiful, brown-feathered carrier shearwater. His head twitches in my direction as he stares at me down the length of his beige beak. "Why do you think his name is Chip? He used to bite the edges of my bookshelves and leave woodchips all over the floor of my cabin like some sort of savage."

"It's almost like he's an animal," Hyde says sarcastically.

"He doesn't have diseases, right?" Harrison fixes his glasses and smooths his auburnish hair back in its middle part. The humidity makes it droop across his forehead and down the sides of his head. "Will I catch something from this?"

"You'll be fine," Hyde reassures him. "Chip is a clean man like the rest of us."

I reach into the cage and scratch the feathery scruff on his neck, which is a dull white color compared to the rest of his body. "Cleaner than the nasty birds they keep in the outposts."

"Is that why you bought…" Harrison hesitates and clears his throat as he awkwardly slips out of his threadbare brown jacket. "Chip? For cleanliness?"

"That, and it's much more convenient to send letters from anywhere without having to find the nearest outpost." I smooth out his feathers and turn to Harrison. "He has a keen sense of direction and is trained to recognize the scents for more than a dozen cities in the Commonwealth. I keep the scents in pouches in my desk on the ship."

"Is that why the outpost smelled like vanilla? That's the scent?"

Hyde narrows his eyes. "Have you never mailed anything by bird before, Harrison?"

"The town I grew up in wasn't on the coast, and we didn't have any reason to mail out of town, anyway." He tugs at the collar of his shirt. "A mailman always delivered the mail to us."

I grab the folded parchment letter at the bottom of the cage and quickly skim it. "The ship has left port and the crew is waiting for my go ahead."

Hyde rubs his hands together. "Excellent."

"Oh! I got this, too." Harrison pulls *The Padstow Sun* newspaper from his back pocket. "It's the afternoon edition."

Hyde takes it as I set the letter down and glance at the window of our inn room. We are situated on a hill overlooking the city, and I'm blinded by the sunset glowing off the black glass roof of the Armada Academy. Shiny white marble walls and pillars stretch toward the sky, acting as a beacon amidst the hubbub and thrum of the city it watches over.

It would almost look beautiful if it weren't run by a bunch of morons. Such a waste of an amazing idea to get the sharpest maritime minds in one place to strengthen the city.

On a hill directly across from where I stand, the vast mansions and palaces of the aristocracy are speckled throughout a thicket of green. I can only imagine what the Walkers' perfect little angel is doing now.

Perhaps she isn't there. Perhaps she left the ceremony and went straight inside the command post to plan the next steps of her hunt for me.

After she fled into the night with my errand boy in chains, she sought out the buyers listed in the logbook, who folded and told them of the other places I did business besides Lexington. She found my allies and had them arrested, and every other person I worked with turned their backs on me, because who could ever trust a man who'd gotten his associates killed or jailed?

The news ran the same story for weeks about how the disgusting dog of the sea had finally met his match, but they never knew that under the shining lights of courage, the golden girl and the navy she sails under were just as corrupt as they claimed the people they hunted were.

The trading I do may be messy at times, but at least I never lie or cover up anything I do for the sake of preserving an image. And they have the nerve to call me a villain.

While I may not be a hero, I do know that heroes don't snatch innocent boys from their families in the middle of the night with no one there to protect them.

"'The audience at the ceremony was somber, yet energetically excited for the new young captain to finally take her place in the Captain's Hall,'" Hyde reads from the paper. "'She is yet another example of the strength and resilience the Walkers portray daily.'"

I roll my eyes. "Biased garbage."

Harrison wrinkles his brow and pushes his glasses up his nose. "That doesn't sound so terrible."

"It's fake." Hyde creases the paper and quirks one eyebrow. "These people keep the news in their back pocket so they'll say what they want to keep their image clean in the public eye."

"If they were as virtuous as they claim to be, then we would not be here vying to get Kearon out of jail," I say.

"When are you meeting your contact?" Harrison asks. "Speaking of that."

"Tomorrow morning," I say. "So you don't have to worry about doing anything else for me while we're here."

"Good." He anxiously adjusts his vest and breathes deeply. "I don't like walking around in enemy territory. I don't know how you do it, Captain. They don't even know who I am, and it makes me nervous!"

"I know you're still new to the crew, but you will get used to it eventually." Hyde creases the newspaper parchment again and tosses it to Harrison, who fumbles to catch it. "It's fun."

Harrison eyes me warily. "We have very different interpretations of the word 'fun.'"

6

NESTLED in the beating heart of the city and sitting at the apex of two streets is a squat brick building with a sagging wooden roof, where dewy lantern light leeches from the open doors and windows. Moss covers the exterior, except in random places where it's been torn down so the brick could be resealed from the years of wear and cracking. A large sign with red blocky letters spelling "The Tab" gently swings back and forth over the open door.

Vaughn breaks away from my side to walk in with Charles and Miles, but Callie lingers, sensing my sour mood as my pace slows.

"Why do you seem tense?" she asks over her shoulder.

"More so than usual?" I reply bitterly.

She faces me with a scowl knotting her brow.

I cave and shift my jaw. "Did you listen to The Shining Star capsule?"

Her expression loosens. "Oh."

"You'd think I'd learn how to deal with it after living under a magnifying glass for years." My face burns as I shake my head. "Having the audacity to lie to the public like that—"

"It's what they do." She shrugs. "They're going to do whatever it takes to attract more listeners."

"But it's different when it's a flat-out *lie*." I groan, throwing my head back in frustration. "We've always been in good standing with the reporters there! And if I'm being honest, I'm more upset that they're lying because people are gullible and will believe it. It ruins faith in the Armada if people think we're lax on our standards. And they're *supposed* to be unbiased. They aren't a gossip outlet like The Shout is."

"Well, whoever it was is new and probably doesn't understand the gravity of the idiotic things he says." She rolls her eyes and slides her hands into the pockets of her black coat. "We've been dealing with that since Kon was arrested."

I lean against the building and fold my arms as a chortle of laughter sounds from inside the bar. "I don't think I have much room to complain to you after your family's name has been dragged through the mud by them for years."

She waves me off. "You get used to it."

I sound like an angry fool. I take a deep breath and tuck my hair behind my ears. "I'm sorry. I keep letting this bother me way more than it should."

"Don't be sorry. If someone tried to tarnish the thing I've worked my entire life to achieve, I wouldn't take too kindly to it either. Even then, does it really matter what they say now that you're here?" She holds up her fingers like a picture frame. "The youngest, greatest captain of the last century does not need a bunch of moronic reporters worshipping the ground she walks on."

"Or spitting on it?" I ask wryly.

"Yes." Callie flashes her teeth and matter-of-factly tilts her head. "You're catching on."

I concede with a smile and duck my head.

"Momma, look!" Across the street, a little boy with wild red hair tugs the skirt of his mother's dress and points at me. "Look! A sailor!"

Callie casually moves her coat to cover the pistol on her hip and nudges my arm. "These are the interactions that matter, anyways."

She's right. I take a deep breath and stand up straight.

"She's wearing a jacket like one!" The boy yanks on his mother's arm. "Do you see?"

She glances at me with a flushed face as the boy drags her toward Callie and me. "I'm so sorry. He talks nonstop about the boats."

"It's okay." I grin and step forward, straightening my coat. "You don't have to apologize."

"Look!" He runs up, holding a little toy sloop carved out of wood. "It's the fastest in the Commonwealth!"

I make eye contact with Callie as I frown and kneel in front of him. "Really?"

He nods eagerly. "Uh huh!"

"Well, *that* can't be true," I say, injecting faux disbelief into my tone. "The ship that *I* get to sail with is the fastest in the Commonwealth. And the Armada."

He gasps as I pull the Seal from my coat pocket and hold it in my palm for him to see. His jaw falls to the floor as he reaches for the coin. "You're a captain?"

"We heard about her on the news earlier," his mother says to him. "Remember? This is Captain Walker."

He turns back to her and jumps up and down. "Captain Walker!"

I chuckle and pocket the coin. "What's your name?"

He beams at me. "Henry!"

"Maybe once you get through the Armada Academy and become a sailor, we can race." I poke his shoulder. "We'll see who's *really* the fastest in the region."

Henry laughs again and runs back to his mother. She mouths a silent thank you as the two of them walk away.

"Did you see that? She's a captain! A real captain!"

My chest grows warm as I stand back up, still smiling. Callie's stone-cold expression finally cracks, and she grins. "You're quite the celebrity, Ems."

"Hardly." I dust off my hands. "I'm just being nice."

"'Nice' is what that little boy is going to remember for the rest of his life," she says, taking a deep breath. "And that's what the others who *know* you will talk about. Forget what the headline chasers say."

I tilt my head and narrow my eyes at her. "When did you become so thoughtful?"

"It's not thoughtful. I don't think the people who don't know you are worth your time, anyway," she says bluntly, stepping through the door to the bar. "So why worry about it?"

As she enters the bar, I glance back at the sunset, which is a backdrop to the ship masts that bob up and down in the distant harbor.

And I wonder.

How far will those you know really be able to take you?

. . .

"All right, Ems. What d'you wager?"

I pick a speck of dirt out from under my fingernail. "You give up drinking for the rest of your life and become a respectable member of society?"

"Funny." Miles takes off his red coat and tosses it to the side before rolling up his shirt sleeves. His arms are only slightly smaller than his ego. "And you'll give up your and Charles's library? Reading is boring."

Callie and Vaughn are sitting together on a bench against the wall, seemingly deep in conversation. I watch them curiously for a moment before turning back to my brothers.

Charles knits his brow. "You did not just equate being a drunkard to enjoying reading."

"I am not a drunkard. I enjoy a drink. There's a difference." Miles picks up one of the throwing knives and squares his shoulders to the target. The throwing lane is sectioned off with scratched wooden walls so nobody catches a blade in their bourbon, which has happened before. I've always found it odd that the owners chose throwing knives over cards, dice, or other objectively safer forms of entertainment for a bar full of drunks, but I'd be lying if I said I didn't enjoy it.

"Do you remember that technique I told you about?" Charles grabs my wrist and adjusts my grip as I take aim. "Hold the flat part of the handle so it's facing up."

"Right, right, right," Miles waves him off. "Emery?"

"Twenty novas." My tongue skims my teeth. "But I want to go first."

"Fine."

I run my finger along the flat of the blade and bring my arm behind my head. My chest tightens just as the blade passes my ear, and the knot releases as it leaves my hand. It sticks about two inches out from the bullseye with a satisfying *thunk*. Nearly half the blade is embedded into the red-painted middle ring, between the blue bullseye and the yellow outer ring.

Miles raises his eyebrows. "Impressive. Who has the score?"

"I do." Vaughn appears beside Charles and grabs a piece of paper and a pencil from the cup that's screwed into the wall next to the stall.

"That's three for the captain. First to twenty-one without going over. No cheating."

He winks at me, and I grin.

Miles's motion is faster, and the knife strikes the blue bullseye with a startling *thwack*. Wood chips fall to the floor below the target.

"Five." He waggles his brows at me.

Thud. Bullseye. "Eight," I smirk back. "You're not beating me."

He swears as he misses his next shot and hits the outer yellow. "That blade was crooked. I remember seeing it last time we played."

"Oh, sure." Callie leans against the edge of the stall and folds her arms. A crease sits between her brows. "Blame the tool."

Miles gives her a dirty look.

"Your form is too rigid," Charles pipes up. "If you just—"

Thud. I hit the blue. "Thirteen, Vaughn?"

He smiles at me. "Thirteen."

"Come on, Emery," Miles mutters. His next throw is in the red, and he goes to eleven.

The game ends two throws later at twenty-one when I hit the bullseye in the dead center, taking me to twenty-one. My chest swells with pride as I turn to him and smile, drawing upon as much annoying-youngest-sibling energy as I can muster.

Miles shakes his head. "I used to beat you at this every night without fail. Charles, you remember that, don't you?"

"Oh, of course." Charles throws him a bone. "You were absolutely *fantastic* to watch. Just *enamoring*."

"Yes, I was." Miles steps out of the stall and wrinkles his nose at me. "You wouldn't be good if it weren't for me, Emery."

"You stroke his ego too much," Vaughn murmurs to Charles with a crooked smile.

Charles grins and jokingly nudges Miles's shoulder, and Miles whispers something that has all three of them laughing. Callie glances at me and boredly arches her eyebrows.

"You want to go, Charles?" I ask, tossing the knife in the air and catching it.

He waves his hand, shooing me away.

"Cal?" I offer.

Callie shrugs, but takes her mark and loses twenty-one to fourteen.

"Guns are better," she claims. "If we go to the shooting range, it's over for all of you."

Vaughn perks up, his spine straightening. He loves a day at the shooting range more than anyone.

"Sore loser," Miles mutters to Charles.

Callie spins around. "What?"

"*What?*" Miles raises his eyebrows innocently. "I didn't say anything."

Vaughn and I exchange a quick glance and grin at each other again.

"Let me in." A man with short curly hair approaches with a suave, sideways grin. His teeth seem to glow in the lamplight.

"Lieutenant." I return the smile to Kennali Spaulding, the best weapons expert in all of Padstow and the commanding artillery officer for his pirate-hunting crew.

"That was quite the ceremony you had this morning." He twirls one of the knives in his scarred, slender hand. "I was impressed."

"Thank you for being there. Is your crew with you?"

"Some of them are, and they're eyeing to best you after I do." He flashes his teeth at me. "I've gotten better at this since I played you last."

I glance behind him and see a few members of his crew gathered around a nearby table, eagerly watching. A few of them still wear their striped gray uniform coats.

"Challenge accepted." I smile and step aside as I clasp my hands behind my back. "You first."

He hits the yellow ring, and I nail the bullseye on my next three throws. I hit an intentional shot at the red and the yellow, and the game is over before he breaks double digits.

"Have some mercy." Kennali's brow furrows as he drops his remaining knives. They clang together as they hit the floor. "Good grief, Captain."

"I'll try." A man from Kennali's crew comes forward, though I don't know his name. He has curly red hair and a pockmarked face.

We play a round, and he gets a little closer than Kennali, but still loses twenty-one to seventeen. A woman from their table jumps up to try her hand, but she also falls short.

"Showoff." Miles rolls his eyes and crosses his arms.

"Okay, okay." Kennali steps in to defend his crew's honor. "How about this, Captain? If we can find someone in the bar to beat you, then you owe everyone drinks. Everyone in the room."

A sailor at a different table raises his half-empty mug. "I second that!"

I glance back at my brothers and the twins. Miles shrugs and nods, but Callie and Vaughn exchange uneasy looks. They're technically on duty, but most of the people in the bar are my family's colleagues and acquaintances—*my* colleagues and acquaintances. I don't think they need to worry.

I make eye contact with Charles, who smiles and rubs his hands together.

"And so the slaughter begins!" He laughs. "Who wants to take on the undefeated champion?"

My feathers ruffle at the attention, but people start lining up along the side of the stall. Vaughn's paper collection quickly grows as he keeps score, and the pile of wood chips on the floor grows and grows until there's enough to use as kindling for a fire. The line of people shrinks one by one, and by the end, my elbow and shoulder ache after so many throws.

I turn back to Callie and the boys and grimace, my competitive fire nothing more than a pile of ash. "Is that it?"

"You are nineteen and oh." Vaughn strikes a line through the most recent score. "Are you throwing in the towel?"

I rub my sore shoulder. "I'd like to."

"Anyone else?" Kennali calls out to the crowd, though he's lost his gusto as well. Everyone stands around and kicks at the dirt on the floor.

I sigh at the glum crowd and drop the knife in my hand. "You know what? Everyone gets free drinks because I'm calling the game now. My treat!"

The crowd disperses with shouts of gratitude and excitement as they maneuver toward the bar. I blink the exhaustion from my eyes and force a smile.

Miles nudges me, sweat beading on his forehead. "Are you really paying for everyone's drinks? I'll help."

"Same here," Charles says as he knits his brow. "That's a tall order."

I wave them off. "Don't worry about it. It was my idea."

"Nineteen and oh is a new record, believe it or not." Jessie, one of the barhands, takes one of the papers and scribbles my name and the number nineteen before tacking it to the wall with one of the knives. She smiles at me and claps softly. "Very nice, Captain."

I force a chuckle, which unintentionally becomes a scoff.

Jessie flicks her braid over her shoulder. "Do you guys want anything before the onslaught begins?"

"I'll pass, but thank you," Charles says, adjusting his collar and undoing the top button of his shirt.

"Drink of choice, Miss Riggs?" Miles dramatically offers Callie his elbow. "My treat."

"I'm on duty." She scowls, pushing his arm away. "And frankly, you should act like it, too."

"I was just being polite. I have *no idea* where this attitude is coming from." His chest sticks out even more than usual as he huffs a sigh and turns away from us. "So *dramatic*."

Callie rolls her eyes and follows him to the bar, and Charles glances at me with a bored grimace as he unbuttons the cuffs of his red coat and trots after them.

I touch the chain around my neck and turn to Vaughn.

"I've never heard of anyone buying drinks for the losers." He smiles and runs a hand through his spiky black hair. "How *humble* of you."

"I know most of them anyway and needed to say thank you for coming today," I say with a suggestive grin. "But I might need help hauling all of that money back up here."

He chuckles, a sound that deepens my smile as we start toward the storage room stairs on the opposite side of the bar. "You are not very subtle."

"What did subtlety ever get anyone?"

Vaughn and I wade through the crowd to the storage room, and I run my fingers along the rough stone wall as I step lightly down the dark, damp stairway. Each wooden slat of the staircase is half-rotted and creaks under my weight in the dark, and when we reach the bottom, Vaughn strikes a match and ignites the lantern on the rickety desk against the wall. It casts a dim yellow light across the dank room. There are a few splintered cabinets pushed up against the stone walls, along with some locked chests, crates, and chests of drawers, concealing enough secrets and stories to fill libraries.

I pull off my coat and lay it on one of the crates as I take a deep breath to relax my shoulders. I cuff the sleeves of my blouse as chill creeps down my back.

Vaughn casually perches himself on one of the chests and sighs, his head dipping to one side. The sleeves of his black coat slide over his hands as he grips the edge of the crate. "How large of a tab do you think is growing up there?"

"Large enough that I probably should've kept my mouth shut." I reach under the neckline of my shirt and unclasp the metal chain around my neck. Attached to it is a small bronze key, its head as thick and round as a nova coin.

The wall opposite the stairwell is a mosaic of eleven iron vaults, and four counts up from the floor is mine, perfectly at my eye level. I unlock it, and the stacks of novas inside reflect off the flickering lamp-light, covering the entire bottom and nearly stretching to the top of the iron box.

"I'd say. . ." Vaughn's mouth puckers as he looks up at the wooden ceiling. "At least two hundred and fifty novas. Assuming nobody gets greedy and goes back for seconds."

"Never underestimate how greedy one can be when given a hand-out." I grin back at him and start piling twenty-five-nova coins into my left pocket. I accidentally knock one of the small stacks over and begin rebuilding it, ensuring each coin lines up perfectly with its neighbors.

Vaughn watches me, his brow furrowed. "Mickey and Jessie's sharp eyes wouldn't let that happen. Do you remember how Mickey caught that man drugging someone's drink a while back? He was wiping down a table on the other side of the room and saw a man drop something into one of the mugs on the counter."

"Eagle eye." I finish perfecting the coin stack and reach into my right pocket for the Seal, letting it twirl between my fingers. "Do we know what ended up happening to that man?"

"Technically, I'm not supposed to say," Vaughn replies coyly, smoothing his mustache. "You know, confidentiality and whatnot."

I turn and raise an eyebrow at him. "Yeah?"

He puckers his lips and tilts his head to the side. "I could get in trouble with my father. I don't think you'd want that."

I smile and fold my arms.

He sighs. "Well, since you're *so* convincing with that gorgeous smile, I can tell you that the man who did it will be rotting in his cell for a very long time. A handful of the other prisoners were made aware of his intentions, and I don't imagine it'll be a pleasant stay. My mother and father made sure of that."

"Isn't that fantastic?" I lock the safe and tuck the key under my shirt once more. "I don't see anyone jumping out to scold you, so I think you're safe."

He dramatically smacks his chest. "Ah. What a relief."

I laugh, despite how stupid the joke was. Sometimes I wonder if he's genuinely trying to be funny, or if he does it because he knows that no matter what, I'll still smile. The way his eyes twinkle as he speaks in an airy, teasing voice is so endearing.

Vaughn's eyes lose their playful sheen as they fall to my pocket. "May I see it again?"

"The Seal?"

He nods, and I walk over to where he's seated.

He pouts his lips in thought as he runs his fingers over the engravings, where the heads side is the rectangular crest of the Armada, and the tails side is my name carved in coiling calligraphy, all outlined with red.

"Beautiful," he whispers.

I'm standing in front of him, and our legs are touching. The height of the chest he's sitting on brings us eye to eye—black dots of stubble pepper his face like little flakes around his thin mustache. He's very handsome, but his comforting presence is all that occupies my mind.

I exhale softly and close my eyes.

"Are you okay?" he asks quietly.

"I finally feel . . ." I pause and let my head tip to the side. "At ease."

"Oh?"

"I feel like everyone's been looking at me all day. Like I live in a jar."

"I was worried about you," he mumbles, his fingers intertwining with mine at my side. "You seem to be handling it nicely."

"The attention has always been there," I reply softly, "but this is all anyone is going to talk about when I'm around. Talking *about* me as if I'm not even there."

"The youngest captain ever isn't something that follows others around as it does you."

I bite my cheek. "That and the fact that my parents run the Armada."

But what *don't* they see? Nobody was there when the sun hadn't broken the ocean's horizon to watch me getting to know the ships, learning their heartbeats and how to control them. They weren't in the Academy classrooms in the late hours of the night when the doors were locked and poring over books on history and theory until the candles were burnt to nothing. They didn't see me perfecting the knife throw, or the rifle shot, or the swordplay in the wee hours of the morning on the beaches. None of it. My name was in the Academy without the slightest push from my parents. I started low and clawed my way out just like everyone else.

They only see what The Messenger and The Shining Star cast light on and bend shadows around.

But the one truth I wish they'd see is that the only life I ever dreamed of since the attack was a captain's. A captain who would find pirates like Warren Chadwick and keep them away from those who can't defend themselves. The captain who would stop the merciless murderers and catch the traffickers; who'd be what Padstow needed in a moment of weakness and a shield for its citizens.

I dig my nails into my palm and grit my teeth, my vision unfocused. "I don't wish it were different," I whisper, "Because if it were, I wouldn't be here. That's a price I can pay."

"Of course." Vaughn notices me fidgeting with the key and wrapping the chain around my index finger. "If there's no pressure, then it doesn't mean anything, does it?"

"True."

Pressure provides promise. If I close my eyes, I can see a life of success panning out exactly how I want, straight and glowing. There's a life with my family, with Vaughn. There's a career I can be proud of, where there is peace on the seas, and where people don't have to be afraid anymore.

I can practically touch it if I reach far enough.

Neither of us speaks for a moment, but Vaughn reaches up and brushes loose strands of hair from my face as he cups my jaw. He smiles softly.

I frown. "What?"

"It's funny how you worry so much about the news and how everyone is watching you, but less about the people who want you dead."

"I won't be dead unless they are first," I mumble, glancing at the floor.

His eyes crinkle.

My skin starts to ache. "I am going to watch them all swing from a noose and rot in a cave until they die if it's the last thing I do."

He gently grabs my wrist and slips his thumb under my fingers, causing them to relax.

I keep fiddling with the key and staring at the wall over his shoulder, my chest buzzing with an animalistic desire to hunt, just like we were hunted. Padstow's pirate hunters are strong, but they were caught off guard the night Warren Chadwick came to town.

Chadwick was the backbone of a deal gone awry that two of Padstow's most successful traders had taken part in. Aleksander Nowak and Coy Hadley grew greedy and hired Chadwick to intercept a shipment of gold bars that a trader from Blazer Point, another major city in the northern corner of the East, was transporting to another city in the Northern Estates. This mystery gold trader had pulled out of a deal with Coy and Aleksander months previous, and the two men wanted to resell the captured gold and recoup what they believed they lost in the previously foiled deal."

Once Chadwick saw how much gold was really aboard that ship, he demanded a larger payment than Coy and Aleksander had already set. Since the conniving duo already had the ship and the gold in their possession, they sent Chadwick away without as much as a single nova in his pocket, but this dog would not go down quietly. He was a young, inexperienced pirate captain looking to make his name mean something. And he did.

He returned to Padstow within a week. What started as a targeted attack against the two families turned into a muddled city-wide brawl as the night went on, with hordes of different pirate crews he'd recruited burning and looting and killing like savages. A group of them breached the grounds of our house in the middle of it, and one of their bullets burst through the door and caught my father in the side.

The only time I saw Chadwick was at the end of the chaos, when the dust settled over a bloody, ash-filled morning. Bands of citizens were dousing the fires burning across the city, while others were screaming at the loss of their friends, neighbors, and families. My mother was watching my father as he lay in the hospital, pale and unconscious, while doctors dug the bullet out of his ribs.

And I, a scared fourteen-year-old Academy cadet who barely had the strength to hold a rifle, ran to the harbor as moans and cries of agony followed me like ghosts. I stood on the dock as Chadwick sailed into the sunrise, abandoning the mess of bodies and burned buildings he'd left behind.

I saw what those degenerates had done to my home and to the people I love. I saw the terror that came when nobody was there to keep it in check, and from then on, I dedicated every ounce of time I had to learning their patterns and how they think so I could catch them. I was enamored. I *am* enamored.

Vaughn reaches for the key, and our fingers touch. I blink, suddenly remembering where I am and where he is, touching me. His knuckles graze my neck.

"Are you sure you're okay?" he mumbles, brow knit and eyes weary with concern.

I nod, though the images of my father's blood soaking the floor of our house and the sounds of screams echoing off our ceiling replay in the back of my mind like a capsule on repeat.

Vaughn takes my hand and brings my knuckles to his lips. He touches the key with his other hand.

"Let me hold onto that for you while you sail," he mumbles against my skin. "You wouldn't want a pirate like Chadwick getting his hands on this, would you?"

Be present. I take a deep breath. *Be with him now.*

"I suppose not." I set my hands on his shoulders and let them snake into a clasp on the back of his neck. "Unless I can convince you to learn how to sail and come with me. It wouldn't matter who had the key at that point."

A smile curves across his lips. The dimples on his cheeks transform the stirring anger in my heart into a light, warm pitter.

My fingers slide under the collar of his shirt as I let myself smile. "That could also mean lots of quiet time away from here, you know."

"Oh, I'd love that." His voice is so deep that it makes the hairs on the back of my neck stand on end. His arms wrap around my waist. "I could stand some silence for a change."

I lean forward and kiss him. Vaughn is not a gentle creature in the dark like he is elsewhere, and his strong arms stay locked around my waist as we kiss. He tastes vaguely of sweat from being in the crowded, musty bar, and his lips curl into a sneaky grin as his hands reach up and tangle in my hair. "If someone comes down here—"

"They won't." I press my lips against his again. "You worry too much."

I perch myself on his knee, and he cradles me tightly and kisses me deeper and deeper, and it makes me giddy. His kisses grow sweeter as time passes, and his lips are surprisingly soft against my neck and my jaw.

A few moments later, he cups his hand at the base of my skull and touches his forehead to mine. He takes a deep breath. "Please let me hold onto it for you," he whispers. "That's part of our whole future locked away and only accessible by that key."

I open my eyes and pull back slightly.

"What?" His eyes flash with brief dismay.

"You said *our* future."

I have imagined a thousand futures with him that I thought were out of reach. The long hours at sea have been hard on our relationship at times. He isn't a trained sailor and couldn't come with me, nor do I think I'd let him and put him in harm's way—though that hasn't stopped me from yearning.

"Say the word when you're ready, and it can be." He reaches for the key, but I grab his hand and squeeze his fingers.

"You're starting to worry like your sister," I whisper playfully.

Something flashes behind his eyes, but it's gone in an instant. "Emery."

"*Our* future." I grin at the thought, and warm tendrils spread from my chest to the rest of my body. "I would love that."

"Eventually," he chuckles, kissing me again.

The sound of breaking glass echoes across the ceiling, and we both look up as the thunking footsteps are replaced with shouting.

Vaughn and I untangle from each other, and I grab my coat and hastily slip into it as I sprint up the stairs.

Through the gaps in the crowd, I can see two people tussling on the floor, one of whom I immediately recognize.

"Hey!" I shove my way through the group. "Miles!"

He regains his balance and spits bloody saliva onto the wood at his feet as I yank him back by the collar of his shirt.

Charles appears on his other side. "What is the matter with you?" he hisses.

"You say *anything* like that again and you'll regret it," Miles snaps at the other man. "I'll make you regret it!"

"Oh, shut up," he belittles. He was one of my opponents in the throwing game. "What good reason would they have to lie about that?"

I grab Miles's arm. "What is going on?"

"He was talking about what the news said and had a little more to add on to it." He's glaring daggers at the man. "Do you want to tell her what you said about her, or should I?"

"Stop." I glare at Miles, my chest tightening. "Don't."

"You have no idea what you're talking about if you believe a word of that," Charles says authoritatively, squaring his shoulders to the man.

"Nobody wants you rich brats in here anyway." He pushes Charles into the crowd, and Miles lunges forward again. I grab fistfuls of his shirt and dig my heels into the floor, though it's like trying to stop an ox. My boots skid against the wooden ground.

"Easy!" I snap at him.

"Look at the prissy baby being saved by his sister." The man rolls his eyes and takes a drunken step backward. "Not like she can do much for herself anyway."

Miles shoves me out of the way, but he meets the man's swinging fist, and I flinch as my brother's nose snaps under the impact.

Vaughn springs forward and tries to wrestle the man away, but another jumps to the man's aid and pushes him off. Chaos erupts as random patrons jump in to either fight or try to stop it, accompanied by shouting and shattering glass. Mickey and another bartender leap out from behind the counter. The crowd pushes me back as I stretch my arms forward to grab Miles, but he disappears in the wave of people.

Someone shoves me in the back, and I catch someone else's bony knee in the jaw as I fall forward. Sharp pain zips through my wrists as my hands collide with the floor.

A pair of arms hook under mine and hauls me to my feet.

"Are you okay?" Callie shouts over the chaos.

"Where's Charles?" I wince and rub my face. "We need too—"

"Everyone knock it off!" The second bartender's voice booms over the noise. He yanks Mickey out of the scrum as a full glass of booze flies through the air and lands in the crowd. Someone cries out in pain, but despite the commotion, movement near the front door catches my eye.

Someone clothed in all black and has a triangular hat pulled snugly over his head, but icy blond hair peeks out just under the rim. His head turns, which reveals a sharp nose and jaw.

And time stands still as I stare.

Chadwick.

He bolts out the door and disappears into the dark. Without a second thought, I pull away from Callie and sprint across the bar, past the bloodied patrons and Riggs patrolmen who have shown up to quell the chaos.

"Emery, wait!" Callie shouts after me.

The night air is chilly and whips across my face as I sprint outside, my vision tunneled like a dog's when chasing a cat down an alleyway.

He must have followed us home to rescue his errand boy. He might be planning another move to get close to me, just like he's tried and failed at in the past.

What if it's both?

The possibilities and questions are a whirlwind in my rigid mind as I run.

But when I finally stutter to a stop in the middle of a deserted street, he's nowhere to be seen.

7

"Good morning, good morning! Today, your Messenger comes to you on a beautiful spring morning in the aftermath of a ruckus-filled evening involving the Armada's newest jewel. Reports have trickled in that Emery Walker, who was inducted into the Captain's Hall just yesterday, was caught in the middle of a fight at a local pub that resulted in numerous arrests. Authorities from the Riggs patrol were quick to the scene, and many witnesses claimed to have seen Captain Walker fighting various patrons of the Tab, which is a popular drinking spot in town. Others said that—"

"I love the smell of slander in the morning," I mumble as we pass a dress shop with the news blaring from an open window. "Don't you?"

Hyde wrinkles his brow as he glances at the spindle on the windowsill. He wears a tri-pointed hat that shields part of his face, just as a precaution on the off chance someone from Emery's crew or any other sailor who's been with her during her attempts to catch me is out and about. I'd rather not run the risk of one of them recognizing him.

"Does slander have a smell?" he asks me.

"Yes." I gesture to the bakery on our left where a baker is stretching and folding a giant lump of dough. "Right now it's sourdough."

"—safe to say it's not looking great for the young pirate-hunting captain thus far. Other reports have said her older brother, Armada boatswain Miles Walker, was also involved in the scuffle, but The Messenger is waiting for an official statement from the Riggs patrol. In other news, import rates have decreased in the last two weeks, according to Stanton family reports. Jameson Stanton came out and said that the ports in all of Padstow's major trading partners' cities have been under attack by pirates. Authorities from—"

In the distance, the clock tower sounds to mark the nine o'clock hour. It isn't a bell, but a high-pitched whistle that tweets nine times and rips apart the eardrums of everyone within a ten-mile radius. I wince and rub the side of my head as an ache pulses through my temples.

"You didn't have to be there in the first place, you know," Hyde mutters in my ear. "You'd still have your beard, at least. I can still see your face clearly enough even with the hat and wig."

"I wanted to make sure people were *talking* about what the news said about her, Hyde. Word of mouth spreads like a disease, especially here." I glare at him. "You knew this was going to be risky when I asked you to come with me. Would you rather be on the ship doing nothing?"

He gives me a dirty look and keeps walking, though his limp looks especially bad today. I watch his awkward gait, and his twisted leg seems to bend under each step.

"We can rest if you need," I suggest, glancing from side to side. "I'm sure that bakery has coffee or pastries we can snack on in the meantime."

"It's fine," he mumbles.

"Hyde."

"I'm *fine*." He clenches his teeth in frustration. "I can manage."

"It'll feel better once this plan is in motion." I try to keep the mood lighthearted and quell his anger. "But the other day, I overheard Harrison talking about how he assisted with a prosthetic installation about the time you broke it last year. I think you'd look stellar hobbling around with a peg leg, but I digress."

He snorts, trying to hide his smile.

"I appreciate that you're here," I reiterate. "I wouldn't have left you on the ship. I shouldn't have said that."

He wrinkles his nose. "Gee, you really know how to make a man feel special, don't you?"

And that's what I get for trying to be nice.

We walk in silence until we're out past the edge of the business center of town, where the shiny brick and plaster buildings morph into crumbling stone and rotted wood shacks. We turn the corner onto a quiet, dark street where the windows are shuttered with splintered planks and the doors are shackled shut. It's the one eerie dead area of the bustling city, where eyes watch us from the cracks in the concrete and whispers follow our every step.

Hyde glances over his shoulder and keeps a hand on his pistol as we pass a group huddled at the entrance of an alleyway. "Warren, if this is a trap—"

"Then fire away." I look back at him to confirm his composure before opening the door to a shoddy shack wedged between two stone buildings.

I'm not sure what the shack was used for, though the smell would indicate an abandoned slaughterhouse, reeking of old blood and rot. I wrinkle my nose, and Hyde mutters a curse under his breath.

Quite honestly, it's a mess otherwise. There are tables lining the walls with various maps of Padstow marked with tiny pins and scribbles of handwriting. Leatherbound journals and ink pens are scattered across the desks, and rusted lanterns hanging from the ceiling do little to light the space. A few maps and pens are scattered across the floor.

In the back, looking as stressed and sweaty as I've ever seen him, Eldon Riggs is talking to one of his black-clad patrolmen. He glances at us and dismisses him.

"Be thorough!" He barks after the guard, who flinches as he shuts the back door.

"What is going on?" Hyde demands.

"You." Eldon points a scornful finger at me. "This is your fault."

I scowl. "I need you to narrow that down a little, please and thank you."

"That little stunt you pulled at the bar last night has set my entire police operation on fire! She saw you!"

My face relaxes. "Ah. Did she tell you that?"

"My twins told me. Why did you even have to be there in the first place?" Eldon scrubs his thinning black hair and shakes his head. "I could have sent someone else to make sure whatever it was you had planned worked!"

"You know better than anyone that if you want something done correctly, you do it yourself," I reply. "I had to start the conversation with two sailors to make sure her dimwitted brother overheard. It went perfectly."

"Perfectly," he mutters. "I should put you in charge of the fake investigation to search for Warren Chadwick, and you can see how *perfectly* it goes. I don't have time for this! You've put my entire family and the other guards in a bad spot with the news, which is worse than where we already were, by the way. Every single family in the upper class is going to be talking about this by noon!"

I bite my tongue. He's so irrational.

"Well, it's a good thing I've offered a way to help you strike back against a few of them." I try to hide the scoff in my voice, but he picks up on it. "Lest we forget."

"You'd *better* do well on your promise or I will expose every lie and back alley deal you are running in this city," he snaps. "I have too much on the line for you to be acting this way!"

And how much does he think *I* have?

I concede with a smile, having neither the leverage nor the energy to argue with him. "I apologize. I had a disguise at the bar, but it was lost in the scuffle. I promise not to cause any more trouble right now."

He grunts in response.

"I can . . ." My lips twist as I roll my weight from my heels to my toes. "I can increase your cut of the spoils as a reparation once this is finished, if it'd make you feel better. It should cover a decent chunk of what you'll lose from whatever these families pay for your services."

His tongue pokes out of the corner of his mouth. "Fine."

"Excellent." I fold my arms. "Now, what do you have for me?"

Eldon gestures for us to sit in the two chairs pushed under one of the desks. I stay standing, but Hyde sits to relieve the pressure on his leg, wincing.

"Do you want the good news or bad news first?" Eldon asks with a quirked brow.

I wrinkle my forehead. "Humor me."

"Luckily for you, Judge Gordon is a predictable twit," he deadpans, digging through one of the drawers. "He arrives at the courthouse at the exact same time in the morning and comes home at the exact same time every night in his chauffeured carriage. One guard drives the horses while the other sits inside with him. He insists they always be with him, so your best chance is to wait until he's alone inside his house."

"And then drag him back across town to the harbor?" Hyde raises his brows. "I don't think so."

Eldon drops a scribble-covered map on the table, which I spin to face me.

"What would make him divert?" I ask. "Doesn't he go out with his wife? Is he ever at that fancy dancing hall down the road or out to dinner?"

"He's addicted to his work," Eldon mutters, slumping back in his chair. "He's either at home or the courthouse running the city."

Hyde rubs his leg. "It's almost as if his job is *very* important."

I space my fingers out across the map. My forefinger rests on the harbor, and by my estimation, the courthouse sits no more than a hundred yards away. The surrounding buildings consist of government offices, the main headquarters for the Riggses and their patrols, and the Armada's main command outpost, whose stone walls stretch nearly the length of the harbor.

But where is the weakness? I wonder.

I purse my lips. "The judge might break his routine if his little golden girl comes calling for help." I glance at Hyde. "Perhaps?"

He shrugs. "Maybe."

It plays out like a stage show in my mind. "Let's say she writes to him and conveniently asks him to meet . . ." I make a *tsk* sound and point to a street corner pressed against the mountains. "Here. We can use a carriage, can't we, Eldon?"

"What for?" he asks.

"Transporting him to the harbor. I know it's a short walk, but we can't risk anyone seeing."

"I could arrange it," Eldon sighs, rolling a pen between his fingers.

I meet eyes with Hyde again. "You're a better writer than me. Could you—"

"Of course. Should we aim for distressed? Friendly? Conversational?"

"Have some fun with it." I shrug. "Why not?"

Eldon's confused eyes flick between the two of us.

I grab a discarded pen and circle the area on the map. "You said the areas closer to the mountains aren't as busy, so can we work here? Can you *ensure* we can work here?"

He studies the map for a bit. "I'll see what I can do."

"Perfect." I take a deep breath. "And what of Miss Walker?"

Eldon's fingers drum on the desk. "I'm not worried about her as much. Her guards are just waiting for instructions. I'm not sure what her schedule is like now that she's been inducted, but from what I've been told, she's going to interrogate your errand boy and get to work quickly on finding you."

My jaw clenches. "Is that so?"

"You should really know something else, too." He looks at me warily and glances at the back door. The tension in the air is thick like the dough in the bakery we passed. "The judges under Gordon have been working to make the piracy penalties harsher. Their first step is eliminating trials for people accused of it and appointing two judges to handle the investigation rather than the prosecutors. And this is all just a rumor, but based on the investigations Gordon has been running on your errand boy, they may be fixing to send him to the Pereculum."

A single shiver traces down my spine.

"They think they have enough to convict him."

"Without a trial?" I say exasperatedly. "That's abominable!"

"Again, it's all just a rumor." Eldon wipes his sleeve across his forehead. "But that's all the more reason to get the boy out with haste."

My stomach rolls.

Most of what is known about the mysterious prison is loads of he said, she said, where someone claims to know someone who was stationed there or some other long-winded connection. The rumor is that sailors who are arrested by Padstow and Osecola of the Eastern Commonwealth and Turtle Point of the Northern Estates and convicted of piracy will be transported to the prison island, locked in an underground cage, and left to rot.

But that's all we know about it.

Some claim that it doesn't even exist because there's been no proof besides the word of people who have been stationed there—or the word that's been passed along. Allegedly, those soldiers have been sworn to secrecy under threats to their lives, but it didn't deter the rumors.

The ones that I have heard the most consistently is that the Pereculum is where sailors go to never see the sun or feel the wind on their face again. They say that prisoners live, eat, and die in hell. Kearon would not last a week.

My fists curl as I snatch the map off the table and storm toward the door. A pencil snaps under my foot. "Then we need to move quickly, because that could happen any day."

"Warren, wait." Hyde grunts as hobbles after me.

I whirl and point my finger at Eldon. "I want as much information as possible about Miss Walker's routine by tonight so we can set this plan in motion. Written, please."

He looks taken aback as he rises from his seat. "I suppose I—"

"Lovely. I'll come pick your notes up tonight."

Hyde's injury is only a blip in the back of my mind as I race down the street. He winces in pain behind me as he hustles to keep up. "What are you doing?"

"We need to get the rest of the crew here and ready to move." I fold the map and shove it into my pocket. "This isn't going to work if Kearon is gone. I'll write to the ship and have Harrison send Chip while you write the fake letter."

"Bloody hell," he mutters. "Going down in a spiraled frenzy like this is not a good look."

"I've brought Padstow to its knees in a frenzy before." I clench my teeth. "And that's bold of you to assume that we'll go down for this at all."

8

Emery

AN EERILY SILENT house makes a great echo chamber for my thoughts, bouncing and ringing in my ears like the clapper in Padstow's bell tower.

They follow me into the kitchen. This morning's news reel is sitting on the counter next to the spindle, untouched since Elle set it there in the early hours.

But I grab an orange from the fruit bowl beside it and walk away.

In the living room, I stand at the window that stretches from the marble floors to the polished wood ceilings, and stare out at the sunrise as the city basks in its dewy morning rays. I glance down and bite my tongue.

My mother appears beside me and, for a moment, we stare in silence at the city. I do my best to keep the orange peel in one giant piece as I tear it away from the fruit, but I grit my teeth in annoyance when it rips.

"Morning, Ems," she mumbles.

"Hi."

A few beats of silence pass.

"I left the Kyotic book on your desk. It was a good read."

I say nothing and stare straight ahead.

She winces and touches my cheek, right where the bruise is. "Emery, your face."

"It'll fade." I recoil from her soft fingers. "Callie pulled me away before the fighting got worse."

"Before it was worse for *you*." My mother sighs. "Not your bone-headed brother."

Miles couldn't keep his swollen eyes open as we dragged him

home, and his nose was bent so far out of shape that none of us dared to look at his face.

Charles did the heavy lifting to help carry him home alongside Vaughn, who was bloody and exhausted from the fighting. He and Callie dropped us off and left without another word, much to my confused frustration.

"Vaughn was trying to protect him, too," I snap, pushing the thought away. "I don't want any more bad things said about the Riggses because they were trying to do their job."

I regret the sharp tone as soon as it leaves my lips. I grimace and turn back to the orange.

My mother takes a deep breath. "Well, considering how the night went, I'm glad it wasn't you who came home with a broken nose. I can only imagine what that man would have done to you if—"

"Mother—"

"I didn't mean it as a jab at the twins." She glares at me. "I'm just saying—"

"That man knew who I was. It wouldn't have gone that way."

"You don't know that. You say that like you're invincible."

Sticky orange juice leaks between my fingers. "I didn't think I was in danger, and that instinct has never failed me."

Her eyes fall to the lush flower garden in front of the window, where white orchids sprout from the mossy ground.

I swallow my pride and glance at the ceiling. "I'm sorry for snapping," I mumble. "I have a lot on my mind."

"You have a big day ahead, don't you?" Her eyes crinkle, and she sighs again.

"What?"

"I don't think I'm ready for you to leave on that ship again."

I blink and look up, a little taken aback. "What makes you say that?"

"It's not that I don't think you're ready." She meets my eye. "Just. . . please don't go anywhere alone. I'm just worried that whatever target you had on your back before has doubled in size."

I swallow.

After telling the twins and my family that I saw Chadwick at The

Tab, it took nearly thirty minutes for my father to convince my mother not to order me to be locked in our house until Chadwick was found, though she fought tooth and nail. She tried to invoke every power she had as my commanding officer, but my father was able to pull her off the ledge.

Her hands smooth over my shoulders anxiously. "You have to give each of those pirates hell." Her voice trembles slightly. "You must stay on your best game the entire time and not let up for a second, or you're going to get hurt. Perform like you've been taught, and don't forget who you are and the name you carry with you. That will always be with you at the end of the day when this isn't." She grasps my hand and runs her thumb over my captain's ring.

My chest deflates at the sad sheen over her eyes. Sad, but proud. "Mother—"

"I'm not going to risk losing you like I almost lost your father. Promise me that you'll do all of that." Her eyes are glassy. "Please."

I'll never forget the terror on her face from the night of Chadwick's invasion. It makes my skin prickle.

So for that, I will. For my father's life and my mother's terror, I will.

I take a deep breath. "I promise."

She leans forward and kisses my forehead, and I rest my head on her shoulder as we embrace. Her stiff posture relaxes, but the moment is short-lived as a swift knock at the door breaks the silence.

I swear under my breath and swallow a bite of orange. "They're early."

"Go." She takes the orange peels and kisses my head. "I love you. Be safe."

"I love you, too."

Charles races down the massive spiral staircase and meets me in the entryway as I slide into my coat. He's fixing his curls, particularly the one that hangs across his forehead.

"How's Miles?" I ask, cramming my feet into my boots.

"Still pulverized." He shudders. "Father said a doctor is coming to reset his nose later today."

"I want to see him." I yank the laces of my boots taut. "Is he awake?"

"No."

I straighten the collar of my coat and take another deep breath, and Charles sets his hand on my shoulder.

I stop. "What?"

"What's the matter? You seem antsy."

"Why wouldn't I be antsy?" I huff, fidgeting with the collar.

Charles narrows his eyes, but I open the front door and duck past him, stealing his chance to reply.

The twins mumble their hellos and follow behind us. I keep trying to meet Callie's eye, but she keeps her hand on her pistol and stares dead ahead as if I'm not there.

Charles mutters his annoyance at skipping the usual carriage ride, but the walk to the outpost and the harbor wakes up my mind, fully clearing it of the biting anxiety. I roll my shoulders and set my jaw.

It's early enough that the streets are silent, save for our footsteps on the cobblestone road as the sound echoes off the strip-style brick buildings. They stretch the length of the street, with some containing businesses and others used as residential spaces. The corners and perimeters of the windows and doors are accented with mossy gray stone. Everything is tight and stacked in the heart of the city, but the closer we walk toward the harbor, the older the architecture becomes; towering marble pillars support the roofs of squat, white granite structures, and there's more space to move about.

I try to catch Vaughn's eye before he and Charles break off toward the harbor for Charles's teaching shift at the command outpost, but he barely spares me a grin as the two of them disappear down the long cobblestone path.

My cheeks burn in angry embarrassment.

Callie falls into step next to me, and I don't hold back on her. "Are you going to tell me why you haven't spoken to me since we were at The Tab, or will you stay mute?"

"I was up all night dealing with the mess." Her jaw is tight. "A mess that *you* technically made."

I stop dead in my tracks. "I'm sorry?"

She turns to me. "Well, if you hadn't jumped into the fight—"

"I didn't *jump* into anything!" I say defensively.

"All three of you jumped in!" she snaps. "All because Miles couldn't handle a few stupid comments from two drunken idiots!"

"Don't act like you wouldn't have done the same. *I* would have done the same for any of you!"

"That put Vaughn and me in an awful spot, Emery. The only chatter anyone is going to care about is how two core members of the Riggs family failed in their assignments to protect their charges, and it wouldn't have happened if all of you had just stayed out of it!" She turns away and stomps off.

"I will say whatever I have to to set the story straight," I say, jogging to catch up to her. "My word matters more now that—"

"Yes, now that you're a captain." She rolls her eyes and angrily rolls up her sleeves. "It also matters how *we* perform now that you're a captain. It matters how *we* act now that you're a captain, and it matters how w*e* look to the rest of the world, and right now we look like the incompetent idiots that the news and the upper class say we are!"

"No, no, no," I say sharply. "I'll go down to The Shining Star and The Messenger myself and—"

"Stop." She shakes her head and waves her hands. "Just stop, Emery. You can't fix everything, and you run around acting like you can when you know that's not true. Your new status doesn't change that, and you're out of your mind if you keep thinking it will!"

That hits like a slap to the face, and my chest swells with anger. "Fine, then!" I bump her shoulder as I storm past her. "If anyone comes asking about what happened last night, don't expect me to be singing your praises about anything. How do you think that's going to sound?"

I don't bother checking if she's still behind me as I veer toward the Armada's command post.

Control, I remind myself. *Be in control.*

I rake my hands through my hair and inhale, and when I finally glance behind me, Callie isn't there.

I should report her for abandoning her post, but maybe she was right. Charles and I jumping in didn't exactly stop the fight.

I don't have the space for that to be weighing on my conscience, so

I adjust the knife sheath at my side to divert my attention and keep walking.

The command post is easily double the height of every other government building in the area. It's also the only one made completely of gray stone bricks, mostly so it protects the rest of the town from cannon fire. It stretches across three-fourths of the harbor and has six towering spy nests, where soldiers peer out into the horizon with long, bronze-plated telescopes. The Riggs patrolmen prowl the various arched entrances like animals on the hunt, watching for danger.

"Can we trust the Riggses anymore?" I can hear the news outlets whispering in the back of my mind. *"What have they done to deserve our respect?"*

". . . Callie and Vaughn Riggs are not fit for the role they've been given . . ."

In the harbor, the *Chaplain's Heart* bobs gently up and down beside the other Armada ships. She's smaller, though about five knots faster, which shaves anywhere from hours to days off of travel time.

Off in the distance, the waves and trading ships coming and going sparkle under the sunlight as I walk down the hill. I keep my eyes on the horizon, on what's ahead and what I'm working toward.

The building Reese works in is the shiniest, whitest one in the whole sector. I squint and shield my eyes from the reflecting sunlight and ascend the steps. I smile and nod at Ollie, one of the Riggs cousins.

"Captain." He nods with a warm smile as he opens the door for me. "A bit warm for a coat like that, no?"

"Thank you," I say. "And yes, it absolutely is."

It's not much cooler inside, and sweat trickles down my back. I roll my shoulders and stretch my neck as Melanie Tatis eagerly waves at me from behind the secretary's desk, which is the only piece of furniture in the massive white entryway.

"Good morning, Captain Walker!" she squeaks.

I put on a grin. "Good morning Melanie."

"I can officially call you Captain now." She giggles, standing on her tiptoes to be seen over the massive mahogany desk, her brown curls bouncing like springs. "I'm sure you've heard it a thousand times, but congratulations. It's truly amazing."

"Thank you. How is Philip doing? Did he recover from the honeymoon seasickness?"

"Yes. Now all he talks about is wanting to go back to Turtle Point and *actually* experience it since he was so sick for most of it."

"Everyone in my household has been going on and on about the vows he wrote for the ceremony," I chuckle softly. The tension in my mind begins to diffuse. "Nobody knew he was such a poet."

"Ugh, I know." Melanie places a hand over her chest. "I want them framed and hung on my wall."

"My mother knows a few skilled calligraphers who could turn them into decoration, if you'd like that." I drum my fingers on the wood. "I'm pretty sure they charge by the letter, but they aren't terribly expensive."

"Oh, I wouldn't want to heap something else onto your plate, Captain." She waves me off. "Another time."

"No! I insist. Consider it a late wedding gift from me personally." I lean over the desk and lower my voice. "I will not associate my name with the boring silverware my parents gave you."

"The silverware is beautiful . . ." She sighs and shakes her head. "But all right. Can I drop the vows off at your house?"

"I can come by here tomorrow morning and pick them up."

"You're too much, but thank you. I assume you're here to see the judge?"

"Is he here?"

"Yes." She points to the hallway off to her left. "He just returned from an evidence review."

"Thank you, Melanie."

She blows a kiss as I walk away. "Anything for my favorite captain!"

The door to Reese's office at the end of the hall is propped open with a wedge of wood, but I knock anyway.

He looks up from his desk, and I don't miss the shadow hanging over his face before he forces a smile.

"Captain."

"Your Honor." I smile, keeping my facade better than he does as I sit across from him. His face droops with exhaustion. "Did you have a long night?"

"Me? I heard *you* had quite the evening." He pushes his wiry glasses up his nose and frowns at the bruise on my cheek. "Are you okay?"

"It's nothing." I purse my lips and shoot him a look that I hope warns him not to ask further.

He doesn't budge. "You're very tense. What happened?"

I wrinkle my nose and stare out the window. The early morning sunlight streaks through and makes all the darkly-colored furniture look brighter and richer in color. Reese's bookshelf is empty, save for the white vase of red snapdragons sprouting from the opening. The petals look like hungry little mouths looking to feast on the dust coating the shelf.

"Why the snapdragons, again?" I ask, ignoring his question. "I know that's what you proposed to Penny with, but why?"

"They have been known to symbolize protection." His eyes narrow. "Everyone needs protection. The Riggs patrolmen protect the people, but in essence, that is my job as well. That's the job of all of the judges. We uphold the law, which is protection for the people."

"Beautiful," I mumble absentmindedly as I stare at the flower.

"Penny keeps the white ones around the house because she thinks they're prettier, but I've always been fond of red."

"I am as well." I grin, tugging on the lapel of my coat.

"Red was mine before it was ever yours, Captain," he chuckles. "Believe that."

The tightness in my chest has finally loosened. "Not at first. It was the Ridgewoods'. Annette Ridgewood wore a red snapdragon in her hair almost every day at the Academy."

"Annette." Again, he seems taken aback but masks it with a frown. "I'm surprised you remember that."

How could I not? Red was defiance for her. Not many students in the Academy had to work through the dregs and fight for a spot on the class list as hard as she did. Her relationship with her family was always rocky, and they refused to pay for her to attend. Rumors floated, as they usually do, but we never knew the reason they fought. We still don't.

The agreement that was barely agreed upon was that if she passed the entry exam and kept near-perfect grades, then she could attend despite having neither the money nor a maritime history in her family. She was the talk of the Academy before she pulled her records and disappeared from Padstow without a trace.

"At least you have the snapdragons all to yourself now," I say.

"Yes. That was one positive of that ordeal." He smiles dazzlingly. "Penny has been experimenting with cross-pollinating the dragons in our garden, and she was able to get a beautiful shade of violet a few days ago."

I open my mouth to respond, but catch myself. *Stay focused.*

"I'm sorry. I didn't just come to chat." I press my fingers into the desk. "I want to interrogate Kearon Romney myself before you proceed with his sentencing."

"You're quick, aren't you?" He smiles knowingly and hands me a piece of paper.

I scan the report of previous interrogations. "The fact that he was standing with his hands in Chadwick's safe is enough to convict him, right?"

It should be enough to have him locked in the Pereculum until his bones turn to dust.

"He swears on his life that he had no idea who Chadwick really was," Reese replies.

I scoff and roll my eyes. "That can't be true."

"We've had three different people interrogate him over the last two weeks, and he's said the same thing." He hands me more paper. "Chadwick was paying him to watch over the vault and handle his money. He said Chadwick never told him where any of it was coming from or going to."

I shake my head. "Regardless, he's still an accomplice. Willing or unwilling."

"Correct."

I run my sweaty palms over the legs of my pants. "Has Lexington's chief judge written to you about this anymore?"

"Yes, and he and the majority of the judges in that city aren't upset, believe it or not." Reese sits back and folds his arms. "The boy's parents are lobbying to have him extradited, but the judges' majority feel we have jurisdiction because the original attack happened on our soil. We have all the evidence, anyways."

"And did he mention anything about . . ." I pause, searching for the right word. "There wasn't an issue with the fact that we didn't have a warrant?"

Reese shakes his head. "For now, most of them agree it was an 'extenuating circumstance' and don't want to press charges."

I exhale in relief. We received the anonymous tip that Chadwick had a vault in Lexington late at night, and in the frenzied panic of my crew preparing to set sail, I ignored the protocol to petition Reese or one of the other judges for an arrest warrant. Any other instance of a city's navy sneaking into a foreign city in the middle of the night would be an act of hostility.

I force the uncomfortable thought away and change the subject. "Did Kearon tell you about the book we found?"

Reese rubs his neck. "He did, but he didn't know who the people listed in the book were. Chadwick cleaned up nicely so if anybody was suspicious, the boy couldn't give anything away since he doesn't know what's going on."

I stare at the desk, my fingers tapping with buzzing energy.

Bang.

The sounds of that night echo through my mind.

My mother is screaming.

I'm screaming.

Pirates everywhere.

The images are crystal clear in my mind.

I only heard the bullet as it cracked through our front door and struck my father in the side, and I didn't know Chadwick had pulled the trigger until Cassie Dorenbasch told me. She ran one of the most notorious jewel smuggling rings in the North and part of the East, and she was a business partner of Chadwick's whom he'd recruited to help in the attack. She ran up our driveway after my father was shot, taunting us through a broken window and saying how many people she and Chadwick had cut down to get to our house. Her psychotic laugh echoed in my nightmares every night until I finally caught her two years later.

Even though her confession resulted in numerous arrests, it wouldn't be enough until I had Chadwick. It *isn't* enough.

I exhale through my nose and smooth back my frizzy blonde waves.

"I'm glad you stopped by, actually." Reese adjusts his position in his massive, throne-like chair. "I've already talked with Captain Park and Admiral Van Pelt about this, but you're leading the investigation back to Lexington. My only ask is that you be thorough with the reports you write. It makes it easier on my end."

I look up. "Really?"

"Really." He smiles, albeit strained. "If you can handle a challenge."

I sit back in near disbelief.

Challenge accepted.

"Okay." I stand and dust off my pants, my heart beating with excitement. I grab the interrogation papers he showed me. "Okay. Do you have copies of these I can take? And the warrants, obviously."

"No sneaking in like last time." He winks. "I'll have Melanie draft them, and they'll be signed and on my desk the morning you leave."

Yes. Finally.

I grin. I can practically see the sailors on the *Chaplain's Heart* now, commanding the ship with enthusiastic vigor. *My* ship. *My* crew.

Reese chuckles.

"What is it?"

"Your enthusiasm is charming." His grand smile folds into a wince as he glances at my captain's ring. "I know you're sick of hearing it—"

"Then please don't say it." I wince in return.

"All right." He sighs. "While I *am* proud and know you're going to be amazing, I'll also say that I trust you more than anyone else to handle this."

"Handle catching Chadwick?"

"Not just that." He gently takes my hand and traces his thumb over the ring. "Pressure, politics, ploys." His throat bobs. "Whatever it is. You can handle it."

Ploys?

I frown. "Reese—"

"There's just a lot going on right now, that's all." His smile is still strained. "But if it all goes downhill, you know where to find me, right? Lounging on the beaches in Kahu."

"Kahu?" I wrinkle my brow. "Why not Hana Kailea or any other major island down there? Or are you talking about that trip Penny suggested?"

"I might have something set up there." His smile slips off his face. "Well, I hate to shoo you away, but I have a few cases I need to prepare for." He grips my shoulders. "Be great, okay? Even when things are hard."

I nod warily.

"Go. I'll be fine."

Reese is not one to lie, but I leave his office with the nagging feeling that he is following me like a shadow.

9

Emery

"My crew is slated to leave for Lexington in two days, and I've alerted the Riggses about Chadwick's potential appearance in town, but I wanted to ask you to alert your crews to do the same." I swallow the knot tightening in my throat as the entire pirate-hunting corps stares at me. Each is scattered in various seats across the charting room. "I want all eyes searching for him."

"That information stays within your crews," says Captain Park, the corps's commanding captain. "We are not inciting mass panic."

Hector Hadley raises his hand. "I can talk to Eldon Riggs about stationing my crew at the harbor to increase security since we aren't on a patrol rotation right now."

"Sure. If he says yes, then so do I." Park glances at his wristwatch. "We're over time. Does anyone have any questions about their assignments?"

A few captains shake their heads.

"Then you're all dismissed. Thank you."

I exhale softly as everyone's attention shifts away from me.

Behind me, Park touches the giant map spanning the wall, which is covered in little colored pins marking the whereabouts of pirates around the world.

He reaches into a bowl sitting on the table and wedges a black pin in the dead center of Padstow. The darker the color, the more important the threat.

My eyes drift over the dozens and dozens of pins pressed into the map, and unease stirs in my stomach. I have only seen this map a handful of times, all during my time as a navigator when Captain Martinez, the *Chaplain's* previous captain, included me in the corps meetings. Each time the number of pins on the board has shrunk, but there are still too many. There will always be too many disgusting pirates to exterminate until there are zero pins on the map.

"Nice debrief, Walker," Park mumbles to me as he passes. "I've got great expectations of you."

I smile and nod politely. "Thank you, sir."

A hand appears on my shoulder, and I turn to see Hector Hadley smiling at me. "Nicely done, *Captain* Walker."

My smile grows. "Good to see you, Hector."

Of the other captains, he is the closest to me in age, despite being a full seven years older. He has a kind, dazzling smile and wavy brown hair that reaches his shoulders.

"I'm so sorry I missed your ceremony yesterday." He sighs. "My crew and I were on rotation and just got back this morning. I haven't even been home yet."

"It's okay. Where were you on rotation?"

"Just below Turtle Point. The sailors from their navy were talking about another new captain who's been making his way across the Estates." Hector knits his brow. "Dasher. Have you heard of him?"

"Yes," I reply. "Captain Scott was on rotation in Piersford specifically watching for him. What were they saying about him?"

"Apparently, they'd heard that he travels on twin ships with two crews." The two of us turn and walk out together. "He can cause havoc in two places at once, so he's covered twice as much area."

"And that means he's twice as likely to be caught," I counter. "He obviously isn't that smart if he's doing that."

Hector shrugs and runs his hand through his greasy hair as we descend the winding staircase just outside the charting room. "I'll ask Scott more about him."

As Hector and I near the ground floor, I hear Fallon's voice echoing off the stone walls of the command post. She and a few other captains are locked in conversation.

"—in the crossfire," she's saying. "Luckily, there weren't very many who saw, but it was just an accident."

I frown.

"How many died?" Captain Mont asks, rubbing his bearded chin.

"Six, officially." Fallon presses a finger over her lips. "Other civilians are unaccounted for, but you didn't hear that from me."

I bristle.

Fallon gave her debrief before I did mine, and she talked about the arrest of a potential pirate accomplice. She didn't mention anything about a gunfight.

I open my mouth to ask her about it as I step off the staircase, but I'm cut off.

"Walker!" Captain Ripley's slimy green eyes flash with amusement as Hector and I join the group. He twists his blue-and-silver captain's ring absentmindedly. "Has the student stress worn off yet?"

"I'm still waiting for the headache to go away." I grin.

"Where are you headed next?" Fallon asks.

"Are you interrogating the boy?" Ripley presses. "I wonder what you'll get out of him that the other interrogators haven't."

I clear my throat. "Judge Gordon said I could interrogate him tomorrow morning."

Hector scowls at Ripley. "How did you know that? This isn't even your case."

"People talk." Ripley shrugs. "It isn't confidential among us."

"I don't think it's a good idea to stick your nose where it doesn't belong," Hector scoffs at him.

I quietly excuse myself from the conversation, and Fallon falls into step next to me.

"You fit into the room like a hand in an old glove." She slings her arm around my shoulders and jostles my gait. "I'm impressed. It took me a bit longer to get comfortable debriefing everyone, but you did great."

"What were you talking about civilians for?" I ask. "Did something happen during your last arrest?"

"Nothing major." She frowns. "Why?"

"Nothing major?" I wrinkle my brow doubtfully. "What does that mean?"

"Don't worry about it." She glances over her shoulder as we step into the sticky humidity. "That arrest was just a bump in the road. Now,

I can focus solely on Dasher, and we'll hopefully send him you-know-where soon."

I eye her skeptically, squinting in the sunlight.

"Listen, I have to meet someone, but I'll talk to you again before I leave." She pats my shoulder and runs off. "I promise!"

I stop and watch her go, my stomach in knots, just like it was when I watched Reese Gordon's countenance fall.

10

THE NEXT DAY, my crew creeps through the back streets, slinking under the cover of the morning shadows where the authorities can't see them, and soon there are ten of them standing in my room.

Hyde opens the door to Brooks and Gil, two deckhand platoon leaders, who push inside and wipe sweat off their faces.

"I hate this city," Brooks spits as he rips open the top button of his shirt and shucks his brown, threadbare overcoat. "Hills and valleys! Not a flat road anywhere!"

"He got lost." Gil bends down to pet Chip in his cage. The bird nips at his finger. "Three times."

Brooks smacks his arm. "As if *you* had any idea where to go."

"Stop fighting," Kit, my master gunner, chides. He rubs his tan, buzzed head and slumps back in his chair. "We've been waiting for you for almost thirty minutes. I'm starving and want this to be over."

I point the tip of my knife at Kit and raise my eyebrows as I stand at the front of the room—or what I've deemed as the front. Hyde sits beside me in his cushioned chair as the rest gather around the table or sit on the dusty floor.

"Now that everyone is here—" I glare at Brooks and Gil for being late. "—are you ready to listen? I wouldn't have called you here if it weren't urgent."

Darren, my best shooter, steps forward with his arms folded and eyes ahead, signalling everyone else to settle into silence.

My tongue curls in my mouth as I glance at the ceiling. "I have been told that Padstow is changing its policy to more severely punish those accused of piracy, and Kearon is caught in the middle. They want to send him to the Pereculum without a trial."

The room goes dead still as they stare at me with wide eyes.

"What?" Tahj, one of my boatswains, breaks the silence first.

"How can they do something like that?" Kit throws his hands in the air.

Hyde scowls. "None of you should be surprised by this."

"Does he know?" Brooks demands as he throws his coat onto one of the beds. "Kearon. Have you talked to him at all?"

"Yes," I say. "I visited him two days ago, and he's okay—"

"As okay as one can be rotting in jail," Hyde mutters.

"—and he's going to be fine." I shoot Hyde a dirty look. "I called you all here so we could set the plan in motion and get him out before they move him, which could quite literally be at any second. Harrison is down there right now watching the prison, and I need someone to go down there with him."

"I can." Darren raises his hand. "I brought my guns in case."

"Excellent. Hurry."

"You said it was just a rumor," Brooks goes on as Darren leaves. The door clanks shut. "How do you know Eldon Riggs isn't conspiring and lying to catch you in a trap?"

"Because they would have shot me between the eyes the second I set foot on the dock if that were the case." I smooth the map I took from Eldon over the table, straightening the tiny fold in the corner. "Plus, I just increased his payment to calm him down after what happened at the bar the other night."

"Sounded fun. I wish I'd been there," Gil mumbles to Tahj.

Everyone squeezes around the table to see the map, and Hyde peers over my shoulder and hands me a pencil. He stands on his strong leg and leans against my shoulder for balance.

"This is where Eldon said we can move Gordon and Miss Walker." I circle the street corner near the mountains, where an abandoned apartment building stands. "Hyde is writing a faux letter from her to Gordon, asking him to meet her somewhere close by so we can get him inside the building. We should have Miss Walker there by then, if her bloody bodyguards cooperate." I roll my eyes.

Tahj flicks one of his black dreadlocks out of his face. "What's our timeframe for this? Mine and Darren's."

I list it out as simply as I can. At sundown, when the light is dying,

Tahj and Darren will give the letter to Eldon's nephew to deliver to Gordon's mansion. Per Eldon, they'll switch with the Riggs guards to drive Gordon's personal coach to the area. While that is happening, the second team, consisting of Gil, Brooks, and Hyde (who was very insistent despite his limp), will lure the golden girl in all her shining glory to the building.

"Do not forget the key she keeps around her neck," I drill into the three of them, my eyes lingering on Hyde a bit longer because he's my most reliable. "Do. Not."

"Got it." Hyde glares at me and gestures for me to move on.

"Mikhail and Alexis will go with you to get the key and race back to The Tab to get the money." I make eye contact with the two of them as I point to the map, and they nod.

Alexis raises his crooked index finger. "The employee you talked to will still help us get it out, right?"

"Yes. Give him his cut and get out. Tahj or Darren will come to help haul it out as well."

Kit will have rigged a bomb on the opposite end of the city to draw attention away from all of us rowing back to the *Lost Commandeer,* docked and guarded by the Riggses on the backside of the island to make sure nobody comes too close.

I trace that path, where I will take Emery, her money, and her title with me, leaving Gordon behind with a proposition.

He will exchange Kearon for Emery on the threat to her life and suffering, but once I have Kearon in my hands again, Emery will disappear with me, and the young captain I've hired will ensure that Gordon, Admiral Van Pelt, and anyone else involved in this mess will be found with a bullet between their eyes.

I smooth out the map again, now marked with my heavy hand. The tip of the pencil is splintered.

"I need all of you to do your best tonight," I say, looking each of my sailors in the eye. "You're all more than capable, but each part needs to run smoothly. Can you promise me that?"

They nod.

I stand up straight and nod in return, glancing out the window and at the glistening Armada Academy, glowing with the morning sunlight.

The tension in the room seems to relax a bit. Gil grabs the wadded-up edition of old news and skims through it.

"Did anyone else see the bakery down the road from here?" Kit twists in his seat to look at the others. "Their bread looked like a cloud. Who wants to come with me?"

"Stomach with legs," Tahj mutters to me, and I nod.

"Just bring some back." Brooks collapses onto one of the beds and sighs as he runs a hand through his wispy golden-brown hair. "I'm taking a load off."

"Not in my bed, you're not." Hyde throws the dead pencil at him. "Get up."

"Did you see this?" Gil approaches me with a scowl and points to the passage Hyde read to Harrison after the ceremony.

"These people are insufferable," I mutter and roll my eyes. "The 'strength and resilience the Walkers portray' is a fad. The middle child of that family is a hotheaded moron who was shoved into the Academy because of his parents' status. How convenient nobody seems to talk about *that*."

"Now that you mention hotheads, wasn't her old captain in the spotlight a while back because of a scuffle that happened on one of their hunts?" Alexis asks, opening the top button of his shirt. "Or am I thinking of someone else? What even happened?"

"No, that was him," Hyde answers as he collapses into the chair again. It squeaks under his weight. "The captain beat the daylights out of a prisoner to get the whereabouts of another smuggler in the area."

Alexis wrinkles his brow. "And no one noticed when he came back half beat to death?"

"They claimed the use of force was justified. I think Emery corroborated that story in his defense."

"How do you all know this?" Tahj scowls at the rest of the group.

"Eldon," Hyde sighs. "He's in the know about everything."

"Does Kearon know anything about Emery?" Gil asks me. "Would he have recognized her?"

"I doubt it." I shrug. "His parents don't even own a news spindle, and I don't think Lexington's Shining Star outlets print pictures on their news like Padstow does."

"What do they know about this?" Brooks asks, cuffing the sleeves of his shirt and tilting his head as he sits up. "Just a story you've told them?"

"They know that I was involved in a bad business deal, and their son was caught in the middle." I sigh. "It really means nothing because this is going to be sorted out, and all will be well. It's a blip."

"I wouldn't call your wrecked reputation a 'blip,'" says Hyde, tucking a wad of tobacco into his cheek. Brooks snatches the stash from his hand and tosses a piece into his mouth.

"The devil's advocate has returned." Kit rolls his eyes.

"The devil's advocate would like to go back to being paid regularly." Hyde leans forward to glare at him. "And if you suggest building illegal weapons as an avenue again—"

"It's so lucrative!" Kit grips the edge of the table, and everyone visibly shifts in annoyance. Brooks glances at me and puffs out his lips.

"Places like Motilla and Corzéon *kill* for weapons developers because trading for gunpowder and lead is a nightmare there," Kit insists. "Nobody else wants to do it because making weapons takes time, but I can show everyone—"

"Sometime soon, Soto," Alexis interjects, mostly just to shut him up. He reaches up and presses his palms to the ceiling, stretching his arms and wincing. "Just not now."

"I have a potential connection for jobs in Midway, so everyone can relax," I tell the group. "But Hyde is right. The Armada seizing my money was a major blow financially and otherwise. It'll be fine once people see what I've done here. We'll regain the reputation we've lost and move on from there."

My resoluteness seems to ground them, and for a moment, it grounds me as well. Even Hyde drops his attitude and nods, though it may just be the tobacco.

"So . . . pastries?" Kit jumps up and jingles a bag of coins. "Anyone?"

11

Emery

Interrogations are always riveting.

One of my favorite parts of Academy training was learning to interrogate. After six weeks, I could negotiate with a pirate for hours to wear them down and break them. I learned how to sit across the table from the worst murderers and thieves the world has ever known, and I can look them in the eye without faltering.

The first time I interviewed one, I held eye contact with him throughout the entire conversation, even as he spat and swore at me with a hatred stronger than acid. I didn't flinch or let my composure slip, even though my heart was about to burst in my chest. If I faltered, I would lose. If he faltered, I would win.

But, before now, I've never had to speak to one who breaks down before the conversation even begins.

There is a dripping, teary sheen of fear in Kearon Romney's eyes, and a gaunt shadow hangs over his greasy face. He watches me warily through the iron bars of his cell, the chains on his hands rattling as his fingers twitch.

I send the prison guard from the hall. It's Kearon, myself, and rows of hollow, lifeless prison cells who've held countless others like him before they were shipped to the Pereculum. I wonder if he's contemplated his fate. I *hope* he has.

I fold my arms and lean against the stone wall opposite the cell door, holding the silence.

His chin quivers. "I told them everything already."

I narrow my eyes. "Did you?"

"Why'd you send the guard away?"

"Because I want you to focus on me."

Kearon blinks rapidly. "I would never lie. I know what you've done to the pirates you've caught and I—" His voice catches, and he shifts in his spot against the wall. He isn't a total coward; if that were true, I'd expect him to be trembling in the corner like a frightened rabbit. His chest rises and falls with shaky breaths. "I'm not one of them. I swear on my life."

"That's all the more reason to lie." I tilt my head to the side. "To protect yourself."

"I'm not a liar." Something like a whimper stirs in his throat. "My mother or father could tell you that easily."

"I bet they could just as easily say how much they needed the money you were receiving from Chadwick. They're first on my list of people to talk to when I go back to Lexington tomorrow."

He grips the cell bars, and the chains on his hands clang against the iron. "They have nothing to do with this. Please. You can't—"

"I won't hurt them. I'm just going to have a conversation with them." I shrug off my coat and set it on the bench adjacent to the cell. Kearon eyes the knife and sword sheathed on my left hip.

"What exactly did Chadwick tell you when he told you he'd start paying you to handle his money?" I ask, folding back the sleeves of my shirt.

"He just asked if I wanted to make more money than I was making at the Green Sailor, and I said yes. He never told me anything else." He tugs at the collar of his black jumpsuit. "I already told them that."

"If he wanted anything withdrawn or deposited . . ." I pace in front of the bars. "What did he tell you then?"

"He just told me the amount and to make sure that it was documented correctly."

"Document?"

"How much was taken out or put in on any given date. I had a little book I kept inside the vault."

I raise my eyebrows dramatically. "The other interrogators didn't say anything about a book."

They did. I flipped through that book myself before it was locked in the basement of the courthouse with other pieces of evidence.

"That's what I told them!" he yelps. "I promise!"

"We never found a book or anything like that in the vault when you were arrested."

"I-I know that's what I told them. I swear."

"Why is your story changing so much every time you tell it?" I press him, hoping the confusion will cause him to slip up.

His lip quivers.

"Maybe your parents are involved in this, and you're just not telling me the truth." I crouch down so we're eye to eye, pressing the pads of my fingers into the dusty stone floor for balance as I lean forward. I carry the lie a little further. "And that would make them witnesses or accomplices, and under Padstow law, all people who fall under that category have to be detained until the investigation is over."

"They aren't!" The tears in his eyes spill over as he continues to buy the lie. "You can't! Please."

"Word for word, what did Chadwick tell you each time you touched any of that money?"

"I don't . . . I can't remember what he said *exactly,* but it was the amount he wanted taken out or put in. I don't think he ever told me why."

"You don't sound so sure. It's been a long time, hasn't it?" My tongue skims my teeth. "How good is your memory?"

He drags his hands down the side of his face. "He didn't tell me anything about anyone. I don't know where any of it came from."

I clench my jaw in anger. "But you have to understand how strange it was for me to find you with your hands in Chadwick's filthy money."

"I-I know, but . . . well, I already said . . ." He blinks rapidly and shakes his head in a panicked frenzy.

"It's okay." I tilt my head, holding his gaze. "I know he has a gift with words and could cajole a king to give up his crown, but you *were* there. You *did* willingly choose to work with him, didn't you?"

"Well, yes, but—"

"Then he offered you a spot on his crew where he promised you more money, didn't he?"

"No!"

"He told you he could raise your parents out of poverty, right?" My tone drips with poison. "That you could be their hero and make them proud?"

"He is not a con man!" Kearon's voice cracks like glass. "I trust him!"

Bang.

I blink as the memories surface without warning.

My mother is screaming.

I'm screaming.

Pirates everywhere.

Something snaps in my mind, and I grab the collar of Kearon's uniform through the bars. He yelps as he grips the bars to keep his face from cracking against the iron.

"You're not convincing enough to keep lying in custody. It's not a good look." I snap. We're so close that I can feel his frantic breathing on my eyelashes. "What else do you want to say? Your words are numbered, so I suggest you choose carefully."

"I don't know anything!" He blinks rapidly. "I just watched his money and made sure nobody ever broke into the vault!"

"So he could keep funding his crimes?" I seethe.

"I don't—"

"Yes or no?"

"I don't know!" He winces and tries to wriggle away from me. "Please, let go."

"Chadwick must have paid you a boatload if you're willing to go to jail rather than sell him out."

"No he didn't!"

"Liar." All I see is red.

"Please—"

"Pirates lie all the time."

"I'm not a pirate!"

I angrily shove him backward, and he sprawls on the dusty floor. The shackles on his hands and feet rattle.

"When I get to Lexington and find out everything you've told me isn't true, you're going to be in a world of hurt." I snatch my coat off the bench and storm down the hall. "Believe that."

Charles flinches when I stomp down the stairs from the prison.

"He's lying," I snap, my boots kicking up dirt on the ground. "How stupid do you have to be to work for a man like Chadwick without realizing who he really is? How did he not hear rumors about him?!"

Some of the other guards' heads turn.

"Emery." Charles grabs my elbow and glares at me. A few of the Riggs guards turn in our direction.

My face is hot as he leads me away from the prison into the beating sun. "He's playing the terrified victim, and I'm not buying it," I spit, ripping my arm free. "I'm not buying it for a second."

"What are you going to do?"

"I'll drag his parents back here in chains and *break him.*"

Charles blinks.

I stop walking and smooth loose hairs from my bun behind my ears. Nerves, whether anxious or angry, cloud judgment, and I must quell them.

"He's going to crack," I vow. "I'll make sure it happens if it's the last thing I do."

That cowering, sniveling fool. The way his voice shook and his hands trembled . . .

It'd be a lie to say I didn't take pride in seeing him like that, knowing I was the one who put him there for associating with Warren Chadwick.

I straighten my spine and set my jaw. This isn't how a captain acts.

"You understand you have enough accomplishments on your ledger, right?" Charles folds his arms and knits his brow. A loose blond curl falls in his eye. "I don't think your reputation is jeopardized if he doesn't confess."

"It's not about that," I say as we start toward the massive metal gate that surrounds the prison. "It's about Chadwick paying for what he did to our home and almost killing our father, Charles. It's about *all* the others he's killed and stolen from! If this is the first step—"

"We didn't *see* him shoot Father," he retorts. "Are you sure it was even him who orchestrated it? Are you *sure* it was him you saw sailing away?"

"I know he did!" I whirl around to face him. "And does it really matter? We know it was him because Cassie Dorenbasch—"

"Was smart enough to save her own skin and defer to Chadwick as the mastermind!" Charles exclaims. "For all we know, it was her who started this."

"So I should just leave this alone?" I scowl at him. "Should I let one of the most dangerous pirates in the entire world run amok?"

"That's not what I'm saying." Charles grabs my elbows again. "You *weakened* the most dangerous pirate in the world. It's been weeks, and he would not have wasted a second attacking us if you hadn't hit him right where it hurt." His grip tightens. "Why don't you focus on that instead of fretting about the past? You're winning, Emery. Do you understand that?"

I stare into his blue eyes, as sharp and bright as our father's. Charles, more resilient and gritty than the best of us, was quick to move on from the attack. Some were spooked, and others were bitter like me, but it took me a long while to understand that it wasn't because he didn't care. He has always been an anchor in the swirling sea, unshaken and unbothered. I wonder what it's like for him.

He raises his eyebrows, and I exhale slowly. "Don't stroke my ego."

He drops his arms. "It was the only way to calm you down."

I roll my eyes and tilt my head from side to side, stretching my neck. "That doesn't change the fact that Kearon is a liar."

"Of course." He smiles. "I never said he wasn't."

My fingers curl around the hilt of my sword, and I sigh, shaking my head.

"I'm glad I came with you," he says as we pass through the gate, and the Riggses return our identification papers. "I can only imagine the ruckus you would've caused otherwise."

I glare at him.

The gears in my head spin as we descend the hill. Kearon is quite an actor . . . unless he *is* telling the truth.

Should I not have taken the sharp approach? Would he have been willing to tell me more?

The begrudging answer is yes. In some cases, they've asked the female soldiers or Riggs patrolmen to question suspects or other people involved in cases because of their softer nature, and in lots of cases, it's worked. It might've worked with him had I not started accusing him right off the bat.

I exhale, trying to dispel my frustration.

"Has Callie been acting standoffish toward you?" Charles asks, puffing the stray curl from his eye. "Trying to coax Vaughn into conversation has been like yanking teeth."

"I wouldn't know." My fingers tighten around the hilt of my sword. "She abandoned her post yesterday after I confronted her."

He wrinkles his sweaty brow. "What happened?"

"She had the audacity to blame us for what happened at The Tab. Miles . . ." I grit my teeth. "Miles is a dolt who doesn't have a filter and should have kept his mouth shut, but no one would have rolled over if they'd taken a hit like he did. She knows that better than anyone."

"Well, that doesn't mean fighting is the answer," he says matter-of-factly. "Especially in a bar."

"You know that's not what I meant." I hit his arm. "Why do you say things like that when someone is upset?"

"Callie's feelings are somewhat justified, though." He ignores my question. "The news hasn't been too kind to the Riggses today." He rubs the back of his sweaty neck. "Especially The Messenger."

Even though I shouldn't, I still ask. "What did they say?"

His lips twitch in discomfort. "Just reemphasizing how the Riggses can't do their jobs correctly and how Gordon and the other judges should vote to pull their funding."

Something about his tone is off. I frown at him, but he won't meet my eyes.

"Charles."

"Emery."

"What else did they say?"

His throat bobs up and down as he glances at the ground. "They found a way to rake our name over the coals by saying what Callie said to you. That *we* started the fight."

"Of course," I say bitterly, rolling my eyes.

"Everyone's been talking about the Riggses, mostly," he says quickly, as if to cover it up. "Everyone I've spoken with has been fixating on that in conjunction with when Eldon's brother was arrested for smuggling criminals out of jail. I don't think the Riggses' reputation will ever recover."

I know it won't. My parents' and my private, anonymous testimony against Callie and Vaughn's uncle will ensure that, because one of the men he was aiming to help escape was a pirate that I had arrested.

They don't know, and it will always stay that way. They'd never speak to me again if they knew, and if they found out I lied to them about it . . .

I sigh.

"I know." He raises his eyebrows lazily. "It's exhausting."

Vaughn waits for us at the bottom of the hill where the prison rests, thoughtfully tapping the hilt of his pistol. He looks at Charles and me and smiles. *Forces* a smile. I understand what Charles was saying about dragging conversation out of him, because Vaughn's replies are all terse, not playful like I'm used to from him. His eyes keep flicking to me sheepishly, as if he's hinting at something he wants to say.

Or perhaps something he wants *me* to say.

I huff and quicken my pace to walk in front of them, trying to regain my composure and focus on the more pressing matters. My crew and I will meet later this afternoon to go over preparations for departing for Lexington, and that genuinely excites me.

Despite the destruction he's left in his wake, from the smoldering remains of ships floating across the ocean to the bodies tied to his name, Chadwick kept his tracks clean, which is something other pirates don't consider. He plays a quiet game of smuggling, but he isn't innocent when collecting the goods. He's fueled by greed, just like any other. I've seen it in his eyes each of the times we've met. He is a fascinating creature to watch.

I readjust my thoughts. *Lexington.*

The owner of the bar where Chadwick's vault is will know something. The people who lived there had to have noticed the lanky, blond-haired snake slithering around their town.

And I am going to find answers, even if it kills me.

I wonder.

Were you there the night my father almost died?

How many people died that night because of you?

How many lives were ruined because of you?

12

Emery

I RUB the exhaustion from the day out of my eyes as I slide my mother's Kyotic poetry book onto one of the three ceiling-high book-cases in my room. The sunset streams through the curtained window and casts everything in dewy yellow.

I run my finger along the cracks of the book's leather spine and sigh, the sound echoing across the large room. Charles's doing, no doubt. He complains about water getting on the books when I'm sailing, but he snaps their spines like a monster who has no respect for books.

Looking at the hardback poetry collections and dog-eared fairytales from my childhood with the intricate designs on each cover is calming to my ever-creaking mind. It slips into a comfortable numbness when I flip through the pages after an exhausting day, as if each story is a familiar home I've lived in before. Charles, my mother, and I have lived a thousand lives through them without having to ever leave the house.

I climb the sliding ladder to the second shelf from the top and am wiping away a few dust bunnies—who have gathered for their bi-monthly meeting—when a knock at the door shatters the silent bliss.

I bite my cheek. "Come in."

Vaughn pokes his head inside and smiles at me. His spiky black hair is greased back instead of resting in its usual middle part. "Hello."

My stomach prickles with disdain. "Hi."

"May I come in?"

I lazily gesture to the room as I turn back to my books.

"I just met Elle." He shuts the door and kicks off his boots. "She's such a darling. She offered to take my coat, and I think I made her feel bad when I laughed. I told her she didn't have to worry about me in that sense."

I don't say anything as I adjust one of the other books until it slides perfectly into place next to its shelf-mates.

"What is it?" He takes off his black uniform jacket and frowns, coming to stand at the base of the ladder. "Something wrong?"

I twist my lips as I descend the ladder. "Just a lot on my mind. That's all."

"Oh, I should've known. You always rearrange the books in times of stress."

I scowl at him. "That's not true."

"Yes, it is. Look." He purposely stands so his body is pressed against my back, and he balances his outstretched arm on my shoulder. The baggy sleeve of his white uniform shirt tickles my cheek. "That one used to be on the bottom shelf." His other hand creeps up my arm on the way to the third shelf. "And that series was on the tippy top." He gently grabs my chin and tips my head up, grinning. "It wasn't like that before."

"Aren't you so observant?" I narrow my eyes.

"Oh, I try to be. It's part of my job, after all."

We lock eyes. His are such a beautiful shade of green, like a piece of the lush mountain ranges is trapped around his pupils. He playfully bites his cheek and tilts his head.

It's really hard to be angry at him when he's staring at me like *that*.

Someone bangs on the door, and it flies open, causing us to jump.

Miles shuffles into the room with a blanket wrapped around his head and shoulders. Two white strips of hardened plaster are molded to his swollen nose to protect it while it heals.

"My head is throbbing like someone is taking a mallet and smacking, smacking, smacking." He pounds his fist against his palm with each smack.

"Then why are you out of bed?" I break away from Vaughn and take Miles's arm. He leans into me and sighs.

"My key is missing," he whispers.

"The one to your vault?" I sigh. "Again? Is that why you came in here?"

"I stood up to get water and it was gone." He blinks like a sloth and wrinkles his purple and black eyes. "I swear I took it off and left it on my dresser."

"You're lucky nobody knows where those vaults are."

"I was careful this time!" He winces and touches his forehead. "I don't know. Maybe I wasn't."

"—walk away for two seconds, and—" Callie stops short in the doorway when she sees Vaughn, Miles, and me. My chest tightens.

"Come here, Miles. You quite literally look like hell." Vaughn gives me a look as he moves forward to escort Miles back to his room.

He sniffles and winces. "Ow."

"Tell me more," Vaughn replies. "Where can I look?"

"I checked under the dresser, but . . ."

Callie closes her eyes and rubs her nose as they exit.

I snip the tension short before it can grow. "Callie—"

"No." She holds up a hand. "You don't have to say anything because you're right. I would have done the same thing if it were Vaughn."

"You would've punched a man in the face?" I ask, somewhat jokingly.

"If he deserved it, then yes!" She drags her hands down her face and starts pacing like an anxious animal. "I'm so sick of being criticized for doing my job by all of these people who have *no* idea what it's like. They'd never get out of their silks and their linens but still think they have a *right* to talk about us and how we aren't good enough, and the scandals, and . . ." She never finishes her sentence and plops down on the edge of my bed. Her eyes are red and rimmed with exhaustion as she ducks her head.

"You're right." I sit on the black comforter with her, swallowing my pride. "But what I did certainly didn't help."

"It wasn't just you," she mutters. "I shouldn't have said that yesterday."

I fold my hands in my lap and stare at them for a moment. "I'm sorry I put you in a bad spot. I didn't think I'd escalate the situation, but . . ." I trail off, apparently having nothing else to say, either.

Her eyes shine with tears, and she closes them.

"I'll say something to the news," I say quietly. "Next time they come pounding on the door—"

"They were here?" She frowns at me. "When?"

"Early this morning." I fold my hands together. "I could've used your excellent deterrent skills. Where were you?"

"I-I was just at the office by the harbor for most of the morning." Callie tugs on her collar. "I went to look for Charles, but I couldn't find him."

I frown a little. "Wasn't Vaughn with Charles this morning?"

She blinks rapidly before stuttering, "I don't . . . I don't know. He left the house before me. Vaughn did." Her face turns pale. "That's not important. I'm really sorry. I don't think you make stupid decisions, either. That was shortsighted of me."

"It's okay. I'm not mad."

She still won't look at me, her expression as stony as a mountain range. It only softens when I touch her arm and pull her into an embrace. I can feel her body relax as she sighs and rests her forehead on my shoulder, her weariness rubbing off on me like charcoal on paper.

I tighten my hold. I owe her at least a thousand of these from my dead-tired Academy days, when the exhaustion was so heavy that I would just lie my head on her shoulder and cry.

"Roll with the punches," she'd say to me. *"Throw it right back and you'll manage just fine."*

"You're really not mad?" She looks up at me with bleary eyes, twisting her braided ring.

I nod, touching my own ring. "Not anymore. I promise."

She stares at the floor, but her expression is still tight with guilt, with her twisted lips and wrinkled forehead.

"When are you off?" I ask.

Callie glances at the small clock ticking on my desk. "In an hour."

"Will you stay tonight? The crew and I leave for Lexington tomorrow morning."

Her eyes crinkle as she winces. "I forgot all about that."

"Tell your father I need protection more so out there than I do here." I grin and nudge her arm with my elbow. "You're too good to prattle around someone else's heels like a lost puppy. Tell him I insist, rules be damned. *I* say you don't need to be a sailor to be in *my* crew."

She finally smiles, albeit a bit sadly.

"His nose is making me squirmish." Vaughn comes back into the room, his hands slung on his bony hips. "It started bleeding again."

"Gross." Callie squeezes my hand and grins softly before standing up and snatching Thea's miniature beach painting off my writing desk. "He might like something to look at, don't you think?"

I shrug. "I don't think he can see that well, but sure."

Vaughn narrows his eyes as Callie scoots past him and disappears down the hallway.

I bite the inside of my cheek and stare at the sharp outlines of his jaw as he stares into the hall, his lips puckered. His full, rosy lips should not be commanding this much of my attention, yet here we are.

I force my gaze to the wooden floor as I feel his weight nestle onto the bed beside me.

"Are you two okay?" he asks.

"She and I are fine." I frown at the doorway. "But I don't know if I like the idea of the two of them alone."

"I love that the youngest sibling is overprotective of the older ones."

"I'm not protective of him. Miles gets around enough, and I don't want Callie to be one of the notches in his belt." My fingers dig into the velvety comforter. "I'm going to kill him for treating her that way if he does."

"She'd kill him first." Vaughn grins fondly. "I don't doubt it for a second."

I narrow my eyes at him and lean back, supporting my body with my arms stretched behind me.

He anxiously taps his foot on the black rug running the length of the room. "Are *we* okay?"

"That depends." I tilt my head. "Are you going to tell me how you feel, or will you just keep awkwardly smiling at me and pretending nothing is wrong?"

His cheeks flush, and he inhales deeply. "I was angry like Callie, but I'm fine now." He reaches across my body and grabs my waist, turning me to face him. "I'm sorry. That wasn't right of me."

My eyes drop. "You knew I would have helped resolve this."

"I know, but . . ." His jaw muscles twitch as his fingers trace my side. "I was just angry. My father has been on my and Callie's case about everything for the last two days, especially since you told him about seeing Chadwick. But that's not important." His head lolls to the side as a lazy smile traces his lips. "However stressful it's been for you, I can empathize with it tenfold."

He teases, but his eyes are heavy like his sister's.

"I'm sorry," he mumbles, lacing his fingers with mine. "I won't leave you like that again. I promise."

I concede, scooting closer to him so our knees touch. I fix the wrinkles in his shirt, my knuckles brushing the wiry muscles of his chest and shoulders.

"I do want you to know," he leans closer to me, lowering his voice and smiling suggestively. "I don't like the idea that we're not the only sneaky lovers in this house," he says.

I wrinkle my nose. "Sneaky lovers?"

He raises his eyebrows at me.

I glance to the side, pondering for a moment before letting a smile curl my lips. "I don't know if sneaky is the word I'd use."

"Well, what does it make us?" His head tilts upward. "Sneaky is the perfect word. I'm not perfect, and I wouldn't particularly paint you as a saint."

I snort as he leans down and kisses me, pressing his hands against my back and pulling me close.

"*You* come into *my* room and say that," I laugh softly, scrunching my fingers into his spiky hair as we continue. "The audacity."

He pulls back and frowns at me. *Down* at me. I'm tall, but he's lanky, like a literal stick figure that's almost a head taller than me, even when we're sitting.

I brush a loose, greasy strand of hair out of his eyes as our lips meet again. He snakes his arms around my shoulders and holds me tight.

I savor it, closing my eyes and focusing on the warmth of his arms and his lips as I drape my knee over his. His hands, usually gentle and caressing, tremble slightly as his arms lock me in a tight embrace, and his fingers untuck my blouse and press into the skin underneath. His kisses start soft, deep, and slow, before quickly growing frantic and rushed. His breath is shaky.

"Vaughn," I mumble.

He doesn't hear me. He keeps his mouth firmly pressed against mine and balls the hem of my blouse in his shaky fists.

"Hey, hey." I grab his face and pull back, breathing hard.

It takes a moment for his steely eyes to focus, and he blinks rapidly. "Sorry."

"What's the matter?"

He swallows, his grip relaxing as he pulls away. His head droops. "Distracted."

I think I know why. My heart twinges as I wrap my arms around his neck, pulling him down so his forehead rests against my shoulder. I press my lips to the side of his face and hold him there for a moment, willing the nagging dread of tomorrow away.

"Do you have to leave?" he mumbles against my ear. "Am I allowed to say that I want you to stay here?"

I wince and bury my face into his soft black hair, and his pulse beats against my cheek. I should be home quickly, just like with the last trip to Lexington, but if we find and pursue another lead for Chadwick, there's no telling how long it will be until I get back.

Even then, every trip is hard regardless of length because there's always a chance something could go awry and I won't come home. It's happened to others.

It isn't just him I'll miss. I won't have Callie to lean on, or my brothers to banter with, or the wisdom of my mother, or the resolute reassurance of my father.

I will have the parts of my heart that make me feel alive in the creaking of my ship and the freedom of being on the ocean, but the other parts—the most *important* parts—will be here. I hate it, but I'm used to having my heart split between my two homes. If only I could cradle each piece to my chest and have it all at once.

But it's just for a few days. Perhaps they'll be the most important few days of my life, but a few days nonetheless.

He reaches under the collar of my blouse and traces his fingers across my neck. They curl around the key chain.

"You can come with me," I say softly, my heartbeat slowing. "A quiet ship out on the water is like heaven."

His shoulders slump, just slightly. "You'll have to tell me all about it when you get back."

"Not if you come."

He sighs.

I kiss his cheek again. "I love you."

"I love you to the end of forever," he mumbles into my neck. "Do you know that?"

I close my eyes and nod.

For the first time in days, my mind is silent.

Until it isn't.

Someone knocks on the door, and Rose, another of our housemaids, pokes her head inside. "Emery, I'm so sorry to interrupt, but one of the couriers is here. Vaughn, you and Callie have been summoned to report to your father."

His lips pucker with disappointment.

"It's okay, Rose." I try to smile. "Thank you."

She shuts the door.

"I'll come see you before you leave tomorrow morning."

My heart sinks as he hops up and slips back into his jacket, but before heading for the door, he pulls me to my feet, grabs my face, and kisses me again. I melt into it, my spine tingling as he pulls away and grins at me. "Goodnight."

I can still taste him as he leaves the room.

13

As the night grows old, it is like waiting for a painting to come together as the sunlight dies, fading from a bright, earthy orange—when Tahj and Darren *should* be moving in with the letter for Gordon—to a sullen lavender—when the judge and Emery *should* be delivered here—and then a navy blue that's nearly black—when we *should* disappear.

But we don't.

The stars appear. The oil lamps scattered around the city begin to burn out as patrons retire for the night.

And all is still. No one showed.

I pace across the lobby of the abandoned apartment building Eldon said we could work out of, sweat dripping down my back and my heart racing in anxious anger. They must have been caught. After the *weeks* I spent deciding who I wanted in which position, those dimwits weren't careful enough to—

The door bursts open, and Darren runs in without Tahj or the judge.

"What's going on?" I snap.

"Gordon wasn't at his mansion." He pants like a dog and rests his hands on his knees, his pistols swinging from his hips. "His wife told the Riggses he hadn't come home yet."

"What took you so long to get back here? Where's Tahj?"

"We were sitting waiting for Eldon's nephew to bring Gordon, but Tahj left to find Hyde, Gil, and Brooks while I came back to you."

"Well, where's Eldon's nephew now?"

Darren throws up his hands in exasperation.

How is the leader of this bloody city *missing*?

How convenient. How oddly convenient. I could almost laugh.

"They should be here soon." Darren wipes the sweat off his forehead. "It's—"

The sound of footsteps crunching in the dirt outside catches our attention. Darren sticks his head through the door.

"Where's the captain?" Harrison's far-off voice is raspy. "He needs to find Eldon and—"

I slip past Darren with my hat in hand and find the doctor awkwardly jogging toward us.

"What's going on?" I demand.

"Now, I can't be sure . . ." Harrison pulls off his fogged-up glasses and blinks sweat from his eyes. "There . . . There was a prisoner being transferred onto one of the ships—"

"Kearon?"

"It looked like him," he pants. "I couldn't see his face, but he was still in his prisoner's clothes."

I swear under my breath and grab Darren's sleeve. "Wait for Hyde and the others and tell them—"

"Captain!" Brooks and Gil emerge from around the corner and wave, followed by Tahj and a limping Hyde.

"Her guards weren't there like Eldon said they'd be," Hyde speaks before I can. "We waited in position and they never showed."

I pull my hat on my head and dig in my pocket for our room key. "We have a bigger problem right now." I toss the key to Gil and beeline for the harbor. "Find Kit and the others and meet back at the inn."

"All of us?" Darren asks.

I don't answer. I hear Harrison's voice trail away as he explains what he saw.

The apartment building is just around the corner from the harbor, and there's only one group of Armada soldiers still there at this hour. Two of them climb aboard a two-mast schooner, escorting a boy in a black prison uniform with a mop of messy hair aboard.

I stare in shock as Hyde's uneven footsteps crunch in the dirt behind me.

My mind races faster than a jackrabbit. There are nine of us total and only six soldiers. All of us are armed. It would be quick. We could storm aboard the ship and kill them all in an instant.

My eyes drift to the left. The soldiers aren't the only sailors out still, as a group of merchants stands at the bottom of their trading sloop's gangplank just a few ships over from the schooner.

I step back into hiding and brush past Hyde without a second thought. I don't wait to see if he follows.

The Riggses' oval command outpost comes into my view moments later, stretching high into the sky. One of Eldon's pudgy, good-for-nothing nephews is already waiting outside the stone walls. His expression is grim, but I barely acknowledge him as I push the door open and rip my hat off my head.

"Eldon!"

He whirls around from the desk he's bent over and holds up one finger. Luckily, he's the only one in the room. "Warren, wait—"

"Your explanation better be fantastic," I spit. "What's going on?"

"My nephew got to Gordon's door, and his wife said he hadn't come home." He holds up his hands like he's trying to calm a tiger. "When he went back an hour later, he still wasn't there, and another hour passed—"

"Bloody hell," Hyde mutters, rolling his eyes.

"Where were his escorts?" I demand.

"He gave them the rest of the day off and told them to go home."

"Why?"

"I don't know. We're searching the whole city." Eldon shakes his head. "And my twins—"

"Didn't do their jobs because they're a pair of cowards," I snap. "With all else falling apart, I could have had at least Miss Walker in my hands tonight. Why didn't they bring her out?"

"They said—"

"I don't care what they said! We had a deal!"

"A deal that they did not want to be part of in the first place!" he shouts. "You're going to have to find another way. My daughter was just here and told me they resolved whatever squabble they had with her and don't want anything to do with this."

"Why are they still loyal to her after everything her family did to get your brother arrested?" I roll my eyes. "I want to talk to them."

"Absolutely not. You aren't going anywhere near my children."

"Then you can kiss goodbye any chance you had to get back at those who've dragged your name through the mud." I fold my arms and lean on him a bit. "I can find a way. I thought you'd love a taste of justice for your family and for Kon, but I suppose that's not the case."

His jaw is tight.

"All the lies and things they've said . . ." I trail off and narrow my eyes.

Hyde frowns at me. "Warren?"

My eyes scan the room, and they land on newspapers and news reels discarded on a writing desk wedged in the corner. The anger that was once bubbling in my chest has settled.

"How easy it is to believe a lie when it's presented so believably," I mutter, wandering to the desk and picking up the paper.

Hyde grabs my shoulder. "Your inside man at The Shining Star," he whispers. "Can he fit another story into the paper before they're printed tomorrow?"

I squeeze his forearm and grin. "You read my mind."

Eldon looks at us like we're speaking nonsense.

"It will be a small bit we show the twins to make them think Miss Walker said something she didn't," I explain to him. "Though I'm sure there's plenty she *has* said in private. It isn't a lie."

The knot in Eldon's brow disappears, and I smile and clap him on the shoulder on my way to the door. "Bring your twins here and I will convince them to betray her. Or your daughter, at the very least. I will handle everything tomorrow morning, and they won't question it again. Just make sure they are here."

He snatches my wrist and glares. "You will *not* command me in my own office, Chadwick."

"Then don't consider it a command," I shrug innocently and pout my lower lip. "It's an offer that you're going to take because you're a smart enough man. Won't it feel nice to finally have a break from the constant nagging and ragging from the people who hate you? Once Miss Walker is missing, that's all anyone is going to talk about."

His jaw tightens as the thought tumbles through his head.

"This may be your only chance to seize back a bit of power, Mr. Riggs." I tilt my head. "How devastating it would be for you to miss it."

Eldon drops my wrist and steps back, his tired eyes crinkling. "Eight tomorrow morning. A minute later, and I lock the door."

I smile and tilt my head as I grip the handle on the door, satisfied.

Hyde grabs my sleeve as we exit into the darkness. I can smell tobacco on his breath. "Why do you think this is going to work?" he hisses.

"We are simply pivoting," I say, pulling my hat snug on my head. "I am going to get my hands on Miss Walker, and she is going to tell me where Gordon has run off to and anything about that blasted prison they run."

"You seem so unbothered by this." Hyde angrily gestures around. "Kearon is gone, Gordon is gone, and as far as I care, so is Emery. Whatever you're going to tell the Riggses tomorrow won't change that."

Oh, I am bothered. Kearon, treated like a dog and locked away, is not a pleasant picture in my mind, nor is the thought of having to tell his parents after I promised that working for me would be simple and uneventful.

And Gordon, slipping through my fingers like a slimy eel . . .

I just chuckle. It's an acceptable way to release my rage that isn't driving a sword into someone's heart or running my fist through a window.

"Why is my resilience unsettling to you?" Air whistles through my clenched teeth as I shake my head. Sweat drips from the tip of my nose.

He rolls his eyes. "First of all, you are not unsettling anyone, so stop acting like some dark vigilante. Second, you talk *daily* about playing a careful hand when you're in a tight spot, and we are quite literally suffocating right now."

I scowl at him. "Yes, but we're still on our feet, are we not?"

. . .

The next morning, Brooks raises his eyebrows as he reads the fake newspaper article. "Your reporter put this together overnight?"

"These people are fantastic writers." I shrug. "It's their job."

"I'm surprised he agreed to slip it into the paper last minute." Gil's eyes narrow as he skims the article.

"He said they don't print the papers until around five or six in the morning," Hyde says, rubbing his sore leg. "He went in before then and included the story in the layout before they started putting paper on the printing presses."

"Are we ready?" I slide into my coat. "Darren, Brooks, Hyde?"

"Yes." Brooks looks up from adjusting the knife sheaths on his forearms—two of many he has hidden all over his body.

I help Hyde to his feet and stuff the newspaper into my pants pocket as Darren opens our room's door.

I hate traveling with an entourage because it draws attention, but there aren't enough eyes in the early morning to notice us.

The still air tells me the city hasn't noticed Gordon's disappearance yet, but I don't doubt that the news is about to make a storm. We pass The Messenger's headquarters, and their metal newspaper displays are full of the fresh news. A young girl with a freckled face waves a capsule at us as we pass.

"There was just a pirate attack about a hundred miles south of here!" she remarks. "It's a great listen!"

I haven't had the time to ponder, but how does prey conveniently disappear hours before the hunter is to take his shot? What are the odds someone told him I was coming?

But if that were true, then he would have told Emery, and she would have run off as well. She's still cozy in her mansion on the hill, as far as I know.

Or maybe she *did* run away. I wonder if Eldon didn't tell me the truth, and his Riggs twins pulled out at the last minute because they helped her escape. Maybe I should have posted someone at the harbor to watch for her departure.

I clench my jaw and take a deep breath.

The morning sunlight blasts the Riggses' office as we approach the door, and I relish the cool air across my forehead as I pull off my hat and step inside the stone room. We are met with voices shouting in an argument, and I clear my throat. "Pardon our interruption, Eldon. Is now a good time?"

Eldon's mouth hangs open midsentence, and he suddenly drops into a chair and purses his lips. I see his daughter's shoulders tighten as she slowly turns around, eyes wide. Her face is framed by the curls that have escaped from the knot on the back of her head.

I smile. "Hello, Miss Riggs."

She watches my crew, wary. "What are you doing here?" Her fingers twitch as her hand slowly lowers to the pistol she keeps on her waist.

"I think you're too smart to be asking a question you already know the answer to."

She glares at her father and then at me. "I'm not doing this with you. My mind is made up."

"You know, I think it's interesting how, despite that, you've made no attempt to stop me." I fold my hands and step forward. "The fact that you haven't warned her or the Armada tells me you aren't necessarily *opposed* to my plan, correct?"

Callie purses her lips, her gaze lingering a bit on Darren's twin pistols holstered at his sides. However quick she thinks her draw is, I guarantee his will be twice as fast.

"You're more forgiving than I am." I shrug. "And that's commendable. My family loyalty is deep as well, but if I knew someone's word had condemned my uncle to the Pereculum . . ." I purposely trail off and shake my head. "Heads would roll."

That struck a nerve that was buried deep in her mind. Her jaw clenches as she glares at the floor.

"I would've been devastated if someone betrayed me like that. When she told you that for the first time, how did you feel?"

She falls right into the trap. "She didn't tell me originally."

I raise my eyebrows dramatically. "She hid from you the fact that she testified against Kon? I thought you knew?"

"I'm not stupid and I can see what you're doing," she snaps, her trembling hand resting on the oak-handled pistol, but she quickly retracts it when Brooks opens his jacket and flashes the collection of blades he keeps secured to his side like an external ribcage. She takes a deep breath. "Vaughn and I love her and I'm not going to sell her out to you."

I may imagine it, but there's a slight hitch in her voice when she speaks of love. A chink in her stubbornness.

"You act like I'm a monster who's going to do something terrible to her," I chuckle. "Everything and everyone will be fine in the end, and you have my absolute word on that."

Callie tilts her head. "You wouldn't go to all this trouble just to scare her."

"I'm not going to *kill* her, if that's what you're insinuating." I roll my eyes. "I don't need that kind of attention right now. She just has to tell me something I need to know, and that's that."

"About what? Your errand boy?"

"You're catching on."

She shakes her head and turns away.

"I don't know why you're defending her when it's clear she wouldn't do the same for you." I press harder, injecting harshness into my tone. "What with your uncle, and what happened at the bar. You've seen what the news just said this morning about that, haven't you?"

"What?" Callie turns, scowling. "What are you talking about?"

"We just picked it up on the way here." I pull the newspaper from my pocket and show her my inside reporter's piece that inaccurately follows up on the events at The Tab, accompanied by a quote to tie it all together like a present:

"The Shining Star *was able to speak with newly Sealed Captain Emery Walker on the matter, where she said this regarding the Riggses' performance: 'It's a shame that it happened, but what's more shameful is that it wasn't contained quickly. My brother sustained serious injuries because of the fight, and it all could have been avoided had our escorts been doing their jobs correctly. I don't see any fault other than theirs.'"*

I study her as the muscles in her jaw begin to loosen, and it falls open in shock. The knot in her brow relaxes.

"Betrayal stings, doesn't it?" I whisper.

In her eyes, there's a shift, a promise that she will turn a blind eye to whatever happens tonight and do what I require. A promise to her family to redeem the hurt they've endured and the slander that's surrounded them.

A promise that means that I now have Callie Riggs wrapped tight around my finger.

"I could have thrown a larger cut of money at you, but why would I let something like this slip under your nose?" I ask quietly, plainly. "It isn't fair."

Her chest swells as she inhales. "No, it's not."

"Show your brother. I'll send someone over with details on how this will go down tonight, and not a soul will know."

Passion burns bright in Callie's eyes, alongside a bitter anger that she may never overcome.

And it's then that I know that my victory is just on the horizon.

14

Emery

I CROUCH NEXT to Miles's bed and gently shake his shoulders, and he inhales sharply.

"I'm awake," he mutters. Crusted blood cakes his nostrils. "Sh."

"I'm leaving," I whisper, dropping to my knees and perching my elbows on his cushy mattress.

His eyelids flutter open as he pulls the cloth away from his squinty, purple eyes. "Help me up."

It's like lifting a boulder, but he's soon perched next to me on the edge of the bed. He sets the cloth next to the bronze music box on the mahogany nightstand. He listens to it every night before he goes to sleep, and sometimes I can hear it twinkling into the wee hours of the early morning.

Not this morning, though. There is an anxious, gaunt air hanging throughout the house.

In it, the beginning of the future I see when I close my eyes begins to grow. Nothing can take it from me now.

Miles clears his raspy voice and stretches his stubble-dotted jaw. "What time will you actually set sail?"

"Not for a couple of hours." I fiddle with the bottom button on my coat. "We need to be gone by ten."

His eyes crinkle as he pulls me into a boarish hug. "You owe me a game at The Tab when you get back."

"Fine, but if you get into a fight, you're on your own."

"I can handle myself, thank you." He pulls back and points to his bruises. "Battle scars."

I roll my eyes. "Yes, scars that prove how you got your behind handed to you."

He scowls and nudges my shoulder with his. "If it had been a fair fight, then it would've gone differently."

I give him one last squeeze. "I love you."

"Love you. Be careful out there."

"I will."

I close his door and pause, my fingers hovering above the brass handle.

My stomach stirs.

Usually, the morning silence is welcome, but now . . .

No. I shake my head and step down the hall toward the front of the house. Charles rushes out from the living room to meet me in the foyer at the bottom of the stairs, combing his fingers through his curly hair.

"I'm late." He shoves his arms into his red coat and kisses my forehead. "I'm sorry."

"It's okay." I stand on tiptoes and hug him. "I'll see you soon."

"You said that you leave at ten, correct?" He grimaces at his watch. "I'll try to come by the harbor, but—"

"Don't rush around. It's okay."

He smiles one final time before slipping out the front door and shutting it behind him. I tighten the laces on my boots, fluff up my hair, and reach for the handle, but hesitate. I glance over my shoulder and peer out of the corner of my eye.

I drum my fingers on the brass and hesitate just a moment longer. I savor the smell of the orchids for what will be the last time in a long while, and I step outside.

Though they protested, I told the twins last night to just meet me at the courthouse so I can set my mind right as I walk. A light breeze rustles the massive palm trees overhead, and despite the humidity, I shiver. My insides twist with the excitement and anxiousness of what's to come.

Even the air downtown ticks with energy. I fiddle with the Seal in my pocket as I near the courthouse.

The granite steps are packed with soldiers being hounded by yellow-clad Shining Star reporters, waving their ink flowing pens as the breeze whips through the pages of parchment they carry. Nearly double the usual patrol of the Riggses covers the ground below the white front steps. The doors are wide open as the legal clerks and officers who work under the judges file in and out frantically.

"—without a trace," I recognize Eldon's sister's voice—Callie and Vaughn's aunt. "His wife is frantic."

My chest tightens as I maneuver toward the steps, but Ollie Riggs stops me by holding out his hand.

"I'm sorry, Captain." His face is grim. "There's a situation. I can't let you in."

"Judge Gordon left a warrant for me on his desk," I say. "I'll be quick."

"Emery!"

I turn at the sound of my father's voice cutting through the crowd and spot his red coat through the yellow and black hordes. He motions me toward him.

"Why aren't either of the twins with you?" he demands.

"I told them to meet me down here." I grab his arm and glance back at the crowd. "What is going on?"

He pinches his lips together, then says, "Gordon has disappeared."

My blood goes cold as ice.

Chadwick.

"He dismissed his private security yesterday afternoon, but no one has seen him since," my father is saying, but I'm distracted, my mind churning as Chadwick's slimy face passes through my mind.

"The harbor has been under tight watch," Eldon reassured us a couple days ago. *"And I can guarantee he wouldn't have gotten through without one of us knowing."*

Or would he?

"No one?" I finally say, exasperated. "Not one person saw him? How does that happen?"

"I don't know, but keep your voice down." My father's eyes darted around the area. Sailors are reporting to their ships, and merchants push carts and wagons with their trade goods across the streets and the dock.

Too many ears. Too many eyes.

"Was it Chadwick?" I ask quietly.

He looks at me warily. "Eldon said—"

"Eldon might be wrong!" I throw up my hands. "How can we be sure? Chadwick wouldn't waste a chance to come and throw things into chaos."

"But why go after Reese for Kearon's arrest? Why not the Armada?"

Unless Reese had a secret.

The thought makes my head spin. Secrets are in no short abundance here, but if he were in business with *Warren Chadwick* of all people . . .

And his odd behavior in his office . . .

What was he hiding?

I have never stuck my nose in the behind-the-scenes bargains and secrets of the people I work and associate with, including my own parents, but Reese's hands have always been clean as far as I knew.

My father glances over my shoulder. "That isn't all, believe it or not."

I frown.

"Kearon Romney was transferred to the Pereculum last night."

"Conveniently at the same time that Reese disappears?" I scoff. "Did he approve it beforehand?"

"I don't know. It was a decision the entire judge's council had to make, and I don't know how he voted."

I take a step back and purse my lips. "It has to be Chadwick, Father. He must be hiding well enough for the Riggses to miss him. What if he went after Reese?"

"All for an *errand boy?*" My father shakes his head. "Why?"

My thoughts are like a whirlwind circling my head. "Kearon probably knows more about Chadwick's operations than we thought. We need to lock down the port and search the whole city for him. Every inn, every abandoned building, every house—"

"Stop." He grabs my shoulders. "You sound manic."

"It's not manic when the chief judge is missing!" I gesture to the crowd. "It's not manic when we're talking about the man who almost *murdered* you!"

He purses his lips and sighs, dropping his head. "If so, then who do you think he'll go for next? Perhaps the girl who arrested his errand boy and started this in the first place?" His grip tightens. "You need to stay with both Callie and Vaughn at all times. Go find them."

"Commander Walker!" A woman in a lilac Messenger vest waves and approaches us. "Is there anything you can tell me about Judge Gordon's disappearance?"

My father's media mask comes up as he turns to face her. "The Armada has no details. The Riggses are more equipped to . . ."

Before the reporters can hound me, I slip away from the conversation and jog to the Riggses' outpost, my heart still pounding.

. . .

"*. . . missing from Padstow . . .*"

"*The judge has not been seen since yesterday afternoon . . .*"

"*. . . conspiracy? Hiding from a bad deal, perhaps? It wouldn't be surprising.*"

"*. . . other judges are scrambling to elect an interim chief who can lead the city until Judge Gordon's return . . .*"

"*. . . the only question left is, where is Reese Gordon?*"

Callie yanks the capsule of the spindle in the *Chaplain's Heart's* captain's quarters—well, it's *my* quarters now. So is the mahogany desk, the four-poster bed on the upper level, and the caged burrow currently housing a black shearwater that will deliver letters when the time calls. Maps decorate the walls where there are no windows, and lanterns swing from the low-hanging ceiling, their rusted chains creaking with the movement of the ship.

I fold my arms and stare through the window at the back of the room, out at the sea and the sun falling below the horizon line.

Too coincidental. Too convenient.

That's all I can think of.

My fingers twitch. My parents' commands were for me to stay with both the twins for protection, while the vile monster that *I* know the most about and whose behaviors *I* know best is potentially roaming Padstow. I've been waiting here for ten hours, and I'm losing my head.

Where are you hiding? Where can I find you?

And why does it feel like you're right under my nose?

"Emery."

I blink and turn to Callie. "Sorry, what?"

She picks at the skin around her nails. "What are you going to do if you can't get the warrant to leave?"

I clench my jaw and ball my fists. "If he is here, I don't even want to leave. I want to go after him myself."

She gives me a look of warning.

"I know," I deadpan, resisting the urge to roll my eyes. "You'd lock me in the brig downstairs if I stepped out of your sight for a second."

She turns away and bites her cheek.

"Is something wrong?"

"I'm fine," she grumbles, but she won't meet my eyes. "This day just needs to end."

I watch as she turns away and continues picking her skin. "I'm jealous that you're hiding your anxiety better than I am," she says.

"Anxious isn't the word." I clear my throat and straighten my spine. "Antsy is. *Annoyedly* antsy."

She takes a shaky breath and rakes her hand through her black curls.

I tilt my head and sigh. "Cal—"

"I don't know why you want to be out searching, anyway, when you know he wouldn't hesitate to slit your throat." She cuts me off and paces the room like a caged tiger. "Why?"

"It's no different than being on a hunt." I frown. "If anything, it's safer now that we're in our own territory."

She blinks rapidly, clearly flustered.

"Callie, what's going on?"

Vaughn opens the door with his black jacket draped over his arm. His eyes are weary, and his white uniform shirt is wrinkled and untucked. He grimaces at me. "I could not find your father or the warrant, and no patrols have seen anything suggesting that Gordon or Chadwick is here."

"*None of them?*" I step back. "Please tell me you're joking."

"The Armada is running around looking for Chadwick, and the patrols are out for Gordon, but there's nothing." He scratches his head and puckers his lips. "I'm sorry."

I exhale through clenched teeth and press my hands over my mouth.

"The patrols have been scouring the city and talking to potential witnesses for hours, but there's been nothing." Vaughn rubs the back of his neck. "He's a ghost."

Callie mumbles something to herself.

"Captain Scott is outside waiting for you as well," Vaughn says to me, though he won't look me in the eye either. "She wanted to see you."

"Now?" I grumble, adjusting my sword belt. "Why?"

"I don't know."

I grip the hilt of my sword as I walk past him, but I stop. "Vaughn."

He finally looks at me. I glance between the two of them. Callie's lips are tight.

It's just the stress of the day weighing on them.

Right?

I don't know. There's something they aren't telling me.

I squint in thought for a moment, then step carefully outside.

The humidity is stronger on the water, and that just adds to my bitter mood. Fallon stands near the gangplank, her hair slicked back and pulled into a tight bun. She's dressed in her full sailing attire of the striped gray captain's coat and shiny black boots. Like mine, hers has intricate embroidery along the hems and cuffs.

She smiles as I walk up to her. "Captain."

"What are you doing?"

"Checking on an inferior." She frowns. "Rough day?"

"If you want to call it that," I mutter. "Why are you in uniform?"

"My crew is leaving on rotation again in Marshland."

"How did you get a warrant?" I scoff. "I've been waiting for one so *I* can leave!"

"It's just a rotation." She waves it off. "It's not that big of a deal."

"Who authorized you to go? The judges—"

"It was the admiral, and he agreed with me!" She crosses her arms and shrugs. "I guarantee if you ask him, he'll do the same for you. It's too chaotic, and besides, you left without one for Lexington last time."

"That was a more pressing situation than a rotation, Fallon," I say irritably. "I'm not dodging the rules again."

"All crime is a pressing situation. Especially piracy." She wrinkles her forehead. "And as weak as Lexington is, they won't care. It's not like we're staging an invasion."

I stare at her and scowl, but all I can think of is what she said after the corps's meeting

"Other civilians are unaccounted for, but it's six. You didn't hear that from me, though."

My insides turn with discomfort, and I turn my gaze away.

"If you need backup, just write to me. The bird you've got in there is good at its job." She hands me a small canvas bag of scent. I look in and see that it's full of pine needles, which I assume is Marshland's scent for the birds to follow. "You look good. The pressure hasn't been weighing down on you too badly, right?"

I grit my teeth. "I've been fine."

"I'm glad." She rubs my shoulder and smiles as if all is well. "We'll catch up with each other later. Good luck."

I watch her go. She carries herself like she isn't dragging secrets behind her, but I don't stew in it for long. I have barely turned to storm back into my cabin when movement on the dock catches my eye. A flash of light gleams in my vision, and I squint and recoil.

When my vision focuses again, I scan the dock for the source of the light, and my stomach drops.

Limping, hot-headed, tobacco-chewing *scum.*

What is he doing here?

Hyde Kensington keeps glancing over his shoulder as he hobbles forward, holding what looks like a small handheld mirror to direct the sunlight right into my eyes. He holds my gaze for a moment before limping around the corner.

"Cal! Vaughn!" I race back to the door and throw it open. "Pirates! Hurry!"

My vision tunnels as I run down the gangplank. I can catch him. He lumbers like an injured deer around a corner on the north end of the harbor, where the smaller merchant ships dock. I draw my sword and sprint.

"Emery, wait!" Callie calls out.

I don't stop. My racing heart and tunnel vision won't let me.

"Hyde!" The winding streets are deserted as I zip through them, drawing my sword and the pistol that rests against my ribs. "Stop!"

I round the corner and barely see him duck into an alley and vanish. I sprint harder, but by the time I make it through and out onto the next street, he's disappeared again.

I whirl around. There's an abandoned apartment building nestled at the base of the mountain, and I break toward the door before stopping dead again.

The trees and bushes behind it rustle, despite the still air.

I pull back the hammer of my pistol and run into the trees alone. If I lose him, it won't matter if I have backup or not. I can take a cripple, especially if I'm armed.

The air in the thicket is stiflingly thick, and the greenery blocks out the dwindling sunlight. Cicadas and other creatures of the jungle buzz in chorus as I crouch and listen for Hyde's uneven footsteps, my finger hovering over the trigger.

Snap.

I move toward the sound, my heart pounding and mind sharp. I glance back for any sign of the twins.

The sound of a bush rustling snatches my attention, and I leap toward it. More footsteps—these sounding more even-gaited—rush through the trees to my right, and I drop to the ground as a single gunshot cracks through the air.

Then, silence.

My heart pounds.

Dead, eerie silence. Even the insects seem to have vanished.

My grip on the gun tightens.

"Emery?" Vaughn's voice echoes in the distance.

I scramble to my feet and rush to approach him. I nearly trip over a fallen branch. "Here!"

Where is he?

The tightness in my chest remains, and I freeze in my tracks. My intuition screams at me.

Get out. Get out now.

A hand grabs my elbow and nearly yanks me off my feet. My back collides with a warm body as its arms snake around my ribs and shoulders.

"It's me! It's me!" Vaughn hisses in my ear, lifting me off the ground with ease. Saliva lands on my skin. "It's okay."

"What are you doing?" I wince, squirming in his hold as my toes scrape the ground. I drop my sword to free one of my hands to wrench him away. "Vaughn, let me—"

"I'm so sorry." His clammy hands reach under the neck of my blouse as he grabs the vault key and snaps the chain with a hard tug. Another hand grabs my wrist and snatches the gun out of my hand.

"You're lucky she didn't shoot me," a husky voice grumbles behind him.

What?

Panic claws through my body as Vaughn's hold relaxes, and as I twist away from him, I'm met by a circle of pistol muzzles, trapping me in the center. Their wielders are breathing heavily and staring at me with wide eyes, ready to pepper me with bullets if I dare to run.

A hammer clicks. Vaughn is aiming at me, staring at me down the length of my pistol, gripping my vault key in his other hand.

Time stands still, and no one moves.

"What is this?" My heart begins to sink. I step toward him, but he steps back, aiming the pistol right between my eyes. He shakes his head and clenches his jaw.

I blink. That's all I can do through the tense shock. "Vaughn . . ."

He doesn't say a word. The charming warmth in his eyes is replaced with a cold, metallic grit that I have never seen before.

I blink. My eyes must be tricking me. This can't... this wouldn't *happen.*

I'm pulled back to reality as another set of hands grabs my shoulders and yanks me backward. I writhe and kick until an elbow drives into my ribs and a hand clamps over my mouth, but I scream. I scream in panic, praying someone somewhere will hear me or see what's happening.

Shaky hands fumble with the knife sheath and sword belt on my hip, and I notice a thin, pale line around the left little finger. I glance up, seeing that the silver earrings I gave as a gift are missing.

Callie.

No.

Why?

"—four counts up from the floor. Next to Charles's." Vaughn's voice. His hair hangs limply in his eyes as he hands my key to Hyde. "It's going to be a lot of money to carry."

"We picked up everything from the other vaults already, so it's fine," he answers. "We'll leave your cut at the bar."

"That timing was nice," someone above my head mutters. "I'm surprised she saw you, Hyde."

Hyde's brows flash upwards. He buttons up the brown vest he wears over his yellowing shirt and rubs his muscly arms. "Me too. I didn't think she'd come outside."

"I told you it would work," Callie snaps. "Why do you all sound so surprised?"

My muscles ache from exertion as I try to wrench free, but the hands are like rough iron clamps on my arms, shoulders, and ribs. I helplessly watch Callie slip my sheath into the inner pocket of her coat, but she won't look at me. Anger radiates from her like mist as he stretches her wrists and sighs.

Why, why, why? It's the only word that bounces through my mind.
What did I do?

"Would you hold still?" a lighter voice snaps overhead. Something sharp presses into my side as the hand over my mouth wrenches my head back. "Good grief."

I glance back and forth between my protectors, my friends. My sister. My lover.

Not anymore. A whimper stirs in the back of my achy throat.

"Is that all?"

And that voice. Light. Mature. Echoing in my mind for years as I've chased it.

I summon what little strength I have and manage to throw my captors off balance, but my head snaps to the side as a blunt object cracks against my skull.

I see sharp blond hair, a sharp nose, a sharp jaw, and—before the blackness overtakes my vision—a sneering, triumphant smile.

15

THE MORNING SUNLIGHT breaks the horizon and streams through the windows of my cabin as Padstow becomes nothing more than a blip in the distance.

And it was like I was never there, which is quite a far cry from the last time I departed the city.

The carriage Eldon promised us transported Emery, myself, and a few others back to the harbor while Darren and Tahj led a small team back to the bar for her money. We gave the owner his cut, Eldon and the twins their cut, and we were on our merry way.

My chest swells with pride as I sit at my desk, where my trophy awaits.

Her red coat is beautiful, threaded with golden, hand-woven embroidery that adorns the cuffs and seams. There is a secret pocket on the inside breast, and when I run my fingers over the buttons, I'm shocked to find that they're real gold, stamped with a capital W. I throw it on the desk with a scoff of disgust.

Hyde looks up from his pen and logbook, where he's working at the round table in the corner.

"The ego of these people is disgusting," I spit. "All for a coat."

"Ninety-eight, ninety-nine," Darren murmurs, adjacent to Hyde, his back hunched as he counts. "Hundred." He slumps back in his chair and groans. "So far, it's nine million, two hundred thousand, eight hundred novas."

My eyes widen with excitement. "And we're not even halfway there."

"Correct." Hyde smiles and claps the sharpshooter on the shoulder. "Very nice, Darren."

I let myself grin. "Indeed."

"Thanks," Darren mutters, brushing his greasy brown curls behind his ears.

"Go switch with Brooks or Tahj and take a break, why don't you?" I suggest.

"Yes, sir." He pushes away from the table and exits my cabin. "Fine by me."

I can't hide my giddy grin as I stare at the pile of coins and over-flowing bags on the floor around the table. Stray coins dot the rugs in front of my bookshelves that line either wall.

"What exact time did we leave last night?" Hyde asks without looking up from his writing.

"It was 1:46. Winds were from the southeast."

Hyde copies it in the log. "Thank you."

I stare at the coat again and rub my fingers over my mouth, my thoughts wandering.

I am winning, but this fight is far from over.

"Tell my parents I love them if you can get back." Kearon's eager smile haunts me more than his last words. I should have known better than to let a boy come too close. There was a time when *I* was a boy who grew too close to this twisted game, and look where I am.

I wonder what determines who gets the noose and who gets the gold. In this case, the gold is mine. She's locked away and will tarnish and rot as long as I have a say in it.

I notice a loose thread on the coat's left sleeve, and I pick at it. It unravels in a long, twiney strand.

Hyde snaps the log shut and sets it on my desk. He sticks the pen into the pocket of his shirt. "Whatever will you do when I'm not around to write your logs for you anymore?"

"Die." I touch my chest and sigh. "I despise it."

"It takes five minutes."

"Writing is tedious," I say as I slide the book into one of my desk drawers. "Why on earth would I do it when you can? You're so gifted."

"It doesn't take a genius to write a logbook."

"Of course. Why do you think I have you do it?"

He scoffs with a grin. "What does it say if even *you* can't even write them?"

"Well, one of us is a captain and the other isn't." I smile and swipe my hands across his shoulders like I'm dusting them off. "Lest we forget the distribution of power here."

"Aha." Hyde licks his lips. His eyes fall to the new collection of trinkets on my desk; her rings and earrings are laid out in a neat row in the middle of the polished wood. The red and gold captain's ring sits in the center.

I glance at the pockets of her coat and slip my hand inside, and I gasp. "How could I forget about you?" I hold the gold Seal between my index finger and thumb. "Look at that."

"Give it all to Kearon's parents to sell it off." Hyde brings one of her earrings to his face, studying it with narrowed eyes. "They deserve it after everything that's happened."

My spine shudders at the thought of having to tell them what happened to their son. It killed me the first time, and now I have to sit down and share that their son's fate is—according to some—worse than death.

Not is. Could be. *Won't* be. Not if I still have a say.

"I'm going to kill her once this is over," I mumble absentmindedly, narrowing my eyes at the intricate engravings on the coin. "I'm going to rip her to shreds for this and for everything before."

Hyde folds his brawny arms. "Do you want me to go see if she's awake?"

"No." I set my jaw and stretch my neck. "I will go down there later. I want to see her face the second she's awake, and then you can have her."

"Well, I'll be outside waiting, in that case." He pops up onto his toes. "Don't make me sit for too long."

I gesture to his leg. "You've waited long enough. Your family has, too."

He smiles at the mention of his sisters and father and shuts the door behind him.

I pick up the Seal again and stare at it.

A "W" on one side, and a ship on the other. It fits nicely into the palm of my hand and looks even better on the desk with the other spoils of hers I've collected. All gold for a formerly golden girl.

16

CREAK...

    Creak...

    Creak...

I inhale sharply as an aching jab pulses through my temples. My memory is blank.

The stabbing intensifies, and I groan. My neck and back are cramped with tight, excruciating pain, and something hard presses against the knobs of my spine. It's dark when I open my eyes, and cold, rusted chains encircle my wrists, binding them behind my back and around what feels like a wooden support beam.

I tug at them on instinct and choke back a panicked sob, the metal cutting my skin and digging in tight. Holes pepper my memory.

I see Callie stealing my knife and refusing to look at me, and Vaughn handing me off to—

"Hello."

Him.

Slimy, sarcastic, despicable *him*.

My eyes adjust, and I see Warren Chadwick fold his arms and lean against a stack of barrels, one of many in the hot, musty storage room. I can hear the faint sounds of ocean waves lapping against the walls.

He tilts his head, carefully and calculatedly watching me. Neither of us speaks for a long moment.

I clench my teeth as I hold his gaze. He has consumed my mind and robbed me of my peace on so many sleepless nights as I've paced the halls, obsessed with the moment I would finally see him behind bars or with a bullet between his eyes.

The fiery passion in my chest burns its brightest every time I see him in person, but now, everything is oddly silent. I swallow the knot in my throat. When we've interacted, I've always stood across from him with a weapon in hand, but seeing him still—*being* still, trapped, confined—is different. Terrifyingly different.

His sharp jaw muscles twitch. "It's rude not to return a greeting, you know," he sneers.

I don't speak. I can't. Every word, every biting remark seems to die on my tongue before it can escape.

He rolls his eyes and pushes off the stack, adjusting the sleeves of his black-as-night coat. His icy blond locks are combed back and styled neatly. "Usually, you can't shut up, but now I have to pry to get you to talk?"

"What did you do?" My voice shakes and my head pounds. My mind grapples to fill the gaps in my memory, but there's nothing there. Nothing besides the memory of Callie's angry eyes and Vaughn pointing a gun at my forehead.

"There were lots of moving parts involved in this, though your cooperation was invaluable," Chadwick replies. He adjusts the lapel of his coat so it lies straight.

Nausea rolls in my stomach as I move my legs, finding my ankles are bound as well. "No, I didn't—"

"Oh, you did." He narrows his eyes. "You ran into my trap. Your guard was lowered. I thank you for it, honestly."

My senses sharpen just a little. I flex my fingers and notice my rings are gone, and so is my coat. I swallow and dig my fingertips into the splintered floor, willing the nausea to pass as my heart pounds in my ears.

"The two of them were willing." Chadwick sighs dramatically and holds out his hands. "I suppose the years of beratement and mistreatment finally got to them."

"No." My voice shakes. "They wouldn't have."

"Oh, they would." He speaks like a teacher scolding his subordinate. "I know, for one, that near the end, Callie did not like being at your every beck and call at every moment of the day. As for your Vaughn . . ." He laughs a true, hearty laugh. "He is quite an actor. I was impressed. His feelings *might* have been real at some point before this, but I digress. The nail in the coffin was that little statement you gave the courts about their uncle."

I shake my head as the words drop like sludge from my tongue. "They didn't know that—"

"Well, obviously they did or they would have never agreed to this." He rolls his eyes. "I don't know if it was Gordon who spilled the beans or someone else, but come on now. This is your fault. You're not that dense, Miss Walker." He chuckles. "Or *Captain,* I should say. Captain Walker." His voice drips with mockery. "All eyes are on the captain at last."

His disdain for me is thick like fog. I can practically hear the gears turning in his head as he glares at me.

I learn forward, tugging on the chains. "The Armada will know I'm gone." My voice trembles. "How did you plan for that?"

"*You* planned for that, actually. They think Captain Scott asked you to join her as she left, and you were gone like that." He snaps his fingers. "The twins will corroborate that story until the day they die."

I squeeze my eyes shut.

But somewhere, deep in my heart, I can understand it. The Riggses were always at the bottom of the ladder and were the footstool for the others.

But I never thought that they . . . My family would never . . .

The pain in my chest is so unbearably heavy that I can't think straight.

Why? Why? Why?

Chadwick chuckles darkly. "Quite nauseating to think about, isn't it?"

"Someone had to have seen . . ." I lose my breath before I can even finish the sentence. My tongue feels like a shriveled leaf rotting in my mouth. "How?"

"Money talks. Eldon couldn't save his brother from the Pereculum, so why not target the man who put him there and find some semblance of justice?" Chadwick's eyes grow dangerously dark as he angles his head. "And what about the justice for an innocent boy who you *stole* in the middle of the night? What right did you have to barge into Lexington?"

"He wasn't innocent!"

"He was! Try to make that make sense, and try to justify shipping him to the Pereculum just like you try to justify everything else you do!" His voice echoes through the small space. "Tell me why I have to knock on his parents' door and explain to them that their son is as good as dead!"

"And you thought targeting Reese and me was going to free him? Is he here too?"

"No." Chadwick rolls his eyes. "Gordon, that pathetic wretch. He somehow knew I was coming for him and ran like a coward."

My headache spikes, and my thoughts are slow as I try to process everything. I test the chains, and the rust scrapes across my skin. "If you were going to kill me, you would've already done it, so what's this about?"

He turns and chuckles, and venom drips from his voice as he speaks. "That's a stupid question with an obvious answer. You didn't expect to, one, ruin my life and those of my crew, and, two, take my innocent errand boy and get away with it, did you? My initial plan was a simple trade where Gordon and Van Pelt would exchange Kearon's freedom for yours, but what with recent events—"

"You think I know where Reese is, don't you?" I curl my shaky fingers against my palms. "You think he'll rescind Kearon's sentence."

"There's that cheeky intuition I've come to know." He snaps his fingers and winks. "Such a bright mind."

He leans over and picks up a news spindle and capsule from the ground, and I watch as he gives it a spin.

"*—thing doesn't seem to be right in Padstow paradise like we've all believed. Last night—*"

"What is this?" I scowl.

He touches his lips and points to the spindle.

"*—that there was a robbery within the Walker estate, and the reports that are trickling in say. . .*" The reporter pauses, and he clears his throat. I recognize him as the one who reported the night after my Sealing, downplaying the event as a result of my parents' meddling and position in the Armada. "*Reports are trickling in and saying that this* *was a plot orchestrated by none other than the family's newest captain, Emery Walker."*

My blood freezes.

"Authorities have yet to find the young captain-turned-thief, and The Shining Star invites anyone with information about this to come forward to your closest news outpost to—"

"What did you do?" I demand.

Captain-turned-thief plays again in my mind.

"Here's how this is going to go." Chadwick folds his arms and lets the capsule play on. "You started this entire ordeal weeks ago when you took Kearon, and now I'm collecting my dues. You can be a help or a hindrance, and the only thing that's hanging in the balance is your precious name and image."

I listen, though I'd like to pounce like a lion and rip him to shreds.

"You know better than most how powerful a negative word can be. What do you think will happen as that collection of words begins to grow against you?" He narrows his eyes. "Where is Reese Gordon?"

"I don't—" I stop short.

"If all goes down the drain, then you'll know where to find me." Reese's voice whispers in the back of my mind. *"Lounging on the beaches in Kahu."*

Is that why he told me? So I could find him after he ran from Chadwick?

But if he knew, why didn't he warn me that Chadwick was coming for me, too?

"I wouldn't tell you even if I knew," I spit, the lie rolling off my tongue with ease. "And there's no guarantee he knows where the Pereculum is, either. You won't get Kearon back no matter how hard you try."

"Don't be so cavalier." He narrows his eyes. Shadows outline the edges of his face like black ink.

"If this is just for Kearon—"

"It's for Kearon, it's for me, and it's for my entire crew!" he shouts, the sound echoing through the small space. My stomach clenches. *"You set my operations behind for months when you wrecked my name and* took all my money. *You* put my entire crew out of work and ruined everything!"

I keep my tone level. "Anyone who decides to follow you deserves anything that's coming to them."

"Where is Gordon?" Spittle flies from his lips. "Where?"

"I don't know."

"Does he have other houses in different areas of the region? Is he being harbored by an official on another island?"

I stare him straight in his icy eyes and set my jaw.

"Come on. The twins told me how close the two of you were. He must have told you something." Chadwick eerily keeps his composure and turns his back to me when I don't answer. He paces like a creature in a cave. "Think very, *very* carefully about the decisions you're going to make over the next few days, Miss Walker, and think about how cooperative you want to be while we travel. Everything that's about to happen rests on your shoulders."

The reporter's voice drones on as dread settles its cold, dead fingers over my shoulders and digs into my sore muscles.

He'll tear down the tower I've worked so hard to build one brick at a time.

But no. The words of all the teachers I've had over the years, including my mother and father, whisper in my ears after each day in the Academy.

"Win."

"Do not stop until you're the last one standing and do whatever it takes to win. The challenge is yours."

The challenge is blond and has the eyes of a venomous snake, but one of us is going to lose, and it's not going to be me.

"Padstow is going to know it's you behind this," I say at last. "They won't leave a captain behind."

"How? Everyone thinks you ran off with Captain Scott and are a thief." He smiles like a charmer, lips curled and teeth shining in the dim light. "The only theatrics here are the ones you've been acting in for years, Miss Walker. The curtain isn't there to protect you anymore." He turns toward the door, but stops short. I frown.

"Think carefully about how you'd like this to go," he gently reiterates, his back facing me. "That is my current proposition. You've spent time dragging my name through the dirt, and I think it's time you experienced the same." He glances over his shoulder and smiles. "Who will you be at the end of this? Walker, the captain? Or Walker, the fraud?"

The door clanks shut.

And oddly, my mind is silent.

For a few heartbeats, it stays that way.

Until it's not. Until I'm suddenly hyper aware of each sound, each smell, each sensation on my skin. The air is thick. Hot. Uncomfortably hot. Dust floats across the dim lantern swinging from a chain in the middle of the room, and I want to leap from my skin, my clothes, from the hot, sticky prison I'm suddenly very aware of.

Panic doesn't rest with time, I've come to learn.

The metal digs into the bones in my wrists and ankles, and I resist the urge to yank and tug until my skin bleeds and my bones crack under the pressure. My chest constricts with each panicked breath as I bring my knees to my chest and duck my head, swallowing a whimper.

The dread from being trapped in one spot and unable to move has always been an anxiety I've never been able to shake. One too many negative experiences, when hunts have gone wrong, are cemented in my psyche.

The difference here is a matter of personal vendetta.

He took my mother's earrings. My rings. My coat.

I grit my teeth.

"Cooperative and calm, my teachers' voices echo. *"Cooperative and calm. Don't do anything to provoke them."*

I can be cooperative and mask calm for a little while. Maybe.

So much fell to pieces so quickly that I don't even know where to begin worrying. Nothing seems to exist outside of the bowels of this disgusting ship and the dim lantern swinging in the center of the room.

Creak, creak, creak

I wrap my fingers around the chains and yank in frustration.

I should have seen it. There were enough hushed conversations and whispers between the twins that should have given it away, and I was a fool to ignore them because they are my friends.

Friends. Traitors.

The hours crawl by, and I am dredging every single conversation and interaction from the last few months for a sign. Any sign. The whispered conversations between the two of them and the constant bitterness about the bad press and mistreatment should have been enough.

I should've known. I should've *seen it.*

I knew from the conversations between Callie and me in the late hours of the night that the judgments from the aristocracy weighed on her mind. I reassured her. I comforted her. I promised that none of it ever mattered and that it wouldn't change the fact that she was my strong, resilient best friend who I'd walk to the ends of the world with no matter what.

Nausea bubbles in my throat as my eyes well with tears. She saw into the darkest corners of my life and was there despite everything, but I don't think she knew how much I cared for her.

And him.

I let a phantom touch me and kiss me so ardently, and I believed he loved me. It was too real for it to have been an act.

"I love you. To the end of forever."

The worst part is that if he were unhappy, he never would have told me. He exemplifies nothing but strength and admirable resilience.

Which indeed makes him quite the actor.

My chest swells with anger as I stifle a sob, and another, and another, until the hole clawing its way through my chest is so wide that it might never be repaired. I strain against my restraints with so much force that my arms shake alongside each heart-wrenching sob.

His touch was too gentle for it to have been a trick. Her loyalty was too rich for it to have meant absolutely nothing.

Though it seems yours never meant anything to her. The doubt creeps in. *Their uncle is in jail because of you, and you told them nothing.*

Nothing. Nothing.

It echoes through my turbulent mind for a very long time.

17

HYDE SIGHS and rubs his temples. The skin on his knuckles is split open and red in the lantern light. "You know, this was entertaining for the first fifteen minutes or so, but I'm *really* starting to lose my patience."

Another fist jabs into my side, and I double over in the chair, groaning and gasping for air.

"*That* wasn't even that bad," he mutters above my head.

I squeeze my swollen eyes shut and hold my ribs with my shackled hands. Blood drips down the front of my shirt, and I squeak out a word despite my throbbing, split lips. "Hyde—"

"Oh, spare me." Hyde rolls his eyes. "I'm not in the mood to listen to you prattle on unless you're going to tell me what I want."

"No." I force myself to sit up and breathe, however painful. "I was going to compliment your form. It's surprisingly good considering you can barely stand straight."

My nose cracks under his fist as my head snaps to the side. The other pirate in the room—a man with brawny hands—has to hold me upright by the shoulders so I don't tumble onto the dusty floor. My head hangs as I grit my teeth, stealing from Hyde the satisfaction of hearing my pain, even though there are about a thousand screams lodged in my throat.

Hyde stretches his fingers and curls his lip. "Goodness. You are just the *worst*, you know that?"

I touch my nose, and my fingers come away bloody. The broken bone and cartilage scream like a twig that's been snapped under the weight of a boar.

"I hope you know Warren is the only barrier stopping me from strangling you to death for going after my family," he growls, grabbing my aching jaw. The shackles jingle as he jerks my head upright. "Every time I write to my sisters, they write back worried that the Padstow Armada is going to show up and take them away like you threatened."

I grimace and try to twist out of his hold. "I didn't threaten them," I mutter, though I barely remember that day. It's been over a year . . . or two years? All I remember was the anger from finding that Hyde wasn't there.

"That's not how they remember it." He tilts his head. "You were looking for *me*. You should have left *them* alone."

"I thought they knew where you were."

"Well, that wasn't true, was it?" His grip tightens, and I wince. His breath reeks of tobacco.

"Stop." My breath hitches.

"Didn't you keep pressing them for answers and threatening to arrest them if they didn't cooperate?" His thumb digs into the cuts on my lips, and they sting with pain. "Didn't they beg *you* to stop?"

He reaches up and presses his thumb into my nose, and I cry out. Spots dance in my vision as I rip my head away from his grip, breathing hard. Tears well in my eyes.

"And I'd love to return the favor on this." He lifts his twisted leg and presses his foot directly onto my knee. "When you pushed me and ran, did you hear the sound of the bone breaking? I won't snap your shin in half, but I learned this new move to twist someone's leg and pop their hip right out of its socket. Why don't I show you?"

I clench my sore jaw and force myself to glare at him, though it's like staring into the eyes of a rabid bear inches away from ripping its prey to shreds.

"Where is Gordon?" he spits.

"If I knew, why wouldn't I have told you already?" Another spike of pain jams through my head, and suddenly, two of him appear in my field of view. He catches my chin as my head droops.

"We're not done." The smell of tobacco mixed with blood is nauseating. "Stay awake."

"Then direct your fists elsewhere," I rasp.

What did my teachers say to do in moments like this?

I don't know. There's nothing inside my skull besides bone-splitting aching and agony.

Hyde steps back and stretches his thick arms over his head. I tense, praying he'll aim somewhere other than my face as I swallow a sob.

"I genuinely don't understand what you gain from protecting Gordon when he's a liar," he says. "Do you know how many secret dealings he shared outside of the law? For someone whose entire career is based on telling the truth and upholding the law—"

"Reese isn't like that." I cut him off.

Hyde chuckles bitterly, flashing his yellow teeth. "You should know better than anyone how shiny the upper class pretends to be, especially after how you betrayed your best friends."

My heart twinges, and I look away.

"How do you think it felt when they found out?" He leans down, favoring his left leg and perching his hands on his knees so we're eye to eye. I could hit him, but I don't trust my double vision or that he won't snap my jaw clean in half with another punch. "You were putting up a facade when their family was going through the wringer, and I guarantee others thought nothing of you, just like you thought nothing of them. You can pretend all you want, but the difference here is that Gordon doesn't care about you. Why do you think he took off without warning you that we were coming?"

My cheeks burn.

"It's a bit odd he disappeared just before Warren was about to catch him, isn't it?" He narrows his eyes, his tongue skimming his chapped lips in disdain. "So he either didn't know that you were involved in this plan as well, or he intentionally left you behind. You better hope it's not the latter."

"You're a lousy manipulator," I snap, but my heart isn't in it. A dark voice whispers that he may be right. If the twins betrayed me, what's to say Reese wouldn't do the same to protect his own skin?

I grimace and bite my tongue, resisting the urge to scream in frustration. I should be en route to Lexington right now, not dealing with the confusing grief of disappearance and betrayal.

Hyde folds his arms and waggles his eyebrows. "You're right. Why do you think Warren asked me to do this?" His elbow rears back, and I flinch, the chains on my hands rattling as I hold them out in front of me.

He chuckles jeeringly and signals for the other pirate to leave.

I sob in relief as I slump back in the chair, and almost every bone from my waist up throbs with each heartbeat. The pain is indescribable, as if someone splintered my skull and face open with a hammer and wedge.

"Well?"

Oh. I forgot he was standing in the corner, arms folded and expression taught. My throat tightens as I duck my head.

Chadwick raises his eyebrows. "He's content to keep doing that forever, but I don't think you are content to sit through it."

"If I knew, I wouldn't be putting up with this," I say quietly, my lips and face aching with every word. I close my eyes and will the bile in my throat to subside.

"That would be a fair point if it weren't a lie." His eyes roll to the ceiling. "Miss Walker—"

"I'm telling the truth!" I exclaim a little too desperately. My shaky hands grip the chain connecting my shackles as I lean forward. "I already said if I knew where he was—"

"You should know better than anyone that my patience is thinner than ice." He glares at me, staring down his long, sharp nose. "Do not test me."

"If anything you said was true, then why do you think I would defend him? My family was the closest to him, and if anything was going on—"

"Then *obviously* you would have spoken up about it, wouldn't you?" he mocks. "You would have come to save the day to appear virtuous to the others."

"That's not true."

"You speak so much of justice when none was served to Aleksander Nowak and Coy Hadley for the night you and I met. Do you remember it?" Chadwick narrows his eyes. "I remember it. I remember how they didn't take the blame for anything, even though *they* were illegally smuggling gold." He smiles politely. "Isn't it interesting how I caught the most trouble from that, and everyone turned a blind eye to the two of them for causing it?"

"I didn't. I went to Aleksander—"

"And if I recall, wasn't it you who constantly shifted the blame to me with the media?" He sucks his teeth. "Why not call out the men who instigated it all in the first place?"

Bile rises in my throat again, and I have to duck and resist the urge to vomit.

"They covered it up," I breathe, the air choking up out of my throat. "Coy and Aleksander paid off the news outlets and anyone who threatened to expose what really happened. I fought it, but no one listened to me."

Chadwick gestures to himself and grins. "And so enters the scapegoat."

"That doesn't change how you attacked Padstow and tried to kill my father," I snap.

"You have no proof that it was me!" He points his index finger and shortens the distance between us. "This is ridiculous, and you know it. Now you've operated on false information that has sent an innocent boy to jail! To *die!*"

Chadwick grips either edge of the chair so I'm trapped between his lean arms. Our noses are inches apart, and he smells like woody ash. "You lied to your own friends about their uncle, you've lied about me, and you've lied to the public for years about everything to keep this virtuous little image of Padstow alive and breathing. And paying the news to keep that image of yours spotless—what sort of gallant captain acts that way?" Venom drips from his lips as they curl over his shiny white teeth. "Your ambition and work ethic are admirable, but you are not the upstanding figure that you think you are."

Something stirs deep in my chest as I clench my fists. "And what does that make you?"

"Imperfect." He pushes away and turns to the door. "But at least I don't lie to myself and others about it."

It clanks shut and locks.

My skin crawls with discomfort as I wriggle out of the chair and land awkwardly on my hands and knees, groaning in pain. I spit blood and curl up on the floor, and the tears fall. Every inch of my face and ribs throb, and warm blood from my nose coats my split, stinging lips.

I'm no stranger to fights, but the relentless bare-knuckle blows from a man who could single-handedly row a barge across the ocean . . .

My breath hitches. No.

My fingers curl into fists. Crippled, cowardly, pathetic Hyde Kensington will *not* break me, and neither will the monster he works for.

Chadwick can hold Coy and Aleksander's vices over my head, but I will stand firm in my actions. The *correct* actions.

That is, unless Kearon had never broken the law, my conscience whispers. *Unless he really was just a bookkeeper.*

His cries and pleas the night of his arrest still echo in the back of my mind from time to time, but so does Aleksander's pious insistence that he was innocent. Both were in the wrong.

I don't doubt this ordeal is only about forcing Reese to repeal Kearon's sentence, but a twisted game of revenge he's going to play with me until one of us gives out.

I stifle another sob as I press my hands into the floor and force myself to sit, slumping against the section of the wall that isn't blocked by barrels and crates. The rattling of the chains is the only sound that fills the dark hold as I press the collar of my shirt to my dripping nose and suck slow breaths into my aching chest.

Reese must have a good reason to have left without warning me. He *must.*

I tell myself it's the truth because I cannot take the soul-crushing agony of another betrayal.

My eyes slide shut as I listen to the gentle waves lapping against the side of the ship, and the pain subsides to a dull throb. The dread of the situation settles into my racing heart. Chadwick's threats echo in the back of my mind as if it's a hollow, stone cavern, dark and devoid of hope.

Despite it, I smile, because if I don't, I'll burst into tears and suffocate myself with more crying. The thought of what my family must be going through with what the news has said, the twins' betrayal, and the pain of my near-shattered bones . . .

I wonder if this is how Miles felt after that night at The Tab.

I could chuckle. I don't know if it's actually funny or if it's delirium from all the blows my brain has taken.

Pain is so *exhausting* to be in, physical or otherwise. It pays no attention to time or circumstance—however damning those circumstances may be.

I rest my head against the wall and bring my knees to my achy chest.

And how damning this one is...

. . .

A crash jerks me awake, and a voice swears from behind one of the stacks of crates.

I manage to lift my head and squint through the dark, through the swollen, throbbing muscles around my eyes. This is the first decent view I've had of my prison, which is nothing more than walls of barrels and crates rising above my head like trees in the jungle. The chair from my interrogation sits in its same spot near the wall on my right, and I can barely make out speckles of blood on the grainy wood floor in the dim lighting.

A silhouette appears in the shadows ahead of me, dragging a large crate that scrapes across the wooden floor. She grunts from the exertion.

She?

Chadwick doesn't usually employ women on his crew.

I frown, my eyes straining in the dark.

The mystery woman stands upright, and the light catches her round face, dull cheeks, strong jaw, and round button nose. Her mousy hair looks gray in the poor light and is knotted neatly on the back of her head. Bangs fall onto her forehead and down the sides of her face.

My stomach drops as I realize.

The mousy hair and round features of a Ridgewood.

It can't be.

"Annette?" I mumble.

It *is* her. She's dressed in a white blouse and black corset, laced boots, and tight-fitting pants. It's a far cry from her pressed Academy uniforms and gowns of the Ridgewood habit.

All I can do for the moment is stare in shock, and she does as well. She blinks at me.

Here? Why?

Hope immediately latches onto the back of my mind. My parents invited her to dinner at least once a month, and despite the buzz surrounding her, we all admired her steadfastness and unwavering persona. I'll never forget the devastation I felt when learning of her disappearance. We were the only girls in some of our classes at the Academy and would occasionally study together. She could have easily been in my position. There's no doubt.

"Emery," she replies curtly, returning to the crate. She produces a small metal tool from her pocket and crouches to unscrew the bolts holding the lid in place.

I wince as my head throbs. My lips are sticky with blood and feel swollen and stiff as I try to talk. "What are you doing here?"

She ignores me, and her tongue sticks out of the corner of her mouth as she works.

My fetters rattle as I sit up straighter against the wall, my neck and back cramping from being arched for so long. "You look well."

"Hm."

"Is this where you disappeared to after dropping out of school?"

One of the bolts falls out and clatters to the floor. "Not quite."

"Why?" I curl my tongue in my dry mouth, wincing. "What happened?"

"I don't make it a habit to converse with the prisoners," she says snootily, narrowing her eyes at me.

I set my head back. Fine.

She mutters something under her breath as the tool slips out of the next bolt head.

"I can help you if you let me loose."

"Ha. Clever." Her head cranks to the side. "I definitely haven't heard that one before."

The door, partially obstructed from my view by a stack of barrels, swings open, and a young man struts inside, ducking so he doesn't hit his head on the low ceiling. He lifts his eyebrows when he sees me.

"Lewis," I clear my prickly throat. Every word clings to it like dust. "Or Lucky, I should say."

"You remember me?" Lucky plants his hands on his hips and grins. The movement wrinkles his cobalt coat, which looks about a size too big for his twiggy frame. "She remembers me, Annette. I thought that since it's been a while since we met for the first time—"

"What do you want?" She turns to him, annoyed.

"Vey needs a patch for his vest." Lucky raises his lanky arm. "The seam under his arm keeps ripping."

"Tell him I can fix it later if he comes down here and gets the material. I ran out of fabric upstairs, and the extra is buried under two other boxes. I'm not lifting them." Annette rips the final bolt out of its socket and pushes the lid to the floor with a clatter. She bends over the crate's edge and retrieves a pistol, beautifully crafted with dark wood and accented with orange paint. "Will you take that to Hyde, please?" she asks, handing it to him.

Lucky whistles as he turns the gun in his hand. "She's a beauty. Why?"

"Because the barrel on his other one is cracked."

"Is that all?" He wrinkles his forehead. "Just an errand run?"

"Yes." She grunts and lifts the lid back onto the crate. "Goodbye."

"Fine." Lucky winks at me before spinning on his heel and exiting. "Captain."

Annette gets back to work inserting the screws, exhaling in frustration as a strand of hair falls into her eye.

I rack my memory for things to say, but she pauses and turns her head.

"Captain." She frowns at me. "That has a nice ring to it, doesn't it?"

I blink, surprised.

"Did you get to stay on the *Chaplain's Heart?*" she asks.

"I thought you didn't talk to the prisoners."

"Your run has been historic." She grunts as she twists one of the bolts into place. "I admit that I would have liked to know how it ended."

"You could've been on that stage, too. What is Chadwick promising you?" I press, leaning forward and ignoring my throbbing ribs. "Is it some sort of revenge against your family?"

"Take a hint, would you?" She rises and drops her hands to her sides in exasperation. "Honestly, Emery. Stop it. Nothing has changed."

"Yes, it has!" My face throbs. "You were not a vagrant, Annette. My parents loved having you over, and everyone thought you were going to do something amazing. Reese told me just the other day—"

"I could not care less what *Reese* has to say about me, especially after how he shipped Kearon away without a moment's thought," she snaps, kneeling in front of the crate again. "I am not Chadwick's puppet. I owe him more than you will ever know."

"That makes you sound like a puppet."

"And what are you?" she scoffs. "Fitting right into the mold everyone expected you to and living for the expectations of the aristocracy?"

"*I* wanted that," I say sharply. "I was not manipulated."

Her composure is as steady as a stone wall as she tightens the final screw. "Neither was I."

"Annette, please." I lean forward, letting the chains rattle to keep her attention, though for what? Spite cannot be reversed so easily.

"I am not your friend." She dusts off her pants and heads for the door. "You can try to cajole all you want, but this matter is between you and Warren. You won't buy yourself out of this like you have before."

18

Warren

"I FOLD, WARREN," Hyde mutters.

I show my hand, and Hyde throws his cards on the round table in my cabin. "Every time with you."

"Stick to poker." Lewis waggles his eyebrows at Hyde. "This game is more fun."

Hyde folds his arms. "It's only fun to you because *you* made up the rules."

I turn to Lewis and narrow my eyes. He squints his bright blue eyes in return, and the orange sunset gleaming through the window casts his body in a halo.

"Captain."

"Lewis."

He puckers his lips and rearranges the cards in his hand. "How many times do I have to tell you to call me Lucky?"

"I refuse to refer to you by that. It's childish."

"Fine."

"The last three days have been quite peaceful since we left Lexington." I tilt my head. "I'd hate for that to change."

"I'm aware. Lexington *was* quite nice." Lewis narrows his eyes. "I *stand.*"

"Ah." I raise my eyebrows and smile. "Are you sure?"

His eyes roll to the ceiling in thought. "Yes."

I show my hand to him, which is a king, a jack, and two tens. He sucks air through his yellow teeth while he shows his.

Four aces.

My jaw drops. "You slimy little rat."

"I don't think you're the best card player on this ship anymore, Captain." He grins like a clown and pulls the stack of painted wooden chips across the table to him. "Especially with the games that I make. Where can I cash these?"

"Over the side of the ship." I drop my cards and fold my arms. "Just jump."

"Sorry, but no. I told my mother I'd visit her on our next hiatus, and I can't disappoint her." He starts gathering his cards and looks up at me with a gloating grin. "Speaking of which, in her last letter, she asked me to give you her best." He flicks one of the chips to me and winks. "You're welcome."

"Get out." I toss the chip back at him. "Or I'll throw you overboard myself."

"Thank you!" he calls over his shoulder as the door clatters shut.

Chip startles awake in his burrow, his head twitching to the side. His niche sits just behind my desk and is built into the back of my ship. It's lined with leather to mimic the warm conditions of a real shearwater burrow. The space is the size of a hatbox, if not slightly taller and wider, and is full of leaves, twigs, and fine straw. The burrow has a wire cage door with a sliding latch in the front for my easy access.

"He's such a nuisance." Hyde rolls his eyes, scratching the scruff that's begun to grow on his face. His knuckles are still scabbed from his conversation with Emery.

"You were chipper like that once," I say, piling the chips into a leather sack.

"Sure, but I never acted like a fool like he does."

I scowl at him. "Why are you still bitter?"

Hyde has had a bee in his bonnet since we left Padstow and broke the news to Kearon's parents in Lexington. He was basically mute as we walked back to the ship after our conversation with them, and I might as well have been walking alone.

Between her stomach-wrenching sobs, I promised Kearon's mother and his silent, stoic father that I had a plan. I was not going to leave their son behind, even if I had other intentions elsewhere. If Emery falls, if Gordon falls, then the integrity of the mighty Padstow crumbles. But within that, I have been dreaming of Emery's demise since the night she arrested Kearon. Since the day I met her, quite honestly. I will ruin her for what she has ruined.

"I'm not bitter," Hyde mumbles.

"I'd be bitter if I beat the pulp out of someone and they still refused to speak." I drum my fingers on my desk. "Harrison told me to tell you to leave her alone because too many hits to the head can—"

"I do *not* care." He glares at me. "After what she did to my family, she could die from her injuries, and it still wouldn't be enough for me."

I frown, but his anger is justified. It was an early morning about a year ago when she and a few of her crew members broke into his house looking for Hyde as a way to get to me. Except he wasn't there. He was with me. Still, she ransacked his entire house looking for him and took his father into temporary custody as a way to get Hyde's attention. She terrorized his younger sisters and told them that their older brother and father were going to die if they didn't tell her where he was.

Hyde is a natural protector, and it tore him to shreds knowing he wasn't there to defend his family. When he was growing up down the street from my mother and me in Midway, he'd protect the lizards, snakes, and other critters that crossed the road so they wouldn't be stepped on or crushed under a wagon wheel. He fought bullies who picked on his sisters, but he couldn't protect them when it mattered most, and he deserves nothing less than his own version of justice.

"Speaking of your family . . . " I flip the mood and eagerly lean forward. "Did you open Jamie's letter? What did she say?"

That, finally, causes his guard to drop. He smiles and runs his meaty hand through his wiry hair. "She got into St. George's School and is leaving in a couple of months."

My chest warms with pride. "That's fantastic!"

Hyde's smile turns somber. "Warren, I don't want to take more of your money to pay for her school. My father said he—"

"Ah ah ah. No." I wave my hand. "I don't need to hear it."

"That's not fair."

"It's perfectly fair. Your sister will become the best doctor the world has ever known, and that will be that. I need no thanks otherwise. Take whatever more you need from the Walkers' stash."

He purses his lips and sits back in his chair. "Okay."

"And to add to our fountain of good news, guess what I officially received in the mail?" I move to my desk, open one of the drawers, and hand him an open cream-colored envelope. "I've been meaning to show you this, but having to be out on deck to help sail has kept me busy."

He slips the letter out and reads it silently, his expression changing the further his eyes travel down the page. He looks up, shocked. "So soon? How is Derrick so sure that's where the ship will be?"

"It takes the same course between Ely, Marshland, and Crookston each week." I trace my finger across the wood of the table in the pattern Derrick described to me weeks ago. "The furthest it ever gets from land is a point between Ely and Crookston, and that should give us time to get in and out with ease. Each time he's written to me, he's complained nonstop about how this ship has been a burden on his trading operations for months." I roll my eyes a little. "It's a bit exhausting to listen to."

"How will he know that we actually accomplished what he's asking?"

"He told me the captain wears a silver and black ring on her left middle finger." I rub the calloused skin on my palms. "She wouldn't part with it unless she were dead, so he asked that I bring it to him when we meet with him later. She runs in the same level of scum foolery that the Walkers and the rest of Padstow run in."

"Dead," Hyde repeats. "We're starting off strong, aren't we?"

"Of course." I continue on my high horse. "I've heard her name tossed around a few circles because she's illegally boarded ships and the like."

The grandfather clock upstairs plays its echoing chime, and I stand up.

"When you write to Jamie again, tell her I said congratulations," I say to him as we exit the cabin and step into the moist evening air. I squint at the blazing orange sunset that splays over the ocean and the rest of my ship. "We'll tell the crew of our *other* good news once we're closer."

"Any news is good news in the middle of nowhere."

I turn to the source of the new voice. Annette is perched on the railing with a needle in her hand, concentration knotting her brow. A string of black thread is pinched between her teeth as she stitches a patch on someone's shirt.

I frown. "Annette."

"Captain," she remarks without looking up.

"I made you my navigator so you wouldn't become the ship's mother and be forced to fix everyone's thing." I tilt my head. "Is that a good way to describe it? *Mother?*"

"We are currently on course, and nobody else knows how to sew." Her concentration is iron. "It passes the time."

"Kit's banjo isn't enough entertainment for you?" Hyde wrinkles his brow as the gunpowder rascal begins plucking the strings from the bow. He lies on his back with his knees bent as the twang echoes to the back of the ship where we stand, and we all wince as he hits a sour note. He raises his head off the deck and glances around sheepishly.

Hyde smiles. "I think 'mother' is the right word, to answer your question, Warren. She ensures we are headed in the right direction and fixes our clothes." He leans down and rests his hands on his knees so he and Annette are at eye level. "I know for a fact she loves us all *so* dearly like a mother would, don't you?"

Annette rolls her eyes as she pulls the thread through the next stitch.

I clear my throat. "Hilarious."

Hyde laughs and stretches his arm overhead before he joins the rest of the crew in their sullen leisure on the main deck. Warmth fills my chest when he smiles and joins Brooks, Gil, and a few others as they share a drink from a glass flask being passed around.

Since we're coasting with the breeze, there isn't much that needs to be done above deck. There's only Mikhail acting as lookout, perched in the foremast crow's nest, and Vey at the helm on the quarterdeck below us.

Usually, the evenings are loud and lively, but my crew's exhaustion hangs in the air like mist. We're short-staffed enough from Emery's previous purging that the dying sunlight every night marks the death of everyone's energy. Some of them are curled up against the side railing, snoring, while others glumly lean against the wood railing, their heads resting on their hands as they drink their exhaustion away. Against the starboard railing, Gil takes a long swing of a bottle of rum and exchanges it with Hyde for a wad of tobacco, and the two of them sigh in unison.

Ten more sailors would do wonders for them. I need them before my crew starts abandoning me because of the workload.

"Are you enjoying your revenge?" Annette's voice pulls me from my thoughts, her brow furrowed as she focuses on her sewing.

"I will when I see how she looks after rotting downstairs for a few more days," I reply.

"She's very resilient, you know." Her lips twist. "She thought whatever camaraderie we shared before this would cause me to help her."

I wrinkle my forehead. "Really?"

"Oh, yes." She slices the needle through the fabric. "She's quite a bargainer. That hasn't changed in five years."

I fold my arms. "And you? Have you changed?"

"I am as you see me." Her eyes flip to me as a soft grin crosses her rosy lips.

I smile, my cheeks warm.

Watching her work is quite a wonder. I stare a bit longer than I probably should, but her slender fingers work so masterfully on the stitching that it's like watching a dancer flit across a stage, gliding and spinning to a tune only she can hear.

How entrancing.

How beautiful.

19

Emery

"I THINK you're wasting your time."

"I would rather be safe than sorry. The captain isn't going to be very happy if she turns for the worse. These have been festering for almost a week."

"It smells like something has been festering for a week," someone mutters. "Disgusting."

My mind stirs. *Has it really been that long?*

I lost track after about two days of fading in and out of consciousness. Periodically, I'd wake up with a stale slice of bread and a mug with about three swallows of water inside, but it was rare that it stayed in my stomach—it usually ended up in the bucket against the wall because of the nausea from my head injuries. That, combined with the smells of living in the same room for days on end, has made for a nasty combination.

My bruised eyes are heavier than barrels of sand as I peel them open. Two blurred figures are standing in the doorway, and one of them kneels in front of me. "Miss Walker, can you hear me?"

This person is new. I don't recognize his voice, but I weakly lift my head off the support beam, wincing in pain. My wrists throb under the shackles.

He gently holds the sides of my skull with his fingertips and studies my face for a moment. "I can't see in the dark. Can we take her upstairs?"

"Are you sure it's that bad?" This voice belongs to Lucky. "The captain isn't going to like that."

"I won't be long. I promise."

Lucky blows a raspberry and sighs. "All right." He crouches to unlock my shackles from the support beam and pulls me to my feet without warning.

"No! No!" I gasp, my head throbbing. The room seems to spin under my wobbly feet. "Wait!"

"It's okay. We're just going to see the doctor." Lucky steadies my shoulders and pats my arms after relocking the shackles at my front. "Can you walk?"

Barely, and I lean on Lucky's shoulder more than I'd like to admit as we exit the room and ascend the steps at the end of the cramped corridor. When we emerge, we're still below the upper deck, but the air here is fresher than in the storage room. Yellow lanterns light the closed space, and cannons and gunnery line this deck from one end to the other, with bits of the sun streaming in from the square portholes.

My eyes have been in the dark for so long that the glimpse of light on the deck above us is blinding, and pain shoots through my skull. Crates of supplies are neatly arranged between hammocks that are strung between the support beams, and the sharp smell of alcohol and gunpowder burns my nose.

Lucky leads me up another set of stairs. More hammocks are suspended between wooden support beams and beside planks of wood that have been screwed into the walls to make actual beds, though the mattresses are thinner than pieces of paper. They are suspended from the ceilings and above the portholes with rusty chains, accessible by rows of protruding slats screwed into the curved ship walls between the portholes. Some of the hammocks hang awfully close to the cannons, and I can only imagine trying to sleep comfortably with flammable gunpowder and lead only a foot or two away from my face.

I can hear the pirates jeering before Lucky and I have even emerged from below deck, and my skin crawls. I almost close my eyes to shield them from the blinding sunlight, but I want to see what's in store for me. The humidity clings to my skin as we emerge. A few of the pirates' bitter eyes follow me as I pass, like sharks watching a guppy.

I stare right back. Chadwick has ingrained his hatred into each of them well, but I stare right back, their names and faces bouncing across my memory.

There's Kit Soto, the Cordova-born bomb expert. He keeps a box of matches in his right pocket.

Brooks Scobell, tall, tan, and handsome, with a knack for knives, which are hidden in pockets all over his body. His tongue skims over the mole near his lip as he and I make eye contact.

Hyde Kensington, Chadwick's merciless shadow, enforcer, and first mate.

I have spent time learning about them in the hope that they would lead me to Chadwick. I've seen their faces every night before I go to sleep, visualizing the moment when I would catch each of them. Tahj Eckles, Darren Patrillo, Alexis Keetch, Mikhail Dubrov . . . I count off their names as I pass them. Most of them are younger than thirty, but not one of them is older than forty, according to the intel my crew has gathered. They're all well put together for sailors, let alone pirates; their skin and clothes are surprisingly clean, which is odd considering that most sailors don't keep more than three or four sets of clothes on board at a time.

I regain some of my balance and nudge Lucky's hand away as we climb a final set of short stairs. My legs shake as we enter the doctor's cabin, which sits at the bottom right of a triangle of cabins. The largest of the three sits atop the triangle and is the blond snake's den, if I had to guess.

The doctor leaves the door open, letting in the fresh breeze and the sounds of life from the ship. He instructs me to sit on the edge of one of his padded examination tables, and I listen, my feet dangling as I take in my new surroundings. A long, squat cabinet spans the length of one wall and has various bottles and jars arranged in neat rows sitting atop it, colored brown, green, and yellow by the odd concoctions inside them.

I spot a few framed pictures of the doctor with an older man and woman, as well as a girl who has the same smile and bright brown hair that he does.

But, like the lower decks, the cabin is clean, all per the captain's picky requests. It even smells like flowers and herbs, similar to the scent of orchids. The knot in my chest loosens as I take slow, deep breaths, relieved to not be locked in the dark.

Lucky wrinkles his nose as he gets a clearer look at my battered face. "Ouch."

"I've seen a lot worse, if it makes you feel better." The doctor pulls up a wooden stool and sits in front of me. He wears a gray cotton shirt under an unbuttoned gray waistcoat, a relic from a dapper suit that no ordinary pirate would wear. On his lap sits a tin box of supplies, containing flasks of mystery liquid, long pieces of fibrous cotton, and a pair of scissors.

"It's not worse than Hyde's leg, Harrison." Lucky folds his arms. "You should have seen that. Someone pushed him down a flight of stairs . . ." He trails off when he notices me staring at him, and his jaw drops. "Was it you?"

"Lucky—" Harrison starts.

"That's terrible!" Lucky holds up his fingers so they're spaced about four inches apart. "They had to cram *this* much bone back into his leg and drill it together with screws and brass plates! It oozed and bled like a volcano."

"Would you like to wait outside?" Harrison turns to him, his ears red. "Well, obviously you can still watch, but—"

"Oh, no, no, no. Of course." Lucky waves him off and winks at me before leaving. "Let the magician work his tricks."

Harrison blinks again and adjusts his glasses. "He is dramatic. Don't tell anyone I said that, though."

I clear my scratchy throat. "Noted."

"Now, let's see. The other cuts will heal fine . . ." The doctor bites his cheek and gently grabs my chin to turn my head to the side, spying the long cut near my eye. He wrinkles his nose.

"What?" I ask.

"I should have stitched that right after it happened," he laments. "It's going to leave a really bad scar."

"How long is it?"

"About two inches." He stands up and grabs a few bottles and an empty mug from one of the cupboards. "I'll just have to clean it and hope for the best."

I watch him curiously as I fiddle with the thick chain links between my shackles, testing for any give or weakness. The rust scrapes my fingertips.

"Have you always lived in Padstow?" Harrison asks me out of the blue.

I frown and watch him measure out oddly precise amounts of the mystery liquids and pour them into the mug. "Yes."

"What about your parents?"

What is he playing at?

Whatever it is, I can play too.

"They used to live in Bloomington." The scabs on my lips rub against one another as I speak. "They were married young and moved there shortly after. To Padstow, I mean."

"Bloomington?" Harrison turns back to me, eyebrows raised. "As in *Northern Estates* Bloomington? That's quite a far cry from Padstow."

I squint. "They hated living in a small place and went to build a name for themselves."

"And they did." He gestures to me. "Obviously, you did too. My sister felt the same way before she went to school in Kerrisberg, but she didn't enjoy being a small fish in a massive ocean. We grew up in Osecola." He mixes the brew with a spoon and reaches for another ovular tube in the cupboard. "She's enjoying a job in Santa Clara right now."

"Did Chadwick ask you to bring me up here as an excuse to extract information?" I tilt my head. "What is this?"

He turns and holds up his hands in surrender, one with the mug and the other with the spoon. "I'm not his plant. I promise. I told him that if your injuries were left untreated, it could cause problems, and I don't think he wants to deal with that later. Problems like infection . . ." His mouth hangs open as he thinks of more to say, but he just takes a breath and hands me the mug instead. "Never mind. This hopefully should help with the pain."

I hesitate. The chains jingle as I lift the cup and swallow, and the cuts on my lips burn from the bitterness. I wrinkle my nose and set the mug next to me as he starts rummaging through more cabinets. He takes a small bottle, pours its clear contents into his hands, and rubs them together. Droplets fly and land on the wooden counter.

I drag my tongue along my front teeth. "How do I know you didn't just poison me?"

"Oh, I would never!" He whirls around with wide eyes. "It was just a mix of herb concentrates and opium poppies for the pain. I didn't mean to—"

He pauses when I pucker my lips and tilt my head.

"Oh." He blinks. "You weren't being serious."

"What gave me away?"

"Sorry." Harrison frowns as his face turns pink. He adjusts his glasses. "The poppies might make you a little drowsy, but . . . never mind." He returns to his stool, still rubbing his hands, and the smell of alcohol makes my nose curl. He uses the scissors to cut the cotton sheet into small squares, and he wets one of them with liquid from another bottle. "This will sting."

"This isn't my first go 'round."

"Good," he sighs, pressing it against the cut near my eye, and I wince. He repeats the process with the other cuts on my face and lips before using a watered-down cloth to clean away the dried blood. He notices me staring at him oddly and smiles, revealing a dimple in his left cheek.

"Chadwick hasn't conditioned you to his way of thinking yet, has he?" I ask.

He frowns as he drops the rag onto the floor. "What do you mean?"

"You wouldn't have offered to examine me otherwise."

"It's my job."

I narrow my eyes.

Harrison presses on either side of my nose with his forefinger and thumb, presumably feeling for any pieces of bone that are sticking out of place. "I am not God, and I don't judge. I treat regardless of what everyone says."

"Regardless of what everyone says or what you believe?"

"Both, but the former in this case." He peeks inside my nostrils. "The chatter is quite . . . interesting, though."

I narrow my eyes, studying his clean-shaven face, shiny hair, and unwrinkled clothes. The glasses on his hooked nose strike me the most. Most sailors don't bother with them because they get knocked around and broken so easily.

"You're not the type of person I'd peg as a pirate."

His focus is unwavering. "I think that's why the captain wanted me to be his doctor. I graduated at the top of my class."

"Then why are you here?"

"I owed a favor. My father was about to lose his practice due to a misstep during surgery, and the captain stepped in to pay the legal fees."

"And Chadwick pressured you into this by using that as leverage."

"I offered to be here, as a way to thank him, but I was told we were just moving supplies and goods for business. We've transported lots of things over the last few months."

I scoff. "You're joking."

"All of the scuffles we've gotten into have been with people who aren't totally innocent." Harrison shuffles the cotton sheets into a neat stack. "It's been tax collectors and politicians who have a scandal or two up their sleeves. Or other sailors who've done worse than him."

"You don't sound convinced." I press him. "Where do you draw the line then, Harrison?"

His lips twist.

"Does all of that justify burning and looting their ships?" I snap. "What about the ships of innocent traders you passed along the way?"

He flinches. "He said they weren't innocent."

"You're a fool if you believe anything he tells you."

He doesn't get to defend himself because Lucky barges through the door, causing both of us to flinch.

"We're arriving," Lucky announces. "Are you done?"

"What?" Harrison twists around. "Already?"

"Arriving where?" I demand.

Lucky just shrugs and rolls up the baggy sleeves of his cobalt blue jacket. "We're early, apparently."

Harrison drops the cotton patches and scissors back into the tin. "Okay. Fine."

Lucky turns his back when someone outside calls his name. When

Harrison jumps back up and returns to the cupboard, I lean forward and snatch the scissors out of the tin while both men aren't looking. My heart leaps at the perfect timing. I mask the jingling chains with an exaggerated cough as I slip the scissors into my sleeve and push the pointed tips into the inner hem of the cuff.

Lucky pulls me to my feet again and leads me out under the blistering sun. The crew is scattered across the deck, scurrying like ants. Brooks is waiting on the main deck, smiling smugly as he twirls one of his knives.

"Don't step too far out of line," he jeers, taking my elbow and ushering me along as Lucky walks ahead of us.

My eyes linger on the ring of keys hanging from Lucky's belt as he walks away. They're loosely secured with a strand of fabric, and one of them looks like the silver cylinder that would unlock my shackles.

Hyde stands at the bow, and he has an identical key set on his waist, right next to his sword. Chadwick stands beside him and relays calls to Lucky, who then commands the boatswains.

Chadwick isn't wearing his coat, and his hands are raised almost like a conductor signaling his orchestra. He leaps into action like a cat when one of the boatswains begins to slip and loses hold of the rope holding the mainsail, and Chadwick catches it before the canvas comes tumbling down. He helps the boatswain back to his feet and the two of them tie the sail together.

He looks up when we approach. A patronizing smile crosses his face as he cuffs his sleeves, revealing pale, veiny forearms. "Good morning."

I clear my throat and wrap my fingers around my chains. The steel scissors are cold against my skin. "I wouldn't call it 'good.'"

"You're right. This weather is disgusting." He tugs on the collar of his cream-colored shirt and sighs as he studies my face. "Harrison cleaned you up nicely, didn't he?"

"What is this about?"

"Have you thought about what I said?"

"My answer hasn't changed."

"Oh, don't play like that, Miss Walker." He shakes his head. "I'm sure Gordon has heard the news of your robbery by now and won't feel as burdened by your betrayal when you tell me where he is."

I bristle and clench my jaw. "I am not a traitor."

"They'll call you a lot more than that if you don't cooperate."

"Ship in the distance!" a voice shouts from the sky, and I look up at a man leaning over the rails of the crow's nest. "Ship in the distance!"

My heart leaps. I crane my head to see over the side of the ship, but Brooks grabs my shoulders and keeps me in place.

"Last chance, *Captain.*" Chadwick uses the word with spite. "What will it be?"

I hesitate for the briefest moment before shaking my head. "You're lying."

"Pity. At least we'll have a bit of fun with this." He claps his hands and cups them around his mouth. "Everyone, to your positions!"

Hyde pulls out his new pistol and gestures to the left. "Nothing funny from you. Under the stairs."

I glance one last time out at the ocean to catch sight of the new ship before Brooks ushers me forward. We're approaching the ship quickly. It reflects almost black in the sun and is smaller than most galleons, which makes it faster than most. Its two masts support white-as-snow sails, and it's not until we're close that I see the red, yellow, and blue stripes of Padstow's flag flapping in the wind.

My stomach drops.

That's the only view I get before they push me underneath the staircase to the quarterdeck. Hyde grips his pistol with both hands while Brooks draws one of his many knives. He traces the tip across his neck as a silent warning for me, but I'm too distracted, fearfully watching through the slatted stairs as we approach the other ship.

Whose is it? I wonder.

Chadwick pulls a black leather hat over his eyes and crouches behind the ship's wheel as Lucky climbs atop the wooden railing, holding one of the riggings for balance. "Hello!" He cups his other hand around his mouth. "Hello? Can you hear me?"

The whole ship is silent as we wait for a response.

"What business do you have?" a voice in the distance calls back. "You fly under no flag!"

"Well, yes, that is true. I was wondering if I could speak to Captain Scott. Is she there?"

Scott. Padstow.

"Fallon." I lunge forward and try to shout her name again before Hyde smacks his hand over my mouth and wrenches me back into my spot under the stairs. He jams the muzzle of his pistol under the bony part of my chin.

Some pirates watch the exchange, but others have their hands on their weapons and stand eerily still, waiting. Kit, Darren, and a few others are noticeably absent. Lots of others are.

Despite the weakness and pain, I wrench in Hyde's grip. He clicks the hammer of his gun.

"Dare me," he spits in my ear.

My heart pounds as I helplessly listen to the exchange, fearing I already know how this will end.

20

I WATCH from my hiding spot as Lewis taps his foot on the railing until Captain Scott's voice echoes in response. She shields her eyes from the sun and waves, standing on the railing and holding the rigging for balance. Her sandy brown hair whips in the wind. "This is Captain Scott!"

"Ah, Captain! Hello!" Lewis plays the diplomat well, much to my jealousy. Given my stellar reputation with Padstow, every soldier should have a general idea of what I or my ship looks like, and I don't doubt Captain Scott would have recognized me. That left the fun, acting part of this job up to someone else. She shouldn't recognize my ship with its new coat of dark paint, either.

"It's good to see you!" Lewis calls. "I'm glad I was able to find you."

"May I ask what this is about?" Even though our ships are only about fifteen feet apart, her voice seems faint in the distance.

"Yes, of course! My apologies. We're on passage to Crookston and were told that your ship would be here in case we needed help."

She pauses. "Who told you that?"

"Some of the merchants in Ely's harbor said so. We were just passing through to meet friends and overheard some conversations and whatnot. There is quite an interesting bunch of traders there, I've noticed. And from what I've heard, they're *very* good at their jobs." Lewis chuckles heartily. "Kudos all around!"

I glance at the water as the tail end of a dinghy disappears around the back of Captain Scott's ship.

"Would you be able to drop anchor?" Lewis calls. "We're in a bit of a predicament and could use some help. We are *very* short-staffed and need a hand for just a minute."

There's silence again. "Why aren't you sailing under a flag?"

"See, that's part of our predicament. When we were docked in Ely, someone forgot to secure our flag properly, and it blew away in the wind." Lewis makes a show of shrugging and scratching the back of his head. "Quite amateurish, I know."

She pauses, briefly considering the oddity of the situation. "Let me see what we can do. I don't—"

An explosion sends shock waves through the air and causes the Armada soldiers to lose their balance. Those closest to the blast scream and fly backward, and my sailors throw tow lines and hooks to the other vessel and begin to pull us closer to them. The end of our gangplank crashes against the other ship, and our deck empties as my sailors charge, guns blazing and swords glinting in the sun.

I pause for a moment to locate Captain Scott in the chaos. The Riggses told me she is a captain known for bending the rules and turning a blind eye if it means gaining an advantage, but her skill is not to be ignored. She fights bravely beside her crew like any good captain would, even in an inevitable loss like this.

Like flipping a page in a book, my mind shifts into focus as I cross the gangplank. My eyes dart through the commotion and lock onto my target. Bullets fly. Bodies fall. She still fights as if her crew has a chance.

And I'm almost there when I see a glint of blonde from the corner of my eye.

. . .

Emery

Hyde readjusts his footing, and the keys jingle on his hip. His grip relaxes slightly, allowing me to drop my hands and let the scissors slide into my palm.

We both flinch when a bomb explodes.

I pray that Hyde's trigger finger is disciplined as I duck away and jam the scissor blades into his thigh. He shouts in surprise, and I drive my elbow into his jaw with all the force my weak body can muster.

Brooks turns around and catches the iron of my shackles in the face before shouting in pain and hitting the deck like a sack of flour. I snatch Hyde's keys from his waist and yank the scissors free, dodging Brooks's hands as he swipes at my ankles from the deck.

I sprint across to the other side with the energy of an animal freed from its cage and toss the shackles aside once I've unlocked them. The world seems to spin around me and my throbbing head as bodies hit the water left and right. Bodies of gray-coated soldiers whose names I don't know. Gray-coated soldiers whom I've trained with. I shudder.

One topples over the edge and lands in the water a few feet away from a dinghy. Kit, standing on one of the benches, is thrown off balance as he feeds a black line through one of the cannon portholes. The boat is filled with black explosives and what I realize are gunpowder lines. Another boat on the other end is doing the same thing while the chaos persists overhead.

No.

Distracted, I almost trip over the leg of a soldier, and his cold, lifeless eyes seem to follow me as I grab his sword, clutching the scissors in my opposite hand. My lungs burn from the sudden exertion.

A hand wrenches me back by my shoulder, and I narrowly avoid a sword edge buried in the side of my neck. I swing the sword hard and connect with the pirate's midsection, and he screams in pain as I push him down and run through the chaos.

One of the Armada soldiers makes eye contact with me. His greasy black hair is plastered to his face with sweat, and my heart leaps.

"John!"

He and I were in a history class together at the Academy, but that knowledge doesn't stop him as he raises his weapon. "Don't move!"

"They're going to blow up the ship." I hold up my hands, realizing how ridiculous I look, bruised, bloodied, and armed with a pair of scissors and a dead man's sword. "Please. We have to stop them."

He watches me warily. "But the news—"

"Whatever you've heard isn't true," I plead. "I'm being framed."

A smaller explosion sounds at the other end of the ship.

"John, please," I beg. More and more bodies fall. "Everyone on this ship is going to die if we don't hurry."

He glances from side to side and groans. "Fine."

My heartbeat spikes as we maneuver through the fray. "They're funneling explosives through the portholes below deck."

"Did you see them?"

"Yes. We need to gather more soldiers and—"

I spot Fallon, but her back is turned, and she doesn't see Chadwick breaking toward her with a white-knuckle grip on his sword.

No.

In a panic, I grip the scissors just like the throwing knives in The Tab and let go, but someone bumps me from behind and ruins my aim.

The scissors fly, fly, fly—

. . .

Warren

Something slices through the delicate skin of my ear.

My knees slam into the desk as blood drips down the side of my head, giving Captain Scott enough time to notice my advance and flee. A pair of shiny, crimson-dotted scissors clatter to the deck beside me.

The world seems to melt around me as I fall forward and catch myself with my hands, the sight of the shiny blades twirling through the air replaying like a broken news capsule over, and over, and over in my mind.

Move! My mind screams. *Move now!*

I can't. It could have slit my throat. It could have thrown me off the edge into the dark abyss where we all end up sometime or another.

Pound. Pound. Pound.

A bead of sweat trickles down my spine like a lone raindrop in a monsoon. I touch my chest.

A nearby gunshot shatters my paralysis, and I scramble back to my feet, blood leaking onto my collar.

Emery has disappeared.

I blink to refocus my vision and whirl around, watching.

The gray-coated crowd is thinning as more bodies topple into the water, dead or alive. I spot our dear captain scrambling to help her wounded, her coat colored more red than gray from the blood of her fallen soldiers, but it's useless.

The others begin to see that to be true. A few drop their weapons in surrender and look to their captain as my crew encircles them, jeering and shouting profanities.

I beeline toward Captain Scott. She's shaking the shoulders of a dead man whose coat is decorated with metal pins of valor.

"Lieutenant!" Her voice trembles with desperation as she grabs his pale face. "Dane! Wake up!"

I clear my throat as my shadow is cast over the two of them, and I watch her spine go rigid. She shakily climbs to her feet and is met with a sword point under her chin.

I grin, though my chest aches with terror. "Hello."

Her jaw tightens as she slowly raises her hands. "Chadwick."

"Captain Scott." I glance to make sure another surprise attack isn't hiding over my shoulder. "The pleasure is all mine."

I wedge my index finger and thumb between my teeth and silence the chaos with two sharp whistles. Like bees called to their queen, my crew shouts to their fellow sailors and scurries back across the plank to the *Lost Commandeer*.

Bravely—or stupidly—Captain Scott uses my temporary distraction as a chance to run, but I snatch her wrist and pull her close, my sword edge resting against her ribs. My eyes flick to the ring on her finger as she stares at me wide-eyed.

"I don't have much time, so answer quickly, please." I tighten my grip, and she winces. "I'm looking for a certain missing judge. Would you happen to know anything about that?"

Her brow furrows.

"You don't hear much of the news out here, I'm assuming. If you tell the truth, the rest of your crew can live." I glance around. "What little of them are left, that is."

Quick as lightning, she draws a knife from the small of her back and strikes, but I knock it away. Her breath catches as my sword penetrates her ribcage.

I purse my lips and grin. "Where do you think you can run to?"

The first bomb below deck explodes.

. . .

I don't wait to see Chadwick's reaction as John and I skip steps to the lower deck. Piles and piles of iron spheres pool on the floor around the gunports. It takes every ounce of strength I have in my fingers to lift one and throw it back out, and it lands in the water with a loud *splash*. We work quickly to throw the others out.

"What's going on?" John grunts as he picks up another. "Where have you been? I heard—"

"It's a long story." I pause as the room begins to spin around my aching head. "Do you remember the boy I arrested who worked for Warren Chadwick? He—"

"Is that who you threw the scissors at?" The color drains from his face. "That was Chadwick?"

"He's setting me up." I wince as another bomb tumbles out, and my stomach drops when I see how many are spread across the deck below each cannon. The gunpowder inside them is going to blow us to dust.

At least not yet.

Two sharp whistles sound out from above the deck, and there's a grunt to my right as someone's hands push another explosive through. Kit and I make eye contact as I lunge forward to stop him. The end of my sword catches his hand, and he yelps in pain as he loses his balance and falls backward into his boat.

I poke my head outside and spot Darren's boat a few portholes over as he pushes more bombs inside.

"John, hurry!" I duck inside and point to the bow end of the ship. "Over there!"

He lifts his rifle and leans out of the porthole as an explosion behind us shakes the boat and knocks both of us off balance. Chips of wood fly through the hold, and I scramble back to my feet and stare at a gaping, jagged hole ripped across the wood on the stern side.

John groans as he tries to regain his footing. Half of his face is marred with bloody scratches.

I move to help him, but only manage one step before another bomb goes off. Shrapnel flies, and my ears ring as John's body is thrown backward, now a bloody, mangled husk that slams into the opposite wall. I don't even have time to react before Kit reappears and lunges through the porthole to grab my arm. I lose hold of my sword as he yanks me through the space and into the dinghy. I cry out as I fall headfirst and stretch out my other arm to catch myself. Another explosion pierces the air.

No, no, no.

My shoulder pops awkwardly as my extended arm collides with the floor of the dinghy, and my hip hits the squared edge before I fall onto my back.

The water on the dinghy floor soaks into my clothes like spikes of ice. My breath hitches as I reach for the edge of the boat, but a sharp, stabbing zing shoots through my arm, limp as a corpse's. I fall backward and gasp in pain as another explosion pierces the air.

Kit presses his boot into my good shoulder to keep me still as he collects the oars. He shouts for help as we float back to the *Lost Commandeer,* and the last thing I see before Fallon's ship is engulfed in flames is the imperfect captain herself, clutching her bloody abdomen and staring at me with a look of terror in her eyes.

She slumps over the railing and doesn't move again.

21

Warren

MY BLOODY HEART won't stop pounding.

I don't know if it's the loud explosions from the burning ship, or the groans of the wounded, or the clanking of wood on wood below my feet as Tahj, Alexis, and Darren reload the dinghies back onto the ship, but it's making my brain itch.

My chest loosens a bit as I spot Hyde, alive but unwell. Gil and Annette are helping him limp toward Harrison's cabin, and his pant leg is stained red. Droplets of blood follow the path they take

I press my hand against my ear, my skin sticky with my own blood and sweat. If she hadn't missed her mark…

The moment plays in my mind again. And again. And again. I *cannot* expel it from my memory.

Speaking of the devil, Brooks and Kit are wrestling her back onto the ship as she screams and thrashes. Brooks's lip is split, and it looks like one of his teeth is chipped.

They practically carry her across the deck as she writhes. Her bruised eyes land on me, and then on Captain Scott's black and graphite ring on my finger.

"You monster!" She lunges and nearly slips free from Brooks's hold as Kit wraps his arms around her midsection and lifts her feet off the wood. "Murderer!"

"I gave you options, Miss Walker." My voice trembles more than I'd like. "This was all avoidable."

"Fallon had nothing to do with this, and you knew that!" Her voice is raw as she wriggles again. Black streaks of gunpowder cover the front of her blouse, matching the bruises on her face. "You knew!"

"You know what else I knew?" I snap. "*I* knew about those civilians who were caught in the crossfire in the South. Did she get her comeuppance for it or not?" I gesture to the burning ship. "Why is her life worth more than theirs?"

Kit jerks her shoulder back, and she gasps in pain.

"Should we discuss all the other lieutenants and captains who have taken rotten deals to imprison innocent traders just because they crossed the wrong leaders?" I spit.

"You don't know what you're talking about!" she snarls.

"The Riggses told me more than you think. Captain Scott deserves exactly what happened after what she did in the South. And after what you did today . . ." I laugh bitterly. "You will have a *world* of hurt headed your way very soon."

She fights like a rabid dog and continues to shout at me as I turn away. Lewis assists the other two in wrangling her below deck. Even then, her annoying voice echoes from below the floorboards.

My solace is brief. The flash of the scissors and the sound of explosions are still ringing in my ears.

It doesn't leave. Neither does the apparition of my blood pooling across the deck, had she not missed her mark.

I shudder.

No.

My crew is more injured than I am, and I cannot be this jittery for them.

Those who aren't injured tend to those who are and work to keep the ship on course for a short time. Chaos follows chaos, and I'm conscious of myself once again when Tahj places his hand on my shoulder.

"Three," he mumbles in my ear. "Vick, Pietro, and Jack."

I exhale softly. "They don't have families to alert, so that's good. Will you gather whatever belongings they had in their bunks?"

He reties his dreadlocks at the back of his head and nods. "Of course."

"Thank you."

I step through Harrison's door to find him tending to Hyde's scissor stab wound. Hyde's jaw is so tight and swollen that it looks like his teeth might splinter in his mouth, and his eyes are burning with anger.

Harrison's hands are shaky as he pushes back Hyde's rolled-up pant leg. "T-tools are never misplaced," he stutters, his fingers shaking. "Never. I-I didn't mean to—"

Hyde grabs the doctor's face with surprising gentleness. "*You* didn't stab me. I'm not angry at you."

Annette has Gil sitting on one of the cots as she bandages his elbow. Brooks waits behind her with a bloody rag pressed to his mouth, shaking his head.

I sigh. "You're lucky she didn't stab you in the neck, Hyde. Or you, Brooks."

"*She's* lucky I don't throw her over the front of the ship and watch the barnacles chop her to pieces," Hyde snaps.

"I'll rip her teeth out! Look what she did!" Brooks flashes his maw, and half of his left front tooth is missing. I grimace.

Annette raises her eyebrows, and Harrison turns pink and ducks his head.

"Ninety-nine times out of one hundred, that doesn't happen," I say. "And it definitely won't again."

"Because she'll be a bloody husk floating in the ocean?" Harrison asks.

"You're catching on." Hyde claps him on the back so hard that he loses his balance, and his glasses fall askew on his face.

I take a deep breath and curl my fingers into fists.

Annette approaches me with narrowed eyes, and she touches my face and presses a pad of cotton against my ear. "What happened to you?"

"She tried to kill me with a pair of scissors," I whisper. "She almost did."

Annette's fingers are warm, and mine graze hers as I hold the cotton in place. She only pulls away when Hyde's breath catches in pain. His back slams into the wall. "Ow!"

"Sorry." Harrison sets a bottle and a soaked towel on the floor.

"It's not very deep." Brooks leans over Hyde's leg and squints. "Or is it?"

Harrison puckers his lips and blanches. "Don't look."

"What?" Hyde reaches over his blood-soaked pant leg to feel the wound, and Harrison fumbles to stop him.

"It's going to get infected from your nasty fingers! Stop!"

"Will *this* get infected?" Lewis demands as he storms into the room, holding up his index finger, which is red and puffy. "She's a biter. She almost bit Kit's ear off when we were making sure she wasn't hiding any more weapons."

"Degenerate," Brooks mutters, rolling his eyes.

"I know none of you want to babysit, but she stays fettered at all times, and someone needs to sit outside that door or in the room with her," I say. "After we stop in Midway, she isn't going to leave the hold again. She's causing too much trouble."

"That's too kind. String her upside down by her ankles over the side of the ship and let the blood run to her head." Brooks perches on one of the cots. "I want to see her eyes bulge."

Lewis piggybacks with a laugh. "String her by the toes!"

Harrison fixes his glasses. "All of you are horrible. She could die if you did that, just so you know."

So could you.

The thought makes my heart skip again, and I turn toward the window with a clenched jaw.

Annette rolls her eyes as she secures Gil's elbow wrap. "You're all dramatic."

"Don't pretend like you wouldn't be first in line to do something like that, Annette," Lewis retorts. "Especially after the lies her parents spread about you when—"

"It wasn't *them specifically* who spread them," she mutters.

Mikhail enters the cabin and leans against the doorway, but doesn't speak right away.

"Are there more?" Harrison sighs, holding a needle and a spool of thread. "Please tell me there aren't."

Mikhail raises his eyebrows. "No, but anyone who can still walk needs to come sail the ship because we're starting to drift."

"Brooks, Gil?" Lucky rolls up the sleeves of his coat and stretches his knuckles.

"What? No." Brooks peels back his lip to show his chipped tooth. "I'm wounded."

Mikhail rolls his eyes, and I slip past him as the squabble continues. It's giving me a headache.

My cabin smells like paper and wood, a stark contrast to the sharp sting of alcohol and earthy herbs in Harrison's. My desk sits in front of a wide window that looks out on the endless sky and sea, and casts the room in sunlight. Bookcases are pressed against the walls, lined with books and little trinkets I've collected from my travels. A handful of framed pictures decorate the shelves as well, including one of my mother and another of Hyde and me when we were boys.

I let go of the cotton pad on my ear and grip the edges of my desk, taking a deep breath. Chip squawks at me in his enclosure and nips at the cage door.

It's over. Death whispered in my ear, and I ignored him.

The door opens, and I turn to snap at the intruder, but I see it's only Annette. My fists relax.

Her lips are puckered. "Are you all right?"

"I am." I put on a charming smile, a facade. "Miss Walker is miserable, and one of the many pests in the Armada has been exterminated."

Her rosy lips twist as she looks me up and down.

I have never been a coward, but this nagging anxiety about death started manifesting itself about a year ago, more frequently arising when I lie in bed and stare at the dark ceiling in the middle of the night. It weighs on my mind since one of the primary challenges of my job is to avoid it when I'm defending myself from attacks. Every crack of a bullet or flash of a blade locks my mind in a debilitating awareness of death. Of the end. Of the knowledge that I am going to fade into nothing and no longer hold control.

I watch Annette for a moment, and my heartbeat begins to slow.

There's something comforting about her poised presence juxtaposed to the brash morons downstairs, and sometimes I wish I could have a hundred of her running my ship instead of the loudmouths.

"I want to leave her down there to rot until I find Gordon, if I'm being honest." I quickly change the subject. "If she had gone for Hyde's throat instead of his leg—"

"I don't think she's stupid enough to do something like that. She knows you'll return the favor if she steps too far out of line."

My chest swells as I lick my lips. "Captain Scott didn't know anything about the judge," I say quietly, staring at one of the grainy pictures on my shelf. "Something is *very* fishy about all of this."

Annette tilts her head. "What do you mean?"

"Gordon wouldn't have disappeared right before my plan unfolded unless he was tipped off."

"Who would have tipped him, though?" She crosses her arms. "One of the Riggses?"

"Eldon swore to me that everyone involved was sworn to secrecy." I take a deep breath. "But I don't know. I have no way to tell."

"Have you heard anything about Gordon from anyone else?"

"No. The Riggses are trying to figure it out, and I have people all over the region keeping their ears open." I fold my arms and lean against my desk. "I think finding this mole might be a more pressing matter."

Her eyes are such a beautiful shade of blue. Blue like beach water. My vision blurs as I stare at them, transfixed.

"I think you're right." Her lips twist as she gently touches my jaw and inspects my ear. My skin tingles. "It isn't all lost, though."

My stomach twists as I lean into her touch. "What do you mean?"

"You now have two crimes to Emery's name." She retracts her hand, spotting the bloody cotton pad on my desk. "The theft and the attack on Captain Scott. You can take solace in that, at least."

She's right. The irreversible damage to her reputation and image that will come once the news breaks will be my ultimate weapon, because once her people hear it, who would help her if she escapes?

I glance between Annette's eyes and lips, my jaw tightening. I shouldn't let my nagging feelings of interest overtake my mind, but they have been relentless during the three years that she's been a part of my crew—she brings a calmness to my mind that I cannot generate myself. I grip the edges of the desk and bite my tongue.

She retrieves the cotton and presses it against my ear again, meeting my gaze. "How devastating for her."

"Is that justification enough for you?" I smile in return, and something stirs in my chest, like a twisted knot of satisfaction. It makes my heart race. "Does it cover the damage of what her parents said about you? I hope it covers that and more. I hope it *rips* her apart."

She takes my hand and presses it against the gauze, her fingers lingering on the back of my hand. My heart clenches as the urge to wrap my fingers around hers suddenly enters my mind.

"Don't let your ambition overtake you, Warren," she mumbles. "I'd hate to see it do to you what it's done to her."

22

THERE HASN'T BEEN a funeral for a captain in the Armada for over a decade, but from what I remember, the ceremony is just as somber as the Sealings are. Everyone gathers at the command post for the funeral, and afterwards, Admiral Van Pelt and other high-ranking officials take the captain's family to the very top floor of the outpost, where there's a massive hall that has the names of every captain who's ever sailed in the Armada etched into the walls. The fallen sailor's name is painted red to signify their passing so it stands out among the others, ensuring that they are remembered forever.

Just like any other funeral, speakers are gathered, and the families in the upper class donate their flowers as a symbol of mourning. Our close relationship with the Scotts means that there will be as many orchids scattered around as sand on a beach, or drops in a monsoon like the one the pirates and I stand in now. Lightning cracks over the ocean a long way's off from where we're docked.

Fallon's mother or father will most likely be asked to speak, and her brother will be called away from his studies at Tarleton with the heart-shattering news that will change his life forever.

Chadwick will without a doubt try to pin this on me, but there's no evidence besides fake witness accounts to prove that I had anything to do with it. They won't believe it.

Or will they?

Will they scratch my name in red because I will be as good as dead to all of them?

The pirates tie Midway's red-and-white striped flag to the pulleys and hoist it like a beacon in order to blend in with the other ships in Midway's harbor, though I don't know who'd be able to see it in the rain or in the pitch-black night sky. I wonder how much money Chadwick has doled out to Midway's public officials to keep them from arresting him on sight.

It's so dark that I can't see more than a few feet ahead of me as the rain stings my eyes and soaks through my coat. I woke up with it next to me one morning in the hold. I don't know who left it, but I've been wearing it like a shield even though it's wrinkled and covered in snags. It hangs off my body like a limp shell as I'm escorted down the gangplank, Brooks walking in front and Gil behind. For a moment, I contemplate shoving Brooks off the plank out of spite and watching him topple into the inky, icy water, but my attention shifts to the other members of Chadwick's crew trudging across the dock, their clothes soaked in the rain.

What could they be planning for me now? What could be worse than watching my fellow captain die?

If that's even what I am anymore.

I keep my head down and try to support my injured arm against my body, though the short chain on my shackles makes that difficult. Each step is another muscle-throbbing and metal-clanking reminder that I have never been more alone. Fallon's eyes haven't left my mind. Neither has John's shrapnel-riddled body.

I wonder what my parents and brothers think when they hear the news.

Will they believe it?

I have spent days wondering and praying that my family has rebuked what's been said. I wonder if the weight of my absence is weighing on them as much as it's weighing on me, like a boulder crushing my heart.

And as much as I've tried to fight it, thoughts of Callie and Vaughn cross my mind. I long for the feeling of Vaughn's hands in my hair and the taste of his lips, and I am disgusted that I miss it.

I clench my fists and keep my head down. We wander down a poorly lit and muddy street. We seem to be taking backstreets and alleyways to avoid being spotted, though I don't see any witnesses to our entourage. Each foggy window and wooden door is shuttered to keep the rain out.

Chadwick leads the pack, with Annette and Hyde close behind. By my messy count, there are about fifteen pirates with us.

Mud flips up onto my black pants and trousers. The crew behind chatters and laughs with each other, so whatever we're about to walk into can't be that serious.

Can it?

I wipe water from my eyes as we enter a well-lit section of Midway, which is just as luxurious and pristine as any neighborhood in Padstow. The brick and clay buildings are exquisitely tall, with candles and lantern lights glowing from the curtained windows. Eventually, we approach a rain-soaked brick house with a slanted roof and a balcony on the second floor, where an intricately cut railing wraps around the entire structure. Vines and other greenery intertwine around the metal, and potted plants hang from the canopy that stretches out over part of the road. Lanterns line different sections of the brick, and each window is outlined in white stucco that arches across the top.

We enter into a courtyard with an overflowing fountain stretching toward the sky, and we walk under more lanterns strung across the opening like stars fixed on long strands of wire. Some of the crew retire for the night, breaking off from the procession to climb the wrought iron spiral staircase to the second story. Gil touches my back and guides me through a metal door that leads inside.

I wrinkle my nose at the smell of tobacco smoke and alcohol. The floor is wooden and wet, reflecting the yellow candlelight that spills from the various chandeliers and candelabras drilled into the maroon walls.

We veer left and enter a huge sitting room with velvety violet couches, antique armoires, bookshelves, a grandfather clock, and other clunky decorations. The room connects to a dining hall with a long mahogany table and at least twenty cushioned chairs.

On one of the sitting room shelves sits a stout crystal vase of red orchids, and a ring of petals circles the bottom of the vase. I stare at them a little too long.

Someone brushes past my injured shoulder, and I flinch as pain zings through it. I notice a young man and an older woman looking over rolls of parchment at a desk in the back of the room. The desk is decorated with various glass statues and other trinkets.

The man is tall and has ashy brown hair that's cut close to his head, and he wears a plain black shirt with matching pants. The old woman has her graying, wispy blonde hair pulled up in a neat knot on the top of her head, and she's dressed in a black-and-white overcoat that matches Chadwick's almost perfectly. Even her sharp, time-worn features match his, from the hooked nose to the angled jaw. She purses her rosy red lips as we approach.

The captain smiles and goes to greet her. "Hello, Mother."

Mother?

Is this where he lives?

"You're late," she snaps, rising from her seat to hug him. He towers over her by at least a foot. "I had to recall the carriages because I didn't think you were going to make it."

"It's a miracle we got here at all. Do you see the weather?"

Thunder cracks overhead, and the jewels on the chandeliers rattle.

"Hm." She raises her eyebrows and looks to the crew as they shake the rain from their clothes and hair. She doesn't even acknowledge me. "Is this it?"

"Some found other arrangements, and the rest are watching the ship." Chadwick slips out of his coat, which drips water all over the floor.

"Goodness, Warren. You left them out there to be drenched?"

"They'll be fine. They're working in shifts and will switch tomorrow morning."

"The cooks left some dinner for all of you in the dining room," she calls to the rest of the crew. She seems unbothered by the puddles everyone leaves all over the floor. "I can't guarantee how warm it is since you're all here later than anticipated."

They aren't fazed. Each pirate speaks their thanks and says hello to Chadwick's mother as they move into the dining room. Chadwick shakes the mysterious young man's hand while Hyde leans over and hugs Chadwick's mother, despite the staggering height and weight difference. "Good to see you, Louise."

Annette smiles and kisses Louise on the cheek as they exchange brief conversation. Her bangs are plastered to her forehead from the rain, and Louise reaches up to fluff them up in a motherly manner.

Annette, whose own mother sobbed daily to mine about her runaway daughter. Annette, who defiled the name and honor of everything she's come from by falling into line with Warren Chadwick.

All I can do is stare. I glance down and wrap my fingers around the chains, realizing how ridiculous I look standing here. Louise must know who I am and that I would be here, because if her son dragged any other injured, shackled, and soaking wet girl into her house, it would raise major suspicion.

Brooks unloops his arm from mine rather roughly, and Lucky touches my healthy shoulder. "Don't make a scene, please." He wipes wet hair out of his face. "This house is old and might collapse if you do."

"Donnie, would you find the rest of the staff and go get some towels?" Louise says to the young man beside her. "And you," she gestures to Lucky. "Take those off of her. There's no need."

"Oh, no, no, no." Chadwick quickly intervenes, shaking his hand dismissively. "We're not going to do that. She's—"

"I don't care who she is, Warren." Louise scowls and waves at Lucky again. "She is technically a guest as well."

Lucky uses his cylindrical key to unlock the shackles and gives them to Chadwick, who shoots me a glare, though I wouldn't be able to do anything if I wanted to. I can't lift my arm to my face, let alone fight my way out of this cave. I would love to rip the candles off the walls and smash each and every ugly little glass statue Louise has displayed on the shelves. Even my mother, with her unique taste, would curl her tongue at how tacky the old bat's house is.

"Don't sit on any of the cushioned furniture while you're wet," Louise commands me. She loops her arm through Annette's as the two of them head for the dining room. "You'll ruin the velvet."

Donnie returns and hands me two towels, but he won't look me in the eye. Others dressed similarly in black cotton shirts and pants bring towels to the rest of the crew in the dining room.

I painfully slide my arms out of my coat and wrap myself in one of the towels, shivering.

It does feel nice to be free—at least for a little bit—and I try to focus on that as I sit on a decorative wooden chair in the corner, draping the second towel over my lap. I watch Chadwick and his crew as they eat, laugh, and drink together like friends. I can't tell what they're eating, but the scent makes my stomach grumble.

At the table, Lucky brandishes a deck of cards and beats Hyde and a few others in a game three times in a row. Each of them gets progressively irritated as he continues winning and drops out to converse with others around the table.

"Come on, just one more?" Lucky plays up the whine in his voice. "I'll go easy on you. I promise!"

Chadwick and Hyde are like peas in a pod as they chat, though Chadwick keeps glancing into the living room, watching me like he's the owner of a mischievous puppy. Annette sits on his opposite side and listens quietly to the conversation, only chiming in occasionally. She nudges Chadwick at one point and whispers something into his ear, and he smiles, brushing his fingers against hers.

My chest swells bitterly. If I squint—*really* squint—it's like I've never left Padstow, and I can pretend I am at The Tab or another tavern, watching a crew enjoy each other's company. I can pretend it's my crew unwinding after a long day on the open water. Or it's a group of friends gathering for the first time amidst a busy schedule. It's a dinner between families who share a bond that others don't.

And it's a thing I fear I may never experience again.

In the short future, there are no fun dinners with the Gordons, the Stantons, the Nowaks, the Scotts, or anyone. There are no late nights at The Tab watching Miles and Charles argue about something stupid, combing through our library with my mother, or talking sailing and swordplay and sailing with my father. There will never be a chance to confide in Callie or listen to Vaughn's sweet, subtle voice in my ear ever again. No more training sessions with Fallon. No chance to lead a crew of my own to hunt pirates and protect the region.

Nothing.

The word echoes in my mind as I stare at the floor, my eyes burning with tears. My chest aches with exhaustion.

But I *will* get back to Padstow and take back what little of that I can. I don't know what will be the same with my name circling through the news, but I will find a way back to it if it's the last thing I do.

The clicking of boots breaks my trance. Louise Chadwick enters the room, walking with a lifted chin as if a book balances atop her head. She sits next to me, and I frown at the plate of food in her hands.

"I suppose you weren't expecting to meet the mother of your public enemy number one, were you?" she asks politely.

"I didn't think he had one." I use one towel to wipe my nose, which crackles with pain. "I assumed the ground split open one day and he crawled out of hell."

Surprisingly, she laughs, pressing her hand over the silver necklace that rests on her chest. "I've heard many negative things about my son, but I think that's my favorite. It's clever."

I stare at her for a moment until she hands me the plate. "Eat. You look like a twig. My cooks are the best in the entire Commonwealth, and grew the potatoes themselves, which I'm sure is an upgrade from whatever backstock Warren keeps on his ship."

I wouldn't know. Withholding food and water is another trick he's pulled from his sleeve.

I have to set the plate on my lap and eat the chicken, potatoes, and vegetables with my left hand as my right sits limply at my side. Even though the food is cold, it still tastes like euphoria. I could swallow it whole if I knew I wouldn't be scolded by the old bat as if she were my own mother.

"Your face looks terrible," she says, commenting on my bruises, cuts, and scabs. The cut near my eye is puckered and irritated. "You'd think that doctor could clean it up a little nicer, but I suppose not."

I don't answer. She and I sit in silence for some time.

"Why did he stop here?" I ask, letting my curiosity win.

"I know he had some mail directed here that he needed to pick up, and he always comes by with his crew to make sure they have at least one respectable meal every once in a while." She clasps her hands around her crossed knees. "Plus, I enjoy the company."

My fingers curl around the damp towel on my lap. I use the prongs of the fork to gesture at the extravagant living room. "Did he pay for all of this?"

"The house? Oh, no. This was all my doing." Her breath catches, and she turns away, coughing into a cream handkerchief. She winces and clears her throat. "Forgive me. I've been dealing with a stubborn illness."

I look around at all the antiquities. "So he grew up like this."

"Not in this house. And he was not pampered—let me make that very clear." She holds out her knobby finger and glares at me. "He learned well after his father died. I spent a number of years organizing trades and investing my money wisely, and I advised Warren to do the same." She sighs. "But he enjoyed the thrill of being on the sea. It called to him."

"You call what he does a thrill," I mutter.

The audacity she has to think that he is on some moral high ground when he's murdered dozens of people and has become rich off of smuggling and breaking the law is infuriating.

He stole from *my* family.

He *murdered* Fallon.

"Sailing is a thrill, and I would assume you know that well," she says matter-of-factly. "He believes in fairness and sees what he does as—"

"No," I snap, the fork clattering on the ceramic plate. "You can't actually believe that."

I guarantee she would not be defending him if she hadn't been practicing it herself at some point.

"That's a bold statement coming from someone whose side is just as dirty as you're claiming his to be. You're only choosing to see the worst and ignoring how bloody your hands actually are." She turns up her nose. "I didn't raise a fool."

"Kearon was not innocent. Neither was anyone else he's told you about working with or the others who attacked Padstow. None of them were!"

"I didn't say anything about them." Louise narrows her watery-blue eyes and tilts her head. "You're a little too keen on believing you're on the right side of any discrepancy, aren't you?"

Her response catches me off guard, and I blink. "What?"

Louise twists her cherry-red lips and smiles. "You aren't going to get to the other side of this unscathed, Miss Walker." She stands up and moves to her desk, and she brings back a news spindle and a Shining Star capsule. She slips it onto the rod and gives it a spin. "I don't guarantee a lot, but I believe in that."

"Shining Star! Shining Star!" It's the blasted reporter from the capsule we listened to the night of my Seal. *"We have a breaking story emerging out of Crookston, where two days ago, a patrol ship from Padstow's Armada began an unsuccessful attack on a pirate crew that was passing by. The Armada's ship, commanded by Captain Fallon Scott, was destroyed in an explosion about five miles out from Crookston's port, and authorities from Crookston and Padstow are still trying to count casualties. No one is sure which group is behind this, folks. Other ships that were patrolling the area reportedly saw an unmarked ship leaving the area where the blast occurred. Witnesses say that on board was none other than Padstow's Emery Walker. Obviously, The Shining Star can't confirm if it was she who set the explosives, and though it seems like a stretch, the young captain has not reported for duty in two weeks and has seemingly disappeared from the city. And certainly, living under the pressure and expectations of a powerful family can't have helped her mental state. Ladies and gentlemen, is it unreasonable to believe that all of these combined factors have created a red-coated monster?"*

I throw the towels down and stand. "Nobody will believe that. It's ridiculous."

"Authorities from Padstow have been combing the region in search of the young captain for the theft of the Walker family's money, and the Armada has posted wanted signs in neighboring islands such as Lexington, Ivins—"

"Lots of people believed what was said about all of the scandals in Padstow and the things that have been said about my son," Louise says sternly. "Alongside that, how suspicious is it that you haven't come out to try and defend yourself?"

I bite my tongue. It's one thing to soil someone's name, but to keep them hidden away where they can't defend themself is twice as damaging. Her son, though a snake, is not stupid.

She sits back in her chair and grabs the capsule to stop it from spinning. "All they will focus on is the negative things they're being told. Just like you do."

I have to turn away so she doesn't see the tears of frustration welling in my eyes.

Chadwick waltzes into the room with his hands in his pockets. "All the dishes are ready to be washed."

"Thank you." Louise takes my plate even though I'm not finished. She glances at the dining room, which is now empty. "I assume they're all off to bed?"

"Yes. They all sent their thanks on their way upstairs."

"Good." Her eyes dart back to me one last time before she turns up her nose and exits into the dining room. "Goodnight, Miss Walker."

I awkwardly rip the capsule off the spindle with my left hand and take it to Chadwick. "You can't keep doing this."

"Why not?" he scoffs. "You've all done the same."

"You are blaming me for the murder of one of my associates!" My voice trembles.

"*You* blame me for your father's injury, which I had absolutely nothing to do with."

"Witnesses *saw* you on our doorstep! You aren't fooling anybody!" I inhale shakily. "All of this just for Gordon—"

"No. This is for Kearon," he clarifies. "All you have to do is tell me where Gordon is, and it'll be done."

"I don't believe that."

"So you'd rather keep playing this game than find out if I'm lying?" He grins and tilts his head. "I think we both know which one of us is going to last longer than the other, if that's the case."

"What exactly do you think you'll gain from doing this?" My fingers begin to tremble. "Do you think dirtying my name is going to—"

"See, it's that and more." He slowly creeps forward, closing the distance between us as I step backward. He widens his eyes. "Padstow is not the golden beacon on the hill that everyone should aspire to emulate, and I'm sick of you pathetic frauds pretending it is. You all say one thing and act the complete opposite, and you have no right to criticize me or anyone else about anything."

"Then you should be going after the entire judge's council or the Armada and not just Gordon and me," I snap. "Why aren't you doing that?"

"Oh, if I can get to you, then I can get to everyone!" Chadwick spreads his hands. "You're the best that's ever come out of Padstow, Miss Walker. If I can twist your image in their eyes, then their faith in the image they've created crumbles." He rubs his fingers together like he's feeling for sand. "If Gordon reverses his decision and releases Kearon from the Pereculum, then it *all* crumbles."

"Kearon was . . ." I trail off. His name is sour on my tongue.

You did not have the evidence. The voice of doubt whispers quietly in the back of my mind. *You had no right.*

He rolls his eyes. "You are not invincible. Look around. You are a liar who loves being in control and having a say in what happens to the people that you've exerted power over."

"Stop." My throat tightens.

"Every time someone called you Captain, it was a stroke to your ego and helped you rise a peg higher, right?" He tilts his head. "You shine on that pedestal and are nothing without it."

Am I?

I turn away again.

"Where is Gordon?"

My throat tightens. "I don't know."

He sighs, unamused. "If you're going to be stubborn, at least don't lie about it."

If this is how he's exacting revenge on me, I can only imagine what he'd do to Reese. I can't let that happen.

You have no bargaining power. The voice grows louder. *You have nothing.*

But Gordon has done too much good for me to betray him like that.

I wince and rub my shoulder as it aches again.

Chadwick clicks his tongue. "Miss Walker—"

"I won't resist you anymore if you call off the hunt." My voice trembles as a tear rolls down my cheek. "I can't . . . I don't know—"

"I have friends who could pay your family a visit to see if they know. They'd be more than willing to"—his lips pucker—"*extract* information from them."

"No! Please."

Ah.

Too eager. Too easily set off, and *exactly* where he wants me to be.

The devil grins. "I know you're trying to cling to whatever power you have left, but I suggest you heed this advice." He leans down to my ear, so close that I can feel his slimy, salty breath on my skin.

"Let go."

23

Warren

I AM LIVING IN A PAINTING; the airy song of the birds echoes from the trees as the sun rises, casting its dewy glow across the city. Stone and brick blend with the backdrop of palm trees and greenery, and in the distance, the *Lost Commandeer's* masts stretch high into the sky as the ocean sparkles in the dawn.

My deckhands did a fantastic job wrapping and tying the sails to keep them out of the wind, but I watch as the sails suddenly drop and expand to their full size. I ordered them to begin prepping the ship for cast-off at dawn so when the multi-hour process of guiding the ship out of the harbor was finished, all we'd need to do was row to it in the dinghies.

I lean against the balcony railing on the second floor, my sleeves growing damp from the rain residue. I roll them up and inhale the crisp morning air. It distracts from the smell of smoke and death that's been burning deep within my nose for the last few days.

Because of *her.*

She has lived on the back of my mind like a rotting sore, festering and oozing until she's consumed every thought in my mind.

How can I ruin you? As I open my eyes in the morning.

What can I take from you? As I clean my teeth at night.

And sometimes, if I squint, I can see the end result of this, where she is nothing and has nothing, when the consequence of hypocrisy has finally caught up to her.

Shining Star! Shining Star! The fake headline echoes in the back of my mind. *Have we really spent this much time promoting a fraud?*

Perhaps yes, they have. Perhaps once this is over, they can finally move on and find someone adoring.

Perhaps *I* can finally move on.

My mother hobbles outside and joins me. She's dressed; the black lines around her eyes and pink blush on her cheeks pop out.

Neither of us speaks for a few minutes.

"When are you meeting Derrick?" she asks me.

"In an hour." My spine stiffens. "He told me he has a few leads on where Gordon might be."

"Hm."

A bird caws in the distance.

She turns to me. "Why do you seem on edge?"

I frown. "I'm not on edge."

"What happened? Why is your ear bandaged?"

I close my eyes. "It was a pair of scissors."

"Scissors?" She scowls "Who is attacking you with a pair of scissors?"

I don't answer.

"Don't ignore me, boy," she huffs.

"I don't want to talk about this right now."

"Fine." She pulls the sleeves of her black blouse over her hands. "We can talk about how your night guards need to do a better job. It was deplorable. The two I saw were asleep outside Miss Walker's door both times I went to check."

I close my eyes and purse my lips. "Were they?"

"Why weren't you checking on them? The girl was awake all night blubbering like a baby, but she could have escaped. You're lucky that room doesn't have any windows. You need to be more careful. I know you didn't parade her through town and into my house in chains just for something like that to happen."

"It wouldn't have been a parade if you'd kept the carriages waiting for us," I mutter. "Who's watching the door now?"

"Hyde." She raises her eyebrows "I thought it was brave considering he told me she almost killed him, but that's his character."

The silence returns.

"You haven't heard anything about the judge, have you?" I ask.

My mother sighs. "I haven't. I'm sorry."

I wrap my fingers around the iron railing and exhale through clenched teeth. "How does the most important man in the entire Eastern Commonwealth fall off the edge of the map like this?"

"Well, what did the Riggses say? Did you read the letter I left in your room?"

"They just said what the news has said. The Armada is actively looking for him *and* Emery. His wife knows nothing, and nobody saw him leave port, either." I narrow my eyes at the sunlight. "Someone tipped him off that I was coming."

"Who?"

"I have no idea."

"Why wouldn't they have tipped off Miss Walker, then?"

"Annette said the same thing." I trace a circle on the railing. "I don't know. Emery shouldn't have known about my money in Lexington, either, yet she was there that night. Only Kearon and my crew knew."

"So someone is selling your secrets," she says. "I told you to be careful about who you let in your circles, Warren."

I purse my lips and take a deep breath.

"I think you should be focusing on that instead of whatever it is you're going to do with Miss Walker," she presses. "If you let this go on any longer—"

"Mother, there are more than thirty people on my ship who could be doing it." I throw one hand in the air and scoff. "How do you expect me to manage that *and* everything else?"

"You're putting too much energy into dragging her down when you need to be trying to reclaim the sailors you've lost."

"She deserves everything that she's getting after what she did to Kearon. And for all the phony arrests and corruption she stands in front of. I'm not just going to drop everything with her."

"Well, you need to do *something*." She cocks her head. "If you're going to dedicate this much time to what you're doing, then you need to give hell to whoever stands in your way and win."

She's right about both, as much as I hate admitting it. It fuels her ego.

I look at her a bit longer. Her gaze is fixed on the horizon, always watching for what's to come.

"And don't you dare compromise your values for any of it," she mumbles. "I taught you better than that."

"Of course."

The clock tower in the distance chimes at the hour.

As if on cue, she lurches forward and breaks into a nasty coughing fit. I grab her shoulders to steady her, and it sounds like rocks are clattering around in her lungs. She's pale by the time she stands up.

"Mother—"

"I'm fine." Her eyes are watery, and she clears her throat. "I'm fine."

I wrinkle my brow and support her frail frame as she leans into me.

"What do you need?" I ask, my chest tight. She's more hollow every time I see her, and I worry she may blow away in the wind. "What can I do?"

"You're already caught up in your own burdens." She glares at me again. "You don't need to bear mine."

I exhale softly. I learned not to argue with her a long time ago.

She grips the handrail and takes a deep breath. "I'm okay. I promise."

"Are you sure?"

"Go make yourself presentable to meet Derrick. You look like you rolled out of bed five minutes ago." She scowls and ruffles my blond hair. "Who taught you how to do your hair like that?"

"It's the wind, Mother." I push away from the rail and start back toward my bedroom. "And if you'll stop scolding me, I have something for you."

Before she enters my bedroom, I'm already holding out a leftover bag of the Walkers' novas.

She scowls at me. "What is this?"

"Donnie said there were still payments remaining on the house, and now that I'm a little more stable on my feet—"

"Absolutely not," she snaps. "I am doing fine for myself, thank you very much. I do not need your handouts when you've got your own issues you're trying to resolve."

"You're so dramatic." I don't roll my eyes at her for fear she might poke them out. "It is only the right thing to do. I'll give it to Donnie if you won't take it. Please tell me you'll use what's remaining to see a doctor."

"I don't need a doctor." She scowls. "They're just going to tell me what I already know."

"And that is?"

"That I'm old and need to rest." She pinches her lips. "Imbeciles. If they knew of *half* of the things that would crumble if I weren't there to oversee them—"

She stops short when I chuckle, despite the tension hanging in the air. Her expression relaxes as she purses her lips and sighs. "I'm not carrying that bag downstairs."

"I didn't expect you to." I kiss the top of her head and disappear down the steps with the novas jingling at my side.

24

DERRICK ADEN IS NOT a subtle man, so it makes no sense that he would choose a quiet, secluded bar deep in the thicket of the city for me to meet him.

Hyde and I climb out of my mother's carriages after the ride over Midway's rolling hills and valleys. The buildings are tall enough to block the sun, but the humidity seems denser between them, especially with throngs of people pushing their way through the streets. Cart owners and swindlers are shouting for the attention of the passersby, like seagulls begging for food scraps on a beach.

The sights and sounds and annoyances are a welcome distraction from my mother's feeble condition. I straighten the lapel of my coat and set my jaw as I face Derrick's bar.

It's a squat stone structure with two swinging doors and a long line of windows stretching around the perimeter. Hyde spits his tobacco on the ground and wipes his gray sleeve across his face before we enter. He puts his hands on his hips and looks around at the homey yellow room, with cutesy flower pots and plants scattered along the shelves. Dim candles and lanterns are perched across the low-hanging wooden rafters. Other than us, there are about five people in the bright space, three of whom are working behind the counter.

"Charming choice." He glances back at me and smirks. "I can tolerate it."

I blink the salty sting of sweat from my eyes and shake off my coat, ignoring him.

Derrick is sitting in the corner, and he smiles and waves us over. His graying golden hair is cut close to his head, and he's let a well-trimmed beard grow in since the last time I saw him. I frown at his casual attire until I see the wooden crutch propped against the wall.

I gesture to it and raise my brows. "What happened to you?"

"It's degenerative." He tries to stand, wincing. "Nothing exciting."

"No, don't bother." Hyde swoops in and takes his hand and elbow.

Derrick grunts as Hyde lowers him back into his seat. "Thank you."

"Time has not been very kind to you, my friend, has it?" I smile and shake his hand.

He laughs, a booming sound that bounces off the low ceiling. "Not all of us are blessed with oily, twenty-something-year-old bones like yours, Warren."

"Please tell me you have some good news for me," I say as I sit across from him. My chair scrapes against the dusty cobblestone floor. "I'd really love a victory right now."

"It sounds like you already have some. People have been talking about the news."

"Good things?"

"Great things!" He taps his thick fingers on the table. "They believe it all. They're shocked to think Walker would ever turn her back on Padstow, but people are buying it up like cheap booze. And the things they're saying about her are shocking. I can't believe how nasty people can be sometimes."

"Has anyone said anything else about Kearon or what happened?" Hyde asks.

"Lots are scrutinizing Padstow about the legality of the arrest, and there's been lots of talk of Cassie Dorenbasch and the others who were arrested the night you were there." Derrick points to me. "They're questioning if those arrests were valid after what's come to light about Kearon."

I nod and tap my heel on the ground. "Good."

"I've heard your name thrown around a few times for jobs, but I'm assuming you're finishing your little vigilante escapade."

Hyde scowls at him, and then at me.

"Is that not what it is?" Derrick glances between the two of us in confusion.

"That's a dramatic way to phrase it." I slide Captain Scott's ring off my finger and hold it out for him to see. His eyes light up. "But I suppose you could call it that if you'd like."

"Scott." Derrick scoffs, as if the name tastes like lantern oil in his mouth. He twirls the ring between his calloused fingers. "Thank you for quelling that thorn in my side."

I smile, which hopefully masks my suspicions. I wonder if it may be him who alerted Gordon, directly or otherwise. His social web is intricate, and while he and I owe many things to each other, bribery is an enticing beast. Emery and the Riggses know that well.

"You know, I can list at least ten others who have personal drama with Padstow's Armada." Derek clasps his hands on the table and sits forward. "Do you realize how quickly we'd run the world if they weren't there to mitigate it? And if we gathered enough sailors to provide enough resistance—"

"I will begin to think of that again once I find Reese Gordon." I chuckle. He brings up this spiel every time I see him. "I will *think* about thinking about it."

Hyde frowns. "Am I missing something?"

"We have always tossed around this idea of a full obliteration of the pirate hunters." Derrick beams at him. "It's bold, but it can be done. One at a time, just like plucking berries. Scott is just the beginning! We could strike now. With Gordon soon rescinding the Pereculum sentences—"

"And Emery's image in question," Hyde points out.

"Right. We could recruit enough for targeted attacks across the Estates, the Commonwealth, and the South." Derrick laughs heartily. "I can hear the headlines now!"

"'Padstow in shambles.' 'The Armada crumbling to pieces.'" I let myself smile. "What a world."

"You must consider it after this." Derrick sits back. "With your name attached to this, sailors will flock, Warren. *Flock.*"

"That all depends on whether I can find Gordon first." I lean forward. "Please tell me you have news."

"News for myself." He chuckles. "I didn't realize he'd dealt with so many pirates and hushed deals until I started asking around. No one I spoke with knew any specific details of his whereabouts, and most people are just going off rumors that he's actually been hiding in Padstow this entire time."

"And that's all they said?" I ask.

"The gossip that seems to have the most grounding are these two." Derrick reaches into his pocket and unfolds a parchment newspaper dated from yesterday. "This is in Gatlon, where someone happened to snap a picture with someone who looks like Gordon in the background."

Hyde and I lean in and study the grainy photo. I squint at the man in the background, who has Gordon's round build and short, stringy hair. The only thing he's missing is the wiry glasses.

"This is corroborated by a man who swears he saw the 'missing Padstow judge' checking into the inn he works at in Gatlon. Gordon has not been seen checking out, apparently, and the man says he works there all day, every day, and constantly sees patrons coming and going."

"Who are your contacts there?"

"The Valentine siblings."

The name tickles familiar in the back of my mind. "You're sure they—"

"Absolutely," Derrick swears. "They have eyes all over the city, and I've been doing business with them for years. I trust them."

Hyde glances at me warily, but I ignore him. "Okay. What else?"

Derrick continues. "The other is a bit shakier, but more eyewitnesses are saying they've seen him at the mailing outpost in Hale'iwa. My contacts there are incredibly reliable, though, so I wouldn't dismiss it entirely. If he isn't in Gatlon, then someone there might know where he's going."

Hyde nods. "That's promising."

"I would move quickly, because this could change at any moment. Gordon isn't stupid. From what I've been able to gather, there haven't been any payment records in his name or anything of the sort." Derrick shrugs. "He's covered his tracks well."

"Yes, he has," I say bitterly, gritting my teeth and digging my fingers into the splintering wood of the table.

"Why doesn't his wife know where he is?" Hyde asks me. "She could have told the Armada, and they would have found him by now."

A light, wispy voice speaks behind me. "Unless he stayed silent because he never wanted to be found."

My blood turns to ice as I whirl around to see a young man dressed in a wrinkled charcoal coat. A single curl of black hair falls across his forehead.

"Who are you?" Derrick demands of the newcomer.

"No attempt to cover one's tracks is perfect." He smiles. "But perhaps a larger team is required to help locate them."

I grab the collar of his shirt and bring his face to mine, ignoring his stale breath as it hits my nose. His slimy brown eyes flick to me.

"You should not be here," I hiss. "What are you doing?"

He grabs my wrist and licks his lips, still grinning like a madman. "Being proactive, Captain." He extends his other hand to Derrick. "I apologize, Mister Aden. My name is Isaiah Dasher, and I am going to be the reason we find Reese Gordon."

25

Emery

I'D NEVER THOUGHT I'd feel emotional sitting in the moist, chill breeze of a post-thunderstorm morning, but it's heaven compared to the stuffy, choking humidity of Chadwick's hold.

Rather than being swollen from the beating, my eyes are swollen from crying as I sit on a wet bench in the courtyard, slumped against the brick house. My coat sits in my lap, and I cling to it like it's the only thing that means my old life isn't dead—a life that included a man who loves me, a life that showed my hard work and dedication paying off, and a life where I am a captain.

I am also alone but not unwatched; the crew is outside to enjoy the earthy smell of the rain, but Lucky and Hyde periodically glance at me. Hyde sits on the cobblestone with his back against the brick and chews tobacco like a cow chewing cud. He tries to offer some to the others, but they decline. Lucky wrinkles his nose and slowly inches away from him.

Even though they're at ease, their eyes are too sharp for me to dash toward an exit. The widest exit is the archway of the courtyard that we entered through last night, and any other holes or cracks are guarded by pirates.

I touch the corner of my eye, and I can feel where the scar is forming from my eyebrow nearly to my cheekbone. I was able to look at the nasty thing in the mirror of the bathroom that Louise commanded her servants to prepare for me. It had an intricate water pump system, so I could scrub the dirt and blood out of my hair with relative ease despite my injury. The gray blouse and black pants they left for me in the vacant bedroom were fresh, and the material feels almost new.

I stare down at the loose threads of my coat and wrinkled edges that Callie smoothed out a lifetime ago. I can just make out the tiny holes in the lapel where Vaughn pinned my family's orchid.

I close my eyes as tears well in them again. I didn't realize they felt so much animosity about their uncle's situation despite the horrible things he did, but the fact that they didn't tell me stings even more.

I wonder if they've been stirring the pot in Padstow and fueling Chadwick's lies. I wonder if the Armada is looking for me or what my family must be thinking. They have to know I wouldn't disappear after finally achieving what I've dedicated my life to.

Or maybe they think that is the perfect reason to leave. Maybe they're convinced the pressure and expectations were too much, just like they were for Annette.

My thoughts spiral. I bring the coat up and cover my mouth, taking a deep, shaky breath.

Maybe Reese Gordon is listening to this and thinks of me the same as everyone else probably does. Maybe he wouldn't feel anything if I betrayed him. Maybe he believes me evil, and it won't come as a surprise if Chadwick shows up in Kahu looking for him.

I can only imagine what else Chadwick has in the pipeline for me, and my chest tightens. The physical torture from Hyde's beating could be multiplied in about a thousand grotesque ways. He could even commission the Riggses to go after my family.

Nausea bubbles in my throat as I squeeze my eyes shut.

"You know where to find me." Gordon's voice echoes in my thoughts. *"Lounging on the beaches in Kahu."*

I could…

I grit my teeth. I couldn't. Chadwick's hatred for me and my home isn't going to stop if I give Gordon away. I have been trained to withstand the horrors of the pirate underworld, but even that idea isn't as resolute in my mind as it might have been at the beginning of this nightmare.

Speak of the devil . . .

Chadwick emerges from the house wearing his usual black attire, and his hair is sharp and shiny. He greets his crew and whispers something into Brooks's ear, whose eyes flick briefly to me.

I frown.

Chadwick pulls Hyde to his feet, and the two of them leave the courtyard and climb into a maroon horse-drawn carriage. I wonder why, but not for long. If it means we have to wait for them to come back before we board the ship again, then I'll happily sit here all day and sweat until I'm nothing but bone.

Or perhaps not.

Brooks pushes off the house, and he and Gil approach me, motioning for me to stand. I do, keeping my injured arm clutched to my chest with my coat draped over it before either of them can grab it. Gil puts his hand on the small of my back as they usher me inside the house. Instead of going left into the sitting room, we veer right down a long, barren hallway.

"What are you doing?" I demand.

Brooks claps a hand on my injured shoulder, and I flinch. "We have a few hours of downtime and thought it'd be a perfect time for a chat."

He rolls up his weather-worn sleeves and reveals matching black leather sheaths on his forearms. A polished wooden knife handle pokes out just above his wrists.

"Cut the drama," I say with as much fervor in my voice as my anxiety will allow. "Hyde wasn't able to beat anything out of me, and if you think you're more intimidating than him, you're delusional."

I shouldn't have said that. You never want to anger the man with the knives.

Brooks suddenly grabs the collar of my shirt and pins my back to the hallway's maroon wall. A knife appears under my chin.

"Brooks," Gil warns. "Take it easy."

My throat tightens.

"Weapons are the great equalizer." Brooks narrows his eyes and bares his teeth, one of which is chipped from where I hit him with my shackles. "And bruises heal faster than cuts, *Captain*. Would you like to find that out for yourself or tell me a little information about the judge?"

"I already said—"

"I'm less patient than Hyde." He forces my chin up with the edge of the knife as it presses deeper against my throat. His lips curl. "You'd better speak quickly."

The thought briefly crosses my mind, but I set my jaw and put on a brave mask. I swallow and glance at Gil, who scratches the back of his greasy black head like he's bored and has better things to do.

Someone clears their throat, and all three of us look at Lucky walking casually toward the scene. He pockets his hands. "I don't think Louise would appreciate it if you left blood all over her floor."

Brooks makes a dramatic show of twisting his head and glancing down either side of the hall. "It's a good thing I don't see her . . ." He notices me supporting my limp arm and raises his eyebrows. "What's this about?"

He grabs my arm and jams my shoulder into the wall, and it takes every ounce of strength I have not to scream. Spots dance in my vision as I cry out and keel over, dropping my coat at my feet. Gil sucks his teeth.

"I wonder what's torn up in there." Brooks narrows his eyes and levels the tip of his weapon at the socket. "Shall we open up and take a look? Harrison would be proud of how clean my incisions are."

"Stop," I plead, my voice tight.

"Oh, come on. It won't take long." His grip tightens as he leans close. "Unless you can say where the judge is."

"What is going on?"

Brooks lets go of my arm at the snap of Louise's voice, and I groan, holding my arm against my body as he steps back. We all turn and see Louise on Annette's elbow at the end of the hall, dressed in a black blouse with white pants. Annette is in her corset and black pants, and her hair has been pulled back into twin braids.

"Brooks Scobell," Louise snaps, pointing an accusatory finger at the group, "If you think you're going to run a full-scale interrogation in my house—"

"I would *never* make a mess in your house, Louise," Brooks says innocently. "It's just that screaming is much better contained indoors than out."

"Oh, spare me." She rolls her eyes. "While you're here, you will keep the peace in my house or sleep outside. I won't have it."

"But—"

"It won't be an issue, Louise." Lucky cuts Brooks off with a glare. "Right?"

Brooks's lips curl as he sheathes his forearm blade. He smiles with affected sweetness. "Not at all."

Louise's scowl drills into him as he slips past her and storms outside. She rolls her eyes. "If he keeps acting like a child—"

"You're welcome," Lucky mutters to me as Louise continues complaining to Annette. He picks my coat up off the floor and hands it to me. "Hyde is ruthless, but imagine crossing the man who sleeps with a blade in his hand. If you're thinking about sharing something about the judge, I'd do it before he gets angry."

I press the back of my head into the wall, my shoulder throbbing. Whatever is injured is irreparably worse now. "I wouldn't betray him even if I knew where he was."

"You don't actually believe that *we* believe that, do you?" Gil knits his brow and folds his tattooed arms. "That you don't know where he is?"

"Why would I lie after everything that's happened?" I gesture to my face, my heart still pounding.

"Because maybe Gordon is more valuable than we initially thought." He shrugs. "It's your secret to tell."

"Come sit down." Louise motions for us to follow her and Annette back into the ugly living room. "Heaven forbid you do this civilly instead of cutting each other open and putting holes in my wall!"

"There isn't a hole," Gil mutters, rolling his eyes.

"That may be difficult as civility isn't their nature, don't you know," Annette says with a small smile. She helps Louise into her desk throne.

"I can at least *hope* they don't act like a crowd of degenerates in my home," says the bat, pointing a gnarled finger at me. "Especially that one."

I glare at the two of them as I settle into the chair I was in last night. Annette glares right back.

"Aren't you living cushily?" I sneer. "Tell me, do you find it gratifying being a kowtow?"

"That's rich coming from the bottom of the barrel," she replies snootily, narrowing her eyes. "Jealousy is not a pretty color on you."

"Jealousy?" I scoff. "Why would I be jealous of a puppet?"

"Stop." Gil rolls his eyes as he props his foot up on the end table. "Good grief."

"Yes, please. Bickering is unbecoming," Louise says to the room, though her comment is mostly directed at me. Annette puckers her lips and turns away, but there are a thousand more insults I'd like to hurl her way.

Instead, I hold my throbbing arm and take a deep breath. Lucky joins Louise and Annette in conversation while Gil watches me. Even though I try to ignore him, my attention falls to his tattoos. Nearly every inch of his long arms has been inked with an odd assortment of drawings, from a mountain range across his left forearm, a clock on his right bicep, and a ship in the middle of an ocean spanning his entire left shoulder. Those are the few that I can make out. The sheer number causes them to blend together, like a child got hold of a black paintbrush and slathered nonsense across a piece of paper.

Harrison enters the room from the hall as he cleans his glasses with the hem of his unbuttoned brown waistcoat. His eyes land on me, and he stops in his tracks. "Are you injured?"

I swallow and glance at the floor.

"Don't." Gil rolls his eyes. "Just leave her alone."

Harrison ignores his comment as he puts on his glasses and crouches in front of me, inspecting my shoulder with a furrowed brow.

"I fell," I mumble, my voice tense from the pain. "During the… attack."

Fallon's terrified eyes flash through my mind. So does John's mangled corpse flying through the lower deck.

"How did you fall?" Harrison asks gently. "What position was your arm in?"

I stick my healthy left arm straight up in the air. "Head first like this."

He gently pulls both arms so they sit straight at my sides and narrows his eyes. He hovers his hand just over the collar of my blouse. "Pardon my reach for a moment. I want to feel if it's dislocated."

His fingers are clammy against my skin as he presses where my shoulder meets my collarbone, and then just outside my shoulder blade. I grimace.

Lucky glances back at Harrison and me and frowns. "What are you doing?"

"If a shoulder is dislocated, you can sometimes feel the arm bone pushed out of place." Harrison meets my eye as he retracts his hand. "It looks and feels like it's still in alignment—"

"That happened to my brother once," Gil chimes in. He reaches up and ties his wavy hair into a knot. "He fell out of a tree and popped it out of place."

"The same thing happened to a friend of Warren's growing up." Louise places her hand on her chest. "His mother passed out when she saw how crooked his shoulder was."

Everyone in the room watches as Harrison gently grabs my elbow and forearm and lifts my straightened arm like a lever. I flinch as sharp, throbbing pain juts through my entire shoulder.

"Sorry." He gently rests it in my lap and pushes his glasses up his nose. "There might be a muscle tear, or one of the sinews might be strained or torn. I can put it in a sling or wrap, and we can see if it heals on its own."

I swallow and nod, blinking tears of pain from my eyes. I slip my strong arm into my coat, and he helps me maneuver the injured one through as a shudder traces down my spine.

"Has anyone seen the news yet?" Louise asks, tucking a wispy strand of hair behind her ear. "Capsule or paper."

"I can check," replies Lucky, glancing at me. "Where is it?"

"I moved the basket to the front of the courtyard for the dunce newsboy." She points at the door. "He always leaves it sitting on the ledge of the—"

She's cut off by the scuffling of footsteps on the stone outside, followed by Mikhail, Darren, and five others rushing inside the house. The metal door slams into the side wall; Mikhail slams it shut and throws the lock into place.

"What on earth are you doing?" Louise demands.

"Sh!" Darren waves his hands, and the twin pistols on his hips swing in their leather holsters.

Mikhail cups his hands over his mouth. "Armada," he whispers.

My head snaps up.

Lucky reaches for the gun on his belt. "You're sure? Where?"

My heart leaps, but Gil senses my intentions and points his knife at me, pressing his finger to his lips. Harrison jumps back and stands near one of the many shelves in the room.

"Brooks ran out to intercept them so we could run," hisses Mikhail. "Some of the crew were able to get up onto the balcony and run to the back of the house to hide."

A hard knock rattles the door, and before I can shout, Gil leaps forward and smacks one hand over my mouth while the other digs into my injured shoulder.

Louise stands and frantically motions for the crew to file upstairs as quietly as possible. They tiptoe like mice in an attic as Lucky comes over to help restrain me, but I kick and thrash like never before.

"Midway Patrol!" The door rattles again. "Open the door or we will forcibly enter!"

I don't care if they arrest me if it means this nightmare is over. I know my family will defend me from whatever charges the judge's council tries to throw at me. I'd rat out the Riggses, reveal where Gordon truly is, and release the wrath of the entire Armada onto Chadwick, his mother, and this disgusting crew.

As she hobbles to the front door, Louise grabs Annette's sleeve. "Show them the back way out."

Lucky wraps both arms around my legs and pins them together as he and Gil carry me up the stairs. The soldiers pound on the door again, and I throw my weight to try and scrape or hit the wall, anything that makes noise and draws attention. Gil holds fast, stronger than stone. Another pirate whose name I don't know holds my other flailing arm, his fingers digging into my muscles.

The second floor consists of wide, maze-like hallways with lots of elegantly carved doors, nothing more than squares of dark brown contrasting with the ugly maroon paint. As the other pirate lets go of my arm, Gil wrenches my shoulder back. The pain is so intense that my vision darkens for a brief moment, but I have to keep fighting. I can't lose my window. I *can't*.

"Where are the shackles?" he whispers to Lucky.

"—impatient," Louise's voice snaps from downstairs. "What is the meaning of this?"

"Does this girl look familiar to you?" an unfamiliar voice demands. "She is a fugitive of the city of Padstow, and we've been permitted to search homes in the area."

"On whose authority? You identified yourselves as the Midway Patrol when clearly you aren't them! That's illegal!"

"They permitted us to be here without them," a second gruff voice replies.

"Then I'd like some proof," Louise spits. "What paperwork indicates that? Did someone tell you she was here?"

"Step back, please."

Lucky motions for Gil to hurry along. Gil keeps his left hand over my mouth and his right arm hooked over my right, and Lucky carries my legs. His twiggy frame belies his strength; it's like fighting against iron clamps holding my knees and shins together.

Annette squeezes past them on her way to the front of the group, touching each pirate's shoulder as she passes.

I try to wiggle out of Gil's painful hold, but the inflamed muscles and tendons seem to shred themselves more with each movement as he keeps pulling my arm further and further back.

"Knock it off," he snarls in my ear. Tears blur my vision as the pain creeps up my neck and down the rest of my arm.

"—ridiculous!" Louise shrieks. "There's nothing you need to search. This house is empty save for my house staff!"

"We'll decide that," a second voice commands. "Step back or you will be prosecuted."

We turn another corner. Lucky grunts and briefly loses his balance as I go limp from exhaustion. The knuckles on my free arm scrape against wood and leather on Gil's hip, and I freeze.

We maneuver around a cream porcelain vase sitting on a metal decorative table, and I act. I grip the handle of Gil's knife and throw it at the vase, which topples onto the ground with a loud crash. Milky white shards clatter across the wood floor.

The others ahead of us flinch at the sound. I reach back and jam my fingers into Gil's eyes. That relaxes his grip as he recoils, grunting in pain. It causes Lucky to lose his balance again and loosen his hold on my legs as he stumbles backward.

I pry Gil's calloused hand away from my mouth. "Here!" I scream. "Up here!"

Gil's hand crushes my fragile nose as he yanks my head backward, and my vision blurs. Sounds of scuffing feet and hushed voices echo around my head as I topple and land facedown on the hardwood, my shoulder and broken nose throbbing in unison.

"Go, go, go!" someone hisses. "Hurry!"

"Move!" Another's foot catches on my leg as they stumble forward.

Get up! Get up! A spike of pain juts through my head.

More footsteps thunder up the stairs and down the hall. "Everybody freeze!"

A gun clicks, but Lucky leaps and tackles one of the soldiers as a bullet rips through the air. Pirates shout in surprise, and some of them take off down the hall or draw their weapons. Metal clashes against metal as I crawl forward using my legs and one good arm. Shards of the vase cut through the fabric of my pants as another gun fires, and someone screams.

My ears ring as I scramble to my feet and run, unaware of direction or space around me. My nose and shoulder ache with each beat of my heart. I duck into one of the rooms and scramble to unlock the latch on the window, praying that they're following protocol, which means at least one of them is surveying the perimeter.

And I'm correct.

I clumsily climb through the window and sprint across the metal balcony, waving my good arm. "Hey!"

The perimeter soldier looks up, blocking the sun with his hand before aiming his rifle at me.

There's a set of stairs leading to the ground, and I cradle my bad arm against my chest as I descend.

"Wait! Wait!" When I reach the ground, I raise my strong arm in submission. "Don't shoot!"

He seems confused by my surrender, but not for long. The crack of a gun rings out from above, and his head snaps back as he crumples to the grass in front of me. I whirl around to see Darren at the top of the stairs with a smoking pistol in hand.

No.

But he won't shoot me. Not fatally, at least.

And it's harder to hit a moving target.

I swoop down and pluck the soldier's knife from his belt and *run*.

26

Warren

DERRICK FROWNS at me as he shakes Isaiah's hand.

I clear my throat and ball my fists. "Isaiah, Derrick and I have worked together in the past."

Derrick eyes him head to toe. "You're awfully young."

"And awfully out of place," I say, widening my eyes. "Care to explain?"

"The Riggses." Isaiah slips out of his gray coat and sits, much to my annoyance. His curly black hair is shorn a bit shorter on the sides and is left fluffy along the top and back, minus the loose strand on his forehead. He rolls up the sleeves of his loose black shirt to expose his intricate Southerner tribal tattoos. "Captain Walker's two bodyguards told me they were close to being exposed for betraying her and needed to escape. In exchange for my sneaking them out of Padstow, I asked for a few more details of your plan." He twists the silver earrings dangling from his cartilage. "I helped them and they helped me."

"You have the twins *here?*" Hyde asks.

"Oh, no," he laughs. "They're long gone. I dropped them off in Port Mariker about three days ago and came straight here to wait for you. I'm not in the business of harboring fugitives."

"Yet somehow you think *this* isn't stupid," I snap, gesturing to the table. "I dismissed you."

"You did, and I did *not* kill the admiral like you asked." He smiles, and two tiny dimples appear in his cheeks. "I have a proposition."

"This should be good," Hyde mutters.

"You should *not* have a proposition." I glare at him. "This partnership died when I told you I didn't need you to kill the admiral anymore. That is final."

"Let the boy speak, Warren." Derrick leans forward and narrows his eyes. "He's being bold."

Isaiah licks his lips. "Why not be bold? When did being weak ever work out for anyone?"

I study his face. He carries himself like he *isn't* a no-name little twit, but like any good businessman, he's there when opportunity appears. It caught my eye when looking for an assassin for Admiral Van Pelt, before the original plan to retaliate against Padstow flopped. The eccentricity didn't bother me because I didn't think I'd have to deal with it for very long.

Derrick raises his eyebrows. "I'm listening."

"Derrick, can you order us a round of drinks?" My eyes flick to him. "Would you mind?"

Hyde stands. "I'll come."

I watch him help Derrick hobble toward the bar before sliding my chair toward Isaiah, halving the distance between us. "Are you out of your mind?"

"I understand you're upset." Isaiah ticks like a clock, whether it's in his rapid blinking or twitching lips. He taps his fingers on the table. "You asked me to step away, but I had an idea."

I glare at him.

"See, Gordon and I have a history, and his disappearance complicates lots of things for me," he says quietly. "He was in a sticky situation about a year ago and needed protection, which I've been providing for him in exchange for goods and other things supplied by the Stantons. They operate the port in Padstow."

"I'm aware," I mutter. "Get on with it."

"So I'm none too happy that my number one supplier has disappeared, and I'd like to pay him a visit." His fingers cease their rhythm on the table.

I frown and purse my lips. "Is that all?"

"No. I can exchange some things for you. You need sailors." He leans forward even more, breaking the imaginary line of personal space between us. He smells like salt and needs a bath—*badly*. "You told me yourself about being short-staffed since your errand boy's arrest, and the others quitting or being captured, but I have more sailors than I need across my two ships."

"I can find sailors," I retort. "That was my and Derrick's next topic of conversation before you cut in."

"You won't find any that are already trained and ready to go like mine are." His lips twitch into a clowning grin. "You'll effectively double your manpower and leave you and your crew less vulnerable."

My tongue curls distastefully in my mouth because he's right. On the off chance we encounter the Armada in their search for Emery, or we're attacked by anyone else, I'd like to be ready. I can't gain an advantage with an ambush like I did with Captain Scott.

"And what would you be asking for from me in return?" I scowl at him, clasping my hands. "I'm not paying you more than I already have."

"Pay me in experience." His eyes are wide and intense. "Pay me in the widespread knowledge that my name is attached to the notorious Warren Chadwick's. I'll never be looked down on again."

I roll my eyes. "Your obsession with status is juvenile, and that's why people treat you as such."

"Padstow doesn't treat me like that." He licks his teeth like a hungry dog, and one of his front canines is missing. "And Padstow! I just heard you and Derrick discussing this. You can't enact that plan with Derrick unless you have more sailors. I know *dozens* of people down south who are itching to fight and wouldn't hesitate to join you."

I tilt my head. The thought is enticing, to say the least. An army there, an army here, and an army in the north to drag Padstow's hunters down.

It sounds too nice.

"You *hate* Padstow. Everyone hates Padstow." Spittle flies from Isaiah's mouth and lands on the table as he leans farther forward. "Just like Derrick was saying, what if we make an example out of Gordon and start picking each of those hunters off one by one? That will show the world that they aren't the beacon of strength everyone thinks they are."

I ponder for a moment.

Bold plans of going toe to toe against the strongest navy in the world aside, I do sometimes wonder how much further I would have gone six years ago if I'd had a boost like he's asking of me now. Seventeen-year-old Warren was oddly similar to this nineteen-year-old Dasher; there's a flicker of fire in his brown eyes that I remember feeling in my chest at the thought of the power and control over my destiny.

Both are young sailors following orders. Both won't cave at the first sign of trouble. Both know what they want, and they'll work tirelessly to obtain it.

"You're forgetting one key issue here," I say at last, narrowing my eyes. "I don't know where Gordon is, and Miss Walker isn't too keen on telling me."

His eyes flash at the challenge. "What have you tried?"

I pay particular attention to his eyes as I explain what's happened so far. They narrow like a snake's and twitch every few seconds.

He grins. "I have an idea."

"Before you say anything . . . " I place my hand on the table between us, and he leans back. "Let me be very clear. If you sign onto this, you are under *my* command. You will listen to my orders, and if you ever step a toe out of line or put myself or my crew in danger, I will abandon you at the nearest port and turn you in to the authorities."

He dramatically smacks his chest. "Abandon?"

I give him a look, and he laughs.

"Okay, yes. I'm sorry." He clears his throat and wipes his mouth with his palm. "I understand."

Hyde has been watching our entire conversation from across the bar, and he wrinkles his brow when I look at him and nod.

"I think I have a job for you, then." I let my lips curl into a grin. "If you can handle a challenge."

He smiles devilishly, but before he can respond, the door bursts open and clatters against the wooden wall.

"Easy!" a woman behind the counter shouts.

Tahj and Alexis rush inside as the door rattles shut.

"Sorry to . . ." Tahj gasps and hunches over with his hands on his knees. "Interrupt."

"The Armada is here," Alexis cuts in. His curly brown mop drips with sweat. "They were knocking on doors and searching homes, and five of them came to the house looking for Emery."

"*What?*" I spring to my feet.

Hyde limps over from the bar. "Did everyone get out before they went inside?"

"I don't know." Tahj rubs sweat off his face. "We ran to find you as soon as they came up the driveway."

I throw on my coat and grab Isaiah by the collar. "Get back to the harbor and stay out of sight in case they recognize you," I snap. "Someone from my crew will come find you."

"No!" He grabs my sleeve as I turn away. "Let me come help. I can—"

"No." I glare at him. "I need you to stay out of the way."

Hyde grabs my arm. "Are you going back to the ship?"

"If they're searching the whole town, then yes." I exhale in frustration. "Even though the whole port is probably crawling with soldiers."

"I can help sneak your crew out." Isaiah grabs my other arm and stares at me with his freakishly wide eyes. "Let me see how many Armada soldiers there are and handle the situation. I can distract them and give you time to hide."

He's surprisingly quick, despite being a clownish spaz. I roll my eyes. "Fine, but do *not* make a scene and do not let them catch you. Tahj, go with him. Alexis, stay with me."

I grab Tahj's shoulder as everyone heads for the door. "He's flighty," I hiss. "Do not let him fly off the handle."

"I won't."

"Derrick!" I shout as we file outside. "Thank you!"

"You aren't staying for drinks?" He turns around with two glasses of bourbon in his hands as the door slams again.

. . .

Emery

Darren's next bullet zips past my leg and drills into the dirt as I skitter around a small patch of greenery in front of Louise's house. I grimace and keep my right arm pressed against my chest, which throws off my gait as I run. Blood from my nose drips down my shirt.

The streets are busy and alive with vendors and pedestrians milling between the massive, whitewashed buildings. It's chaotic enough that no one notices me as I brush by, though if they did, I'd welcome it. The more attention, the better, especially if it's from the Midway Patrol or the Armada. Neither seems to be present here, though.

I glance over my shoulder for pirates, but see none. I check again, and again a little further down the road.

My heart hammers against my ribs.

Is this it? Have I done it?

My breath shakes as I quicken my pace.

Please let it be. Please let it be a step closer to the scent of orchids in the house and the boys' bickering, and the smell of woody paper in my mother's study as we thumb through the pages of literature, and the sight of my father's cheeky grin as we discuss sailing. The excited jitter of the harbor pulsing through the salty air on the morning before a voyage. The comfort of knowing I am not alone.

Please.

I split the crowd and beeline for the harbor. I pick up my pace as sweat runs down my back and face like a waterfall. My attention is drawn to a massive black galleon floating a hundred yards offshore with four rows of cannons and a red, yellow, and blue flag atop the foremast.

There are three ships in the Armada with four cannon tiers—one belongs to Captain Park, one to Captain Embuka, whose seniority sits just below Park's, and the final to Hector Hadley.

I stumble to a stop on the dock before a crowd of sailors and touch the forearm of a burly man with scars on his neck. "Where is the Midway Patrol?"

His jaw falls open as his eyes widen.

I ignore his pause. "Do you know where they—"

"You filthy traitor." He cuts me off, yanking his arm away. Others in the group turn their heads to the commotion. "Get away from me. I hope they lock you away and let you rot."

My heart clenches, and I step back as he stares at me with disgust. Whispers echo through the group.

"Is that Captain Walker?"

Someone grabs my elbow, and I whirl around in surprise. A woman stumbles backward.

"Did you see that? She pushed me!" she shrieks to the crowd, pointing her finger. "She pushed me!"

"She has a knife!" someone else shouts.

My face burns hot from the negative attention as the crowd starts to tighten around the woman and me. Every word I want to shout in defense of myself dies on my tongue.

"Emery, freeze!"

I widen my eyes and turn to the source of the voice. "Hector!"

Yes, yes, yes!

"Everyone move out of the way or you will be arrested!" Hector aims his rifle at my chest as three other soldiers work to clear the crowd. "This is official business of the Padstow Armada!"

I hold my left hand up in surrender as my injured right shoulder screams in pain. "Warren Chadwick is here. He—"

"Stop talking," he snaps, his eyes alight with anger.

"I . . ." I trail off, noticing the slight quiver in his stabilizing hand as it grips the forestock of the rifle. My voice catches when I open my mouth again. "I didn't kill Fallon."

He blinks rapidly and sets his jaw. "Why should I believe that?"

"Hector—"

"She was our *companion*, Emery. You turned your back on the Armada."

"That's not true." Tears spring to my eyes, and I quickly blink them away. "Warren Chadwick is framing me and feeding lies to the news. Do you really think I'd betray all of you? Or my family?"

"Wait, Chadwick?" His face scrunches with confusion as he begins to process what I'm saying, and he lowers his weapon slightly.

"Yes." Hope flutters around my heart as the crowd begins to disperse. "He came to Padstow for his errand boy and kidnapped me as revenge for arresting him."

Hector's eyes twitch as they scan my body from head to toe, and he grits his teeth and digs his heel into the ground. "Drop the knife."

I sigh in relief and let the blade clatter onto the dock. One of the soldiers, a twiggy man I don't recognize, grabs my injured arm, and I inhale sharply.

"Do you have any other weapons?" He pats down my back and sides while the other feels for weapons down my legs.

"No." I glance behind me, but the path beside the dock is still empty. "Hurry. Chadwick isn't going to let you take me without a fight."

"Find the Midway Patrol and keep these civilians in the area." Hector ignores me as he commands another group of eight soldiers who've arrived on the scene. "Don't let any of them leave. This investigation is now open."

"You're not from our government," an older woman snaps. "You don't get to order us around."

"Our presence here is necessary. I need to know if any of you have information that can aid in my investigation," Hector snaps. Two of the soldiers load their weapons and aim them at the civilians, who stir with unease.

"Where's your warrant?" Another man demands. "You can't—"

"The next person who speaks out of turn will be arrested and prosecuted by the Padstow Armada." Anger burns in the captain's eyes as he tightens his grip on his rifle.

My jaw falls. "Hector, wait—"

The soldiers snap shackles around my wrists and lead me away from the group. My boots skitter across the dock as I crane my neck to watch what unfolds behind me. One of the soldiers jams the muzzle of his rifle into a civilian man's chest, and he falls backward. My breath catches as protests erupt from the crowd.

"Hey, stop!" one voice shouts.

"You're overstepping!"

I flinch as a single shot fires into the air to quell the disgruntled crowd. One of the soldiers digs his fingers into my bicep to get my attention as he pushes me along. "Keep moving."

"Gather the others and tell them to return to the harbor," Hector commands his soldiers.

"What about Chadwick?"

"I think she's lying to make herself seem like the victim. Go."

I wince at his comment, but he'll know the truth soon enough. They all will.

We descend a set of stairs that leads to a lower level of the dock, specially made for smaller boats. I'm loaded into one of the Armada's dinghies with a soldier pressed against my left side and another on my right, their arms still looped through mine.

My racing mind and heart begin to slow as two of the soldiers row us toward Hector's ship, and my stomach tingles.

I've done it. My face is bleeding, and my shoulder has been seemingly ripped to shreds, but I've done it.

All that's left is for Chadwick and the others to be arrested. He's smart enough to know not to attack now.

My chains rattle as the skinny soldier on my right wrenches my injured shoulder so I'm forward-facing again. My breath hitches, and spots dance in my vision.

He scowls. "Are you injured?"

"Stop, Hodge," the pudgy soldier on my left sneers. "We have to bring the precious little captain home in one piece."

"Oh, don't be a stickler." The skinny soldier tilts his head and grips hard onto my shoulder. "The judges are going to have a ball with you."

"Let go." I whistle through my clenched teeth to push away the pain. I don't have any room to wiggle away since I'm pressed between the two of them like the cement between bricks.

"Hey," one of the rowing soldiers grunts as his paddle cuts through the water. "Don't abuse the prisoners."

Hodge rolls his eyes, loosening his hold but keeping his hand in place as a silent warning. "Nobody cares about the prisoners."

I curl my fingers, trying to ignore the discomfort twisting in the pit of my stomach. I shouldn't care what they think, but the feeling persists.

It doesn't matter. It shouldn't. Once I'm home and tell everyone the truth, none of it will matter.

Home. My insides flutter at the thought. Home, with my mother's cheerful voice and my family's laughter echoing throughout the house. Tears well in my eyes.

We're fast approaching Hector's galleon, and I finally let myself breathe. We come to the starboard side of the ship, where wedges of wood are screwed into the side. The older of the two rowers uses them as hand and footholds to climb aboard.

Hodge unlocks my hands so I can follow.

He glares at me. "No tricks, or I'll shoot you."

I swallow and tuck my weak arm against my chest before I begin the ascent.

"What are these dunces doing?" the other rower scoffs.

I frown and glance over my shoulder at what he's referring to. A tan-colored sloop with black sails drifts uncomfortably close to the galleon.

"Go," Hodge snaps, poking my calf with the muzzle of his rifle. "We don't have all day."

My heart pounds. It's slow work as I inch up the side of the ship, steadying myself with both feet on one ledge before quickly reaching for the next with my left arm, then repeating the process. My arm shakes as my fingers ache from bearing the weight of the climb, and I'm about halfway up when the shadow of the sloop falls over the soldiers and me. I glance over my shoulder and then down at Hodge and the others. They all turn and watch the ship approach with confused scowls.

"What's going on?" the first rower, who's made it aboard the ship, shouts to the sailors on the other side.

The sailors who stand aboard the sloop are armed with rifles and handheld explosives, shouting and jeering at the soldiers aboard the galleon.

My gaze drops as cannons are pushed through the twin rows of gunports stretching the length of the ship. My eyes widen.

"Get down!" Hodge's eyes widen as he jumps and reaches for my leg. "Get down from—"

He never finishes his sentence as the cannons open fire on the ship.

Warren

I can only think the worst—that they found my mother with a fugitive in her house and will drag her to the Pereculum just like they did Kearon. Or maybe my crew has been shot at like birds, and their bodies and blood are strewn across the streets.

And the Armada will soon do the same to me. Throw my corpse into the black, lifeless pit that is the end . . .

Hyde grabs my shoulder and snaps my trance. I peer forward and see a bloody Lewis, a bruised Brooks, and an outraged Gil sprinting toward us from the direction of my mother's house.

"You passed her!" Gil screams as he darts past us. "She's running!"

Running?

"My mother—" I start.

"Fine!" Lewis's nose is bleeding, and his entire front is doused in red, though I don't think it's his own. "She's fine!"

Alexis draws his sword and tails Gil as the two weave through the crowd and the bustle of merchants and vendors, whose tables and carts contain anything from vegetables to gold jewelry and leather satchels.

I squint toward the far edge of the mass and catch a glimpse of a blonde in the distance before she rounds the corner to the harbor.

"Can I not trust any of you to watch her for *five* minutes?" I snap, pulling my sword and ducking through the crowd. Hyde grips the hem of my coat as Lewis and Brooks fall into line behind him. It's quite literally like wading through mud in a sticky swamp; sellers grab my arms and shove their trinkets in my face as I shove past the pedestrians blocking the street.

It takes nearly five minutes to break from the crowd, but once I do, I round the corner to the harbor. I scan for Emery and instead spot an Armada galleon floating about a hundred yards offshore, with the *Lost Commandeer* floating another fifty to the east. I don't think the Armada has recognized it, considering it's still afloat.

Unless they aren't here for me.

I shield my eyes from the sun and squint at a small collection of dinghies floating beside the galleon, and I can barely see the speck of red and blonde against its dark grain.

My jaw falls.

Hyde's uneven footsteps thud to a stop behind me, and he swears. "Now what?"

The plan I spent weeks constructing begins to crumble in my mind like a stale cracker.

Hyde turns his head to the left and pulls me by the arm into a small patch of greenery directly across from the harbor. "Warren."

I follow his line of sight to a group of Armada soldiers standing around a small crowd of people on the dock. The soldiers have their rifles raised.

"What are they doing?" Hyde mutters.

I glance back at the galleon, where Emery and the soldiers have begun to climb aboard. My jaw clenches in anger. So much for Isaiah distracting them.

Lewis, Gil, Alexis, and Brooks bound around the corner, their weapons drawn. Gil holds out his arm to halt the other three when he sees the soldiers, and they duck into the bushes with us.

"We need to hide." My mind slows down. I can be angry later. "Some of the crew are staying at the Rattlesnake Inn, and I told them to meet at the harbor at noon, but someone needs to warn them to stay there. I guarantee Miss Walker has told them that we are here."

"So we're just going to let them haul her off?" Brooks lazily gestures to the galleon with his blade. "After all the hell we've gone through to get her here?"

"Well, it's not what I'd like to do, but I'm not going to risk my neck to get her back," I retort. "I'm not risking any of yours, either."

"Where's the Rattlesnake?" Gil asks.

"Second Street." I point to the west side of the city. "It's a tall building on the corner, and the signpost has green and yellow letters. Be sure to . . . "

I trail off, my eyes settling on the twin sloops approaching the Armada galleon's stern.

"Hey!" A gray-coated Armada soldier with a crooked nose approaches us, and I instinctively turn to hide my face.

"Hello!" Lewis doesn't miss a beat and steps forward like a chipper man greeting his neighbor. He covers his bloody nose with his hand.

"What do you think you're doing here?" the soldier snaps. Three others stand behind him, their hands placed at the ready on their weapons. "Why are you covered in blood?"

Alexis shuffles in front of me as a shield.

"Oh, just a nosebleed." Lewis chuckles as he tries and fails to nonchalantly cover his blood-drenched front with his arm. I roll my eyes. "We were just on our way—"

"You can't be here," a second soldier commands, his hand drifting toward the trigger of his rifle. "You need to leave or you'll be arrested for tampering with an active investigation."

"We're just standing here." Brooks scowls and gestures to his feet, which have sunk into the moist soil. "You aren't even Midway's authorities! Where are they?"

"Who are you hiding back here?" A third soldier shoves past Lewis and Alexis and wrenches me around before I can defend myself.

He stares. I stare.

His eyes widen in recognition, and just as his thin lips form my name, I knock him clean off his feet with a punch that jolts my entire arm.

Brooks reacts the quickest and swipes at one of the soldiers with one of his knives, and Lewis lunges to redirect a gunshot that cracks through the air. Hyde throws his elbow into another soldier's head while Gil and Alexis team up to attack the fourth, swords swinging.

"Hey!" Another group comes bounding onto the scene from one of the streets that leads to the dock, and the four of us take off. I sprint like a jackal as Hyde and I dive for cover behind the stone retaining wall that separates the wooden dock from the dirt pathway. Frightened traders and merchants flee past us, acting as a temporary screen that gives Lewis and the others time to duck as more bullets fly.

I twist around and pull my pistol from the holster under my shoulder, hitting my mark—one soldier topples into the dirt. I duck quickly to hide my face with the lapel of my coat, praying that my crew will take the rest of the soldiers out before any of us are hurt or killed.

The soldiers surrounding the other civilians take notice of our scuffle and rush over to help. The crowd scatters in a fit of panicked screams and shouts.

"Captain, behind you!" Alexis shouts.

In one swift motion, I grab my sword, spring to my feet, and whirl in a wide arc that takes out two attacking soldiers. Brooks wrestles another to the ground on my left as Hyde lifts his gun and fires at one as he's swiping at Lewis, whose shirt is twice as bloodied as before.

A pistol hammer clicks behind me, and I whirl around as a man with a scraggly brown beard darts past me and fires, not on us, but on the last soldier.

Gil doesn't see that, and he jumps over the wall and raises his gun at the man, but I grab his arm. "Wait! Stop!"

The man aims his pistols at the sky in surrender as the last soldier falls. Long, tangly hair hangs across his face like wavy vines across a scarred mountainside.

"Are you with Isaiah?" I demand.

"Aye." The man's voice is as gritty as chopped-up gravel and rusty screws. "He told us to watch for you."

"*Us?*" Gil demands, knuckles white around the handle of his weapon.

The man points over his shoulder as a few other older, grungy men approach us. Their swords are rusted and dripping with the blood of what I assume are Armada soldiers, and their clothes look as if they've never touched soap and water. One of them is missing some teeth, and another has scaly, oozing patches of red peppered across his face and neck.

My spine tingles with anxious anticipation as they all step forward. I clench my trembling fists.

"He said you're in charge," the scraggly man says. "What's the word?"

"Captain?" Lewis whispers.

I glance at the *Lost Commandeer,* but I cannot flee in the middle of this mess, as much as I would like to. If the Armada didn't know I was here before, they certainly do now. My mind ticks.

"You'll come with Hyde and me to find our dinghies and tell the group aboard the ship to stay put," I say to the scraggly man. "Gil and

Alexis, go to the inn to tell the others to stay at the inn while Brooks and Lewis go back to my mother's house—"

"But the soldiers—" Lewis starts.

"You have to make sure the Armada hasn't arrested her and that everyone got out of the house." My heart pounds violently against the back of my ribcage, for my crew, obviously, but if they've taken my mother or Annette—

Annette.

My breath hitches. "No, Lewis. Nevermind. Stay here, with them —" my arm shakes as I point to two of the old sailors, one of whom has a wooden stump where his leg should be. "—and wait for Gil and Alexis and the others to come back. If the soldiers come here with my mother or Annette, then shoot them. Shoot them all. If Midway's authorities don't show up and stop this *madness*—"

"Warren," Hyde mutters.

My mind races with all the possibilities before me. They have to get out. All of them. There has to be a way. I can't let any of them—

"Go!" I bark at Alexis and Gil, who flinch and spin on their heels before taking off.

Blood pounds in my ears like a thousand drums as death seems to wrap its icy fingers around the back of my neck.

I am not going to die today. Not like this. Not trapped in a corner or shot in the back.

I look to the harbor again, where the two sloops have trapped the galleon in between them. Some of the remaining soldiers on the dock stare, confusion painted on their faces.

"What are they doing?" I demand of the scraggly sailor.

But that confusion quickly turns to shock as Isaiah's twin sloops send a barrage of cannonballs into the Armada galleon, causing it to burst into flames.

. . .

Emery

Without a second's thought, I launch myself off the ladder. I'm still in the air as a cannonball barrels through the woods where I was perched. The icy salt water shocks my body to its core as I plunge beneath the surface, and I can just hear the muffled *booms* of the cannons and see the fiery explosions through the shimmering water.

I keep my right arm against my body and kick upward to break the surface, my ears ringing and eyes burning from the water. I sputter and gasp for air as I watch the carnage overhead. Soldiers attempt to return gunfire, but to no avail. Gray coats topple one by one over the railing of the ship like wooden dolls being knocked off a child's toy shelf.

The sound of snapping wood hits my ears as one of the galleon's masts is split apart by cannonfire. I kick my legs, propelling myself backward as mangled bodies float through the water right in front of me. My nose and mouth dip below the surface with every thrash, and my body shakes with wicked exhaustion that seems to worsen with each choked, saltwater-filled breath.

Hands grab my arms and haul my body out of the water, and I scream as my shoulder pops again. I topple into the bottom of the dinghy as the Armada soldiers row with frantic fury.

"Hurry up!" Hodge screeches. "Faster!"

I cough up water and groan as my arm hangs limp against my side. An acrid scent fills my lungs, and I roll onto my back and watch in horror as black smoke curls from the orange flames engulfing Hector's ship.

Who? Whose ship is attacking?

Wood chips fly as a bullet burrows through the side of the boat. Then another *crack* echoes through the air, and blood spurts from the back of Hodge's left thigh. He screams in pain and drops his rifle as he collapses, rocking the boat and throwing one of the rowers off balance.

I jerk my head in the direction of where the shot came from, and see a pirate aboard the sloop hurrying to reload his rifle. I snatch Hodge's fallen rifle and balance the forestock on my knee. I use my off but uninjured arm to take aim and fire. The pirate's head snaps back before his body tumbles into the water.

The rowers work furiously to propel us from the chaos as the pudgy sailor kneels and presses his hands over the wound in Hodge's leg. "Hold still!"

I scoot away from the pool of blood filling the bottom of the boat, and by some miracle, we arrive back at the dock and scramble ashore in a frantic panic. I glance back at the ship and see a second sloop attacking the galleon from the opposite side, and all I can do is watch in astonishment.

The once-mighty galleon is slowly reduced to nothing more than a husk of splintered wood and bonfire. Gray-coated sailors jump from the deck only to be shot by the pirates, but the sloops are already turning and sailing away from the harbor.

The sheer number of bodies floating in the water makes my stomach turn.

Twin ships.

Oh. I spot the sun emblem emblazoned on the left sloop and the star emblem on the right, and I remember.

Dasher.

Fallon complained of how much of a hassle it was to track him.

But why is he here?

"Where's Midway's navy?" Hodge groans as the group hobbles up the stairs. His face is as pale as ocean foam.

No one gets the chance to respond to his question. The second our group arrives at the top of the stairs, pirates pounce on the soldiers like cats catching mice. The soldier in front of me screams as he's cut down by one sickening swipe across his chest. I scramble away in a panic as a sword blade cuts through the air above my head. The soles of my wet boots slip against the wood of the dock, and I land hard on my knees.

I glance up, seeing that we are not their first victims. The group of soldiers standing with Hector when he was interrogating the crowd now lies off to the side. The captain's body is draped over the retaining wall, with wide eyes and a thin stream of blood trickling from his mouth. His entire back is stained crimson, and his sword is still in his sheath.

He never saw them coming.

For once, I stay down. I groan through the tears of exhaustion and pain, clawing forward with my left arm as I keep my throbbing right one clutched to my body. My knees ache from the impact as I inch forward one pathetic movement at a time.

The sounds of the chaos behind me have ceased, but I keep going. A sob hitches in my throat as my arm gives way, and I faceplant on the dock.

They're dead. All of them are dead.

A shadow darkens my blurry vision, and I brace to die with them.

This is it, the doubt whispers. *This is what you'll be remembered as.*

"Where exactly do you think you can go?"

The voice above me is suave and silky. It sounds perverse coming from its slimy crook of an owner.

I lift my chin and stare at worn, brown boots with sagging straps and rusted buckles. They belong to a boy, younger than me, but whose face I remember well from renderings that were distributed to each pirate hunter.

Isaiah Dasher smiles down on me and tilts his head as the sunlight cascades around him. "Captain Walker. How nice it is to finally meet you."

27

Warren

Mother,

I am fine. I will explain more later because there was a fight at the harbor and we needed to hide. The city was crawling with the Midway Patrol cleaning up the mess the Armada left behind. Lewis told me what happened in the house. That's why I didn't come back to find you. I just wanted to let you know I was fine.

Please forgive me. I couldn't take the risk of being seen. My crew and I had to gather quickly to leave. I don't even know if everyone made it aboard. Our next stop is Gatlon, so please send Chip there with an extra note telling their mail staff to keep him at the outpost until I retrieve him. I love you so much. Please see a doctor.

-Son

MY HANDWRITING IS ABHORRENT, but nonetheless, I fold the letter up and close the envelope with a wax seal. The parchment has been marked with a fake name and return address, and I tie it around Chip's feathery belly with a strand of twine. I grab the scruff of his neck and stick his long beak into a burlap bag of sage—the scent for Midway's mailing outpost—before he takes flight through my cabin's open window, disappearing into noonday sun.

I watch him soar until he disappears in the distance, hoping I'll soon find him and my mother's response in Gatlon. Lewis told me he didn't see the soldiers take her, and I pray that proves to be true.

I rake a hand through my hair and step outside, my heart still pounding. Hyde falls into step beside me as I close my door and trudge down the steps with balled fists.

"How many are dead or in jail?" I mutter to him.

"Zero. But there wouldn't have been a problem at all if it weren't for Emery," he says, glaring at me as we walk. "You were being too soft on her, Warren. She would have broken before now if you'd put more pressure on her, and we wouldn't have been in that situation."

We wouldn't be in *this* situation, either. She and the rest of her fellow soldiers were blown to dust when the sloops attacked. She's dead. She's off my hands forever. I should be glad.

But my key to finding Gordon and rescuing Kearon is gone.

I never imagined her death would be so unsatisfying.

I glance back at Isaiah's sloops as they tail us. I haven't seen him since we split ways at Derrick's bar and I took the group of sailors I met on the dock aboard my ship, but I should take aim with a rifle and shoot Isaiah now.

No Emery. No Gordon. No Pereculum. No Kearon.

Now what?

Annette slips in beside me, and my insides melt like hot butter. I haven't seen her since leaving her with my mother before the chaos, and her usually pristine hair is greasy and disheveled like an ashy bird's nest, with random strands falling out of her braids.

"Are you okay?" I snatch her forearm. "How did you get out of the house? *Did* you get everyone out of the house? What did my mother say? Is she all right?"

"Nice to see you too," she huffs, snatching her arm away. "Everyone who was still in the house escaped, and the Midway Patrol arrived and handled the remaining Armada soldiers. Your mother told me to tell you she loves you."

The knot in my chest loosens, and I remind myself to breathe. Her hands tremble as she tucks them in her pockets and walks away.

I don't see her for hours, as much as I would like to indulge in her calming presence. Despite that, I take comfort in watching my crew sail with new life thanks to Isaiah's sailors, and the sun blares as Midway falls further and further behind us. Everyone sweats and pants like dogs as the day wears on, but we are alive.

I suppose I can be grateful for that.

Sweat burns my eyes as I grip the railing in front of my cabin door and stare at the orchestra of sailors below me.

Kearon's mother's sobs echo in the back of my mind. I cannot fathom that I might have to sail back to Lexington empty-handed and explain that I failed them and their son. All the work I did to get here vanished with a single cannon blast.

I flinch at the sound of a bell chiming behind us, and the whole crew turns to see Isaiah's sun-marked ship floating to our left, while the star one brings up the rear.

Though I don't see him, Isaiah's shrill voice pierces the air. "Permission to come aboard?"

I sigh and wave my arm half-heartedly.

"Permission granted!" Hyde's booming voice returns the call.

Each ship's sailors rotate their capstans, dropping the anchors. I fold my arms as they toss hooks across to my ship to pull themselves closer, and, since the water is calm enough, a gangplank is laid between them.

I turn toward my cabin and reach for the door handle.

"Where do you want her?" A gruff voice asks.

Her?

I whirl around and watch one of Isaiah's sailors carry an unconscious girl in his meaty arms. My jaw falls. Shocked relief weakens my knees as I sprint down the steps and fall in line beside the man carrying Emery. I don't see any indication that she's been bashed over the head again, but she looks surprisingly . . . unharmed. Despite Gil's recount of their fight as he and Lucky wrestled her upstairs, she looks untouched. Her red coat looks darker than usual, and when I touch her arm, I find it cold and damp.

Hyde and I exchange shocked glances.

"Take her downstairs," I answer the man's question, exhaling as we approach the stairs. "What happened? Was she in the water?"

"For a minute, I reckon," he replies. "The crew said she jumped off the boat."

"The *Armada's* boat?" Hyde demands.

"Yes."

"Why is she asleep?" I ask.

"She's squirrelly. Our doctor mixed up a drink that knocked her out."

"I've got this," Hyde whispers to me. He points at something over my shoulder, and I turn.

Isaiah's sailors greet their captain as he marches across the gang-plank and steps onto my ship. He's abandoned the charcoal coat and wears a black drawstring shirt whose sleeves have been ripped off to expose his muscled, tattooed arms. His brown sword belt is so loosely secured that it looks as if it's going to slide right off his bony hip.

We briefly make eye contact, and I don't say a word to him as I storm up the stairs and slip inside my cabin. The door stays open as I start to pace. Flex my fingers. Chew my lower lip.

He hasn't even stepped inside before I start laying into him.

"Does the thought of drawing as much attention to yourself as possible always fly through that thick head of yours, Dasher?" I snap. "Do you walk into every situation thinking, 'How can I make the most noise and endanger the people around me?' Are you *that* dense?"

"If I had done nothing, all of us would be dead!" His hands twitch as he closes the door. "And now we have one less Armada ship to deal with! There were no survivors to report back to them, and no one has the slightest idea where we're going."

"And you are *lucky* they don't!" Red spots dance in my vision like pockmarks of anger.

He chuckles and scratches the back of his curly head. "Lucky. Like your boatswain. I didn't know you were such a jokester, Warren."

My face burns with fury as I glance at the ceiling and silently count to three. "Dasher—"

"All is well." He tilts his head and flashes his crooked teeth. "We're all—"

"The man who carried her here said she jumped off the Armada galleon as your crew opened fire and almost *killed* her!" I sound ridiculous defending her life. "Thereby almost wrecking this plan that you begged me to be a part of!"

Isaiah blinks, but his face stays expressionless. "The gunners may not have seen her, or the cannons may have already been lit. I don't know."

I turn away and drag my hands down my face. My chest and shoulders ache from the stress. "How much of Derrick's and my conversation did you hear?"

"I heard bits and pieces." He clears his throat. "He gave you two leads?"

"Yes. You're going to Hale'iwa to meet his contacts." I spin and point my finger at him, glaring. "You're going to act like a *civil* member of society and not cause issues. You may have saved us today, but that is not going to happen again."

He nods and obediently clasps his hands.

"Tell me you understand."

"I understand."

I rub my fingers across my eyes.

"And if there's nothing there?" Isaiah asks, thoughtfully pressing his lips together. "Hale'iwa or Gatlon. What will happen then?"

"Then Miss Walker is going to wish she'd spoken up sooner," I mutter.

"I have an idea about coercing her into telling you what you want. And it's a *good* idea, mind you." His lips curl as he widens his eyes. "This one I have put a fair amount of thought into."

I fold my arms and scowl at him.

"The Riggs twins told me a lot over the days we were together." He stretches his fingers and flexes them like claws. "Captain Walker is not going to break if you keep hurling things at her, but the second someone she cares about is involved . . ." He laughs again and waggles his fingers next to his ear. "She'll writhe like a worm."

My frown deepens. "What are you suggesting?"

He clucks his tongue. "Hale'iwa is only a day's sail from Hana Kailea. There's a certain friend of hers there whom I know she'd hate to see in danger. A certain…" he sucks in a long, whistling breath and balances on his toes. "…princess?"

I blink, and the realization pops into my mind. "Dasher."

"I grew up there and have friends in every corner of the city who can—"

He pauses when I chuckle, which turns into a hearty, genuine, barking laugh.

"Of course the idea of the Armada chasing us isn't enough for you!" I shout, my voice echoing off the wooden bookcases. "You want the royal navy chasing us as well!"

"They won't suspect a thing! Warren—"

I glare at him.

"*Captain.*" Isaiah licks his lips. "I have thought about this. The princess will be leverage. Captain Walker will crumble under that pressure if we use her."

"That's all the more reason to leave her alone!" I fire back. "I don't involve those who have no hand in the matters I deal with."

"Oh, come on. If this is the only barrier between you and Judge Gordon, then I don't believe that would stand. I'm surprised you haven't done this already, frankly." He shifts his weight onto his right foot and lets his opposite hip pop out. "I would have gone after her brothers or her parents, too. Why wouldn't—"

"Because the more people that I drag into this, the higher the liability!" This *imbecile.* "I'm walking on a ledge as is!"

He insists. "Her morality is such a powerful weapon to use against her."

"Perhaps I wasn't clear." I fold my arms and shorten the distance between us with slow, deliberate steps. "If I send you to Hale'iwa and you disobey me and divert to Hana Kailea, I'm going to *burn you alive.* Do you understand?"

"Okay." He holds up his hands in surrender. "I am following orders. It was just an idea."

I raise my eyebrows.

"A *dangerous* idea."

I lean forward and narrow my eyes.

"A dangerous idea that I swear on my position as a captain that I will *not* act upon." Dimples appear in Isaiah's cheeks as he coyly tilts his head. "How's that for cooperative?"

"I won't believe you can be cooperative until I see it." I point to the door. "You better work extra hard to make that so."

28

Emery

Win, win, win. Do what it takes to win.

How pathetic of any want-to-be winner to sit bound in the bowels of a ship, having done nothing but lose.

My aching forehead rests on my tucked knees as I slowly come to.

No friends, no allies, nowhere to turn.

"Wake up, little rebel," a voice coos in my ear. "This isn't the time to rest."

A shudder races down my spine, and the shackles on my hands rattle against the support beam they're bound behind as I flinch. Two meaty fingers dig into my shoulder, and I gasp, jolting forward in pain. My wrists ache from the shackles.

Someone snickers overhead.

I grimace and press my forehead deeper into my knees. "Go away."

"I didn't think you were actually asleep." Hyde chuckles as he slides down the wall across from me, rubbing his leg. His brown vest is missing, and he wears just a white shirt and black trousers. "Maybe if I were a nicer man, I'd apologize."

My eyes are already well adjusted to the dark, but it takes a moment for my memory to resurface. I grimace and drag my tongue across my teeth to expel the rotting taste in my mouth. The last thing I remember is Isaiah's ship's doctor handing me a cup of mystery liquid after they took me aboard the *North Star*.

I glance around, instantly recognizing my storage room prison aboard the *Lost Commandeer*. I blink rapidly and shake my head as the memories of the dock trickle back to my mind, where Hector's lifeless eyes bore into me just like Fallon's did.

I swallow the nausea in my throat and press my head against the support beam.

"What are you doing here?" I frown at Hyde.

"Guard shift rotation." Lucky drops his blue coat on the floor and folds into a cross-legged seat in the middle of the floor. Two wads of bloody cotton are shoved up his nose, and red speckles dot the front of his gray shirt. The V-shaped neckline and chest are loosely tied together with threaded drawstrings. "Harrison deemed that I have a serious injury that I should be resting instead of helping sail the ship," he boasts. "He called it a . . ." He frowns. "A closed . . ."

"Closed head injury," Hyde deadpans.

Lucky smiles and snaps his fingers. "Elbows to the nose are brutal."

Hyde glances at me. "Oh, she knows."

I scowl at him, and he scowls back.

"What does it say about his crew if Chadwick only trusts the man with one working leg to watch the precious prisoner?" I jeer, my voice trembling.

Hyde leans forward and narrows his eyes. "Oh, I'm sorry, the same crew that has taken down two Armada ships in the last five days?"

"You two just don't stop, do you?" Lucky sighs, flipping through his weathered deck of cards.

I shouldn't be wasting what little energy I have on arguing with Hyde, but it's the only way to make them all think this little game isn't working, even though it is. They can't know about the gut-wrenching anxiety following me through every waking moment, the pain with each heartbeat, the weariness . . . and the thought of telling them where Reese is gnawing on my mind.

My brain knows Chadwick would never let me go even if I told him, but my heart doesn't. My heart longs to be with my brothers and parents and to be home where I can run from this ugly, twisted reality.

"You filthy traitor," the voice of the man from the harbor whispers in the back of my mind. *"I hope they lock you away and let you rot."*

My family would see right through the lies. Anyone who still cares about me will, just like Callie said that night at the Tab.

It's going to be okay, I tell myself. *It's going to end.*

I close my eyes and rest my head on my knees again, my chest aching and tight. Just the thought of her or Vaughn is enough to make my skin crawl.

So stupid. Too stupid to see through their act.

My chains jingle, and I twist my neck to see Lucky inserting the cylindrical key into the locks.

"What are you doing?" They clatter to the floor, and instant relief floods my shoulder as my arm falls limp against my side.

"Here." He sits across from me. The cards are laid out on the floor in two piles. "Want to play?"

"Put the bloody cards away," Hyde mutters through a brown mouthful of tobacco. His arms are folded and his eyes are closed.

"Come on." Lucky gestures to me. "I know you're probably bored to tears. My mother taught me this, and it's really easy. Each person flips over the card on top, and then they bet on whether the next card will be higher or lower than the first. Whoever bets the most accurately is the winner."

He flips the top off his pile. "Look. Since I got a king, I can't pull a higher card, so I'm going to bet lower, obviously." He flips the next. "Four. I get a point."

I pull mine. It's a two. "Higher?"

Lucky shrugs. "Sure."

The next is an ace.

"Yikes. No point."

I clutch my arm to my chest and sit back. "I don't want to play."

"Fine." He reshuffles the cards and cups his ear. "Can you hear that? It's the sound of my mother's heart breaking because you don't like her game." He flicks a card at his companion. "Poker, Hyde? Pretty please?"

Hyde mutters something under his breath and scoots forward. Lucky deals, and while Hyde isn't paying attention, he slips one of the cards up the sleeve of his shirt.

I stare, a bit surprised.

They play. "You have something on your chest." Lucky leans forward and points to Hyde's sternum, using the moment of distraction to slip the card out of his sleeve and into his hand. He wins with ease.

I bite my cheek. I suppose the nickname Cheater doesn't roll off the tongue as nicely as Lucky does.

Hyde sits back against the wall and folds his arms. "Your mother's heart is breaking because you wasted your potential and became a gambler."

"Where is she?" I ask out of genuine curiosity. "Your mother."

"Turtle Point." Lucky gathers his deck. "I was born there."

"Why would you ever leave?"

He quirks an eyebrow. "I wouldn't say I left."

I frown, but he won't look at me. Hyde shoots me a dirty look.

"Chadwick bought me out of an indenture when I was nineteen, and the return was that I come sail with him," he says at last. "Boatswain skills and all."

"Some freedom." I clear my throat. "He bought you out and trapped you in another."

"Is that so?" He narrows his eyes at me. "With one instance, my parents were tricked into selling me to a shipmaster, and I was trapped on a slaving ship and not allowed to set foot on land, and on the other, I get to see my family once a month and send a decent bit of my pay back to them. Is *that* forced servitude?"

"Why haven't you left and gone back to them?"

"Why would I when I have a job like this? I love sailing and I'm making money doing it."

I turn away, shaking my head.

"You're so quick to dismiss Chadwick when you have no idea what he's doing for all of us," Lucky snaps. "You're calling all the things he's done bad when in reality, most of the people he's gone after deserve what they got."

"That's not your job to decide."

"And somehow it's yours?" Hyde scoffs. "What good have you done to merit that? Where does the good outweigh the bad?"

"What he's done for you hasn't changed what he's done to other people!" I shout. "Should I tell you how many bodies I've pulled out of the burning ship wreckage he's left in his wake? How many small coastal towns I've walked through where people are sobbing in the streets because of everything he's done? What *you've* done?"

"Do you know the dirty deals that run out of those small, innocent-looking little towns?" Hyde leans forward. "Is it really a bad thing when something like that happens?"

"It is when innocent people die!"

"Tell that to Captain Scott," Lucky mutters.

"Yes, and some hypocrite you are." Hyde rolls his eyes. "You know better than any of us the dirt that Padstow and the Armada have tried to hide. Look at what happened this morning! The Armada is basically one step from colonizing other cities in the name of 'justice.'" He creates air quotes with his fingers. "That captain's Seal is not the badge of honor you think it is."

I *hate* that what he says stirs something deep in my chest.

I have always turned a blind eye to the captains who abuse their power and the higher commanding officers who let it happen, because I knew when I became a captain, I wouldn't act that way. A good captain is poised, honest, and won't overstep the clear boundaries of power.

But all of that changes when they aren't under a scrutinizing eye, doesn't it?

Look at how you acted when you led that team to Lexington alone. Look how you reacted when you interrogated Kearon alone.

The little voice grows louder and louder in my mind. My entire life has been dedicated to a facade that's hollow and rotting underneath. It can't mean nothing. It *can't.*

Or can it?

It means something because of the things I was *supposed* to do, as if it were going to erase the bad. I was supposed to capture Chadwick and round up the others who are vile monsters just like him, but now I don't think I will.

And that means it will all be for naught.

There's a knock on the door, and Chadwick pokes his head inside. The other two frown at him.

"Give us a moment." He glares at me.

It's always a glare.

29

Warren

"GOOD MORNING, *ladies and gentlemen. Today, the Messenger comes to you after a rambunctious night on the waters between Marshland and Port Mariker, where authorities from Padstow got into a fiery altercation with an unmarked ship. The soldiers on the* Chaplain's Heart, *one of Padstow's most successful pirate-hunting ships, are claiming that Warren Chadwick was aboard the unmarked ship, captaining an illegal shipment of weapons that was headed north. Emery Walker, navigator of the ship and daughter of co-commanders Jonathan and Marisa Walker, was asked to comment.*

"*'We're doing okay.'"* Her voice is grainy on the old capsule. *"'Our crew is a bit shaken, but we're doing everything we can to track down Chadwick. His face is well-known in that area. If you've seen any sign of him, please don't hesitate to reach out. You'll be helping to protect yourself and your loved ones if we can catch him.'"*

I roll my eyes.

"*'We're in the middle of tracking the ship now to seize all of those illegal weapons,'"* she continues. *"'We believe he was traveling north to exchange the weapons with Eden Purdue, another dangerous pirate who frequents the Northern Territories . . .'"*

"Garbage," I mutter, ripping the capsule out of the recorder and tossing it into the pile with the other old editions, including today's.

That record should have gone as follows:

"Chadwick was nowhere near Marshland or Port Mariker the night this happened. You've got it all wrong. It's obvious to anyone with a brain behind their eyes that they're pinning this on me to put everyone on high alert. Pay no mind. The blonde girl in red is a liar."

The next capsule is from the Shining Star and says the same thing about an incident from last year, where a fight—sorry, *altercation*—was skewed to preserve her reputation as a fighter. Almost twenty members of her crew died. She and I were locked in a duel in a cramped alleyway all the way up in Osecola, where I would have killed her had her captain not stepped in to save her.

All of these capsules sit in a box that I keep so I can listen to them over and over, nurturing the raging thoughts that consume every inch of space in my head.

The obsessive hatred and bitterness are unbecoming and give me a headache, but I don't care. The facade must burn, and everyone must know.

I have seen it enough times throughout my life to know that the web of lies and deceit they're spinning will never end well. Spinning the web is what got my very first captain arrested when I was a deckhand scrubbing salt and stray gunpowder off the ship. I watched the body of a good friend of mine tumble into the water when an enemy came to collect a trade he lied about obtaining. When I was a navigator, I watched a fellow navigator be arrested when another lied about his involvement in the burning of a trading company owner's home. I watched my innocent errand boy carted off to prison because a lie was constructed about him.

Lies make the world go round, after all.

I tried not to lie to Kearon, but as much as I tried to keep him as far from my work as possible, he asked me questions about the crew and what it was like to be a sailor. My description of the boundless freedom of the sea would never suffice. He would have to see it; he'd have to breathe the salt air and feel the ocean mist to truly understand it, and it was the one thing I could never give him. That paradise was not worth the pain of the world I work in, and even then, I could not protect him from it.

I close my eyes. The hankering for justice is strong for him, just as it is for Cassie and the others who were with me the night of the attack on Padstow. They weren't my friends, but we shared enough trust in our professional relationship that they agreed to follow me into the chaos of my plan. Once I get Kearon out and back to his parents, I want to go back for them and watch Padstow burn with them, just like Derrick was talking about.

I grab the most recent capsule from my drawer, which is The Shout's newest edition, and set it on the spindle after flicking the cap open. Midway promotes The Shout the most, even though it's a glorified gossip column.

"Shout here, Shout there, Shout everywhere! Our reporters were able to get an exclusive interview with a handful of the aristocrats from Padstow regarding the Emery Walker situation.

"'I'm shocked," said Mariane Hadley, wife to one of the most successful traders from Padstow. "'If I had any idea who she really was when I shook her hand on the day of the Seal, then I would've never done it. Jonathan and Marisa are dear friends, but I would have never.'

"'I can't say that I'm surprised,' Eldon Riggs commented when approached. 'That family always gave my company trouble when we tried to work together. I knew at least one of them would fly off the handle at some point. I think that everything that happens from here onward is deserved.'"

I truly hoped he would feel the sweet warmth of justice, but that might not be so now that his twins are on the run.

"The Armada is considering stripping Walker of her newly claimed title and revoking the rights of the Captain's Seal. Here to comment on the matter is Armada Commander Jonathan Walker:

"'We are conducting an investigation to get to the bottom of this,' he said. 'A decision will be made when the facts come to light.'"

How *damning.*

"Padstow has been in an odd spot considering the situation with Emery Walker, as well as the mysterious disappearance of Chief Judge Reese Gordon. Interim Judge Elijah Phipps has dedicated much of his time to ensuring the public is calm amidst the chaos of those events and the recent attacks on various Armada ships. Many civilians we spoke to referenced the attack from a few years ago, where pirates Warren Chadwick, Cassie Dorenbasch, Darius Reed, and others swarmed the beaches of Padstow and left it in a state of unruly panic.

They compared that to this recent attack and are worried about what that bodes for the days to come."

I stop the capsule and, with the spindle in hand, exit my cabin and cross to the stairway, descending down to the ship's belly. I listen at the door of Emery's makeshift prison. She and Hyde are arguing, much to the surprise of no one. I roll my eyes and rap on the wood as I enter.

"Give us a moment." I glare at her.

"But he was winning the argument." Lewis's shoulders droop as he pockets his cards. "Whatever will we do without knowing who can yell the loudest?"

"Oh, shut up," Hyde grumbles as Lewis helps him to his feet. He makes a rude gesture at Emery as he and Lewis exit.

I sigh and glance at the ceiling.

Emery's injured shoulder is tenser than the other as she holds her arm in her lap and stares at the floor. Most of the bruises and cuts on her face have finally healed, but the bridge of her nose is slightly angled to the left.

I open my mouth, but she cuts me off.

"I don't want to hear it," she mumbles.

I grin. "You're thinking about it, aren't you?"

Her eyes plead with me as she looks up. "We can negotiate anything else."

The mask is slipping. The defiance is finally weakening.

"Your family was on yesterday morning's news," I say, folding my arms. "Or your father was, at least."

Her jaw falls.

"It's a bit odd that it's been nearly a month and we haven't heard much from any of them. We haven't heard much from anyone, really. Not Gordon's wife, not the Scotts." My grin widens. "Or what about your little princess friend Theadora and her family? Or do you call her Thea? Surely with her power and prestige, they would have spoken out."

She bites her cheek and stares at her feet, glassy-eyed. "What did the Riggses *not* tell you?"

The name catches in her throat, and I watch her shoulders tighten as she brings her knees to her chest. She clenches her quivering jaw.

"If it makes you feel better, I don't think they're thinking much about you," I say boredly, stretching my wrists. "So it might save you a breath or two from sobbing in the middle of the night."

She doesn't say anything.

"You don't seem too concerned to hear what your father said about you. Do you want to know?" I spread my hands for dramatic effect, as if the words unfold from my palms. "'We are conducting an investigation to get to the bottom of this. A decision will be made when the facts come to light.'"

Not, *"We don't believe anything that's being said and will get to the bottom of this."* Not, *"We are doing everything we can and won't go down without a fight."* A cold, emotionless punch—not a public defense or rebuke of the story. It hits exactly where I want it to.

My lips curl. "He doesn't care. He isn't worried. *Why* is that, do you think?"

"You won't get far unless you find whoever is selling your secrets," she replies, finally meeting my eyes. "The Armada never works with Midway or their navy, and there was no good reason for them to be there unless someone *told* them I would be. Whoever it is has probably already sent word back to them."

"That's the most useful thing you've ever told me in weeks."

"It's Dasher." She preys on the subject, leaning forward with an eager verve. "It has to be. What is he doing here? Why—"

"Slow down." I hold up my hand and pinch my fingers together, grimacing. "Isaiah told me of dealings he had with Gordon, but I assume you don't know anything about that?"

"I don't." Emery stares at the floor. "I don't know a lot of what he's done behind the curtain."

"She finally admits it," I boast to the imaginary audience.

"Why is Isaiah here?"

What's the harm in telling her? Maybe if I give a bit of leeway, she'll be more open with me.

"Well, he's not *here* on the ship," I continue, watching for any slight shift in her expression that may give away if Gatlon or Hale'iwa is Gordon's hiding spot, but her expression is as guarded as the Pereculum. She doesn't even speak when I'm finished, which I'm not sure how to take. It might just be the exhaustion. Lines are carved into the corners of her sunken eyes.

"I haven't told my crew yet, by the way, so there's no possible way this mysterious traitor would know our destination and could alert him." I shrug.

The skin between her eyes crinkles in thought. "Who told you about Gatlon and Hale'iwa?"

"That's none of your business."

She doesn't press anymore, thankfully. A shadow of worry hangs over her face as she hugs her torso and takes a deep breath. Even though she's stubborn, her weakness is a high that I will never come down from.

She opens her mouth, then closes it.

"What is it?" I ask.

She licks her lips. "Was there nothing else that my family said?"

I raise my eyebrows and spin the capsule again, watching as she desperately tries to mask the pain wrenching through her expression.

She won't meet my eyes, and I know why. From what I was told by the Riggses, her golden, sparkling career is second only to her relationship with her brothers and her parents. Callie specifically told me about the bond she shares with her studious oldest brother and her brash, meatheaded second brother. It seemed to me that bits of them existed as a dichotomy within her. Bits of her parents' strength and leadership skills. Bits of Charles's brain and Miles's doggedness. She is poised, but not shy. She is strong-willed, but knows when to hold her tongue and listen. She is everything anyone would look for in a leader.

Or she *was* everything, I suppose.

If I were kind, outwardly acknowledging her separation from them would be the only shred of empathy she would ever receive from me. My mother has been my lifeline and my greatest teacher in the pressing moments of discomfort, the only constant in my rambunctious, whirlwindish lifestyle. I imagine it's the same for Emery. My words can hound and hound and hound on her, but the ones from her father? One of her greatest teachers?

I can see it in her eyes. And if I can see it, I can prey on it. I can prey on the weak, exhausted little girl instead of the assertive soldier with a reputation to uphold.

I inhale. "Instead of a threat, how about a proposition? You can go home to them, that comfort, and forget about all of this if you tell me what I want to know. I will drop you off at the nearest port."

Her jaw tightens.

Yes. Break. Break.

"I don't believe you," she mumbles.

I narrow my eyes. "What do you gain from protecting Gordon? What do you *lose* from it?"

"It's not about—" She cuts herself off. "I don't gain anything through betraying anyone."

"Ah." It clicks, like a puzzle piece snapping into place, and I chuckle. "I should have known."

She glares. "You *don't* know."

"This is part of the facade, isn't it?" I clasp my hands behind my back. "I think you're still clinging to who you used to be."

"*Used* to be?" she snaps, sitting upright. "Who are you to tell me—"

"The golden, exemplary captain everyone has come to know you as." I tilt my head and skim my tongue over my teeth, sneering. "A good little captain doesn't betray her superiors, does she? When did goodness suddenly mean giving in to the echoes of what's being said around you?"

I adjust the cuffs of my coat sleeve and groan. "Lying is so *exhausting.* Lying to yourself is even worse, Miss Walker. You're too intelligent to waste this much time on it, so why? Especially when Gordon has made it clear that he wouldn't do the same for you."

She huffs because she knows I'm right.

"My offer still stands." I head for the door. "I would at least consider it. Perhaps you'll take it and forget your pride, for once."

. . .

The silence creeps behind me like a shadow, bringing a blank mind.

I watch my crew through my cabin's window, and they seem at ease despite the chaos that they've been around. Kit sits near the bow, twisting the tuning heads on his banjo while the others sit in clusters across the deck. A few of them are perched on a short wooden ledge built into the side about four feet below the railing. Their shirts and weapons are draped over the railing as they dunk buckets on strings into the water and scrub their arms and chests with soap.

All is well. I envy it. They seem unaffected by the chaos swirling around their heads—or if they feel it, they certainly aren't showing it.

I wish I could mask my anxiety that well. First, it was Kearon, then having to change the plan to capture Emery, then my finding my sick mother's worsening condition, then Isaiah showing up, and the chaos and death at the harbor . . . each is another mountain piled onto my shoulders and another thought weighing on my mind in the late hours of the night.

For me, it is odd to be surrounded by death but unaffected by it, like walking through a storm where you are the only one with an umbrella.

I close my eyes and stretch my neck.

We won't be ambushed again. It won't happen because I'm going to find this traitor before he gets any of us killed.

But who could it be?

Lewis is reliable, but are there any other skeletons he's hiding?

What about Brooks and the way he scratches the mole on his lip when he's about to do something he shouldn't? What of Gil, and his calm, reserved demeanor? What storm lies underneath that?

Who wrote to Gordon and to the Armada under my nose? Who could possibly be covering their tracks this well?

It may be the Riggses. Maybe to gain favor with those who have scorned their family.

I don't know.

My eyes flick to Chip, whose feathery chest expands and constricts with each breath, in his burrow, in his trap.

Trap.

I tilt my head.

Perhaps a trap to catch a rat?

Derrick spoke highly of the Valentines. I know they have their dirty fingers in many fields across Gatlon, and I don't doubt they could be useful in the avenue of catching a rat.

Perhaps useful in making our dear little golden girl speak.

The possibilities run rampant in my ever-firing mind, like snaps of lightning behind my eyes.

Just the sight of her broken-down, weary persona justifies the lengths I've gone to for this, but I wonder if what I said was right. A captain wouldn't betray her superiors, but what else is stopping her?

Someone knocks softly on my door, and I turn to see Annette slipping inside. She cocks her head. "Captain."

I smile without meaning to, and all thoughts fall silent. "Miss Navigator."

Her hair is out of its usual knot and curtains her face quite beautifully. She's also dressed in a thin wool sweater that I've never seen before, which is a subtle beige that matches her hair almost perfectly. Her cheeks are rosy from the chill ocean breeze.

She shuts the door. "Do we have our heading?"

"That depends on whether you can keep a secret."

Her blue eyes narrow.

"This traitor we have is somehow in direct contact with the Armada and has been relaying our location to them," I say. "Isaiah will meet us in Gatlon, but I don't want to tell the crew that. We should be fine as long as we don't stay for more than a day or two and give the Armada time to get there after we arrive."

"So..." She bites her cheek. "How are you going to catch this traitor?"

"I want to have the Valentines screen the mail that goes through their outpost when we arrive, and..."

My mind goes blank, almost entrancingly. My heart flutters when a small smile curls across her rosy lips.

"It's the obvious next step." She shrugs.

"I..." I clear my throat. "Do you know who the Valentines are?"

She nods.

"I want them to have their . . . people, I suppose, screen the mail that comes through. I may even have Hyde post up there and watch who from the crew goes to send mail so we know exactly who it is. The Valentines certainly won't know."

"Well, Hyde's not going to be happy about that."

"He's the only one I trust besides you," I say. "And I'd like you to stay with me, if you're willing."

She puckers her lips, though not in disdain.

"I just need to write a letter to them." I turn back to my desk. "*Hyde* needs to write a letter."

"Your aversion to writing is so interesting to me."

"It's such a *bore*," I groan, slipping out of my coat and draping it over the arm of my chair. "Why would I sit in front of a blank parchment trying to come up with a jumble of nonsense that nobody is going to read? What a waste of time."

She folds her arms and pulls the sleeves of her sweater over her hands, and her casual, relaxed persona captivates my attention. Her eyes slink up and down my body. "What else has Emery said to you?"

And the itching returns. I blink.

Emery.

The monopoly this stupid girl holds on my psyche is ridiculous.

They haven't said enough about her, my mind taunts. *They need to believe the bad so the good doesn't stand a chance.*

Stealing her family's money was a stone. Captain Scott's ship was a boulder. This attack on the ship in Midway will be, too.

But more, more, more. There has to be more you can do.

Annette notices my blank stare. "Don't spiral."

"I'm not spiraling." I perch on the edge of my desk. "It's a constant want. A constant, 'What can I do to ruin her? When will all the ruin her and Padstow have caused be paid for by what's happening now?'"

She tilts her head. A strand of mousy hair falls in her face. I stare at it, as if my gaze will magically tuck it back into place.

"The perfect revenge isn't possible," she says. "Perfect is impossible."

I scoff. "You don't know that."

"You've done quite enough. It's *good* enough."

"Is it?" My spine straightens. The thoughts snap, snap, snap through my head, and I blink. "It's not been good enough to force her to tell me about Gordon or good enough to rescue Kearon and the others inside the Pereculum, so obviously I'm doing *something* wrong."

"Warren." Suddenly, the distance between us has closed. She grabs a fistful of my shirt at the rib, which catches me off guard. We lock eyes.

"You sound ridiculous," she mumbles.

"Passion is not ridiculous," I reply matter-of-factly, wrinkling my forehead.

"It is when it consumes every waking moment of your life." Her eyes are like daggers, bluer than the ocean. "There's more to focus on than just that."

She's right. More to focus on, like the shirt collar itching the back of my neck, the feeling of sweat trickling down my back, the way her fingers relax against my torso. Her touch is grounding and surprisingly gentle.

I reach for her other arm, pulling up her sleeve to reveal blood-stained bandages from the scuffle in Midway. I hold her wrist and touch the cottony gauze.

"I think you're deflecting," she says softly, tilting her head to catch my eye, "By talking about Emery."

Stars, her eyes.

"Is this about your mother?"

My jaw clenches again as I stare straight ahead. "Partially." My tongue curls in my mouth. "She needs a doctor, yet refuses to see one. I'm just worried."

I think she senses the slight tremor in my voice, and her eyes narrow on mine as if she can see just how long they've been open in the dark hours of the night as I wonder, hope, worry.

"Is that it?" she asks softly.

"Is what it?"

Annette's lips pucker slightly. She drops her hand, but I catch her wrist.

"This is not a sign of weakness, and I don't want it viewed as such," I say faintly. "Please."

Her eyes flick to her wrist, and then back to me.

I wait for her reaction, her movement, afraid of shattering the fragile air. I wonder if she can hear my heartbeat as loudly as I can.

The smell of her perfume is intoxicating. Somehow, we become so close that I can feel her shallow breaths on my cheeks, and her head tips slightly. Before she can fully pull away, I grab the sides of her head and plant a kiss on her lips.

She loses her balance and presses her hands against my chest, and even though I know it startles her, I relish in the silence it brings to my mind. Eventually, she settles into the kiss and rests her hands on my shoulders, and after a moment, she pulls away, jaw ajar. The flame burns out, and the ticking thoughts return to my mind when she opens her eyes.

We pause, shocked at what just occurred. I blink rapidly. I want *so* badly to kiss her again and let the hours and panic and stress fade into nothing in the back of my mind.

A transaction.

I suddenly step back as a chill races down my spine, repulsed at the thought.

"What's wrong?"

I want it like my lungs burn for air, but I would be a monster to treat her like that.

Would I?

"No." I turn away, rubbing my hand over my mouth. "This is going to be transactional, and I know that's not what you want."

"It doesn't have to be that way," she says matter-of-factly. "If you stop *thinking* of it that way—"

"It's not that simple," I retort.

"It *is* that simple. If you feel instead of think, then it is."

She puts it so simply when it's everything but that.

I ball my trembling hands into fists, terrified to even look at her again. My stomach clenches when she steps into my line of sight and cups the back of my neck. She glares at me and tilts her head. "You're going to ruin this if you keep thinking so much."

My jaw falls as I stare at her like a dumbfounded fool, and I blink. "I suppose you're right."

She pulls my head down and kisses me again, and the silence

returns. The doubt subsides. The anxiety vanishes. It's all feelings, not thoughts bouncing through my head like shouts in a cave. It's the feeling of her hair between my fingers and the silk touch of her fingers against my jaw and neck.

And soon, all that exists is the feeling of her lips curling into a smile.

30

FIVE DAYS after the scuffle in Midway, my crew works in near silence as the *Lost Commandeer* docks and the gangplank drops in Gatlon. Isaiah's crew sticks out like a sore thumb with their disheveled appearances, clashing with my strict standards.

Gatlon's quiet, creaky harbor is shaped like a gigantic capital L, and most small cutters and barges are tied right where the stony land meets the water, making the horizontal part of the L. The larger ships line up along the vertical part, where the mossy dock stretches almost four hundred yards into the ocean.

I step out into the misty early morning air, adjusting the collar of my coat, and Hyde waves to me as he limps ashore and beelines for the mailing outpost. Since Chip is still with my mother—or perhaps already in Gatlon's outpost—I used Isaiah's shearwater to send a letter to the Valentines about my plan, and I requested they send a response to a small city called New Tobac where we stopped to resupply. I only waited a day for their reply and their promise to have guards screen each and every letter to hopefully catch this traitor.

Perhaps this will finally give me useful fodder to usher *something* along. Maybe I won't have to live constantly looking over my shoulder and can focus solely on cracking Emery open once I shoot this traitor and toss his body overboard.

I'm getting *very* tired of living off of ifs and maybes.

I scan the deck, watching for Annette as I maneuver to the stairs. I descend to the lower deck where the charting room is, and I turn the door handle and peek inside. A single lit lantern sits on the circular table, but my attention falls to the blanket-covered lump curled up in the corner of the room.

I crouch beside it and shake it, smiling. "Why do you insist on sleeping down here?"

Annette pulls the blanket back and squints at me, her hair frizzy and disheveled. "You always disrupt my beauty sleep," she mumbles, her voice muffled by the grogginess of sleep.

"I'm so sorry. How can I make it up to you?"

She rubs her eyes and sits up. The neck of her sweater is pulled to one side and exposes her sharp collarbone. "You could stay down here with me and hide from the hooligans."

"You dare insult my crew?" I dramatically smack my chest and hold my other hand out to help her stand.

"I'm just telling the truth," she replies as we rise. She stretches her arms over her head and winces. "You can't fault me."

I wrap my arms around her waist and kiss her, and she melts into it as she stands on her tiptoes and drapes her arms around my shoulders and neck.

My years on the sea have robbed me of a chance at connection like this, but she and I fit together like a hand and an old glove despite the forced abstinence. She gives me the peace I've been craving.

"You don't have to sleep down here," I whisper against her jaw.

"I prefer the quiet." She traces her nails across the back of my head. "I wasn't kidding when I called them hooligans."

"They aren't all bad." I pull back and frown at her.

"I didn't say they were bad, but I have no place in their..." She narrows her eyes. "Boyish conversations."

I chuckle as she presses her forehead into my shoulder.

"Perhaps those boyish conversations will reveal who is betraying me," I say. "I need to go investigate while everyone is upstairs."

She looks up at me and scrunches her face. "If you insist."

I give her another quick kiss and disappear from the room, soon emerging on the deck just above us to sniff out this traitor. I peek under the beds and peel back the sheets, hoping to find a note or a letter hidden away. I look inside the hammocks and check for any loose boards or cracks in the floor or walls, but there's nothing.

"Has anyone seen the captain?" a voice asks above my head.

I angrily wipe the sweat off my brow and storm back upstairs.

After another hour or so of the others packing their things and prepping the ship, half the crew disembarks with knapsacks slung over their shoulders. The other half will watch the ship and keep to the harbor until later tonight.

The Valentines promised us rooms at an inn and someone to escort us there, and I keep my head on a swivel as my group of thirty-five trudges through the dirty streets, following a man wearing a rose on his lapel.

The Dragonfly Inn is a tall, cream-colored building with a slanted wooden roof, and it's nestled in the middle of town. The interior is lit only by lanterns and smells like roses, courtesy of the vase of pink petals and vibrant green leaves sitting at the reception desk.

Everyone shuffles down the narrow hallway to their first-floor rooms. I shut the door when I enter mine, blocking out the noise of the others, and, for once, there's peace. I drop my bag on the polished floor and stand smiling over the en suite bathtub. I get it filled and slip in, relishing not having to wash myself with a salty wet rag and call it bathing. I'd sit in the warm bath for hours if I had the time, but alas, this judge isn't going to catch himself.

Twenty minutes later, I pull on my coat and step into the hall. Gil is leaning against the door to his room, impatiently tapping his foot. He looks cleaner as well, dressed in a rust-colored shirt, a tan vest, and black pants. He's also shaved, leaving nothing but brown stubble along his jaw. His usually greasy hair looks lighter in color now that it's properly washed, and he's styled it so it parts near the side of his head and traces down his shoulders like long, curly snakes.

I lock my door and pocket the key, frowning at Gil's lack of metal-wear. I'm not usually a prude about showing my arms in public, and neither is he. "Where are your weapons?"

He opens the vest to reveal one of Brooks's around-the-ribs sheaths and a pistol holster under his arm. "They're inconspicuous."

"Ah." I grin. "I'm surprised Brooks let you borrow it."

He wrinkles his crooked nose and shrugs. "I wouldn't say he *allowed* me, necessarily."

I watch him for a moment as he tightens the leather straps of the sheath. His tongue pokes out from the corner of his mouth in concentration.

What good would you gain from betraying me? I wonder.

He knows a thing or two about disloyalty. I recruited him after he abandoned his post as a deckhand in Osecola's navy and needed a place to hide from arrest. I'm sure there's a warrant with his name on it floating around somewhere, but he hasn't looked back in over two years.

Or is that the perfect motivation? To gain favor with someone in power who could protect him?

Tahj and Alexis, also clean and prim, open the door to their shared room. Alexis has trimmed and shaped his mustache so it isn't stretching ridiculously far past the corners of his lips, and Tahj has tied his dreadlocks into a knot on the back of his head.

I suspect them less than I do Gil because they've been in my crew twice as long and have always been reliable. Tahj needed work after failing out of school, and Alexis had a petty criminal record he was running from, but never once have they questioned me or my authority.

I suppose today will tell. If Gordon is here, and they defy me, that will be my indicator.

I adjust my collar and take a deep breath. "Shall we?"

31

I press the heels of my hands to my forehead and breathe, willing the knot in my chest to loosen.

"Headache?"

"Mm-hm." I open my eyes as Harrison sits in front of me with his wound cleaning kit in his lap.

Brooks runs a hand through his yellowish hair and glares at me from the corner of the doctor's cabin, and I avert my gaze. He and Hyde are the two I worry about being near the most for fear of catching a knife to the back or another broken nose, and his hand rests on the hilt of one of the three knives he has sheathed on his belt.

Harrison's fingers are cold on my skin as he presses the alcohol-soaked cotton to the cuts, but I barely feel it. My mind wanders far, far away from this moment.

"A decision will be made when the facts come to light."

My father may have just been saying that for the sake of the news. I don't imagine defending me would earn him the support he and my family need right now.

I close my eyes. I just need to find a way home and fix this mess.

If it is even still home. If they'll have me.

If.

If you'd acted quicker to save Fallon— If you'd paid closer attention to the twins and their behavior—

My stomach churns at the memory of Vaughn's whispers. I wonder how long I let him touch me and kiss me after his intentions had changed.

Harrison taps my knee to get my attention and sends Brooks from the room so I can slip my arm out of my blouse and let the doctor rewrap my shoulder.

If I'd paid more attention to what Gordon was doing, maybe I would have known something was wrong. Maybe he would have told me to run if he knew Chadwick was coming if I weren't so self-absorbed.

The voices are like hammers relentlessly pounding the inside of my skull.

Maybe if you'd done better.

Maybe Gordon would have warned you that Chadwick was coming instead of leaving you behind.

I open my eyes as Harrion uses a safety pin to secure the fabric wrappings in place, and he helps me maneuver my arm back into my shirt. The wrappings are wound around the joint, and a long strip wraps around my chest, ribs, and back to keep everything as tight as possible.

Harrison hops up for a moment and returns from the cupboard with a cup of brown liquid. "It's a painkiller for your head, but it might make you a bit drowsy." His lips twist as he motions for Brooks. "It isn't poisoned, either. I promise."

I glance at Brooks entering the room as I lift the cup to my lips. I can't quite figure him out. He's marching to the beat of Chadwick's drum like a mindless puppet, perhaps hungry for his captain's approval? Chasing the coattails of the people above him?

Maybe not. Maybe I just need somewhere to hurl my bitterness that isn't my own situation.

He takes me back to the hold, and the tightness returns to my chest as I sit with my back against the support beam and let him click the shackles around my wrists. My coat lies on the floor beside me.

The smell of sweat and salt radiating off his body makes the hairs inside my nose curl. He tugs on the chain to ensure the shackles are secure, then scrapes his tongue over the chip in his front tooth, the result of our last scuffle. "I'll be back soon enough to return the favor."

Much to my relief, he doesn't stay in the room like the others have. I wrap my fingers around the chains and tug on the shackles, praying that this time, they might just break.

I rest my head against the support beam and close my eyes, which does little to quell my headache, and the pain in my shoulder, and the crackles of pain in my healing nose . . .

The chains slip from my hands and drop to the ground, and I flinch awake as my injured arm goes limp. Disoriented, I blink the blur from my eyes, my heart racing as I brace for one of Brooks's knives to enter my line of sight. "Wait—"

A hand presses over my mouth, and Annette crouches in front of me, her blue eyes wide and stern. She's dressed in a black form-fitting coat, where the ruffled sleeves and neckline of a white blouse poke out from underneath.

"Most everyone is above deck, but I suggest you stay quiet," she whispers. "Come with me."

What?

I blink and scrunch my face as she reaches the door, nodding for me to follow. I clamber to my feet, and each creaky floorboard's moan is magnified tenfold as she and I traverse the maze of catacombs. I forget how large this ship is when I'm crammed in the small storage room.

We ascend to the level just above the storage room, and Annette unlocks one door with a shiny brass key.

Maps and desks with stacks of long, flat drawers line the room's perimeter, but unlike the disorganization of charting rooms on most ships, there's a compartment or jar for every pen, ruler, and tack neatly arranged all over the space. Lanterns sit atop the corners of a world map spread across the round table in the center of the room.

My nose twitches at the scent of ink as Annette shuts the door and locks it again. She tucks loose strands of mousy hair behind her ears and takes a deep, shaky breath.

"You can sit down," she says quietly.

"What is this?"

Her jaw stays tight as she crouches to quietly rummage through one of the cabinets.

I cradle my arm and sit in one of the chairs around the table. "What are you going to say if someone catches you?" I deadpan.

She spins on the balls of her feet and presses her finger to her lips again, her eyes wide. "The crew knows that I am not to be touched or bothered, but they *cannot* hear us or there'll be trouble."

I watch her curiously as she returns to the cabinet. "This is a terrible interrogation," I mumble, stifling a yawn. "You must be Chadwick's last resort if—"

She sets a glass bottle of water and a lumpy canvas sack on the table. I arch an eyebrow.

"It's just meat and bread." She wipes the sweat from her forehead with the sleeve of her coat. "And perhaps a swallow or two of whiskey for the pain."

I peek inside the bag and find a leather water skin—or *whiskey* skin, in this case— to accompany the food, and my hollow stomach grumbles.

"I could have found better medicine, but Harrison doesn't label any of his concoctions." She rolls her eyes.

"Whiskey is a fine medicine." I narrow my eyes. "It's also a fine bribe."

"It's not a bribe." She settles into the chair across from me and folds her hands in her lap. "It's to ease the tension."

I grab the whiskey and down it before even batting an eye at the rest she's provided. My eyes water.

She wrinkles her forehead. "Alcohol on an empty stomach?"

"Quit beating around the bush." I clear my burning throat. "What is this?"

"I want you to hear me out before you make any snap judgments. That's my only ask."

I tilt my head.

She glances at the ceiling and takes a deep breath, her fingers fidgeting in her lap. "When I decided to leave Padstow, the only immediate chance I had to run far, far away was a charter ship that I couldn't afford. I was interning for Gordon at the time, and he was the only one who knew of my situation."

Her attention zeroes in on a knot in the wooden wall to her right. Her throat bobs. "I was running from a household you would have never survived in. All because of a . . ." She glances up again as tears well in her eyes. ". . . drunken, disloyal father who didn't love my mother and me, and a mother who thought I was her little puppet to play with and manipulate."

I raise my eyebrows.

"And Gordon . . ." She trails off, sighing and shaking her head. "I would have never viewed him as a man with a good heart, but he paid for the charter and sent me off with four hundred novas in my pocket. It was just ironic that I happened to run into Warren after."

She lowers her voice to a faint whisper. "You can imagine how I felt when he wanted to unfold this little revenge plot on the man I owe my freedom to, and it wasn't . . ." She winces as she uncharacteristically fumbles for the words. "It doesn't sit right that Gordon did something for me for nothing in return. Writing to him and warning him about Warren was my way of paying him back."

But you didn't warn me, and I was your friend.

But did I deserve it?

What a selfish thought.

Maybe I should have paid a bit more attention to her as she sat quietly behind me in class, or spoken to her as our classmates' wandering, judgmental eyes followed her down the hallway. Maybe that sort of detail could have saved me from heartbreak at the Riggses' hands.

But I was just so wrapped up in . . . everything. Perhaps too much.

My stomach knots as I force the thought away. "So it was you who tipped off the Armada about us in Midway, wasn't it?" I ask. "Why?"

"No. That wasn't me. I'd given Gordon a rough estimate of where we'd be going and when, and he may have told them." She bites her lip. "I told him mailing back to me or anyone was too risky in case anything he sent was intercepted, but apparently he's been doing *something* since he was spotted in Gatlon & Hale'iwa."

"We don't know if he's really there, though."

"Those are the closest mailing ports for people in . . . " She hesitates. "For people in you-know-where who don't own a bird."

I sit back, shaking my head as if that's going to clear the whirlwind of exhausted confusion. I blink the weariness from my eyes. "You know where he is and you haven't told Chadwick?"

"Gordon spoke so fondly of you-know-where, but this little scheme Warren is orchestrating to find him is going to get out of hand." She leans forward, her eyes sharp like piercing blue crystals. "I don't trust Isaiah, either. I think he's a powder keg that's going to explode and put Warren and the rest of us in a really terrible spot."

I toss the empty whiskey skin on the table. "And you're telling me this, *why?*"

"Because you want to protect Gordon as much as I do." Annette presses her palms onto the map. "And because you aren't stupid, you'll take this opportunity to cooperate and ensure that he stays safe."

"Why should I believe you're going to betray Chadwick after kissing his heels for all these years?" I spit.

"Do *not* belittle me like that," she hisses, gesturing to the room. "I am no longer under my mother's thumb or subject to my father's abuse because he let me join his crew as a way to hide. For once, I am a productive member of a family who doesn't look down upon me like scum, and anyone with pride would have chosen this."

"I'm surprised you're so bold as to betray him and think you can get away with it," I say wryly.

"I want to protect Gordon and force that weasel Dasher out of the picture," she insists.

I narrow my eyes and bite into one of the bread slices. "And how do you suggest we do that?"

The sound of creaking footsteps overhead silences her. My blood goes cold as we sit in silence until they pass.

"I want to ruin this plan because I'm worried Isaiah is going to compromise Warren," she whispers, glancing over her shoulder at the door and leaning forward. "And I think the best way to break them apart is by helping you escape and reunite with Gordon."

32

Emery

Escape.

I blink in spite of myself.

Escape?

What a jolting thought.

Annette scoffs a quiet laugh when she sees my blank expression. "I knew you wouldn't believe me."

I swallow. "I'm not seeing how those two ideas are connected."

"There's no way to go after Isaiah directly because I don't have the resources or an unsuspicious reason to, but I think if you escape, it would be a big priority for Warren to go after you so you don't reveal the truth of what's happened or find someone who will. He may abandon Isaiah altogether to look for you."

"I don't think . . ." I trail off. "I don't think anyone would believe me after everything that's happened. Especially with what the news has said."

"That's why you're going to reunite with Gordon. You two can refute all of this together." She gestures above her head. "Gordon has all of my letters warning him of the plan. Your word against Isaiah, elevated by Gordon's, would be invaluable."

I frown and sit back in my chair. "Why should I believe that you're going to betray Chadwick after you just sang his praises for taking you in?"

This time, she doesn't deny that it's a betrayal. She won't meet my eyes. "You have no idea how much of a comfort working in Gordon's office was," she says quietly. "It was the one place where all the behind-the-scenes rumors and drama within my family couldn't reach me, and I owe all of that to Gordon. I am indebted to Warren, but not like I am to Gordon."

Her stoic composure slips as more tears well in her eyes, and she clenches her quivering jaw and glances down.

My stomach twinges. "Why didn't you tell anyone about your mother and father?" I press, keeping my voice as quiet as possible. "Why didn't you tell *us?* My family would have—"

"Because you were like the rest of them," she snaps. "You played the game and stayed in line for fear of scrutiny, and you would have turned your back on me the second it threatened your standing among the others. Just like when you testified against the Riggs brother to keep your good face with the others when it meant betraying your best friends. Just like when Miles was ushered into the Academy when he wasn't qualified to be there."

My heart skips. "How did you know about that?"

"People talk." She sits back and folds her arms. "You should know better than anyone."

My face burns. I should not be arguing with my potential ticket to freedom, but I have to keep defending . . .

Defending what?

"Loyalty is so easily bought out," Annette mutters bitterly, "but Gordon has mine forever. Even if it is at . . ." She hesitates and puckers her lips. "Warren's expense."

"So . . ." I bite my cheek. "Gordon and I reunite, refute all of this, and then what?"

"When you return to Padstow, you will have the entire might of the Armada behind you if Warren decides to attack again." Her glassy eyes flick back to me. "Which I'm sure he won't. I hope Isaiah has the intelligence to recognize that continuing with him is a dangerous mistake and backs away, but if he doesn't, at least Gordon will be safe at that point."

I narrow my eyes. "Why are you so worried about Isaiah? Does Isaiah want to see the Pereculum go down, too?"

"If it elevates his image in the piracy world, he'll do whatever it takes to make it happen, including betraying Warren, I think. Warren doesn't think he's a threat, but after what he did to that Armada ship, I don't trust anything he does." She gestures to her head with an open palm. "There's something wrong with him up here. Not behaviorally or intellectually, but his lust for prestige is not normal."

"You've made him out to be persistent. Why would he back off?"

"If this plan dies and Warren stops attacking you, then Isaiah's hopes of building his reputation by aiding in it will die too. I hope he'll just run away to the next big opportunity." Annette wrings her hands. "I know I'm banking on a lot of variables playing in my favor, but it's the only way to help both Gordon and Warren. That's my compromise."

I watch her, curiosity pinging around the back of my mind. That yearning look returns to her eyes, and she quickly breaks our eye contact.

I glance at my boots. Her offer sounds too good to be true, probably because it is.

"What's the catch?" I ask at last.

Annette shakes her head and tucks her mousy hair behind her ears. "There isn't one."

"Don't say that." I roll my eyes. "There's always one."

"I don't know what image you've concocted of me in your head, but I am not conniving like Warren or the others," she says sternly. "This escape has to be carefully planned, and I suppose the only catch is that you have to be willing to be bold."

I raise my eyebrows. "Bold."

"I know you're brave and won't hesitate or panic when it counts, but I need you to swear that you won't break. If you're caught or this gets traced back to me, you can kiss any chance of returning to your life before goodbye."

I clench my jaw. The word *yes* sits on the tip of my tongue, but hesitation holds it back.

Why?

Distrust of Annette?

Distrust of yourself?

But what if it works? What if she's right and each of those variables plays out in our favor?

I curl my fingers into a fist, look Annette in the eye, and nod. "Okay."

Relief floods her expression, and she sighs. "Gordon told me of a friend he trusts in the Commonwealth who can help reunite you two. His name is Kelsey. If you could meet him—"

"Wait." My heart jumps. "What about meeting him here in Gatlon? How far does he live from here?"

"He lives about three days west from here in Corzéon, but we can't do it here. I have to write to Gordon to tell him you're on the way so we can coordinate a place for you two to meet, but Warren is watching the mail to see if anyone is in correspondence with the Armada." She rubs the arm of her velvety coat. "He asked the Valentines to screen letters coming in or out through the mailing port, so I can't send anything."

"Why not... I don't know. Code the letter? Write it so it isn't obvious?"

"I'd be caught. Hyde is at the mailing post watching who from the crew comes in or out."

I wince and rub my injured shoulder. "And this escape plan . . . Or do you even have one yet?"

She reaches into her coat pocket and procures a sheathed blade no longer than the width of my hand. "I am going to help you as much as I can, but if I'm caught—"

"Yes, yes." I study the sheath, considering the best place to conceal it. It could slip into my boot and is thin enough to fit strapped to the inner part of my shin, but it's too far from my hands. It could fit around the upper part of my arm . . . unless someone grabs me there.

"There's a sliding door that sits just above the waterline where we release the dinghies if the tide is low enough," Annette continues. "But we need a reason to dock so I can send Kelsey a letter. Then right as we leave—"

"I will disappear."

She nods and exhales softly through her nose. "We can discuss specifics later."

My fingers twitch. "How can we trust this friend?"

"I trust him if Gordon does."

I shake my head. "How can you be sure?"

"Why are you so hesitant to—" She realizes it as the words leave her mouth. "No. This isn't like the Riggses' betrayal. I don't think Gordon's friend would—"

"You don't know that," I snap, my voice trembling. "You have no idea who's going to turn around and stab you in the back."

"I love you. I love you to the end of forever."

Pain twinges in my stomach as I look away from her, praying she doesn't see the bitter tears forming in my eyes. I grit my teeth and exhale in frustration.

"I'm sorry about what Callie and Vaughn did to you," Annette finally says. "I know that must be hard to reckon with."

Her tenderness is uncharacteristic. I set my jaw and gently rub my nose with both hands, using the prickling pain to ground myself in the present, even though my heart feels as if it's going to burst from the weight of grief.

"Emery, I know you're exhausted, but if your doubts are going to keep you from helping me with this—"

"I'm fine." I glare at her. "Drop it."

She does, and her composed mask returns. She purses her lips and stands. "You have no idea how badly I want this to work."

Oh, I do. Amidst the confusion of her loyalty to two liberators, I can feel the clawing desperation burrowing into my ribs like a mole.

But even then, it's providing a light that may be able to lead me home.

33

Emery

INSTEAD OF LOCKING me back in the hold, Annette takes me above deck. She makes me swear on my life that I won't make a scene, but with a full stomach, the warm, dewy sunlight on my skin, and a slight buzz from the whiskey, I'd do that and more. Even the throbbing in my shoulder has subsided a bit.

To my surprise, the ship is empty save for the few deckhands left to guard it. Some of them play cards or sit in clusters across the deck, a good chunk of whom are Isaiah's pirates. A few of them send dirty looks my way.

What excites me most is that there's no Brooks, Hyde, or Chadwick to taunt and belittle me, and as much as I'm sure the remainder's suspicion is raised because I'm here, I don't care. The sun on my skin and the bustling liveliness of Gatlon's odd harbor are enough to set my pain at ease.

I sit against the ship's wheel on the bridge deck and close my eyes, pleading with myself.

You can't stop now. You can't let Chadwick win the mind games.

Even though his slimy tendrils have latched onto the dark parts of my mind, I can't.

"You're still clinging to who you used to be," his voice taunts. *"A good little captain doesn't betray her superiors, does she?"*

What a dripping silver tongue. If my past self could gawk at how I'm listening to it now, she'd be very disappointed. She'd wonder how I would ever consider caving to him and his wicked ways.

She doesn't know that the image she crafted of herself was hollow and weak. The bubble she made for herself wasn't as strong as she thought it was. She wanted to be good, but it never panned out that way.

My mind knows Chadwick is a liar, but my heart still aches to take his offer. My friends and my title may be gone, but my parents and brothers will be there waiting for me. They *have* to be, otherwise all of this fighting and resisting will have been for nothing.

But if Annette's plan works, if it all falls into place and I can play the only card left in my hand, then Reese may stay safe and I can see him and my family all again. The hope of ifs and maybes is powerful, especially when that's all that's left to rely on.

I bask in the quiet ambience and warmth of the sun until the sound of angry conversation draws my attention. I open my eyes.

Through the gaps in the wooden railing, I can see a knot of pirates consisting of Gil, Alexis, Tahj, and a few others standing and talking on the dock at the end of the gangplank. They stumble back as Chadwick shoves through them, his face flushed and red. He rakes his hands through his matted blond hair and whirls to talk to his crew. I can't hear what he's saying, but his wired expression and the fact that he's come back to the ship so early tells me what I need to know.

Reese Gordon is not here.

Relief and dread fill my chest like a mixture of icy water and burning alcohol.

On the dock, Gil touches Chadwick's shoulder, but gets his hand batted away as the captain storms across the dock in the direction of the town, alone.

Reese is not here.

I let the hope wedge more deeply into my mind. I let myself think *what if,* and the picture of the end of this miserable, miserable road begins to form. It's sweet like the petals of a white orchid. Like the conical petals of a red snapdragon.

A shadow covers me, and I glance up at a frowning Lucky. He's wearing his cobalt coat despite the heat and has a red strip of cloth tied around his head to catch the sweat at his hairline. "What are you doing up here?"

I squint. "Does it look like I'm in any condition to run?"

He wrinkles his forehead. "You ran last time and almost escaped."

I bring my arm to rest in my lap and wince. The tightness of Harrison's wrap seems to distract from the twinges of pain. "The keyword in that sentence is *almost*."

Annette stomps up the stairs. "Where's Harrison, Lucky?"

"Aren't you off duty?" Lucky's frown deepens. "Why are you still here?"

"The captain asked me to deal with her while the rest of you slack off." She gestures to me offhandedly. "Nobody was sitting in the hold with her when I went to check."

Lucky scoffs and raises his eyebrows. "And you brought her up here and left her sitting *alone*? Are you out of your mind?"

"I was looking away for two seconds. She isn't a child." Her gaze flicks to me. "Even though she continually *acts* like one."

I roll my eyes. She's laying it on a little thick.

A drop of sweat rolls off Lucky's nose as he shrugs out of his coat. His white shirt is completely soaked through. "Well, fine. You can take the captain's scolding when he finds her sitting unattended up here. I'm going to—"

He's cut off by a loud thud, and the three of us turn to see a group of Isaiah's pirates boarding the ship. The group is led by four men shouldering a wooden trunk, and the pirate under the back left corner grunts as he regains his footing.

". . . won't calm down," another pirate mutters as he and two companions continue the train behind the trunk. His gaze drifts and settles on me, and he stops dead in his tracks. "You." He points at me. "You could calm her down."

"'Her'?" Lucky demands. "What are you talking about?"

I tuck my bad arm against my chest and hold out my strong one, signaling for Annette to help me to my feet. Just as I gain my balance, a scream echoes from below deck.

"Who is that?" Lucky grabs the arm of the man who spoke.

My breath hitches in my throat as I surge toward the stairs, fueled mostly by curiosity.

"Emery, wait." Lucky trails me.

I follow the sounds of scuffles and muffled screaming as I race down the stairs and weave through the maze of hammocks and cots. I slip between the mass of musty bodies clogging the walkway, watching the pirates tip the trunk on its side. My stomach drops.

"Her" was referring to the girl who scrambles out of the trunk and flattens herself against the wall, ropes cutting into the fragile skin of her wrists as she thrashes. She's hysterical. Everything about her is pure panic and unfiltered terror as she sobs through the gag in her mouth.

But all I can focus on are the strands of purple and teal woven into her hair—the same purple and teal on Hana Kailea's flag.

"Oh, Thea!" I hurry to her side and pull the gag out of her mouth. "No!"

"Emery, what's going on?" Thea sobs and gasps for air. "What's happening?"

"It's okay. Hold on." Even though it aggravates my shoulder, I reach back to untie her hands, and she throws her arms around my neck, sobbing and trembling like a scared animal.

"It's okay! It's okay!" I lose my balance and sit back on the floor. Pain zips through my arm.

Leverage. My mind snaps with the word, along with a thousand stories of survivors the Armada has rescued who were kidnapped for this very reason.

I should've told him. Now she's going to get hurt, and it's all my fault.

"I don't want to die," Thea wails, repeating it over and over and over again. "That's what they said would happen, Emery. Please tell them I don't want to die. Please. *Please!*"

"Hey," I say raspily, maneuvering to shield her from the pirates. The two groups begin arguing, though I can't hear exactly what they're saying. "Thea, did they hurt you?"

She ducks her head and continues to sob. The sound is drowned out by the noise as the voices meld together.

"We did *not* agree to this!" someone shouts. "Who said—"

"—didn't tell us a thing!"

"Thea, look at me." I grab the sides of her head and level her eyes with mine, ignoring the pain in my shoulder. She's a little older than the last time I saw her in person, though her tear-stained cheeks are plump with baby fat, a gentle reminder that she's fifteen. Only *fifteen.*

So was Kearon.

The thought makes me flinch.

"Did they touch you?" I ask, my voice trembling. "Are you hurt?"

"N-no." She shakes her head and wipes her face with the back of her hand, though long strands of her black hair are plastered to her face. "They were in my room when my father and I came home."

I drag my thumbs under her eyes. "Did anyone see them?"

"They covered my eyes, and I couldn't see. I couldn't scream." Her body and face twitch with erratic panic as she sobs again, her face gaunt. "I'm going to be sick."

I'm not sure who to be angry at, but I hold her tight as pure, unfiltered fear seeps into my muscles. I turn back to see Lucky and Annette break through the crowd, their eyes wide with shock. Lucky joins the argument as I hold eye contact with Annette—her stoic mask is cracked, and she covers her mouth and stares at Thea and me with shocked horror.

I press my mouth to the top of her head and take a shaky breath, wanting to do nothing other than crawl into a hole and hide from the noise and terror. If there was any chance for this nightmare to end, it has certainly sailed, and I can almost see it disappear into the horizon.

34

Warren

"THIS IS RIDICULOUS!" Alexis is the first to speak. "You're going to *keep* her here?"

"You want to risk the wrath of Hana's royal navy *on top* of what just happened with the Armada?" Gil snaps.

My cabin erupts into a commotion of protests that meld together and pound inside my head. Lewis is the only one who doesn't look angry or ready to rip someone's head off, and he watches the group with worry knit between his brows.

For a moment, the noise is nothing but a blur in my ear. My mind ticks with a thousand different ways I could kill Dasher for disobeying me. The shock makes my chest tight.

"Enough!" I scream over the chaos. "That's enough!"

Everyone falls silent.

"I will deal with Isaiah, but the princess—" I stop short and stretch my neck, encouraging myself to speak as I dig my fingers into the edge of my desk. "The princess will be staying here for the time being."

That prompts a collective groan from the entire room.

"We're done for." Gil turns away, shaking his head.

"What good does her staying here do?" Alexis demands.

"How long *will* she stay?" Tahj throws his hands in the air. "Until we find Reese Gordon?"

"Warren, that could be weeks," Hyde mumbles to me. "What are you doing?"

"What's stopping the princess from reporting us to the nearest authorities the second I drop her at the next port?" I snap at everyone. "Now, if you will all stop questioning my authority and forgetting your place in this room, I will continue."

That quiets them, but none will look me in the eye.

"If Isaiah tries to board this ship and torture the princess to make Miss Walker talk, you will resist every action he makes. Is that understood?"

"Well, we're probably going to go down for kidnapping her anyways, so what's the point in avoiding proper tactics?" Brooks flops back in his chair. "It would make Emery talk, and then we can get on with our lives."

"Don't be daft," Annette says snootily. She was so silent that I almost forgot she was perched in front of one of my bookshelves. "You don't want innocent blood on your hands."

Brooks narrows his eyes and points one of his blades at her. "Since when do you know what I want?"

Gil gently pushes his shoulder. "Relax."

"Don't tell me to relax when we're all probably going to end up in jail," Brooks snaps.

I set my jaw. "Please *stop*. This meeting is over. We will discuss more about how I'm going to *kill* Isaiah once I've come up with a plan that won't get all of *you* killed."

That was mostly meant as a joke, but it did not quell the tension. I am breaking the one rule that I've drilled into each of their minds since they stepped aboard my ship, and that is to keep those who have no business in this work out of our way.

"What's our heading?" Gil asks, folding his arms. "Why don't we have any idea where we're going every time we exit port?"

I exhale and glance quickly at Annette.

"Is something wrong?" Tahj snaps. "What are you not telling us?"

I swallow. "I don't want that information to be abused."

He scowls. "Abused?"

If any of them is the traitor, he certainly isn't showing it.

Except for Lewis. He's the only one staring at the ground while the rest of them stare at me in anger.

I snap my fingers. "Lewis."

He flinches and combs back his wispy blond hair. "S-sorry, what?"

I pretend I don't feel rage seeping into my bones. "I don't want

Isaiah to know my plans because he's proven how untrustworthy he is," I say to the group. "I don't want anything getting back to him or his crew, which means everyone here has to stay in the dark, too."

They grumble. Tahj whispers something to Alexis, who rolls his eyes.

Something clicks in my head. "You know what?" I snap, pointing to the door. "Fine! All of you can leave if you have such reservations about my decision. Come back when you're ready to stop disrespecting my authority!"

Brooks smacks the table and is the first out, and everyone but Hyde and Annette follows suit.

"Ridiculous," Alexis mutters to Tahj.

Lewis quickly ducks his head and doesn't spare me another glance.

I slam the door and lock it once everyone is out, which causes Annette and Hyde to flinch.

"Hyde, watch Lewis like a hawk," I spit through gritted teeth. "Go through his things, for all I care. It's got to be him. Why else would—" I curl my fists and resist the urge to run them through the wall.

Why else would they not *listen* to me?

"And Brooks, too," I add. I should have acknowledged his flippant arrogance as a warning a long time ago.

"Why Brooks?" Hyde scowls. "He would chop Emery to bits and feed her to the sharks if you let him. I don't think he'd help her."

"Why *not* Brooks, Hyde?" I clasp my hands. "Why not you? Why not either of you?!"

He blinks in surprise and takes a step back.

"He doesn't mean that." Annette widens her eyes at me in warning. "Does he?"

Hyde rolls his eyes. "You're being irrational."

"Do *not* tell me what I am or am not," I snap, halving the distance between us and holding my finger to his face. "You have no right—"

"That's enough." Annette grabs my wrist. "Both of you."

"You know what, Warren? Why *wouldn't* you use the princess against Emery now?" Hyde demands. "After everything, what's stopping you now?"

"Hyde—" Annette starts.

"Frame her for the princess's disappearance," he spits. "Frame her for it all! Why do I have to spell this out for you?"

"That hasn't worked on her before, and it certainly won't work now since she will focus on protecting Theadora!" I shout.

"Then let me go after her again!" He smacks his fist against his palm. "You won't even have to do anything, but Emery doesn't deserve your mercy. Take the princess out of the room and make Emery think she's in danger. I don't care. But something has to *happen*. If I have to go down there and use the princess myself, I will."

His fury is almost palpable in the air. Annette crinkles her eyes.

"Don't you dare compromise your values for it," my mother's voice echoes. *"I taught you better than that."*

But Isaiah's echoes louder.

"If this is the only barrier between you and Gordon, then I don't believe that would stand."

The thought is all-consuming; a black, twisted rot stirring in the darkest parts of my mind.

Find Gordon, jailbreak the Pereculum, rescue Kearon, get rid of Emery for good . . .

And all the leverage I need is sitting below my feet.

I blink and breathe deeply to expel the thought, but it lingers.

It wouldn't be personal. It's for Kearon. For the mess that Emery has made and the corruption and lies she stands in front of.

"Warren," Annette mumbles, barely audible.

"You won't cross that line, Hyde." My voice trembles. "Promise me you won't."

His eyes flick to Annette. "Maybe. Maybe not." He turns for the door. "We've all been acting a little funny around here recently, haven't we?"

I yank my arm free from Annette's hold once he's gone. "We are safe while we're on the water, so we're going to stay here as long as possible while I figure this out." I fix my coat and stretch my neck again. "End of discussion."

She watches as I start to pace, fidgeting with the lapel of my shirt, distracted. Fixated. Agitated.

How could you let this happen?

"Are you going to say anything?" I snap at her. "Or are you just going to watch me lose my mind and my crew in one fell swoop?"

I sink into my chair and rub my face with my trembling hands.

Getting rid of Isaiah has to be my focus before he does something that lands the rest of us in a dungeon or swinging from the gallows.

Maybe I could poison him and his crew with a cocktail of Harrison's concoctions. Maybe I could sneak into Isaiah's cabin in the middle of the night and slit his throat.

Maybe, maybe, maybe. It all flies through my head like a windstorm.

"Warren."

Her voice is so soft and gentle. It's like a feather tickling the back of my brain.

I look up.

She closes the distance between us and hesitantly touches my shoulder, and my eyes twitch as the thoughts continue to spiral.

Emery.

Theadora.

"Maybe. Maybe not. We've all been acting a little funny around here."

"Warren."

Dasher, Walker, how can I ruin you?

"Don't you dare compromise your values for it."

Why are my thoughts so *loud?*

You're losing your crew, they say. *You're losing control of everything going on around you and there's nothing you can do to stop it.*

Except that I can. Emery would break in an instant if the princess were in danger.

The weight of Annette's hand suddenly disappears from my shoulder, and I blink. She crinkles her eyes and steps back, and the weight of a thousand unsaid words hovers between us.

I should tell her about these awful, twisted ideas, but she would turn up her nose like she has in the past and disappear.

She would despite all you've done for her.

"I need a moment." I leap from the chair and stand in front of the window.

"Warren—"

I don't dare turn to look at her. "Go."

My chest aches as I listen to her soft footsteps cross the room, and then sit in silence after the door rattles shut.

35

I IMAGINE Gordon's house in the Southern Chain to be small and made of straw, nothing that would draw too much attention or suspicion. I imagine him huddled around a news spindle, listening as the world and the people he left behind fall to pieces.

I imagine my mother on the other side of the world doing the same while plucking the petals off a dead orchid. Charles is close by, listening and picking apart each word from the reporter's mouth. Miles is pacing the halls in the middle of the night because he's trying to clear the thoughts of contention from his head. My father is sitting in his study as the candle on his desk burns lower and lower and snuffs itself out.

I wonder what each of them is thinking.

I close my eyes as my chest aches with longing. I just need to get home to them. I will take Thea with me and go from there, and everything will be fine.

Maybe.

Maybe not.

Thea's head rests in my lap, and even though she twitches every once in a while under my coat, she's peaceful. Our new prison, another storage room on the lowest deck, reeks of earthy vanilla, and each barrel is most likely filled with rum or some other drink that I'd really love to taste right now.

No one has come to replace my fetters, either. I'm not sure if Annette leveraged something with Chadwick to allow me to sit freely, but I haven't seen or heard from a single soul since Isaiah's pirates locked Thea and me in this room. Annette hasn't even come to tell me what's going on.

The hours tick by in maddening silence, and my heart pounds at the thought of what they're going to do to her. I have seen what Chadwick is capable of, and Isaiah could be just as ruthless. I sit with bone-chilling images flashing through my mind of what could happen to her. To me. They cycle with the thoughts of what I could have done differently to prevent this. I've tried *so hard* to resist, but nothing has been good enough, and the taunts of my shortcomings haunt my mind.

"You're a little too keen on believing you're on the right side of any discrepancy, aren't you?"

"What good have you done, exactly? Where does the good outweigh the bad?"

"You are a liar who loves being in control. You shine on that pedestal and are nothing without it."

The latter keeps cycling through my mind over, and over, and over. I glance up as tears well in my eyes.

There's no way Reese's word against Chadwick's will be enough to fix the damage he's done to my name. It's ruined forever, even though I did everything right. Even though I had strong intentions to distance myself from the rot in the Armada and wanted to do what was right more than anything.

And what does it say about you that he's torn you down so easily?

Even then, if I were a good person, I wouldn't have turned a blind eye to the Armada's dirty dealings. I don't think it matters how much good I wanted to do.

I force the thought away as my hand shakily combs through Thea's thick hair.

Hours pass like honey dripping from a hive. I must have dozed at some point because when I open my eyes, there are two trays of food beside me, each with a cup of water, a crusty slice of bread, and a few pieces of dried, salted meat.

I slide the trays closer and load all of the food onto one plate. I take a sip of water from one of the cups and take a deep breath, willing the anxious, finicky emotions out of my mind and into oblivion.

Thea's muscles suddenly tighten as she begins to stir.

"Hey, sweet girl," I say softly, brushing her hair out of her face.

"Emery?" she whimpers. "What—"

"It's just me. You're okay."

She slumps against my side when she tries to sit up, landing awkwardly against my shoulder. I tense up in pain.

"S-sorry," she winces.

"It's okay." I try not to grimace and hand her the tray of food with my strong arm. "Here."

Her hands sneak out from inside the coat, and she plucks a slice of bread off the tray. "Is there any for you?"

"It's okay." I force a smile. "I'm not hungry."

She downs one of the water cups in one go, and I hand her the other.

"Is it tomorrow?" she whispers, her voice rippling across the water.

"Yes. You slept through the night."

"Did you?"

I glance down. "Just for a little bit."

Thea pushes the tray back toward me, but I shake my head.

"You don't have to be nice," she insists.

"I'm not a very nice person." I chuckle half-heartedly.

"That's not true." She hands me a piece of meat, which I reluctantly take and swallow. My stomach is so hollow it feels as if it's shrunk to the size of a pebble.

We eat in silence, and she shudders despite the dense air. "What's going to happen?"

My eyes crinkle. "I'm not sure yet, but it'll be okay."

I don't think she believes me. Her face pales, and I can sense her tears before they fall. I drape my injured arm around her as she begins to cry, mumbling something in Kailean.

The neck of her blouse is shifted just enough that I can see a tattoo on her collarbone. I gently pull the cottony fabric back. There are letters inked black in Kailean with a turtle printed next to it.

"What does it say?" I ask gently. "I don't remember seeing this before."

"It's my stepmother's name." Her voice trembles as she absent-mindedly traces the ink with her finger. "Alika. It means of noble kin. She loves the sea turtles, too."

"That's beautiful." I admire the intricate cross-stitched pattern in the ink. "When did you get it?"

"Just last week. I was going to show it to her at a festival happening in a few days, but—" Her voice catches in her throat.

My stomach twists as I lean and rest my chin on her head. She keeps crying, and for a moment, I let her. I want to join her, but instead, I just close my eyes and grit my teeth.

"I have a story to tell you," I mumble into her hair, my voice trembling. "Do you want to hear it?

She looks up and wipes her face.

I take a deep breath and put on my bravest grin. "Did you know I was in a situation very similar to this last year?"

She frowns. "What?"

"I was." I nod. "It was with a different pirate. His name was Art."

"Art?" The confusion temporarily halts her terror, and the tension begins to drop.

"It's a stupid name, don't you think?" I force a laugh. "Anyway, my crew and I had a plan set to ambush him in Corzéon and arrest him, which is a few days' journey from where you live. Someone must have tipped the pirates off that we were coming, because we'd barely gotten to the house where Art was hiding when we were waylaid by his crew."

Thea's eyes shift from panicked to intrigued. "What did you do?"

"We tried to fight, but there were too many pirates for my team of six to handle," I reply. "Everyone except for our cartographer Quint and me escaped the house, but before I knew it, I was sprawled in the dirt with no weapon and a sword under my chin."

"Were you afraid?"

"Of course I was." My brow knits as the memories from that day flash through my thoughts. They are branded into the back of my mind. "I genuinely thought that I was going to die at that moment, but instead, they tied our hands and took Quint and me back to Art's hideout."

"What happened?"

I skip the disturbing details of the night and absentmindedly touch the scar Art left on the right side of my abdomen. "Art wanted to know who told us where he was hiding, but I couldn't sell out our spy, and he was threatening to kill Quint if I didn't cooperate. Eventually, the pirates took him downstairs and left me alone with Art, but there was a trick we learned in the Academy that helped me escape." Even though it hurts, I position my wrists so the bones under each of my thumbs touch, leaving an open space behind them. "When they were tying my hands, I held my wrists just like this so that when the knots were secure, I still had a little bit of room to move them. I started wiggling" —I show the back-and-forth motion where the heels of my hands rub against each other—"and the knots started to loosen. I lunged at Art and was able to get his gun away from him."

Thea gasps. "Did you shoot him?"

"I—" I pause, catching myself. "No. He let me go, and I was able to find Quint, and we escaped. We were able to find the rest of our crew, arrest Art and a handful of his closest associates, and get home safely."

She just stares at me, slack-jawed. "You're a hero, Emery."

I shake my head. "That's an exaggeration."

She twists her lips and holds up her hands, mimicking the positioning with her dainty wrists. "Like this?"

"Yes. You can use it when you're in a bind."

For the first time, she cracks a smile. "A bind?"

I frown, and she ducks her head and giggles. The realization hits me over the head. "Oh!" I genuinely laugh for the first time in weeks and rest my head against the wall. "I did not mean to say that."

"Do you still know Quint?" she asks, trying to suppress her laughter. Two dimples form in her cheeks.

"I see him every once in a while, but he was transferred to a different crew shortly after that happened."

The laughter and light grind to a halt, and Thea purses her lips and stares at the ground, her brow furrowed. "I don't know how they can say all of those terrible things about you when this is what you do. You do good things."

I squint at her words.

She shakes her head and tucks loose strands of her wavy black hair behind her ears. "I don't believe it. Any smart person could see that none of it is true."

They might. Maybe another time, if things were different. Maybe if my world weren't one of fake fronts and falsity.

Thea nearly jumps from her skin as the door bursts open and slams into the wall. Her nails dig into my arm as she shrinks against me.

Brooks stomps inside, twirling one of his knives between his fingers and surging forward.

"Just stay here and stay calm, okay?" I say quietly to Thea as he grabs my arm and yanks me to my feet.

"Wait!" she blurts, her eyes wide with panic. "Emery!"

"It's okay!" I try not to wince as Brooks twists my arm. "I'll be right back!"

I brace for his jeering remark as we march upstairs, but it never comes. My eyes adjust quickly to the sunlight as we ascend the stairs toward Harrison's cabin, but we enter the one to the left of it instead, which reveals itself to be the ship's galley.

Three walls are neatly lined with stacked crates and barrels of food. The fourth wall is a smattering of cabinets and countertops stretching from the windows to the back of the room, and the utensils are neatly arranged on little pegs screwed into the wall.

I flinch when the door clatters shut behind me.

"What a dimwit."

I turn to the source of the unfamiliar voice. Isaiah steps out from a corner of the room and approaches me. His curly hair is frizzy from the dense humidity.

"Don't tell Warren I'm talking about his crew negatively, but that one with the knives"—he points over my shoulder—"is the most annoying."

I know I could hurl all the anger in the world at Chadwick, but Annette was right to call Isaiah a powder keg. I want to scream at him for bringing Thea into this, but I don't want to provoke him. I clench my shaky fists instead.

"Why don't you sit down?" Isaiah slips out of his charcoal jacket and drapes it over one of the crates. He drags another adjacent to it and sits, bringing his knee to his chest and slinging one of his bare arms over it. "Warren wasn't willing to be flexible on a more comfortable meeting spot, so I apologize for that. I preferred my office on the *North Star*, but you know how persistent he can be." He smiles.

I accept his seat and frown at him, rubbing my shoulder. "What has he put you up to?"

"This was not his idea." His eyes are unnervingly wide. "I don't know what you've heard, but I'm not his puppet. We are partners."

"Are you sure *he* knows that?"

He throws his head back and laughs, a high-pitched, airy sound. "You're funny! Warren has never mentioned that about you."

It wasn't *that* funny. "I don't know how you missed it, but the things he's 'mentioned' about me have not been pleasant." I glare at him.

"Of course. It's all a bit dramatic," Isaiah says glumly, rubbing his tattooed arms. "Including this little escapade we're on now. I understand his anger toward you all, but the reward isn't enough justification for risking the Armada's wrath. And now with the risk of the Kaileans chasing after the princess, it's complicated everything. He shouldn't have done that."

The bubble holding my anger pops. "You two had no right to drag her into this," I snap. "You and Chadwick—"

"It was not my idea!" He holds up his hands in innocence. A long scar runs down his left middle finger. "Warren insisted. I warned him that the wrath of Hana's forces would rain down on him, but he didn't listen." He puckers his lips and taps his chin. "Maybe you're right. I don't think he sees me as a partner, and I'm just another peg on his ladder."

"Then why are you still here?"

His eyes flash with cheeky amusement. "You know that our status dictates our power, Captain. Status . . ." He shrugs. "Status *is* power, quite frankly. Who wouldn't want a free life on the ocean with status like his? Who doesn't want the thrill of living on the edge of the world?"

I narrow my eyes, wondering if his erratic personality was discussed in any of the captains' meetings. Fallon must have known at the very least.

"I want the freedom that the power will bring me. I think that what

I want will help you get what *you* want." He leans close and lowers his voice, eyes wide and twitchy. "How do you think that sounds?"

"What do you think I want?"

"The princess safely returned to Hana—same as I—and Gordon's safety. And for this nightmare to end, obviously. Your selflessness is shining through."

I tilt my head.

He balances his elbows on his knees. "Warren is unstable and could snap at any moment, and you know exactly where his anger is going to go when he does." He points to the ground. "He has all the leverage he needs downstairs. I have no reservations about Gordon and only care about the Pereculum, and I can get all three of you out safely. Warren can't. Warren *won't*."

"And why should I believe that?"

"I promise you that I won't lay a finger on Gordon or the princess." He completely ignores my question. "My only interest is the Pereculum."

"Is there someone inside you want to free?"

He shifts his jaw as if reluctant to answer.

I glance up at the ceiling as if the answer has fallen from the sky. "Never mind. It'll boost your credibility to challenge the powers that be and win, correct? Is that what you want?"

Isaiah licks his lips, though I can tell there's more he wants to say and can see the intensity of his ego in his wide eyes. "What can you tell me about the Pereculum?"

"I don't know any more than you do," I say. "That wasn't my concern as a soldier."

"Then it'll be a quick conversation with the judge and an even quicker reversal of the sentences, will it not?" He blinks. "Of course, I don't mean to make that process sound menial. I imagine it must take time for something like that to be approved."

"You didn't answer my question."

Isaiah's head twitches to one side.

"Why do you think I should believe that you will do this?"

His stare is relentless. "Well, it isn't a matter of belief. It's a clock." He clucks his tongue like the seconds ticking away on a clock. "How long do we have until Warren gives in to his urges and puts Theadora's safety on the line to get what he wants?"

My stomach turns.

"His crew is antsy, Captain. You know he'd do anything to keep the peace and keep them from turning on him."

Turning on him . . . ?

"What do you mean by 'antsy?'" I probe, hoping my suspicion is minimal. "Are they just uneasy or are they planning something?"

"That's one word for it." He grins. "'Up in arms' is another favorite of mine. But I don't know if they're planning anything. It'd be a pretty bold move if they tried."

"It's a bold move to go behind Chadwick's back and sneak his prisoners off the ship," I say wryly. "You're very insistent on promising that you can do it."

"I am an odds teller." Isaiah's lips curl into a devious grin. "I don't always promise, but the risk and the odds are in good conjunction with one another. Warren won't notice anything while his crew is at his throat."

My attention locks on his wide brown eyes, and I resist the urge to look away as he stares right back. Annette's comments about him flicker in the back of my mind again.

A powder keg that's going to explode . . .

But maybe an explosion is what I need, not this petty little deal and sob story he's trying to sell me. I know a group who may be more willing to make a deal to save themselves, and they aren't slimy, manipulative clowns like the one I sit across from.

I shake my head.

His mask cracks, and the smile drops as fast as it grew. "I'm sorry?"

"The odds are not there." I stand up. "The odds will never be."

They won't be, unless I get the explosion that I need. Unless I can convince Chadwick's crew to betray their captain.

36

Warren

"TODAY, your Messenger comes to you to report more about a tragedy coming out of Hana Kailea. Princess Theadora Alika Halapua, daughter of King Tanuvasa, has been reported missing. The royal guard reported that the princess left on a deep-mountain excursion and was supposed to return yesterday afternoon, but when her group returned, she was not with them. Kailean authorities are scouring the island in search of the princess, but the excursion team claims the princess was never with them to begin with. The Messenger outpost on the island is still awaiting a statement from King Tanuvasa or Queen Alika, and The Messenger urges anyone with knowledge to step forward and share."

I sigh and rub my temples. How in the *world* did Dasher manage to pull this off?

Chip squawks in his burrow and nips at the wire. He blinks at me expectantly, but I ignore him.

Hyde brought the bird and a letter from my mother back from Gatlon's mail outpost, which provided much-needed solace to my mind —to my surprise, she didn't say a single scolding word, but she demanded to know each detail of what happened and where we're going next. I can only imagine what she'd say now with the circumstances I find myself in.

Behind me, the door creaks slightly, but I don't turn around. I wait for the soft footsteps to approach—an arm loops through mine, and a head rests on my shoulder with a sigh. I tense only slightly at her touch.

I should have gone to her, not waited for her to come to me. Guilt ripples through my stomach as she folds her fingers around mine.

"This news is new," she says softly.

"Tahj grabbed it before we left Gatlon," I mumble, fixing my gaze on the ocean through the window behind my desk. "I've only just gotten around to listening to it."

"—other news, the search for Padstow's chief judge, Reese Gordon, is ongoing. Witnesses from the city of Gatlon claimed to have seen Gordon entering a local inn about a week ago, but there has been no sign of him since that initial report."

So he *was* there. I was just too late.

"Though this is speculation, some sources are claiming that former Armada captain Emery Walker may be to blame for his disappearance. It's known she may have played a role in the recent bombings of two Armada vessels, but investigations from Padstow and others are still ongoing.

"As a result of those bombings, multiple piracy-focused brigades across the Commonwealth have halted their patrols, and we're still continuing to hear of attacks happening in the East's major cities. Neither Padstow's Armada nor Admiral Yanni Van Pelt has agreed to comment on the matter, but it's clear that Walker's actions have sent ripples through the world."

My chest swells with satisfaction.

"The Messenger will report as more information comes out."

The capsule rolls to a stop, and neither of us speaks. There is too much to juggle and too much to say. Too much ambition.

I grit my teeth and look up at the ceiling. "I'm sorry."

"You don't need to apologize for your anger," she mutters, picking at the skin around her nails. "I would have shot him dead a long time ago."

I should. I should do it myself and then interrogate every sailor on my ship to figure out who was sharing my secrets. My fingers twitch, and Annette lets go and replaces the silent capsule with the other sitting on the desk.

"Shout here, Shout there, Shout everywhere!" This reporter's voice is nasally and gruff, as if he's smoked one or two—or ten—too many rolls of tobacco. *"Folks, I don't know what to tell you now, but—"*

Annette flinches as a fist pounds on the door. Even though there's more to say to her, I slip out of her hold and motion for her to crouch under the desk, though I'm sure it's unnecessary at this point. Someone has to have seen her sneaking in and out of my cabin at least once.

I stretch my neck open the door, and Hyde pokes his head inside, tending a wad of tobacco in his cheek. He lazily raises one eyebrow. "Where is Annette?"

My heart leaps. "I don't know. Why?"

"Well, everyone is getting tired of doing nothing, and they'd like to know where we're going," he deadpans, glaring at me. "So would Dasher."

I tip my head forward and can just barely see the bow of the *South Sun* off my ship's starboard side. My blood boils at the thought of the wretched troll captaining it. "We still need to cool off," I say curtly. "Tell Isaiah that we are just continuing southbound."

Hyde's eyes flick down to my feet, then back to my eyes. My chest tightens as the tension in the room—or the tension between us, I suppose—inflates dramatically. He folds his arms and doesn't break his steely gaze, but I glare right back. *He* expects me to say something about our argument, but I did nothing wrong. If he's so bitter, then he can fix it. That is not my problem.

Eventually, I win the standoff, and he spins on his heel and marches away.

"Good grief," I mutter as I shut the door and flip the lock.

". . . what's to say Walker isn't the one who forced the princess to disappear, too?"

I remove the capsule and set it on my desk, suddenly acutely aware of and exhausted from the noise.

Annette's head pops up from under the desk, and she frowns. "Where *do* you want to go? You still haven't told me."

"Cordova." I grab my holster from my top desk drawer and strap it around my left shoulder so the pistol sits under my left arm. "Would you set us on course . . ." I pause. "You do still know where on the ocean we are, do you?"

"Yes." She rests her arms on the desk and tilts her head. "I've been keeping track."

"Okay." I retrieve my coat from the back of my chair and slip into it.

"Where are you going?"

"To talk to the princess. Isaiah asked to speak with Miss Walker up here, so I'm going down there while the princess is alone." I fix the collar of my shirt and tighten the drawstrings, and she leaps out from behind the desk to greet me.

"I'm not upset," she mumbles, grabbing my elbow and raising one eyebrow. "But I'd wish you'd tell me how you're really feeling."

Without thinking, I reach up and touch her hand, my fingers tingling against her skin. I smile. "I'm fine."

Her jaw twitches. "I don't believe you."

My brow furrows. She can see that something is there, but she cannot make out that she has been kissing an obsessed madman—my conscience urges me to tell her that I am closer to breaking than she thinks, but my peace is worth protecting. So is hers.

I grab her jaw with one hand and kiss her abruptly, and perhaps I am an awful person for indulging in this so selfishly, but I do it regardless. It's a welcome distraction.

After a long moment, she pulls away, her eyes unfocused and her lips parted as she falls back onto her heels. I smile, but I don't say a word as I turn and leave her. I didn't lie.

As I step outside, I straighten my sleeves and watch my crew, their expressions, and the way their bodies seem to stiffen as I pass them. Lewis barely spares a glance as I pass by him.

I am losing them, but do they really expect me to drop the princess in the middle of nowhere and let her rip my entire secret wide open? They aren't stupid. I wouldn't have picked them to be in my crew otherwise.

But their trust is slipping through my fingers. The madman whose ships are tailing mine certainly hasn't helped with that, and now I'm left to deal with his messes.

And the ticking in my mind returns.

I descend to the belly of my ship with a lit lantern in hand, and I open the door into one of the storage rooms.

"I don't know anything!" Theadora yelps. Tears are pouring from her eyes like water from a pitcher as she huddles against the wall and tucks her knees to her chest. Emery's coat is wrapped around her shoulders. "P-please don't hurt me. I promise I'm not lying."

I shut the door and exhale softly. "Your Highness—"

"She didn't say anything about you, or about Judge Gordon, or anything of the sort. I promise I won't tell my father or anyone else if you let me go. You won't even get in trouble for it—"

"Your Highness!" I glare at her with wide, angry eyes. "I'm not going to hurt you."

I shouldn't have been so sharp. She shrinks away like a hermit crab retreating into its shell and covers her face with her arms so all that's visible are her bleary brown eyes.

I set my jaw. She reminds me so much of Kearon hunched in his cell, and it makes my stomach churn.

"I promise I won't hurt you," I say again, gentler. "You've done nothing wrong."

"Then why—"

"Dasher is a disgrace who thinks it's okay to loop innocent people into conflicts they have no place in." I lean against the wall and fold my arms. "That's why he brought you here. But I think you already know that if there *is* something Miss Walker has told you, you should probably share it."

She sniffles. "Why?"

"*You* might not be hurt over withholding information, but I can't say the same for her." I crinkle my eyes with pseudo-sympathy. "You wouldn't want to be responsible for hurting her, now would you?"

After a long moment, she shakes her head. "N-no."

"Good." I tilt my head, letting the silence fill the open void. I count to five.

Theadora bites her cheek as she stares at the ground, and I open my mouth to speak.

"You should know that isn't his real name," she blurts.

I blink and raise my eyebrows. "Are you talking about Isaiah?"

She nods. "His real name is Isaiah Hoepa Anahera."

I tilt my head. I should have guessed that, since the name Dasher sounds like it originated somewhere in the Northern Estates or the northern half of the Commonwealth.

"What does it mean?" I ask.

"*Anahera* means 'angel' in Kailean."

I knit my brow and entertain the conversation, even if it isn't what I want. She is malleable in areas where Emery isn't.

"That's ironic, isn't it?" I crinkle my eyes. "Do you know why he changed his name?"

"He's a coward." Anger briefly flashes across Theadora's teary eyes. "He cast his name aside years ago and stole another one to..." She trails off, gesturing around the room. "Do this."

My eyes land on the strands of color woven into her inky black hair. "Family is revered in your culture. Your last name is the most important piece of your identity, isn't it?"

"It is to all Southerners." She holds her knees to her chest. "Or it should be."

"Why would Isaiah leave, then? How do you know all of this?"

"He was a friend of a friend," she replies shakily. "The friend told me how he always felt stuck in Hana and wanted to leave."

"He felt stuck in one of the most prosperous nations in the entire Southern Chain?" I shake my head. "Please. Is that all?"

Theodora's throat bobs, and I watch. I wait for the tension to break her like a knife slicing through a vine, but she remains intact and nods as more tears stream down her face.

She's weak, a voice in my mind snaps. *A weak, pathetic little husk.*

The anger bubbles in my chest before I can stop it, like scalding water bursting from a spring and dripping between each of my ribs. I turn on my heel and slam the door behind me.

Of course Emery wouldn't tell her anything. Of course the dilemma I'm trapped in is the same one I rebuke her for.

I climb the steps back into the sun.

And of course it's *his* fault.

I spot Isaiah as he exits the galley, and sailors jump out of my path as I beeline for my cabin. "Dasher!"

He skips up the steps behind me like a fox and slips inside ahead of me.

"Would you like good news or bad news?" He sinks into one of my chairs and casually slings his arm over the back as if he's a comfortable and welcomed guest.

I glare at him as I shut the door, my knuckles white as I grip the round handle. "Whichever you think is the least likely to earn you a bullet to the back of the head."

"Well, our little captain isn't bending yet, unfortunately, but I'm anticipating she will."

I frown.

"We're missing a nudge." He leans forward. "A nudge you can provide if you use the princess—"

"*No.*"

"She will break, Warren!" Isaiah groans and balls his curly hair in his fists. "You won't even be blamed for the princess's disappearance or what happens to her now. It will all fall on me."

"It isn't about that," I snap. "She has no place in this conflict."

He stares with a sour expression.

My mind wanders.

Who exactly are you trying to impress by not? It demands.

Your dying mother?

Yourself?

Who will ever know?

What a polarizing thought. It niggles in my mind constantly like termites chewing through a wall.

Isaiah's expression twists as he shakes his open palm beside his head. "I'm still trying to understand your intentions here, too. Not with the princess, but this errand boy. All this for a boy you can easily replace in a day."

"Replace?" My face burns. "Replace a boy who belongs to a family that loves him?"

"Are you guilty? Is that what this is about?"

"No, because it's not my fault. It's Miss Walker's."

Isaiah grips the back of the chair and lets his jaw hang open like a dog's, his tongue twitching as it traces across the back of his teeth. "We are *so close*," he presses. "I know that if you would just—"

"Just what, Dasher?" I narrow my eyes and deflect the conversation. "Or *Anahera*, I should say. Am I saying it correctly?"

He blinks, and the muscles in his jaw contract. "I'm sorry?"

"I didn't think of you as a liar," I say accusingly, narrowing my eyes at him. "Perhaps 'coward' is a better term. A coward who ran from a perfectly good life, and for what? I know it wasn't so you could board my ship and pretend like you're in the power position here."

I've struck the correct nerve in that twisted little pea-brain of his. His nostrils flare.

"Do I have your attention now, little *angel*?" I taunt.

He hisses, "Warren—"

"You are going to stay on my ship, and your sailors will remain under my command until I relinquish it. Only then will I consider not turning you in to the authorities for what you've done." I tilt my head. "They will not be as kind to you as I am."

He puckers his lips and stares right into my eyes, undaunted. His fists tremble. "Never call me by that name again," he hisses. *"Ever."*

"Then perhaps it would do you a bit of good to listen." I point to the door, banishing him and the princess from my presence and my mind. At least, for now.

He stands and moves toward the door, but he doesn't take his slimy eyes off of me until he's exited the room.

37

Emery

"I HOPE you know that in doing this, I'm risking my neck for you."
Annette glares at me as she reaches for the charting room's door
handle. "Quite literally."

"Wait." I grab her arm, and she looks up. "Are you sure they won't
go back to Chadwick? *This* group specifically?"

"They've been riled up about what happened for the last day and
have said lots of negative things about him, and I don't think he'd take
kindly to finding out they spoke with you behind his back. It'll be
fine."

"Are you *sure*?"

She thoughtfully bites her cheek. "Don't mention your escape plan,
then. They might not take too kindly to that and might tell him so they
don't get into trouble when it happens."

"But if we stage it well enough, it won't look like someone helped
Thea and me."

"We'll cross that bridge when we come to it." She pushes the door
open, and we're hit with a barrage of arguing.

"—understanding what I'm saying." Brooks jabs one of his knives
into the round charting table and points an accusing finger at Alexis.
"It isn't inherently Dasher's fault. If our *captain* hadn't brought him
here or acted like he's acting—"

"He's not irrational like that!" Alexis snaps at him. "There has to
be a reason why he's doing this. I don't think that—"

"How can you look at what he's doing and think he *isn't* out of his
mind?" Gil interrupts with a scowl on his face. His greasy hair is tied
in a knot on the back of his head. "He's never acted like this before!"

"No, no, no, I think he's right," Lucky cuts in. He's dressed in a sleeveless white shirt that exposes his wiry arms. "When has he ever done something without reason? Even if he didn't consult with us?"

Brooks groans. "He's *not* acting with reason!"

"Boys!" Annette snaps.

Six pairs of angry eyes dart toward us. Alexis and Brooks are squared off on opposite sides of the charting table while Tahj, Gil, and Darren sit in chairs scattered across the room. Lucky is perched on the edge of one of the cabinets.

"If you're going to keep bickering about our captain when he's walking right above our heads, then keep your voices down." Annette locks the door with the key she keeps around her neck. "You're acting ridiculous."

"Our conversation should be the *least* of your concerns with what you're doing with her." Brooks yanks his blade out of the table and points the tip at me. "What is she doing here?"

"She can explain it better than I can." Annette folds her arms and takes a deep breath. "It was her idea."

Gil scowls at me. "What?"

"Hush." Annette presses her finger to her lips and glares at him. "Someone is going to hear you."

They all sit back and stare at me expectantly.

I lower my voice. "We can get rid of Dasher in Cordova, but everyone has to be willing to trust me."

Alexis's jaw hangs open. "I'm sorry, what?"

"Captain didn't tell us we're docking in Cordova." Gil scowls at Annette. "Why there?"

"I don't know," she replies. "Let her speak."

"The public doesn't know that Cordova has pirate hunters in their navy," I say quietly. "They don't brand themselves that way because they think it helps them work discreetly, but they are equipped to handle Dasher's two ships."

"Why are we docking there, then?" Tahj demands. "Does the captain not know?"

"Apparently not," Annette mumbles, rolling her eyes.

"What do you mean by 'handle' Dasher's ships?" Alexis asks.

"Has Thea's disappearance been talked about in the news?" I counter.

"Yes," Lucky answers, frowning. The red cloth tied around his hairline falls, and he pushes it back up. "They talked about it in the capsules we picked up in Gatlon."

"Well, how damning is it if Hana Kailea's missing princess runs into the city of Cordova having just escaped from Isaiah Dasher while he's docked there?"

"Oh my stars," Gil mutters, rubbing his face and staring slack-jawed at me. "You can't be serious."

"Do you really think we're stupid enough to commit to a plan that will cause a massive scene and expose us?" Tahj presses.

"It doesn't have to." I shake my head. "If someone leads Isaiah to a secluded area, and then Thea tells the authorities he's there, it won't cause a scene."

"How do you know that?"

"Running operations like this used to be my entire job," I say. "Believe me. I know."

In the back, Lucky lets his head dip to the side as he narrows his eyes at me. Of everyone in this room, I hoped that he would be the most willing and the most open to trying something like this, but I can't tell if that's true.

Brooks chuckles bitterly. "As Tahj said, you don't actually think we're stupid enough to allow something like this to happen, do you?"

"Why's that?"

"'Oh, I promise I'll only tell them it was Isaiah Dasher who kidnapped me!'" he says mockingly of Thea. "That's ridiculous. I would rat out *everyone* who was involved if I were her."

"And it *was* Dasher who kidnapped her," Darren mutters. "*We* didn't do anything."

"The news and authorities won't see it as that," says Alexis. "Especially with the princess. Her word has more power."

"If I go back into the hold and tell her that the only thing she has to do to return home is to *not* say anything about Chadwick to Cordova's authorities, she would absolutely say yes." I fold my arms and grind my teeth together. "She's not a cheater and a liar like the rest of you."

Everyone gives me a dirty look, and Tahj shakes his head. "I'll believe that when I see it."

"Well, it's fishy that you're insisting she has to be the one to do it." Brooks won't keep his mouth shut. "Any of us could run up to them and say that Dasher is there."

"Well, they would probably take you into questioning immediately," Darren chimes in, rubbing the handle of one of his pistols. "It isn't like Dasher is easily recognizable. If Cordova is secretive like she's saying, they'd probably be suspicious if a random person pointed out someone they've never heard of. Alexis is right about her word having more power."

"Right." The knot in my chest loosens. They're catching on. "Thea's claim is enough grounds for arrest even if they don't know who he is. That will take her and Dasher off your plate immediately. I know none of you trust him. I sure wouldn't."

Lucky and Gil exchange a wary glance.

"I don't want to betray the captain." Alexis plops down in his chair. "It's not worth it."

"You aren't betraying him," Annette chimes in. "If anything, you're helping him. Do you genuinely believe Isaiah has done anything helpful since he's been with us? He caused a ruckus in Midway, and now with the princess being here, there's another navy that has the potential to track us."

"The extra sailors have been nice," mumbles Tahj.

Annette knits her brow. "But besides that?"

Lucky hasn't stopped staring at me since I started speaking, and that makes my stomach turn. His gaze briefly flicks to Annette.

"I hate having the princess here," says Darren. "The captain has talked about how we never involve people like her."

"What people? Rich brats?" Brooks scoffs.

Tahj smacks his arm. "Innocent people."

"But it's not Chadwick's fault," Alexis insists. "It's Isaiah's."

"But Captain's slowly assuming blame by keeping her here," Gil points out. "The princess is terrified because she's been caught in the middle of a conflict she has no place in."

Reluctantly, they all nod or mumble in agreement, but Brooks rolls his eyes.

I glance at Annette. Before coming in here, she told me I couldn't plan my escape in Cordova, but why not? Why not have her write to Gordon while I find a place to hide? Cordova is one of the southernmost cities in the Eastern Commonwealth, and since Padstow is near the northern tip, word of my name or what's happened may not be relevant or important to them.

Why *not* have Gordon meet me there?

I swallow.

It just might work.

If I can pull off an escape in the middle of the chaos, it *will* work.

I finally meet Lucky's eyes, staring at his skepticism head-on.

"When do we dock in Cordova, Annette?" Gil asks.

"Three days." She fiddles with a loose thread on the hem of her black coat. "Though I hope you six make a decision before then."

The group exchanges glances.

"Just us?" Tahj clarifies.

Annette nods.

"And Kit," I blurt. "Kit is from Cordova, isn't he? He'd know where Thea can find their authorities. Would he help?"

The six of them tensely whisper amongst themselves for a moment, and I look at Annette again. Her shoulders rise as she takes a deep breath and purses her lips.

Alexis whirls away from the group and points to me. "You. Out while we discuss this."

Annette unlocks the door, and as I step outside, someone bumps into me from behind.

"Hey—"

"Sh, sh, sh." Lucky cuts me off and grabs my uninjured arm to steady me. He keeps a firm hold on the door handle as it clicks shut, and narrows his eyes. "I can see through this little charade you're putting on."

"I don't know what you're talking about."

"Helping us shake Isaiah and the princess might put you in a favorable position to bargain." He purses his lips to hide a cheeky grin. "I knew you were clever, but I hoped that you would've stopped trying to rebel after all that's been done to you."

I shake my head. "I can tell you don't want to be involved. Going behind your captain's back to help me is too risky for you."

"You don't know that."

I frown.

His eyes flick to the side. "There's unrest throughout the entire crew, and they're becoming divided. Some are just rotten and don't care, but some have their feathers ruffled because of the princess and because of Isaiah. The reason the captain has kept such a loyal following is that he's given his men purpose by claiming his ventures are noble. We go after the politicians and the smugglers who've done worse than us. Not the innocent." His lips purse. "Though that's not the case anymore."

"What?"

He glances over his shoulder and tightens his grip on the handle. "This little game he's playing with you has gotten out of control. We have the blood of two Armada crews on our hands already. Someone else is going to get hurt, and it's probably going to be Theadora caught in the middle of it," he hisses. "Nobody wants to be labeled as a princess-snatcher, and everyone is losing interest in this little feud."

"So what are you saying?"

Someone tugs on the door, but his grip holds fast. "*I'm* not saying anything." His voice drips with urgency. "But nobody wants to be labeled as the traitor who helped *you*, either, so you need to keep your mouth shut after this or it'll cause more trouble than we're already dealing with."

"I'm not doing this for myself," I lie. "It's all for Thea."

"You'll have to convince everyone else of that."

"If you're having doubts, then why not just help me?"

He blinks. "I'm not . . . I don't want—"

"Yes, you do." I press him. "You don't owe your loyalty to Chadwick."

He scowls and drops his jaw. "You have no idea what I owe him, Emery. Do not drag me into this!"

The door jerks open as the handle slips from his grip, and we're greeted by a scowling Annette. "They've decided without you, Lewis."

The group quickly gathers into a huddle as Gil whispers the verdict in Lucky's ear, and the boatswain pulls the group back together like a knot of schoolchildren exchanging secrets in the play yard.

Gil and Darren glance up at me warily as Alexis turns around and folds his arms. "If you think this is going to earn you any bargaining power with us, it most certainly won't."

"I didn't say anything about bargaining." I glare at Lucky.

"You didn't have to say it for us to know you were thinking about it," Brooks snorts. "You're going to frame this as you 'helping' us so you can threaten us if we don't help you in return."

"Well, obviously you *weren't* thinking about it until he told you." Annette rolls her eyes and points to Lucky. "Get on with it before someone comes looking for all of you."

The six of them glance at each other, and Alexis glares at me. "We're not going to take your offer."

My blood turns to ice as my eyes widen. "But—"

"We aren't going to risk him catching us," Gil cuts me off. "That's a stupid game to play."

I stare at them with incredulous shock and clench my teeth. I shouldn't be this disappointed, but I'd be lying if I said I didn't let a small flicker of hope take root in my mind and control my emotions.

And just like a ship sailing off in the distance, that hope disappears into the blazing sun.

. . .

I trudge back to the hold like I'm walking to my execution.

"Forget those insolents," Annette mutters behind me. "I can still help you escape, and—"

"I can't leave Thea here." I spin to face her, stopping both of us in our tracks in front of the door

to my and Thea's prison.

"She'll be fine." She scowls up at me. "Warren isn't going to let Isaiah hurt her, and Warren himself certainly won't—"

"What, you think he's just going to set her free at some point?" My voice trembles. "And trust that she won't tell her father to send his army after you all?"

"I can convince him to let her frame only Isaiah like you were talking about," Annette insists. "That can be the deal Warren offers her if he lets her go. And then Hana Kailea's royal guard will go after Isaiah, and—"

"Chadwick's not going to believe that." I roll my eyes.

"Emery, I have spent every day of my life for the last three years with this man," she hisses. "You might know how he acts as a pirate, but I know *him*. He will pick the quickest way out of trouble, and this is it."

"I can't leave Thea." I pray she doesn't see through the darkness and notice the sheen of tears coating my eyes. I turn away. "I can't . . . I won't—"

"Oh, let it up." Annette snatches my wrist and glares at me. "Don't be the hero in a situation where you don't need to be one. Why can't you swallow your pride for once?"

I don't even have time to open my mouth to respond before a barrage of footsteps pounds on the ceiling above our heads. She and I glance up, and my blood turns to ice when a girl's scream pierces the air.

38

THEY KEEP GLANCING AT ME. Just glances. They don't meet my eye when I pass them or nod in greeting like I usually do.

It seems that the tension in the salty air is a permanent addition to this crew.

I do find a bit of humor in the divide between the crews, however. The sailors from Isaiah's seem to have been isolated by mine, doing their jobs in a separate group—and the groups are not speaking to one another. His sailors don't shy away from me like my own.

I watch each of them as they scurry across the deck, pondering who among them has reason to continue sabotaging me.

But I will find them. I will lock down this entire ship and not let any of them off in Cordova if that's what it takes to keep them from running to the nearest mailing post or alerting the authorities.

They will know their place. They will know what happens when they distrust the man who's given them *everything*.

My eyes settle on Lewis as he ascends from below deck and climbs to Harrison's cabin. A few minutes later, Harrison exits the room, fiddling with a button on his black vest. He flinches when I grab his arm.

"S-Sir?" He stares at the deck and blinks rapidly.

"Harrison."

His throat bobs.

"*Harrison.*"

He looks up. "S-sorry.

I become aware of how deeply my fingers are digging into his bony forearm, and I let go. "Is something wrong?"

"I'm fine." He clears his throat and scratches his neck. "I think I'm coming down with something. That's all."

He slips past me before I can respond, leaving the door open behind him.

Lewis turns as I enter the cabin and close the door. He grins, albeit a bit forced. "Captain."

"Is everything all right?" I ask.

"Harrison just wanted to check on my nose one last time." He gestures to his face. "You know how thorough he is."

"Thoroughly irritating," I say with a forced smile of my own.

His laugh is strained.

Why do we play these ridiculous games with each other?

I frown and cross my arms. "What were you doing downstairs?"

"Downstairs?" He wrinkles his forehead. "I wasn't . . . oh." His cheeks flush with red. "Gil told me he lost something in the bunkroom, so I went to help him look for it."

"Lewis, what's going on?"

He doesn't hold the facade like the others, and he bites his cheek. "Permission to speak freely without fear of repercussions?"

I blink and scowl. "What?"

He exhales and stares at the cabinetry. "You aren't going to like it."

"Speak!" I snap, anger blurring my vision. "What is the matter with you?"

Lewis steps back, blanching. "Captain—"

"I am sick of everyone on this blasted ship refusing to speak to me! Refusing to even *look* at me!"

"I wasn't—"

"You were," I snarl. "You were mincing your words to avoid saying something I wouldn't like because you don't agree with what I'm doing either, do you?"

He swallows. "Everyone is worried that since Theadora is here, someone is going to find out, and—"

"And you think dropping her in the middle of the street where she can tell anyone the truth is going to be better for us?"

"Not if . . ." He winces.

"Not if what?"

"Never mind."

"You know, I would have expected you, of everyone, to understand my position. You aren't an emotional wretch like the rest of them and can understand when hard things need to be done."

"Respectfully, keeping a terrified fifteen-year-old girl locked in the hold isn't . . ." His composure is falling. His face turns red as his lips fumble for the words. "You've compromised everyone's morals and the compass you've held for all of us. That's why everyone is upset."

"I did nothing of the sort!" I snap. "I am trying to clean up the mess Isaiah has made!"

"Well, everyone is a little peeved he and his crews are here in the first place," he says, his tone sharpening. "We didn't have a say in that decision, and compounded with the princess being here—"

"What do you expect me to do?" I slowly close the distance between us. "Where do you think you get the right to question my authority?"

"I'm not questioning anything!" Lewis blinks rapidly. "I'm just pointing out how the crew is feeling."

"Who, specifically?" I press, tilting my head. "Who has said what and when?"

His shoulders tighten as he takes a deep breath. "Everyone."

"But *who?*" We're so close that I can hear his shaky breathing. He's cracking. "Lewis, I have been so kind to you over these years. Do not turn your back on me now."

Sweat beads on his temples as he bravely returns my gaze and clenches his jaw. "It's everyone. I don't know the specifics of who is saying what because I've tried to stay out of it."

"And why is that?" I narrow my eyes.

He stares at me in a way he never has before. I remember his eyes the moment I rescued him from that slaving ship, and I have slowly watched the joy and light return to them as the years have passed. They have always been a window to his thoughts. That window is showing panic.

Disdain and panic.

I clench my jaw. "What are you not telling me?"

"Nothing." His eye twitches. "I promise."

A headache pulses across my forehead as I whirl around and march back to my cabin.

You let him lie straight to your face. You're letting them all get away from you.

My hands tremble as I ball them into fists and pace like an anxious animal in a cage. The

intrusive thoughts come in droves.

You're doing something wrong. If you were doing it right, you would have found them.

Doing *what* right?

I stare out the window as my heartbeat roars in my throat and my eyes sting. I blink until my

vision blurs.

If you were any good, you would have coerced Emery to talk. You would know who this traitor is.

And you think you're good at this.

Pathetic.

My hand snatches one of the books off its shelf and hurls it across the room. It strikes one of my picture frames and cracks the glass front. The pieces skitter across the floor.

I stare out the window behind my desk and gape at the vastness of the ocean.

I slam my door hard enough to crack the glass as I storm back outside and below deck, ignoring everyone's confused stares.

If nobody wants to listen or share, then I will find out myself.

Thankfully, no one is there to see me ripping apart the bed sheets, yanking the hammocks off the wall, and throwing ratty blankets, scouring for evidence of a crime, of a betrayal, of anything.

Piles of linen are soon spread across the floor. I stare at it with heavy breaths, suddenly very aware of my ridiculous actions.

I ball my fists and take a step back so I stand in the back corner, anger stirring my thoughts

like a pot of boiling stew that will spill over at any moment.

I glance down at my feet, and something catches my eye.

The folded corner of a parchment envelope pokes out from under one of the tattered blankets. I

snatch it off the floor and rip out the piece of paper inside. It's a half-written, hastily scratched-out letter:

My feet move. My vision blurs. My pistol is out of its holster and aimed at the sky before I even emerge above deck, and everyone flinches as my bullet cracks through the open air a moment later.

I hold up the letter as smoke curls from the muzzle, sweat beading on my forehead. "Would anybody like to reveal who has been selling our secrets to Judge Gordon?"

Everyone stares at me like I'm a madman.

"I found this downstairs in your bunks!" I snap, turning in a circle so they will all see the envelope. "All of you who sleep in the back left corner where the beds make the L shape, would someone like to explain?"

I repeat the words on the letter, and the silence seems to magnify.

I bark out a laugh because if I don't, I'll explode. I need Hyde. I need Annette. I need someone to confess.

My eyes land on each person who sleeps in that corner of the deck.

Ross. Daniel. Algie. Mikhail.

Mikhail.

That rascal from the North has had a glimmer of darkness in his eye since the day he joined my crew. He looked down the moment I looked at him. I surge forward, and the crowd parts.

He pales. "Captain—"

"Do not lie to me," I say, my voice quiet and even. "Did you write this?"

"It wasn't me." He purses his lips and meets my gaze. "You can check my handwriting. I don't know anything about that."

I move to Ross, who adamantly shakes his head.

Algie and Daniel do the same.

I turn away and crumple the paper in my fist. "You four are suspended. If you even *think* about setting foot off this ship once we dock, you are dead." I spin on my heel. "*Dead.* Do you hear me?"

All they do is stare. That's all any of them do anymore. They stare like I am a bloody madman.

One of them is going to talk if I have to pound the information out of them myself.

My cheeks burn as my eyes flick over the faces of each of my crewmembers; some of them stare with disturbed discomfort while others won't look at me. Isaiah and his sailors stand off to the side, watching in abject fascination. The clown strokes his chin and skims his slimy tongue over his crooked teeth. He watches me with fascinated determination, studying my every move and word like an eager student watching his master.

Tightness stirs in my stomach.

Annette.

Where is Annette?

I can't find her face in the crowd.

I turn on my toes and march back downstairs.

They'd still trust you if you weren't so terrible at leading them.

You would have found the traitor by now if you were paying attention to them.

My mind spins.

This traitor won't matter if I know where Gordon is.

And as Isaiah said, the key to finding that out is sitting just below my feet.

39

ANNETTE RELEASES my arm and throws the door open. The room is empty.

No.

I bolt down the hall without a second thought.

"Emery!" she hisses. "Stop!"

This ship has become so familiar to me that in my blind, panicked frenzy, I can follow the screams to the exact spot they're coming from. Dread fills my stomach in a tight, nauseous wave as I bound up the stairs.

I run through the sleeping deck to find two of Isaiah's pirates dragging Thea between them. The colored strands of thread are missing from her hair, and her face is streaked with tears as she wriggles and screams. They set her on the floor, and she scrambles away from them and backs up against the wall, whimpering and clutching her hand to her chest.

Chadwick stands over her and watches like a fox preying on a rabbit. His face is frozen in a mask of anger, with wide eyes and each livid breath whistling through his clenched teeth.

I rush forward before being stopped by one of the pirates, who keeps his arm locked around my waist as I struggle. The inside of my nose burns from the rotting smell emanating from his body.

"Oh, look who it is." Chadwick frowns pitifully at me, his eyes alight with enough fury to start a fire. He hauls Thea to her feet, wraps an arm across her chest and shoulders, and positions a blade against her throat. "You're a bit late to the showing."

Thea sobs. "Emery, tell him what he wants! Please tell him!"

Chadwick grabs her jaw. "Look at the poor, pathetic princess, *Captain*," he sneers at me. "Whatever will you do to rescue her?"

My mind whirls through the de-escalation phrases from the Academy, but all I can hear is my heart pounding.

Think, think. Come on.

"Let her go." My voice trembles as I struggle to regain my breath. "She has nothing to do with this and you know it."

"All the more reason to use her!" He drops the knife and grabs her hand, squeezing her fingers until she cries out in pain. Her last two fingers are purple, swollen, and crooked like broken twigs.

"What's another finger?" The monster I've come to know is on full display as Chadwick flashes his slimy teeth and squeezes tighter, his knuckles white. Sweat drips from his spiky blond hair and down his temples. "Where is Gordon?"

"Emery!" Thea begs. Her tears plaster her thick hair to her face

Snap.

Her screaming sends a chill down my spine.

"Stop!" My voice is raw from shouting.

"Do you still think I'm bluffing?" His breaths are shaky and erratic, and his hands tremble. "Tell me now, or I swear I'll snap every single one of her fingers."

"Okay, okay!" I hold out one of my trembling hands. "He's-he's in the Southern Chain. He's been there this entire time. I swear to you."

"*Where?*" Chadwick squeezes Thea's hand again.

"Stop it!"

I turn my head to see Gil and Alexis bound up the stairs and surge toward Chadwick. The rest of the group from the charting room follows.

There's another loud pop from Thea's hand before they reach him, and a few others have gathered on the stairs. I finally wriggle free from the pirate holding me and grab Thea while the others push Chadwick back. Her sobs are nothing but raw, unfiltered pain and agony as she cradles her hand.

Shouting echoes through the space, and terror fills my bones. My instincts scream to run where it's quiet, where it's dark, where we are far from the commotion and can hide from it all like children hiding from monsters in the night.

I make eye contact with Chadwick through the crowd of confused pirates gathering in the hold. Annette grabs his arm and pulls him toward the stairs, and even she looks haunted by what's happened.

Everyone keeps glancing back and forth between Chadwick and me, but I don't break my gaze. Neither does he, even as he wipes saliva from his chin. His eyes pierce through me as if he's a demon waiting to bare his claws and rip my throat out.

The demon was well hidden under his cold, calculated mask, but that mask has disappeared.

. . .

The voices mesh together as they bounce off the walls of the doctor's cabin.

"I'm done. I'm *done*."

"This is getting out of hand."

"On three, okay?" Harrison positions Thea's middle finger to realign it while I keep my arm around her body, holding her opposite arm in place as she and I perch on the edge of one of his examination tables. Annette holds Thea's wrist while Harrison adjusts his grip.

The doctor takes a deep breath. "One, two—"

Crack.

Thea cries out and flinches, and my arms tremble as I hold her.

"What are the others saying?" Gil mutters on the other side of Harrison's cabin. "Do they know?"

"Well, they heard the screaming." Alexis folds his arms. "Some of them are arguing with Isaiah's crew."

I open my eyes.

Isaiah.

Chadwick.

This is what happens to pirates left unchecked, and I will kill both of them with my bare hands. I will return to Padstow and reign absolute hell over Chadwick if it's the last thing I do.

Harrison's cabin has become a safe space for the dissenters to speak without fear of their complaints getting back to Chadwick. The noise between them and a shaky Harrison fixing Thea's fingers drones on like the reverberating echo of a bell, pounding, and pounding, and pounding—

A hand settles on my shoulder, and I nearly bat it away before seeing who it belongs to.

"Gil and the others are starting to change their minds," Annette mumbles to me.

I stare at the ground. By keeping my secret, I chose the judge with a potentially shady, secluded past over the innocent girl who was stolen from her home. She keeps touching her hair in search of the colored ribbons and whimpering when she can't find them.

You knew this would happen and you still said nothing, that little voice whispers.

"Emery." Annette nudges me again.

I blink rapidly, speaking quietly enough so Thea won't hear me. "Don't."

Lucky appears in the doorway and comes to Annette and me, glancing at Harrison as he wraps Thea's fingers in leather splints designed for broken digits. I squeeze her tight as she ducks her head, desperately trying to hold back the tears. The guilt is nauseating.

Annette folds her arms and rests her back on the wall beside me. "What's going on out there?"

Lucky stares at his fidgety fingers as he bends the corner of one of his playing cards. "Isaiah is commanding the ship and the crew because the captain hasn't left his cabin. He's brought more of his sailors over from his other ships."

Annette bites her lip and shakes her head. "Emery, tell Theadora that she needs to go along with this plan, or we're all going to be in serious trouble."

"You aren't going to get anywhere without help," Lucky scoffs with a wrinkled brow.

"Which is why you're going to talk to Gil and the others," she whispers, grabbing the collar of his gray shirt. "And if a word gets out to the captain about this—"

"Fine!" Lucky hisses, his face reddening as he glances around the room. "Keep your voice down."

I glance at Thea and clench my quivering jaw as Harrison fixes her fingers. Her fear emanates from her body like mist.

I grab Annette and whisper into her ear. "How will they get her out?"

Before she can answer, the men grow louder, pulling our attention to them.

"The captain will never know," Gil snaps at Lucky, his voice dripping with anger. "Believe that."

"There are a *lot* of things he isn't going to know," Darren mutters.

Annette and I turn as the group of six—Brooks, Gil, Alexis, Tahj, Darren, and Lucky—convene in a tight huddle. I catch only bits and pieces of the conversation.

"—dinghy port downstairs," Gil whispers. "Float her and Kit to shore and have them take off."

"Someone is going to see them. Why don't—"

"No, no, listen to him. That's a good idea."

I force my attention away and gently take Thea's wrist, studying the splints. The leather is supported by four strips of metal that keep her fingers extended, and it's all tied together with small buckles that encircle the broken bones.

I can't even draw the strength to look at her face. I thought the weight of my own grief and torture was unbearable, but this guilt is heavier still.

Brooks stands on his tiptoes to be seen over the shoulders of the others and points one of his knives at Harrison, who flinches. "You're going to keep your mouth shut about everything you just heard and saw. Nothing we say leaves this room."

Harrison inhales sharply and blinks rapidly. "Don't threaten me, please. I don't want any place in—"

"Good," Brooks snaps, widening his eyes. "Then stay out of it."

The doctor shrinks back and nods obediently.

Brooks sheathes his knife and sighs. "Their royal navy is going to skin all of us alive once they see this." He offhandedly gestures to Thea.

"They won't know it was us," Annette says, glancing at Thea. "You're going to tell them it was Dasher."

Thea inhales shakily. "W-what?"

"You heard her." Gil folds his tattooed arms and blows a strand of salty hair from his eye as he glares at her. "If we help you escape, you will not say a *word* about our involvement to your father or anyone else."

"Thea." I gently touch her leg, finally forcing my gaze to meet hers as the knife in my heart twists deeper and deeper. "It's the only way you can go home."

"But—"

"No." My chin quivers as I squeeze her leg and shake my head.

I watch her glassy eyes flick to each pirate, including Annette and Harrison. She pinches her lips and nods. "Okay."

Tahj groans softly and mumbles something under his breath to Alexis.

"All of you need to get out before someone notices we're colluding in here." Annette rubs her temples. "You're giving me a headache."

Brooks rakes his hands through his hair on their way out the door. "We've all lost our bloody minds."

I slip off the edge of the table and grab Lucky's sleeve just as he turns away. "What about me?"

"Sh!" He glances back at Harrison, who drops his tools and ducks out of the room with the others like a skittish sheep joining its flock.

I grab Lucky's arm and drop my voice to a whisper. "How is helping me any different?"

He huffs. "I told you—"

"Jailbreaking the Pereculum isn't going to be the end of this." My voice trembles." All that 'honor' you spoke of will be out the window when pirates more despicable than you are free again, and it's going to cause chaos. And the odds aren't in your favor to fight it, considering Chadwick just lost half his crew's loyalty by keeping Thea and...." I trail off as my voice catches in my throat.

"What do you think you're going to do about it?" he mutters, scowling with his usual snark. "You're not even a captain anymore, Emery."

My stomach twists. I hear Thea wince behind me.

"The Armada is in shambles," he continues. "The news has said there have been three other attacks on pirate-hunting ships in the last two weeks, and most other cities have ceased their operations because of it."

"Who's attacking?" I ask.

"They don't know, but I think people saw how easily the first two Armada crews went down and are seeing that and your tarnished name as a sign of weakness across everything." Lucky drops his hands and shrugs. "I don't know what you expect to do, but whatever it is won't be very helpful."

I glance at Annette, who scowls and pushes off the wall.

"Fine." She dusts off her pants. "I will take care of it, Emery. But Lewis, if you aren't going to help, then stay out of our way."

Lucky's eyes flick between us before he turns and leaves the room.

Annette takes a shaky breath and smooths the wrinkles out of her light blue blouse. Her hands tremble

"Are you okay?" Thea asks quietly.

Annette glances warily at Thea before her eyes flick to the door. "Fine." She clears her throat and turns her head away from us. "I'm fine. I have things to attend to."

I swear that for a moment, the light reflects a sheen of tears coating her eyes. I watch in confusion as she marches outside, leaving the room in silence.

Thea and I are alone and unsupervised, and suddenly, I am no longer the center of everyone's attention. Over a month ago, I would've drooled over the circumstance of being untouched and unguarded, but now I just drop my head and squeeze my eyes shut, exhausted.

I sidle up next to Thea again as her jaw begins to quiver.

"Why does everyone keep looking at me like that?" Her voice breaks.

A month ago, I would have conjured the perfect response to comfort and reassure her, but my mind stays blank.

The guilt spreads through my head and chest like a parasite, until I'm sure that it will consume me and make me nothing without it.

I shiver. No.

My chest swells as I leap forward, my skin crawling as I march toward the door and throw it open.

314

40

Warren

MY CREW SEEMS to listen to Isaiah and actually *acknowledge* him as he makes commands and speaks to them. It makes my blood boil.

I watch them through my cracked window like a haggard recluse. He stands at the helm, having weasled his way into the position I assumed he's had in his sights since the day he approached Derrick and me in the tavern.

I should kill him now. Take aim and strike him right between the eyes like the vermin he is.

What could they even do about it?

A better man wouldn't hide in his cabin like a coward, hiding from the anger of his crew who saw him in a moment of weakness.

And that repellent display didn't even get me what I wanted.

Nor did it stop the crew's secrecy, I reflect, watching Gil whisper something into Kit's ear as they pass each other.

I peer a little longer, my eyes scanning the deck until they land on Annette.

She stands near the foremast, watching Isaiah disdainfully with a pucker in her lips. Isaiah notices her staring, tips up his chin, and signals for her to approach.

When she does, he leans down so his moving lips are mere millimeters from her ear, and her shoulders tighten as his hand creeps to the small of her back.

I ball my fists, willing her to look up and notice me, to spare me a glance and be the only person on this bloody ship who will finally see me.

I turn away from the window and set my jaw as my stomach twists and turns with dread. I glance down at my hands as the princess's screams seem to bounce through my skull.

What were you thinking?

A good captain doesn't act like that. He doesn't betray the rules he's set for his crew.

A good man doesn't spit on the morals his mother has drilled into his head.

I straighten my back as a shudder of pure, icy conviction seizes it, and I flinch as the door flings open.

"Hyde, stop!" I hear Annette's voice before I even turn around and see her chasing him into the

room.

"Did she tell you where Gordon is?" he demands.

"No," I spit.

"Where are they?" He flexes his fingers. "I'll get either of them to talk."

"Stop it!" Annette jumps in front of him on the way to the door, looking like a mouse standing up

to a mastiff. "This has gone on enough!"

"Has it?" Hyde sneers at her. "You're awfully merciful, aren't you?"

She looks past him, and her eyes bear straight through me like needles. Her tone breaks as she stares at me with glassy eyes. "Warren, what were you thinking?"

My heart dies in my chest.

Hyde looks back to me. "Were you planning on doing this all along?"

"—shouldn't be doing this!"

Isaiah's voice grates on my ears. I turn to investigate his tirade and the door bangs open, startling me.

"Chadwick!" Emery storms into the room and lunges toward me in a fiery rampage. Hyde

catches her by the waist and lifts her off the ground before she can advance.

I blink, surprised to see her moving freely.

"You had no right to attack her!" she screams, her nails clawing into Hyde's baggy sleeves. He lifts her off the ground with ease as she writhes and kicks, her face flushed and her eyes brimming with frustrated tears. "No right!"

"I'm happy to see I'm not the only one who has lost their mind." I rake my hand through my hair. "Though I don't know what you think coming in here and acting like a fool is going to do to fix it."

She only stops when Hyde grabs her injured arm and twists. A sob hitches in her throat.

"Okay, okay, stop!" she begs. "Stop it!"

"That's enough," I snap. "Let her talk."

He rolls his eyes and lets Emery sink to her knees as she clings to her arm. Her shoulders hunch as she ducks her head, I'm assuming to conceal the agony and tears streaking her face.

I am a hateful, prideful man for relishing it despite the bigger issue at hand. I watch her with vivid fascination. Annette purses her lips and turns away.

Movement near the door catches my attention, and I whip my pistol out of its holster and click the hammer.

Isaiah innocently holds up his hands as he stares down the barrel with his wide eyes. "Easy, Warren."

"Tell me why I shouldn't shoot you where you stand," I spit, my teeth clenched.

"I've just come to see if she's told you anything." He steps into the room as if he's testing his

weight on a thin sheet of ice. He stares at Emery expectantly, but she stays on her knees as she cradles her arm. She glances up and closes her eyes, and I roll mine.

"Come on." Isaiah's tongue pokes out of the corner of his mouth. "This is just selfish on your end."

I clench my jaw as Emery blinks back tears and stares at the floor. "Don't hurt her again," she mumbles, almost absentminded. She looks at me, and her jaw quivers. "Do whatever you want to me, but leave her out of this."

Isaiah stops his pacing and stares at her, his body and face eerily still. Her shoulders tighten as if she can feel his steely gaze piercing her.

Annette is at my side in an instant, but I speak before she can.

"Annette, can you please send someone to watch the princess?" I ask politely.

Isaiah jerks his head toward me as Hyde raises his eyebrows.

"Quickly, please." I hope the gaze I give her says what I can't: *Please. We'll talk.*

Her jaw falls open for a moment, but she listens and slips outside.

"You think I'm going to go after her next?" Isaiah clenches his teeth and chuckles bitterly. "I love that you still think you're the moral compass who gets to impart his wisdom to the rest of us."

A nauseating wave of self-loathing rolls through my stomach. I can feel Emery's bleary eyes boring into me.

She shakes her head. "It didn't get you what you wanted, did it?"

Something in my expression shows her that her words struck a dark chord in my chest, because she continues to rub salt into the gaping wound.

"It didn't get you what you wanted, and you've lost your crew's trust, but you *love* that feeling of power and control, don't you?" Her voice trembles not from fear, but from pure, unadulterated rage. "Admit it."

Stars, she is just the *worst.* I've had her beaten to pulp and locked in the dark for over a month, yet she refuses to give in.

Even though she's on her knees, even though tears well in her eyes, even though she has no power to bargain, she still clenches her fists and stares at me with zero fear.

It's no wonder the public latched onto her. Who doesn't love resilience?

Surprisingly, she breaks our gaze as she rises to her feet and glares at Isaiah next. "I'm going to find you." Her voice trembles. "When I'm home, I swear I'm going to hunt you down and kill you for bringing Thea into this if it's the last thing I do."

She glances back at me, extending that promise to me as well.

Undaunted, Isaiah chuckles and clasps his hands behind his back. He takes comically large steps across my cabin and stands inches from her, balanced on the balls of his feet as he looms over her with that vacuous, wide-eyed grin plastered on his face.

"I've never bent for Warren Chadwick, the most feared pirate in the Commonwealth." He clicks his tongue. "Why would I flinch for you?"

I make a decision in that moment without any preamble. In another life, I could imagine him reigning terror across the seas and running a successful business venture—but he never will because I can also imagine what he would look like, drained of color as he slowly and painfully bleeds to death on the cold, hard ground.

My fist grips the handle of my holstered pistol as I clench my jaw.

I won't have to imagine it for much longer.

41

Emery

TWO DAYS LATER, Thea takes a deep, shaky breath and rubs her arm with her uninjured hand. Her eyes are glassy as she stares ahead at the hold's door. "I don't know."

"We're dropping anchor in ten minutes," Annette urges her, crouched by her side. "You have to decide."

Thea glances nervously at Brooks, Kit, and Gil. "What if he catches me?" she asks, wiping her tears. "What's he going to do then?"

"He might come after you again if you stay here." Brooks furrows his brow as he wedges one of his blades under his dirty fingernails. "Would you rather do that or potentially escape or risk getting your fingers snapped in half again?"

Thea whimpers and shrinks against me.

"Will you be gentle?" Annette snaps at him. "She's young and terrified."

"She's not much younger than the rest of us." He rolls his eyes. "Certainly not you, Annette."

"Thea, he's right about staying here versus escaping." I touch her arm, pretending that the terror in her eyes doesn't bother me. "Kit?"

"I'll be with you the whole time," he chimes in, twirling a match between his thumb and forefinger. "Well, not the *whole* time, but you'll be safe the second you reach the *marinha* base."

Thea looks at me, her jaw quivering slightly. "Emery—"

"Why don't I go with you?" I throw out the suggestion as a final effort to make my escape easier. I glance at the others. "I'll make sure that—"

"Absolutely not." Gil glares at me. "It's bad enough that we're sneaking *her* off the ship, let alone you."

A bell rings above our heads, signaling the crew to begin the mooring process.

Brooks sighs and stands up from the floor. "Forget it."

"Thea." I grab the sides of her face. "This might be our only chance for you to go home safely, and another might not come along if you don't take this one now."

The bell rings again.

"Princess," Kit mutters impatiently.

She bites her cheek and nods. "Okay."

The knot in my chest unravels. "Okay."

"Good grief," Gil mutters, throwing his hands in the air and turning away.

"I'll come back for you when the rest of them start their distraction," Kit tells Thea. "It'll be quick."

"Will one of you tell me what you're planning?" Annette asks. "What can I do?"

"I'll tell you, Annette," Gil says on his way out the door.

"I'll be one second."

She waits a heartbeat for the rest of them to leave, and she whispers her planned escape route in my ear. An image of each step I will go through crosses my mind, and I nod, my heart pounding in anticipation.

"Count to fifty after the knock on the door," she mumbles at the end. "I'll find the mailing outpost and go send the letter to Gordon and his friend while it's all happening."

Hope flutters in my chest as she rocks back on her heels, staring at the floor. She sucks her teeth.

"I should thank you for doing this for him," she mumbles.

I swallow and stare at the ground. "I should say the same to you for helping me."

Her lips twist. Awkward beats of silence pass.

I take a deep breath. "I'm sorry we all jumped to conclusions about your situation. I didn't realize how terrible it was."

She looks up, blinking in surprise.

"Reese is a good man for helping you."

She hesitates for a moment, then clears her throat. "Yes, he is."

But will it ever undo a ledger of bad? I wonder.

I wait for her to say more, wondering what she's thinking now. She still supported this plan, knowing full well that I would go after Chadwick after this.

I can't figure out why. She speaks of him too thoughtfully for their dynamic to be strictly professional, but however odd her split loyalty is, it doesn't make sense for her to betray him like this. Perhaps, like me, Chadwick has lost the trust of those around him and is losing allies, including her.

Annette takes a deep breath. "When you see Reese, please tell him I'm doing fine," she says at last. "Tell him I hope this repays the debt I owe to him."

"I will."

She stands and dusts off her blue trousers. "Good luck."

"You too."

She smiles and shuts the door behind her.

There's a hollow pit in my stomach, spinning with the same anticipation as the night before my Sealing.

"Stand up there with an even chin and eyes fixed ahead." Vaughn's lips brushed against my ear as he stroked his fingers through my hair. *"You'll blow them all away like you always have."*

My eyes crinkle.

"Are you okay?" Thea asks quietly.

Her innocent voice makes my heart twist. I face her and put on a smile. "I'm okay. Are you?"

She shakes her head and stares at her broken fingers as the tears fall again. "I think he'll kill me if he catches me. I really do."

"They won't catch you." I gently grab her arms and turn her to face me, ignoring the pain in my shoulder. "You're too fast for them to catch. Like lightning."

She smiles weakly.

I squeeze her forearms. "We'll all be home before you know it."

"What will happen to you?"

"I'll write to you as soon as they take me back to Padstow and we get it sorted out," I say, almost reassuring myself. "Judge Gordon will sort all of it out."

"Are you sure?" she mumbles.

I swallow the knot in my throat and nod. "He's one of the most reliable men I know."

She keeps staring at her splinted fingers, and the guilt seems to rip a hole through my chest.

"I'm so sorry," I mumble. "I should have acted faster, but . . ."

She shakes her head. "Please don't stew over it."

That doesn't mean that it isn't my fault.

"Emery." She touches my knee, and I look her in the eye, my breath catching each time I truly study her face, the round baby fat of her cheeks, and her nose, small and button-like.

Very little news out of Hana Kailea ever travelled as far north as Padstow, but what did always revolved around King Tanuvasa and his darling daughter, leading the world of humanitarian work in the Southern Chain. Her pride and love for her people bled into every letter she wrote to me.

Most would say that Chadwick or I are too young to be doing what we're doing, but she is *especially* too young to be here. She hasn't seen the horrible things that the pirates and I have seen, nor does she deserve to be dragged into this twisted, broken world.

And frankly, neither did Kearon Romney. I could have chosen to believe his cries as we dragged him aboard the *Chaplain's Heart*, his screams that he was just a bookkeeper and errand boy who never saw a hint of crime.

Could have. Should have.

Once this is done, maybe there is a way to free him from the Pereculum and send him back to his parents. If nothing else, that's a wrong that can be made right.

I rest my head against the wall and breathe deeply. My body and mind ache with the pain of a thousand lifetimes, from the twins' betrayal, to being taken from my family, to the torture we've suffered.

Tears well in my eyes. I would give anything to go back to the night after the Sealing where Vaughn held me with a love that would have moved mountains, where Miles's cocky grin and brash persona could be seen and felt throughout the room, where the sparkle in

Charles's studious eye seemed to glow brighter than ever, and Callie's quiet, resolute presence by my side seemed immovable.

I hope each of them knows how much it meant to me.

I feel Thea's fingers weave between mine, and despite the dense emotion in the air and the tears in her eyes, she smiles at me.

. . .

About fifteen minutes later, Kit slips inside the hold, his eyes wide with adrenaline. "Are you ready?"

Thea rubs her bleary eyes and throws her arms around my neck. I hold her tight with my left arm as she kisses my cheek.

"I'll talk to you soon," I whisper.

Kit nods at me as he helps the princess to her feet, and soon the two of them are gone.

I inhale shakily and rub my knees. Kit needs five minutes to smuggle Thea off the ship, and that's five minutes that Alexis and Tahj need to keep Chadwick and the others occupied. Five minutes to make it into town and have Kit show her where to go.

I touch the blade Annette gave to me, strapped to my upper right arm and concealed under my blouse and withered red coat. Even though it's dirty and one of the gold buttons is missing, its odd familiarity calms my nerves for what's about to come.

There's a soft tap at the door, and I count to fifty before standing up and slipping outside. Footsteps and voices echo above my head as I creep forward down the long, dark, dusty hallway.

There's an open door on the left, and I peek inside.

Only a handful of the ships in the Armada have such an intricate system for loading and unloading dinghies like this. A large sliding door is positioned at the end of a system of metal tracks and pulleys that help move the boats in and out with relative ease. I steal a glance through the sliding door and see we're moored about fifty yards offshore. The harbor is chock full of other ships, and sailors and merchants are scattered across the busy harbor.

One of the dinghies is loaded onto the sliding track, ready to be cast into the water. The boat is filled with large canvas sacks and small casks, and I rock one back and forth to find it empty.

I grab the large canvas sheet folded atop the pile and step inside the boat, wedging myself in the space between two crates. It takes some wiggling to fit comfortably as I lie on the splintered floor of the boat and cover myself with the sheet.

It isn't long after that the door creaks open again.

"—take to shore," I recognize Mikhail's voice. "It'll take longer since we're lugging more weight."

"It's fine," I hear Annette reply. "I didn't want to wait longer for whoever was leaving next."

The boat rocks as someone pushes it down the track, and it gently splashes into the water. Sweat trickles down the side of my face as the two of them climb inside.

"Do you want help to row?" she asks.

"It's okay," Mikhail grunts as I hear the first oar cutting through the water. He mutters a curse under his breath. "What's back there that's so heavy?"

My heart clenches as the shadow of an arm and hand passes over me. One of the crates shakes, and the bottles rattle inside.

"Just the casks and bottles," Annette says.

"That feels heavier than *just* that," mutters Mikhail. "Are you sure?"

More of Annette's shadow crosses over me as she raps on the other cask. "It's empty."

The tension in my chest tightens as the boat slowly floats through the water. I tighten my grip on the edge of the sheet and clench my teeth as the minutes pass, and soon, we bump into the dock.

"Where do you think I could find people to help carry these bottles to and from the well?"

Mikhail asks, breathless.

"Try going there first to see," Annette replies as the two of them climb from the boat. Her voice grows quieter and quieter as they walk away. "I know a few other cities have people who can help. They might have that here."

I count to one hundred, my heart rate rising with each second that passes. I poke my head out from under the tarp to ensure I'm alone before clambering out of the boat. I wrap the tarp around my head and shoulders like a cloak and race up the stairs to the upper dock.

Cordova's red-and-cream terracotta-roofed buildings burst across the green landscape, their domed and curved shapes like frozen ocean waves. They're very different from the strict, square style of the Commonwealth's northern cities, and I'm tempted to stop and stare in curiosity.

My heart pounds as I slow my pace and move toward a large stone-and-clay wall perpendicular to the harbor. I skitter around the near edge of the wall and press my back against it as I catch my breath.

I peek around the wall and watch the harbor, which looks more like a cove than anything. The massive U-shaped dock encircles a handful of ships moored in the deep water, including the *Lost Commandeer* and Isaiah's twin sloops. Each captain's ship is spaced about ten yards apart, and a handful of dinghies travel between the two boats.

My eyes scan the area, and I spot Annette buttoning her black jacket as she exits the harbor, a pistol on one hip and a knife on the other. A letter sticks out of her back pocket. On the opposite side of the harbor, Brooks and Darren lead Isaiah up the far staircase from the lower dock, and I wonder what lie they conjured to get him to leave his ship.

A bell tower chimes twelve times in the distance, and I move with the flicker of hope igniting in my chest.

Please, please.

I glance around the corner one more time, and my stomach drops. A group of Isaiah's pirates emerges from the lower dock, and they quicken their pace with their weapons in hand.

My heart drops as they take the same route Annette did to the mailing outpost.

42

WHERE ARE YOU, little rat?

I don't plot to kill people very often, but the combination of hatred and unfiltered ambition to do so burns like fire coursing through my veins. I didn't realize delivering death would be such a *rush.*

I weave through the busy street, alive with the rumbling of carts, carriages, and shouts of clashing languages I barely recognize. A group of children kick a ball in an alleyway, and an aroma of garlic, peppers, and spices I don't recognize fill the air.

Despite its rich beauty, the winding curve of the streets and seeming lack of uniformity make it tricky to navigate, where stony roads lead to dead ends and frustrating roundabout loops. Sweat runs down the column of my spine as I dodge between the terracotta-roofed buildings, following Isaiah's general direction. The pedestrians pay me no mind as I quietly slip past them.

The only thing I can't figure out is why Brooks and Darren were with him. The thought is only a whisper through the haze of anger.

I glance over my shoulder and pull my hat lower to conceal my face. I've never run business dealings through here before, but I need the least amount of attention drawn to my face as possible, given the crime I am about to commit.

I can hide from those that don't know me, though deep down, I know nothing I can do will erase the smear on my crew's image of me. Perhaps that's why I didn't tell any of them what I was planning.

I am going to win with or without them. I will.

I blink sweat from my eyes and quicken my pace. Behind me, footsteps fall into line with mine. They follow me as I round a corner. And another corner. And another.

I steal a look over my shoulder. I can't see the owner's face clearly, but his clothes are too casual and ratty for him to be a part of any law enforcement agency here. Nonetheless, I make a show of brushing the hem of my coat aside to grab my knife, hoping to deter whoever this petty aspirant is.

It works for a moment, but unless my ears deceive me, another set of footfalls soon emerges. I swear under my breath, glancing ahead to see Isaiah rounding the bend ahead past a blacksmith's shop.

I sigh. So much for not being noticed.

I stop on a dime, whirling around with my weapon pointed at my pursuers. They're armed and dressed in ragged, filthy clothing that reeks of salt and sweat as if they've spent days at sea.

I smile and tilt my head. "Shall we do this quickly and quietly, or would you like to make a scene?"

. . .

Emery

My lungs feel as if they're full of cotton as I run.

I don't think Annette saw the men behind her.

The cobblestone streets are slippery with dirt and other debris that skids under the soles of my boots. I reach in through the collar of my blouse and retrieve the knife from its sheath.

Like the other mail outposts in the region, Cordova's is marked with a tall, brick spire with the city's red-and-yellow flag waving atop. It stretches above the squat terracotta-topped buildings, and I use it as a beacon as I weave through the maze of the city.

I doubt anyone would recognize me this far south of Padstow, but I turn plenty of heads as I dash through the crowd. I jump over a ratty leather ball that a group of children are kicking back and forth to each other.

I race up a short hill and run straight for the outpost in the distance. Annette and Isaiah's pirates are nowhere to be seen, and dread rises in my throat.

"Emery! Emery! Are you here?"

I stop dead in my tracks and turn in a circle to look for the source of the voice, confused. "Thea?"

"Emery!"

No. I move toward the source of her voice. "Where are you?"

"Here!" She darts out from between two tall apartment buildings. Her clothes are disheveled.

"What happened?" I grab her shoulder and scan her head to toe. "Are you hurt? What's going on?"

"Kit was . . . Kit was attacked." She pants, her face coated with tears and sweat. "They all jumped out of nowhere, and I ran just like you said. I didn't let them catch me."

That's when I notice the sprinkle of blood across the front of her blouse, and my stomach drops. "Where's Kit, Thea?"

Her chin quivers.

"You never made it to the police, did you?" I ask.

"I thought maybe you hadn't turned yourself in yet and I could find you," she stutters. "I—"

"You did the right thing." I squeeze her shoulders. "It's okay."

It's not okay. We are as far from okay as humanly possible.

In the distance, shouting echoes from the base of the mailing outpost tower.

Annette.

I swear under my breath and take Thea's forearm. "Do not leave my side. Do you understand?"

We sprint to the outpost and come to a stop behind the wall that surrounds the tower. The shearwaters screech as they zip through the sky, soaring above the empty courtyard below.

Empty, save for Annette, on the ground and holding her face in her hands, three pirates surrounding her, and Isaiah, cackling like a maniac as he rips open the letter to Reese.

. . .

Warren

When the first sailor attacks, he lifts his sword so far over his head that it gives me a split second to pull mine, parry, and sidestep as he stumbles forward like a drunk. I swing my knife and pivot, but the other sailor is quicker and ducks away, then draws a pistol from the small of his back. I lunge and grab his arm, and the bullet cracks through the air and scatters the patrons in the street like pigeons.

I snatch my pistol from my underarm harness, but the first recovers quickly and knocks it out of my hand. He swings his fist and connects with my jaw. I spin as I hit the ground, and with a desperate swing, I miraculously catch his leg with my blade. He falls back and yells out as blood peppers the stone path.

His partner is on top of me in an instant, landing another hit to my nose and one on the side of my head. I fumble blindly for my sword as he drives his fist into my neck and stares at me with wide, yellow eyes.

With both hands, he raises his knife above his head, and my hands shoot out and grab his wrists before the blade plunges through my skull. My arms shake with the exertion.

And for a moment, time stands still, like the grave.

My mother's face flashes in my mind, wrinkled with disappointment at the wretch that I have become; then Annette's, shadowed with disdain and yearning for who I could have been for her; Hyde, shaking his head because the man who's stood at his side since day one has finally turned his back on him.

No.

I will not die a monster to them. I will not die trapped in this picture forever.

I yell, spitting blood as I jerk my attacker's arms to the side and crane my neck so the knife scrapes the cobblestone an inch from my ear. I thrust two fingers up and into one of his wild eyes; he flies backward, screaming and holding his face. In the distraction, I lunge forward and twist the blade from his hand and jab it into his stomach. He doesn't move again.

The other sailor is hobbling away with his bloody leg, but I grab the dead pirate's gun, and after another *crack*, the injured man collapses in a heap.

My breath shakes.

Move. Move now.

I trudge, spitting more blood and wiping it away from the side of my face.

"Dasher!" I roar. "Come and find me, you coward! Come and—"

I stop, and my shoulders tense,

Bodies. On the ground in front of me. I left two behind, and they seem to have followed me.

I blink.

One lies face down, still clenching his knife like he did when he slept aboard my ship. The other stares at the sky, his twin pistols discarded on the ground.

My body turns to ice.

I crouch and touch Brooks's back, staring in horror at the blood pooling from underneath him and soaking the stone road. His usually tan skin has turned a sickeningly pale shade.

And Darren . . . his throat . . .

I press my hand over my mouth and bow my head, wheezing as I grab the knife from Brooks's still-tight hand and pocket it. I slide his eyelids shut and grab Darren's pistols off the ground beside him. His holsters look wrong without them, so I slip one of the guns inside for him to have just a little longer. My vision blurs as I close his eyes too, and I have to turn away or else I might blow away in the wind.

Shouting in the distance steals my attention, and I force myself to leave them.

Death was just around the corner. Death was inches from my head.

And death be damned if he does not take Isaiah when I'm through with him.

. . .

Emery

"Kahu, Kahu, Kahu." Isaiah cackles as he stares at the letter. Blood inks his tattoos, and what look like bloody handprints coat the front of his white shirt. "I didn't think Gordon would choose such an inferior place as *Kahu,* Miss Ridgewood."

Thea's breath catches behind me, and I squeeze her hand as I peer out from behind a nearby clay building.

Annette winces as she pushes herself to a sitting position and faces him. Blood trickles from her mouth and split bottom lip.

"Now answer me this." Isaiah narrows his eyes at her. "My sailors tell me Captain Walker and Princess Theadora seemed to have disappeared from the *Lost Commandeer*. You wouldn't happen to know anything about that, would you?"

She winces and swallows. "No."

"I find that a bit dubious considering this." He holds up the letter. "All of these little schemes have to be connected."

"Well, you can figure that out for yourself." She glares at him.

Isaiah's lips pucker as his eyes roll to the sky. "Nobody can ever just tell the truth to make things easier, can they? I suppose if I can't take Emery with me, I can just take you."

"Warren will—"

"Warren won't rescue his little belle again after finding out she's betrayed him," he jeers. "Will he?"

I glance at the knife in my hand. It's useless against the pistols the pirates are carrying.

"Annette!" a voice calls in the distance. "Annette, where are you?"

Isaiah's attention snaps up like a dog's. "Find them!" he barks at his crew. "Don't let them near here!"

I drag Thea behind me as I sprint toward the sound of Gil's scratchy voice as he calls for Annette again. About fifty yards from the outpost, we nearly run face-first into him and Lucky on an abandoned street.

"Stop shouting!" I hiss.

"What are you doing here?" Gil snaps at me. He glances at Thea. "Where's Kit?"

Isaiah's pirates leap out from around the corner, and Gil raises his pistol and fires at them. Lucky dives behind the front face of a shop while Gil scrambles to the opposite side of the road to reload. I drag Thea forward and we huddle on the ground beside Lucky.

"What are you doing here?" I demand, grabbing his sleeve.

"I could ask you the same thing!" he snaps. "Gil and I ran to look for Annette and Warren because we overheard Isaiah's sailors on our ship talking about following Warren ashore. We saw a group of them following Annette on the dock, too." He cocks his gun and glares at me with wide eyes. "Your stupid plan wasn't successful, was it?"

A bullet strikes the corner of the building, sending clay shards flying, and Lucky jumps back, yelping.

I lean forward and spot Gil lying on his stomach across the street with his pistol muzzle barely poking around the corner, one eye squinted in aim.

"Where's Annette?" Lucky whispers harshly. "Have you seen her or the captain?"

Another bullet cracks through the air, and Gil is suddenly on his feet with a smoking gun, sprinting after one of the attacking pirates. "Get back here!"

Lucky scrambles to his feet and charges. "Gil, stop!"

I'm nearly on his heels when Thea cries out behind me and is swept back around the corner by an unseen force.

She cries out, "Emery!"

"No!" I leap toward her.

Her captor moves fast despite carrying a wriggling, thrashing Thea. We weave back through the streets, but we veer closer and closer to the harbor. My legs and lungs burn as we ascend a hill that brings the dock into view, and my strides grow shorter with each exhausted step.

Suddenly, Thea buries her teeth into his arm, and he shouts in pain and comes to a stop. She wiggles free and tumbles onto the ground, giving me time to swipe at the pirate with my blade. He knocks my hand aside, and the knife clatters on the stone as I jump on him. My shoulder aches as I hook my elbow around his neck.

"Thea, run!" I grunt as he stumbles back. "Find Lucky!"

The pirate drives his elbow into my ribs before I can make another move, and I lose my grip and hit the ground hard. I grab at his heel as he runs forward.

"Emery!" I hear Lucky's voice behind me.

I grimace as I clamber to my feet, only to be met with the muzzle of a pistol pointed between my eyes. I stumble backward in surprise, bumping into someone and stepping on their toes.

"Easy!" Lucky grabs me and holds out his other hand to the gunman.

I stare over the barrel at Isaiah, eyes twitchy and wide. I look behind us and see four of his crewmembers trapping us in a circle. One of them has a body slung over his shoulder, and my breath catches.

No.

It's not Thea. It's Annette. Blood clots in the hair on the back of her head as her arms hang limp like a ragdoll's.

"Lucky—" I start.

He raises his gun, but the others do the same. The hammers click.

"Ah, ah, ah!" Isaiah rolls his eyes. "Don't be so dense. Drop it."

Lucky grimaces and bends down, tossing his pistol to the side.

Thea got away. At least Thea got away.

I glance back at the harbor, expecting a firestorm coming from Chadwick's ship, but the sound of crumpling paper catches my attention instead.

"Look what I found!" Isaiah chuckles and holds up the letter, staring dead into my eyes. "You didn't even have to betray the judge, Captain. Look how it all worked out!"

I look to my left, down a winding alleyway where a pair of steely gray eyes watches me from under a tri-pointed hat.

I open my mouth, but Lucky, seeing what I see, clamps his hand over it.

"Don't you dare," he hisses into my ear.

"Everyone to the ship!" Isaiah shouts jovially. "We have a judge to catch!"

. . .

Warren

I beat Isaiah's group to the dock as I take cover behind a wall, and I peer around the corner and watch them emerge from the city.

Even with an injured shoulder, two people restraining her, and four weapons pointed at her, Emery thrashes and kicks so much that her escorts pick her up off the ground and haul her across toward the steps to the lower dock. Lewis is shouting something obscene at Isaiah's sailors, and one of them kicks Lewis so hard in the knee that he shouts in pain and collapses. They drag him toward the steps.

My focus is on Annette as her captor follows Lewis's. She slowly begins to stir from her unconscious state as she's draped over his shoulders, and my throat tightens.

What was she doing out here?

What were any of them doing out here?

I glance out at the water, and my stomach drops when I can't find my ship. Panic claws at my heart as I frantically scan over each moored boat, but mine has vanished.

Footsteps scuffle on the road behind me, and I see Theadora run by with Gil at her side. He sees me, widens his eyes, and grabs her, lifting her with ease and clamping a hand over her mouth. She screams and writhes.

"What's going on?" I seethe.

"Lucky and I ran to find you and Annette after Isaiah's sailors followed you out here," he rambles. Sweat-soaked hair sticks to his face as he tightens his hold on the princess. "We ran into them instead, but I don't know how they escaped."

I frown at his uncharacteristic discomfort. He breathes hard and stares at me with wide, anxious eyes.

"Where's the rest of the crew?" I demand. "And the ship?"

"They're moving the ship to get away from Isaiah's in case they attack. His sailors started fighting ours and demanding to know where you were."

"But where is *my ship?*"

"Captain!"

I spin *again* and see Mikhail emerging from between two buildings. "What's going on?"

"They said they were going to circle the island in case Isaiah's ships started attacking us and wait for us to find them on the south side," Gil says urgently. "We need to go."

"What about Isaiah's sailors that were on the ship?"

Gil blinks rapidly. "It was messy. Some jumped off, but our crew was throwing bodies overboard when Lucky and I left."

I turn back to the dock. "Why is Isaiah taking all three of them?" I wonder aloud.

"Emery must have told him where Gordon is."

"But Lewis and Annette?" I demand, but I know the answer to my own question as it leaves my lips. You don't take prisoners unless you want to use them as leverage.

"Marinha! Marinha!" a voice in the distance shouts. *"Rendam-se agora!"*

Mikhail swears under his breath and turns to run, but my feet stay rooted in the ground.

Even though they probably see me as a monster and have withdrawn their trust from me, it hurts to watch more of my crew slip through my fingers.

Isaiah watches with pride as the three new prisoners are dragged forward. The front of his shirt is soaked through with blood, and my cheeks burn with anger.

Emery is relentless as she fights, but in that chaos, no one notices Annette as she weakly lifts her head and looks right at me. Her lip is split and bleeding.

"Kahu!" she shouts, her voice strained. All eyes follow her line of sight to the wall, to me. "He's in Kahu!"

I gasp.

The man carrying her wrestles his hand over her mouth as they all disappear below the dock.

"Move! Go!" I snap Gil. I don't spare a second glance at the group as I run. Gil throws Theadora over his shoulder while Mikhail brings up the rear. I cut away from the city's center, hoping to catch a glance of my ship as it circles the island and praying that whatever head start Isaiah gets on me won't cause me to lose this race.

43

Emery

THE HAMMER-POUNDING throb in the back of my head has returned. It feels like I'm tumbling down a dark tunnel even though I'm lying on my side, and I groan. I keep blinking as my eyes adjust to the dark, but every time I lift my head, it feels like it's full of cannonballs.

Somewhere else in the darkness, someone shifts and groans in pain.

"Who's there?" I croak, tugging at the ropes on my hands. An iron shackle is clamped around my ankle.

"My knee," Lucky's voice moans, and a chain rattles as I see a lumpy shadow writhe in the dark on the floor across from me. His hands are tied behind his back as well. "I can't bend my knee."

I rest my head back on the floor and wince. Luckily, I'm lying on my left side, and my injured shoulder is protected, but it still throbs with each beat of my heart. I cough as nausea fills my throat from all these knocks to the head I've taken. "Where's Annette?"

"I don't know."

I grimace, digging my forehead into the floor.

"Are you okay?" he rasps. "Are you hurt?"

"No."

"Do you see why I was so hesitant to do this?"

"You didn't *do* anything," I grumble.

"Do you know how much drama it would've spared us had you not been so stubborn?"

"Yes, because everything that's happened for the last month and a half is my fault," I spit. "Forget anything that *you* have done and the atrocities that can never be fixed. Forget that because Chadwick didn't get rid of Isaiah when he had the chance, we're trapped down here and will probably die once Gordon is found."

"Warren isn't going to lose this game," Lucky insists, grunting as he rolls over on the floor. "He knows what Dasher is capable of, and he'll come prepared."

"No—"

"Yes," he snaps. I can feel his eyes glaring at me through the dark. "He'll be ready. You've seen all of this firsthand. Warren doesn't *lose*."

I don't say anything, because it's not just that. There are two roads, and each of them leads to Gordon's death, either by Chadwick's or Isaiah's hand.

And then what? I don't imagine I'd be useful to either of them after that. The fear of death has never been a motivator for me before, but it's powerful now.

My head and shoulder throb as I wriggle in my bonds. "Can you stand well enough to fight?"

Lucky scoffs. "You want to *fight?*"

"Not now. We can try to sabotage Isaiah once everyone gets to Kahu."

"I don't think my knee is going to heal within . . . How long does it take to get there?"

"Three days."

Lucky sighs. "Lovely."

I don't say anything, but it worries me that Isaiah took Lucky and Annette as well. Unless Isaiah has plans to use them as leverage against Chadwick once we all arrive, there's no reason for them to be here.

I squeeze my eyes shut, loathing how close I was to something finally pulling off a successful escape. I could practically taste freedom and smell the orchids permeating through my family's house.

"Come here." Lucky grunts as he sits up. "Scoot closer to me."

It takes some maneuvering, but soon we're sitting back to back as he blindly fumbles with the knots on my hands. My fingers begin to tingle.

"There." The ropes fall free, and I turn to work on his. The knots on his hands are impressively tight.

We sit in silence as I work, and he sighs and dips his head.

"What?"

"They took my sword," he mumbles.

"It's a *sword*." I grit my teeth and wedge my finger under one of the loops. "What does it—"

"My mother bought it when Warren freed me. I have no idea how she was able to afford it because she wasn't making much money while I was gone, and I felt guilty about it for months."

The sadness in his voice softens my irritation. I pull the loop free and feel for another in the dark. "I'm sorry."

The ropes fall away and settle into a tangled pile on the floor.

"How did you even . . ." I search for the words and drum my fingers on the floor. "Why were you working on the ship in the first place? The slaving one."

"My mother found a merchant who was willing to take on fresh sailing school graduates, and she signed the contract he presented, not knowing it would trap me in an indenture."

"You weren't of age?"

"Not yet. The man who gave us the contract took me to this tiny island in the Western Territories and dumped me off to the next captain like garbage." He tosses the ropes aside, his face taut with anger in the dark. The vile things he's seen are etched into his green eyes, and I don't think they will ever disappear.

"How did you meet Chadwick, then?" I ask.

"The captain of that ship was setting up some sort of exchange with him, but—"

"Chadwick never does business with slavers." I frown, racking my memory. "Right?"

"Exactly. He didn't know that's what they were."

"What happened?"

"I was so lucky." He snorts. "Literally. You have no idea. Warren saw me working with the boatswains and just started asking me questions. After I told him what happened, he convinced the captain to sell my indenture to him so he could terminate it. I still needed to work, and I love to sail, so it all sort of fell into place."

"What was the captain's name?" I ask out of genuine curiosity.

"Grey. He was arrested by Piersford a year after I was freed."

I remember. It was Piersford's biggest arrest in nearly a decade.

I look up at him. "You were basically recruited from slavery to piracy."

He hesitates for a moment. "What else was I supposed to do?"

"Anything!" I say, exasperated. "Literally anything else!"

"My hand was forced."

"That's a lie."

"Okay, fine. It wasn't forced. But I'd rather die labeled as a pirate than as a slaver," he snaps. "Even my mother understands that."

"She knows what you do?"

"She knows that we ethically trade and only go after those who don't. It's not a lie."

I sit back and bring my knees to my chest.

What would your *mother say about what's happened to you?*

Guilt pools in my stomach. I touch the cartilage on my ears where her earrings used to hang, and Lucky touches his hip where his sword belt used to be. He reaches for the laces on his boots, fiddling with the ratty threads and breathing deeply. A worry line burrows between his eyebrows as he puffs a strand of hair from his forehead.

"You can be more than whatever he's making you into now." I glare at him. "If you feel guilty—"

"You don't know what it's like to be indebted to someone like this." His eyes cut through me like fire through paper. "You will never know."

My heart sinks, though I don't know if he deserves my empathy. It's no wonder he's still loyal to Chadwick.

My stomach clenches when a door swings open and light pours into the room. Two of Isaiah's pirates carry Annette into the room and let her stumble to the floor. She barely catches herself with her bound hands, and she doesn't look injured aside from her swollen jaw, thankfully. They lock a third bolted chain around her ankle.

"Chatty, aren't you?" one of them quips, barefoot and dressed in nothing but rags that hang off his frail, grimy skeleton.

The other ducks into the room carrying a brown sack. "Chatty and *loud.*" His left eye is almost completely gray from the pupil to the edges of the white. He drops the sack near Annette as the skinny one steps into my line of vision.

"A Walker!" A single chipped tooth sticks out of his bloody, yellow gums, and his jittery eyes won't focus. He grabs my jaw and sticks one of his fingers in my mouth without warning, skimming his grimy nail across my teeth. "You'd sell for quite a pretty penny, wouldn't 'cha? Look at those pearls."

I resist the urge to bite at his finger as I yank my head back. The nauseating taste of sweat, fish, and dirt lingers on my tongue.

"What about him?" The blind pirate grabs a fistful of Lucky's hair and tilts his head back. He frowns. "The slaving ships need more deckhands."

Lucky's jaw clenches.

"No, Topper doesn't like boys, remember?" The other licks his lips and stares at me. He grabs both sides of my head and scrunches my hair with his greasy fingers, digging them into my scalp. "But the pretty blonde girls—"

"That's enough," Lucky snaps.

I try to twist away, and I shudder as his nails dig into my hair and hold my head in place. The other comes over to study me like an insect crawling in a jar. The smell of his breath on my nose makes my stomach churn.

"Stop it," Annette says raggedly. She winces as she pushes herself to a seated position. "She isn't going to tell more than I did."

"We'll see about that." The skinny pirate flashes his toothless maw at me as he bends down and unlocks the chain on my ankle. The other hooks his arm under mine and unceremoniously hoists me off the floor.

"Hey!" I wince in pain as he holds my arms while the other rebinds my hands. I barely have the thought to use the trick I taught Thea, keeping as much space between my wrists as possible so the ropes stay loose.

"Emery—" Lucky calls after me, but the door slams shut.

I hope the pirates don't hear my shaky breathing or sense the fear pulsing through my temples, but soon, my senses are overwhelmed by the blinding morning sunrise, the bustling sounds of sailing, and the wetness of the air on my skin. Some of Isaiah's pirates stare at me as we walk across the ship, and cannons are scattered across the deck like sand on a gray, dusty rock. The rancid smell that hangs in the air adds to my nausea.

The single cabin is concealed with royal purple curtains and six brass locks screwed into the wood of the door. The gummy pirate pushes the door open, revealing a cluttered wooden cavern. My nose curls at the pungent smell of alcohol, so concentrated that my sinuses ache after a single inhale. Weapons, from rifles to axes—and even broadswords and maces—line the walls from the floor to the low ceiling. Two tables sit perfectly parallel to one another and are covered in a smattering of navigation tools.

The captain himself is hunched over a map, dressed in clean black clothes with his elbows and shoulders flared like an acrobat's as he maneuvers a nautical divider across the inky parchment. I glance to the side and see an empty shearwater cage next to a propped-open window, wondering who he could possibly be writing to.

Isaiah whirls around with the divider pinched between his fingers, grinning. "Hello."

The blind pirate pushes me forward.

"Sit, would you?" Isaiah gestures to a chair in the center of the room. He turns and drops the tool on the table.

I sit, testing the tightness of my bonds as I gently twist my wrists back and forth. He stares at me without blinking, like a demon staring into a sinner's soul. I swallow as he closes the distance between us.

"So Miss Ridgewood was the rat aboard Chadwick's ship!" he says jovially. "Quite a twist. I wonder what he's thinking now. I hope he isn't too heartbroken about it."

I don't answer.

"My question now is, have you known this entire time where Gordon was, or did she tell you when you tried to hatch this little scheme?" He narrows his eyes.

"What is it to you?"

"Genuine curiosity." He shrugs, as if it were obvious.

I inhale slowly through my nose. "I knew before she told me."

"You resisted Warren for so long, and for what?"

I swallow. "I owe it to Reese."

"You owe it to him?" He raises his bushy eyebrows. "So being stubborn to protect him wasn't just out of the goodness of your little heart?"

Well, when it's phrased that way…

"He is a friend to my family," I say sternly. "None of this should be a concern to you now."

"But it's so interesting." He leans forward and tilts his head. "You are quite a character to study."

His icy tone makes my skin crawl.

"If you knew he was in Kahu, then you could tell me more about this little hideout he's constructed for himself." He dusts something off his hands and turns around. "Miss Ridgewood wasn't very helpful. She swears up and down she doesn't know where on the island he could be, but I think you do."

"What makes you think that?"

"It's not *just* that. Gordon will come if he hears your voice or sees you in danger, perhaps, but we can spare you that discomfort if you speak now."

I grit my teeth. "I don't know where he is. I promise."

He stretches his jaw. "You know, I was hoping to catch both you and the princess in Cordova so I could at least get you to cooperate, but alas." His lips curl. "I suppose one can only break so many fingers, so perhaps she's lucky to have escaped."

My stomach churns as I strain against the ropes, and twinges of pain zip through my shoulder.

"Well, Captain, if you won't be of use to me now, you can stew in the hold for the next few days while we sail." He waggles his eyebrows at me. "Since your pride is the shackle you choose to wear."

"You call me Captain mockingly."

"It's your title. That little thing you want to be remembered for so badly." His snake-like tongue skims his teeth. "What is it like knowing the world and its children have their eyes on you?"

I frown. "I try not to pay attention to them."

"But isn't it gratifying to know that you've left some sort of impression upon them?" His question is genuine. His head tilts as he slowly closes the distance between us, his eyes wide. "That somewhere your name is etched into the folds of history forever? That you will not be forgotten?"

I study him warily, watching the stone-faced, unwavering intensity in his expression. "I am not…" My voice catches. "What others say about what I've done doesn't add to its value."

"Oh, but it certainly has detracted from it." Isaiah clicks his tongue. "Who is talking well of the name Emery Walker with all the negativity surrounding it?"

"None of it's true," I spit, my hands trembling. "That's what matters the most to me."

"But who knows that?" His lips curl into a sneaky, conniving grin. "At least they will remember you more. You remember a killer better than the man who arrested him, don't you?"

I clench my teeth. "Your lust for validation is pathetic."

That struck a nerve. He clasps his hands behind his back and leans forward so we're eye to eye, and my chest tightens.

"What is life worth if we are not accepted by others?"

I sit back in the chair, suddenly seeing what has been present since this conversation started—perhaps it's a little boy, clawing away from the dregs of a society that had turned its back on him, but instead of turning his back on it, he begged, gripping its coattails and replicating its every move to find success. Status. Validation.

"You and I will be remembered as the monsters we've been painted to be. Isn't it thrilling?" He chuckles, high-pitched and grating. "We will not be remembered for what we've done, Captain. We will be known by the things they've *said* about what we've done."

44

KAHU.

Perhaps I should have paid a little closer attention to the handwriting when reading the letter I found in the crew's bunks. It was the same exquisite handwriting on the maps and charts downstairs, and it belonged to an animal who indeed never changed her spots when she left her posh world behind.

I wonder if Emery too felt the gut-wrenching weight of betrayal like I'm feeling it now. There is a wretched hole in my heart, yet my mind is completely silent about it.

"Kahu in the distance!" someone shouts. "Kahu in the distance!"

The voice grounds me in the present. I glance at the horizon's sunset between my bow and stern, wondering when the devil Dasher will appear.

Overhead, Chip screeches and zooms off in the direction we've come from, headed for Midway and my mother. I told her I loved her and not to bother writing until she heard from me again.

If she hears from me again.

The knot in my chest grows.

"Captain!" Vey calls from the helm. "Where are we docking?"

"Um . . ." I check the old, poorly drawn map of Kahu. "We aren't. Stay offshore and circle the island so we can find Isaiah."

Tahj, standing at the bottom of the steps below Harrison's cabin, repeats my command, and it's then repeated by someone further down, so a ripple travels across the entire ship.

Even after everything, I still seem to have their respect and attention. I think the news that Isaiah killed three of their companions and captured two others has lit a fire in each of their hearts, and I pray it keeps burning until Isaiah's body floats in the ocean.

I grip the railing and stare at the tiny speck in the distance. Kahu is the least developed of the other countries in the Southern Chain and has the weakest government and navy. Luckily for them, pirates and other thieves have turned a blind eye to it because there's a whole lot of nothing going on there.

Until now, obviously.

It's a perfect place for a wanted man to hide. It's a perfect place for chaos to brew.

I fold the map and pocket it. "Gunnery at the ready?" I shout.

"Yes, sir!" Joaquin, who ranked just below Kit, has taken over his role as master gunner and is wandering around ensuring everyone is appropriately armed. "They're downstairs readying the cannons now."

I wonder where Kit's body lies in Cordova.

His home. He could have died just down the street from his childhood home.

I force the thought away.

Behind me, Harrison's door opens, and the princess steps out with freshly splinted fingers. She's traded her blood-speckled blouse for a boxy tweed shirt, though I don't know whose it is.

She won't look at me. I watch as she scurries down the steps like a mouse and beelines for the set leading below deck, but she runs straight into Hyde's massive chest.

He grabs her arms and effortlessly pushes her back, planting her at the bottom of Harrison's steps and telling her not to move. He limps up the steps and scowls at me. "You're just letting her run around unsupervised now, are you?"

"She is the least of my concerns right now," I retort.

"Two o'clock!" Mikhail shouts from the crow's nest. *"North Star!"*

I snap to attention and see the sloop anchored about a hundred yards off of Kahu's tiny harbor, but its twin is missing. I stare at it for a moment, squinting through the orange rays of the sunset. I only count ten sailors on the deck, but then I see a collection of dinghies rowing to shore. I beeline for the front of my ship for a closer view and grip the railing to steady myself. I can barely make out two blonde figures sitting in one of the boats. I look past them to the shoreline, where two other sailors are dragging a writhing figure in a red coat between them.

"What are they doing?" someone behind me asks.

The possibilities flip through my mind like pages in a book.

What could the clown possibly be planning?

"Captain?"

I turn as the idea forms in my head and shout for Mikhail. He leans over the edge of his perch.

"Can you see the other ship?" I call through cupped hands.

He peers through his brass spyglass for a moment. "No . . . wait! There!" He points. "Look!"

Sure enough, I spot the bow of the *South Sun* beginning to peek around from the backside of the island. Oddly enough, its crew is rowing dinghies toward the island while the sloop approaches its twin with a heavily reduced staff.

Yes.

"Okay! Everyone listen!" I leap onto the railing and hold the rigging for balance. "A group will go ashore with me to find Lewis and Annette while the rest of you defend the ship from either Dasher's crews or the Kahuans if they realize that their island is about to become a bloody warzone. I want Gil, Alexis, Mikhail. . ." I take a shaky breath as I count off my ten best fighters by name. Not many of my sailors are of Southern descent or look the part, and I pray that we don't gather too much attention.

"Tahj, make sure the princess stays out of the way. Daniel, you're coming with me, and I need you to grab a piece of paper and a pencil." I glance at my first mate. "Hyde, you're in charge."

Gil rounds up the ten as Daniel runs to grab a pencil and paper, and I stare at Hyde, my eyes

pleading. If all goes south, I need to know he's with me and that he's beginning to forgive me for all that's happened; that despite all I've lost, I have not lost him.

The muscles in his jaw twitch, and he nods once. He takes command with such ease as he leaps onto the railing, balancing on his strong leg. He cups his hands around his mouth. "The lot of you left behind, arm yourselves and stay alert!"

. . .

Isaiah whistles a low, haunting tune from the bushes, staring dead ahead at a cottage basked in the dying evening sunlight. Gordon's cottage, made of straw, woven wood, and palm leaves, is nothing that would draw attention or be suspicious to the average eye.

It took time, but the locals eventually pointed out the house of the pale man who never seemed to leave his home and never spoke to any of his neighbors.

Isaiah glances down either end of the crooked dirt road and moves forward, hiding a knife behind his back as he creeps forward.

Bile rises in my throat, and I have to will myself not to be sick. I have imagined this moment a thousand ways in the last month and a half, and it's about to end in the worst way possible. I adjust my wrists behind my back, testing the tightness of the ropes, which are somewhat loose thanks to the trick I taught Thea back on Chadwick's ship. My shoulder throbs.

Isaiah pounds his fist against the splintered door and inspects the shoddy little porch, dusted with straw and palm leaves. We wait in silence for about a minute before he pounds on the door again.

Another minute passes, and Isaiah chuckles and shakes his head. He kicks down the door in one strong go, causing the rest of us to flinch.

The pirate behind me takes my elbow and leads me inside the cottage. Dust floats through the air and makes the hairs inside my nose curl, but otherwise it's still. I don't imagine a runaway would leave the bed untouched, unwrinkled, and unslept-in, nor would there *not* be at least some articles of clothing scattered around or tucked neatly away into a travel bag. A spotless wooden kitchen shows no speck of discarded food, either.

Isaiah crouches down and blows into the iron oven, and a flurry of ashes swirls upwards. He presses his hand on the outside and quickly pulls it back as if it's hot.

"Look." One of his pirates fiddles with a crooked slat of wood on the wall and rips it away. Clothes and shoes come tumbling out, including Gordon's wire-frame glasses. The left lens is covered in spiderweb cracks.

Isaiah walks over and looks inside the hollow space. "Packing was not a priority in a rush, was it?"

I glance down at my escort's pistol hanging limply at his hip. The other three pirates, including Isaiah, are studying the hollow space.

"Good spot to hide money," one comments.

"Or a person."

I twist one wrist slightly to see how much the ropes move, and one strand falls limp against my fingers.

Yes.

I twist again, but my ears prick at the faint sound of rustling dirt just outside the window. I freeze.

"So where is he?" someone else grumbles.

"Not far. He's old and slow."

None of them notices it as it comes again, this time closer to the house.

Isaiah's throat bobs as he turns back to me expectantly. He sticks his tongue out of the corner of his mouth and shakes his head. "I don't imagine that old man has gotten far, like you said, Sydney." He closes the distance between us, and his presence seems to loom over me.

I swallow. It takes all the willpower I have left not to glance at the window, but I don't have to. There's more rustling and a soft thud outside, and everyone in the hut goes silent.

Isaiah reaches for his pistol. He clicks the hammer and silently signals toward the window, and two pirates head for the door, weapons in hand. The captain turns his back and creeps toward the window, and the guard at my flank turns his head toward the door. My wrists writhe and my skin grows hot, and another loop falls limp.

All eyes in the room dart to the window at the loud *crack* of a gunshot and the shouting that follows.

"He's running! He's running!"

Isaiah swears and immediately bolts outside. I shake off the ropes, and in one swift motion, spin on the ball of my foot and snatch the remaining pirate's gun from his holster.

He grunts in surprise as I leap away, but he catches my arm before I can lift the gun. He swings his arm, and I duck, feeling the air whoosh above my head. He reaches for my other wrist and knocks the pistol out of my hand.

I recover quickly and kick the outer part of his knee, and he shouts in pain as the joint pops. He lunges forward and grabs my ankle as I turn to grab the gun, yanking my feet out from under me.

I land hard on my tailbone and scramble from my back to my stomach, clawing for the gun, but the pirate is relentless and twice my size and strength. The weight of a boulder lands on top of my body as hands tighten around my neck. The gun's wooden handle brushes against my fingertips as I grunt in pain. Blood seems to burst in my eyes as he drags me backward.

Crack.

Thud.

The pirate topples off of me in a lifeless heap on the floor. I finally grab the gun, rolling to my back, then hold it up and click the hammer.

"Don't shoot! Don't shoot! It's me!"

My eyes focus, and I freeze.

Reese.

It's odd not seeing him dressed in his pristine gray robes and glasses—the ratty cotton shirt he has tucked into a pair of too-short black trousers is a jarring sight.

But it's him. Alive.

I drop the gun as he reaches to help me to my feet. All I can do is stare for a moment. He pulls me into an embrace, and I nearly melt into him from pure, unfiltered relief.

"I'm grateful for your careful finger." He chuckles, pulling back. He doesn't seem surprised to see me. His tired eyes are shiny with tears, and it isn't long before I realize mine are as well. My tongue swells with the weight of a thousand words I want to say.

He touches my face. "What has he done to you?"

"None of it is true," I blurt as my heart races. "Everything the news said was all a—"

"I know," he says calmly. "I knew he would do it."

"Did you know Isaiah was coming?" I gesture around the room.

"My friends here warned me that someone was here looking for me." He glances over his shoulder. "We have to go. I have a way for us to get off the island." He digs through the hidden closet and returns with another loaded pistol, two knives, and a sword. He gestures for me to retrieve the fallen gun from the floor as he hands me one of the knives, as well as an extra shot and gunpowder, and I set to work reloading the gun.

"When Annette wrote to warn me about what Chadwick was planning, I had to act fast," Reese says as he straps one of the knives to his hip. "I didn't hear about it until after your Sealing ceremony, and Annette didn't tell me he was going after you until later."

"Why didn't you write to Padstow and tell them what was going on?" I demand, my voice breaking. "My family would have—"

"I didn't want my letters to be intercepted by someone with bad intentions or who would twist the narrative." He shakes his head as we exit the hut and step into the Kahuan sunset. "Emery, the rot there runs deeper than you will ever know. I didn't trust that someone wouldn't have gone to Chadwick or would be in league with him. I couldn't do it. I've been trying to set things up for you to be able to clear your name in case we couldn't reunite, and that's been risky enough. Believe me."

"But Annette—"

"She never knew until I started hearing your name in the news, and I wrote to her one time to tell her to help you escape." His eyes crinkle. "I'm sorry, Emery. It had to happen like that for this to have a chance." He rubs the top of his head. "Why are you here with Isaiah? What happened?"

I rehash the story of how Chadwick and Isaiah became tangled in this mess. "Isaiah intercepted the letter from Annette that would have told you to meet me," I finish, stuffing the gun into my left pocket. "He wouldn't have known otherwise."

I didn't give you away. I want to say. *I held out against everything they threw at me.*

I almost open my mouth as if his validation will justify everything I've endured for the last month and a half.

"Funny how it all works out." He smiles, despite the tension.

"Mr. Gordon! Mr. Gordon!"

I turn around. A tall Kahuan boy with a round, babyish face sprints toward us, his feet bare and his tan skin covered in sweat. His eyes are wide with panic as he flails his bony arms around.

"You have to . . . go," he pants. "Kien and I led them all the way . . ." He huffs and looks up at the sky. "S-sorry."

"Where, Sami?" Reese grabs his shoulders. "Where are they?"

"I got too far ahead of them, but they're coming back this way."

"Okay." Reese hands me a knife and the sword, and he reaches into his pocket for a folded envelope. He presses it into my hand and grabs my wrist with a firm grip to get my attention. "Do not lose this. It has everything you need to clean up this mess and expose the truth. You're going to need it in case we're separated."

I pinch the envelope, but there doesn't seem to be more than one piece of paper inside. I frown at him.

"You'll know what to do when you read what's inside." He stares at me with wide eyes. "You *have* to keep it safe, Emery. Promise me."

His urgency makes my stomach clench, but I nod and slip the envelope into my pocket.

He sighs, and despite the uncertainty and the hell of the last six weeks, he smiles at me. A true, charming smile. "Let's go. We're going home."

45

THE GROUP that had Lewis and Annette was long gone by the time we arrived onshore, but as my group crouches in the thicket, we watch as more of Isaiah's sailors flood the island. My knuckles are white against the grain of my pistol as I lead my group of ten deeper and deeper into the island. We keep to the jungle and step lively, following Isaiah's pirates as they traverse the dirt roads in hope that they will lead me to Isaiah, who will then hopefully lead to Gordon.

Sweat drips in my eyes as we creep forward, but my focus is razor sharp. We approach a cluster of huts on an eerily silent street. One of them is missing its front door, and I frown at it.

"What happened?" Gil mutters behind me.

I watch in fascination as a group of sailors appears from behind the hut. Another comes stumbling out of the hut holding the back of his head, and his companions catch him before he faceplants.

"Gone," he slurs. Blood drips down the back of his neck. "They're . . . gone. Gordon and the girl."

"What an astute observation!" Isaiah storms out from behind the hut with two pistols clenched in his fists. "Did you see which direction?"

The groggy sailor shakes his head.

I turn back to my group and stay crouched low as I signal for them to gather around.

"Go east to look for them," I whisper, pointing toward the massive mountain looming in the distance as I look at Mikhail, Porter, Dillon, and Seth. "Take them back to the ship once you find them. The rest of you are with me."

The group of four creeps through the jungle, and I turn my attention back to Isaiah.

"—had to have seen where they were going," he scoffs at the group of six sailors that have gathered around him. "It isn't like they have a place to run or hide! Go find Sydney and a few others to find them. You'd better get to them before the Kahuan authorities do."

I anxiously tap my fingers against my kneecap.

"You two go watch the docks to ensure Judge Gordon and Captain Walker aren't trying to escape," Isaiah snaps as he gestures to the two sailors standing the furthest from him. He turns and marches back in the direction he came from. "Careful not to alert Kahu's authorities. And keep an eye out for Warren's ship while you're at it."

I creep forward, and the rest of my group follows the sound of Isaiah's voice as he ventures out of our sight.

"—going to use those two to draw him out once he gets here," he's saying. "If he hears his precious Miss Ridgewood screaming, he'll come running."

My throat tightens. The dark voice in the back of my mind whispers to abandon her like she abandoned me by writing to Gordon, but I won't. I can't. I fear that love, or whatever this monster is, has its icy claws embedded deep into my heart, and now that I've acknowledged it, it won't let go.

But I will not let the clown lead me along like that. I will not be baited.

I will, however, unashamedly use someone else as bait. If I threaten to kill Gordon and ruin Isaiah's chances of finding the Pereculum, he might release Lewis and Annette in trade.

I grab Gil's collar and bring my mouth to his ear. "Take Nathan and Brahm and keep following Isaiah in case he leads you to Lewis and Annette."

Gil nods and tucks his greasy black hair behind his ears.

The group splits again. Daniel, Glen, and Casper, the final three, stay on my heels as I head in the opposite direction. I have no indication of where Emery and Gordon have gone, but this island is small enough that someone is bound to run into them at some point.

I just pray that I will get to them first.

· · ·

I buckle the sword sheath around my waist as Sami leads us down the street toward the cliff face that abuts the town. Reese keeps glancing at me reassuringly, but unease churns in my stomach. My anxiety insists that pirates are hiding in every bush and behind every palm tree, waiting to pounce like lions.

I hope he can't sense that the facade I've worn for so many years has slipped away, exposing the pent-up panic threatening to claw through my sternum.

Sami cuts onto the next street, which is uncomfortably crowded with children running around and their parents clustered in groups. One of the huts has a massive pit dug in front of its door, where smoke curls from a giant mass wrapped in bright green leaves.

I stick out like a sore thumb, and my cheeks burn as people start to notice the only tall blonde girl stumbling down the road. Sami leaps over a stack of baskets woven with palm leaves before dashing through the trees.

Reese stumbles off the path and huffs and puffs behind me, and I'm at his side in an instant as he hunches over to catch his breath. Sami stutters to a stop ahead of us. "Mister Gordon?"

"I'm fine." Reese exhales. "Just catching my breath."

I grip his arm and glance back at the road, and I see four figures push their way through the crowd of people. The newcomers' drab brown and beige attire is in stark contrast to the Kahuan's bright blue and green robes and skirts. The metal of swords glints in the dying sunlight.

Sami sees them shortly after I do and rushes back to us to pull Gordon along. I draw the pistol and grip it with both hands as I bring up the rear. I continually glance over my shoulder as we weave through the trees.

One of the pirates stops and points at us.

I swear under my breath. "Reese—"

"We're almost there," he says haggardly.

"Almost *where?*"

A bullet zips through the air and rustles the bushes, only a few feet from our path. The crowd scatters as screams ring through the air. Another shot burrows in the dirt a few feet from our path.

I hurry behind Reese and Sami as we approach the towering mountain face. I expect them to veer in one direction or the other, but as we approach the jagged black rock, I spot a small gap that's just wide enough for a person to slip through.

Sami disappears first, but Reese grabs my arm at the mouth of the cave. "Keep your right hand on the wall, or you'll get lost. There's a beach and a harbor on the other side where I have a cutter waiting for us."

He ducks inside, and I take a deep breath and press on. Our trio's exhausted breathing bounces off the walls of the cave, and the slit of sunlight fades behind us.

My heart pounds as my fingers slide along the rock walls on either side of me, which are claustrophobically tight in some areas and manageable in others. The darkness lasts for a minute, and then another, and another . . .

I trip over rocks buried in the sand beneath my feet. "Reese—"

"It's okay!" I hear his voice somewhere ahead of me. "Just keep moving."

My chest aches from panic as I stumble forward, and all I can think about is how this would be such a miserable, terrifying way to die, blind and trapped in the rocky core of a mountain.

More footsteps scuffle through the dark as I quicken my pace.

"—swore I saw them run through here," a gruff voice echoes behind me.

There's a dull thud and swearing. "Agh!"

A gunshot pierces the air, which sends a quick burst of light through the space, and a bullet ricochets off the rocks somewhere.

"Knock it off!" someone snaps. "You're going to shoot someone."

"I can't see!"

"Keep your hand on the wall, then."

Their voices are unfamiliar. I quicken my pace and wave my hand through the pitch black. "Reese!" I whisper harshly. "Sami!"

All I hear are the footsteps of the pirates behind me.

I trip on another rock and fall forward. Pain juts through my shoulder as I land in the sand, and I scramble to my feet as the foot-steps grow louder.

"How many people have gotten lost in here and starved to death?" the gruff voice asks.

I flatten myself against the wall as tightly as I can and grip the knife so tightly that my hand begins to tremble. I shift my footing, and something brushes against my leg.

The sword.

The handle sticks out past my body, and anyone walking by could accidentally brush against it. I blindly fumble to undo the straps, and I wedge it between my leg and the rock wall as the first pirate moves past me. The fabric of his clothes brushes against my leg, but he continues without notice.

I hold my breath and count one, two, more pairs of footsteps. My blood turns to ice as one of them trips on the sturdy toe of my boot.

"Blasted rocks," he mutters.

Mikhail's voice. Bile rises in my throat as I grit my teeth.

Ten excruciatingly long seconds pass, and my hands begin to trem-ble. The last one of the group straggles behind, his feet falling unevenly into the sand. His off-balance gait sends him crashing into me, and the rocks dig into my back. He gasps in surprise as his hands grab me in the dark. "Who is this?"

I yank my knife hand free and swing blindly. The blade scrapes against the rock, and he yelps in surprise at the sudden movement.

One of his hands disappears from my arm as the sound of rustling leather catches my ear. I hit the ground, my elbows crashing into the rocky sand. I feel through the dark and grab at the first thing I can, which happens to be his ankle as he moves to take another step. He yelps as he goes down.

"Seth?" a voice behind us echoes.

"Go back!" Seth grunts. "Porter, find the captain!"

Shadows swirl in my vision as his foot knocks the knife from my hand, and his shoe wooshes past my face.

I blindly fumble for my weapons as I climb on top of him. One of his elbows catches me in the neck as my fingers close around a rock, and I gasp as the blade of a knife slides through the skin on my forearm.

"Get . . . off!" he grunts. My hand smacks against his face, and I bring the rock down on where I think his temple is. He shouts in pain, and I swing one more time. His body goes limp.

Blood sticks to my fingers as I scramble over his unconscious body. The sand clumps on my wound and makes it sting and prickle with a fire that makes my skin crawl.

Another person's heavy breathing and stumbling echoes further down the slot, and dread rises in my throat like bile. I press my left hand against the wall.

Or should it be my right?

It should be my left because I'm going the opposite direction.

My breathing grows heavier and heavier with dread as I trudge forward, frantic now.

No, no.

I stumble into a dead end with my left arm extended, and the rock is sharp against my skin. I whirl around and squint to search for any inkling of light seeping through.

But there's nothing. No light, no sound, no way out.

Voices echo down the cave, but I can't make out who they belong to. I gasp for air as if my lungs are filled with stiff cotton.

I'm going to die in this cave.

I dig my fingertips into the rock and press my other hand over my mouth.

Breathe. Breathe.

If I'm going to die, it's not going to be cowering in this corner.

I hold my hand out and force myself forward.

46

Warren

THE SUN NEARS the horizon as Daniel, Glen, Casper, and I aimlessly race through the villages and jungle searching for Gordon and Emery. We nearly run into clusters of Isaiah's pirates multiple times, and they seem to multiply like spores of disease, popping up everywhere we run. The Kahuan locals peek through the windows of their homes, which tells me that someone has caused terror or panic already.

Nauseating dread fills my stomach. I should have brought more sailors. Or maybe I should have gone to look for Annette and Lewis instead.

I can hear my heartbeat thundering in my ears as sweat burns my eyes. My actions of the last month and a half are flipping through my mind, like each of my mistakes is lined up for all to see. Each mistake has led me to running across this island like a madman.

My pace slows, about fifty yards from the base of a towering mountain, and Daniel, Glen, and Casper pant like dogs behind me as I stare ahead at the giant rockface. Unlike the mountains in other islands, this one is sparsely covered with patches of greenery, while the jagged black rock dominates the sight.

Movement near the base of the mountain catches my eye, and I frown as a figure emerges from the

Porter?

He notices me, glances at Isaiah's sailors a few hundred yards away, and then back at me. He points back in the direction he came from, at the mountain, and I catch on.

I hurriedly wave for my trio to follow, and Isaiah's sailors pay us no attention.

. . .

Emery

"Reese!" My voice trembles as I shout into the dark. "Reese, where are you?"

My hands tremble as I hold one ahead of me to keep from running into the rock, and the fingers of my injured arm against the wall as I move. Voices and scuffling footsteps sound off somewhere in the cave, and I use them as a beacon. I trace my right hand along the wall as I shuffle forward, my eyes aching as they strain to adjust to the dark.

"Reese!"

Silence.

I bite my cheek.

Another voice echoes, and I pause for a moment to listen.

"Emery!"

My heart leaps as I hurry forward, nearly sobbing in relief at the familiar sound of his voice. "Reese!"

His voice grows louder and louder as I run, and soon, my hands collide with a warm, soft body. Reese grabs my arms to steady me. "Are you okay?"

"Chadwick's pirates are in here," I pant.

"We almost ran into them. Sami knows every inch of this cave and we were able to slip into a crevice to hide."

"How did you keep your sense of direction?"

"I'm an expert," Sami's voice squeaks. "I've only gotten lost twice."

"That's not comforting." Reese shuffles through the sand and positions himself behind me. "Where do we go, Sami?"

"One of them ran back outside to find Chadwick," I say.

"Keep your right hand on the wall!" Sami chirps. "We're almost there!"

Shouting echoes behind us, and we pick up the pace. The throbbing cut on my arm fades to a blurry afterthought as Reese holds tight to my hand in the dark, and miraculously, faint beams of light soon shine through the darkness from the end of the cave.

Reese sighs in relief behind me. The voices behind us grow softer and softer as the light brightens. I nearly collapse from relief as I inhale a much-needed breath of fresh air as we near the mouth of the cave.

We're greeted by a narrow beach, and rows and rows of huts are suspended on stilts over the crystal blue and green ocean. Moss-covered fishing boats bob up and down near the shore and are tied to the wooden supports holding up the huts, which are made of seawater-stained wooden planks. Fishing nets, rods, and a hundred other pieces of equipment I can't name are neatly arranged in crates and on racks lined up against the rocky walls of the cove, but I do recognize gunpowder-powered harpoons with massive brass hooks leaning against one of the beached boats. Mist hangs across the cove and blurs the sunset, softening the peach and purple and yellow light.

But that isn't the most breathtaking sight.

Just past the hovering huts, there are two massive ship skeletons propped up on the shoreline beside rows of wooden planks. Scaffolding encases the curve of each hull like a giant row of woody ribs, and there are lengths of rope secured around the horizontal beams of the scaffolding for the builders to tie around their waists, to secure them in place as they work high above ground.

I stare in awe for a moment. I've watched many ships being constructed in my years growing up in the harbor, but it never ceases to amaze me.

Reese takes my hand and leads me toward a small dock positioned to the right of the ships. "Kahu is trying to keep up with the rest of the South in naval strength."

"They've got a long way to go," I mumble, still staring at the construction.

At the dock, Sami jumps into a small cutter with gray sails and chipped blue paint. Two canvas sacks sit at the mast, and Reese climbs in and reaches up to untie the sails as Sami cranks the small windlass at the back of the boat to raise the anchor.

My heart pounds in anticipation as I untie it from the dock. Once the anchor is raised, Sami and I jump down into the low tide shallows and work to push the boat away from shore, seawater sloshing into my boots and drenching my legs.

I feel for the envelope in my pocket as the water nears my waist. A wave nearly knocks me off balance as I climb the boarding ladder and tumble to the floor of the cutter, my shoulder twinging with pain.

Reese helps me to my feet and notices me wincing. "What's the matter?"

"I hurt it weeks ago." I grit my teeth. "It's fine."

I glance back, watching the space between us and the cave entrance, and see Mikhail and Chadwick's other pirates racing down the beach.

Sami throws his shoulder into the boat and gives us one final push. "Go! Hurry!"

Reese and I work silently as a team; he retrieves a large oar from the bottom of the boat and begins to row while I adjust the sail, and the waves carry us away from the dock. I watch Sami sprint across the dock to run from the pirates, but their attention is fixed solely on us as we float away. I hold my breath as Sami darts across the beach and makes it back to the cave.

Thankfully, the pirates ignore him and commandeer another of the small vessels in the dock to chase us. I count only two pirates, but I thought there were at least four in the cave.

No. There were. Seth, the one I fought with, told one to run and find Chadwick.

Nausea rolls in my stomach.

"Will he be okay?" I ask Reese, breathless. "Sami?"

"He's sneaky." He grunts, plunging an oar into the water to guide us further and further out. "They won't catch him."

The pirates hasten their pace, but I turn back to Reese to help steer the ship through the turbulent waves, even though my injured arm has the strength of a toddler's. I keep glancing over my shoulder as the pirates push their boat off the dock.

"What's our heading?" I ask, tying down a rope connected to one of the sails. My clothes and hair are damp from sweat and seawater.

"Anywhere away from *them*," Reese pants. His arms shake as he brings the oar back into the boat and points to two canvas sacks nestled against the mast. "The navigational tools are there. We'll just—"

A loud crack is followed by the sound of splintering wood, and I whirl around to see a brass harpoon hook buried into the stern of our cutter. I follow the line tied to the end and see Mikhail drop the harpoon rifle, and he and the two others begin pulling themselves toward us.

I lunge forward, and my fingers bleed as I try unwedging the hook from the wooden stern. The line is braided tightly around the other end of the hook, making it impossible to untie.

"Knife!" I blurt, turning back to Reese. "Knife!"

They approach us at a terrifying speed. Reese rifles through one of the bags, but loses his balance when an errant wave hits the boat. Their hull bangs into our stern, and before I can retreat, Mikhail grabs my arm and unceremoniously yanks me to their boat.

"Hey!" I tumble to the floor, landing awkwardly on my injured arm as Mikhail points his pistol at my chest.

"Wait!" Reese scrambles to his feet and holds out his hands. "Stop!"

Panic grips my heart in an icy fist as I stare down the barrel of the gun, hyper aware that I am no longer useful to Chadwick or any of his pirates with Reese here. My eyes fall to Mikhail's twitchy trigger finger as it hovers near the mechanism.

"I'll cooperate if you leave her alone," Reese says, his voice trembling. "Please."

I wince as I try to sit up. "Wait—"

"Ah, ah, ah!" Mikhail clicks the hammer and scowls at me when I try to speak. He glances at the other pirates to ensure they're watching me. "That promise better hold true when we get back to shore."

. . .

Warren

The tightness of the cave seems to choke the air from my lungs as my group and I follow Porter through. My crew's haggard breathing bounces off the walls until we reach another opening on the opposite side, and I suck in a long breath of salty air as we break from the darkness. My heart leaps at the sight of Dillon and Judge Gordon himself bringing a cutter to shore. Mikhail has his weapon aimed at Emery, whose face pales when she sees me.

My crew gawks at the construction of the ships perched on the beach, and while it seems the Kahuans aren't as penniless as they appear, I pay no mind. I watch Emery as she climbs out of the boat. Mikhail presses the muzzle of his pistol against her spine and escorts her up the beach while Dillon brings the judge. I meet them halfway to the water, about twenty feet from the cave.

"Your Honor!" I say jovially. "How nice it is to meet you in person."

Gordon focuses on me for a moment, taking in my sweaty, disheveled appearance with a wary eye. He clears his throat. "You're younger than I thought you'd be."

"I'm afraid I can't say the same for you." I tilt my head as I step toward Emery. In one swift move, I yank my knife free of its sheath on my hip, grab her jaw, and hold the blade under her chin as she yelps and grabs my wrist. Her injured arm trembles, and Gordon's breath hitches as he steps forward and holds up his hands. "Wait!"

"So he *hasn't* turned his back on you like I suspected," I murmur in her ear. "How convenient."

"Stop this." Gordon's voice trembles. "It's gotten out of hand."

"You know what I want, Your Honor. I won't make a scene about it. If you tell me where the Pereculum is and rescind Kearon Romney's sentence—"

"Reese—" Emery rasps, but I jerk her head back even further. She winces.

"Nobody invited you to speak," I hiss in her ear. "Quiet."

"If I do that, you have to recant everything that's been said about her," Gordon cuts in. "That's my only request."

"Oh, I'm afraid the damage has already been done." I purse my lips and shake my head. "And I don't think you'd like to watch her die on top of everything that's happened to her, do you? What will it be?"

Neither he, nor I, nor Emery moves for a moment. I have imagined this moment at least a million times since Kearon's arrest, but I never expected it to be this underwhelming.

I stare at Gordon expectantly as Emery trembles under my hold. My grip tightens around the handle of the blade.

Gordon's eyes flip between Emery and me as he stands like a helpless child. "Why all this for an errand boy?" His voice trembles. "All this destruction—"

"Why do you all demean him like that?" I snap.

"I didn't mean—"

"Just the latitude and longitude, Your Honor." I clench my teeth. "Come on now."

"That and you want me to draft an order to have the boy released?" He swallows. "That's it?"

"If we gathered enough sailors to provide enough resistance…"

"One at a time, just like plucking berries."

I hesitate as Derrick's query to me back in Midway whispers in the back of my mind, even though I am outnumbered and possibly outmatched by Isaiah.

But I don't care. If I cared about odds, my success and reputation would be nonexistent.

I can almost hear the headlines now.

Padstow in shambles. The Armada crumbling to pieces.

"Yes, that's all I want," I snap. "I'm losing my patience!"

I watch his expression fall as he takes a deep breath and nods. "Okay. Let Emery go."

"Tell me first."

He says the coordinates, and I watch Daniel scribble them out on the piece of paper I told him to grab earlier for this exact purpose.

Exhilaration courses through my body like an icy river. Around me, my crew breaks into smiles as the tension dissipates.

I've done it.

"Excellent." I unceremoniously push Emery to the side and snatch the paper from Daniel's hand, ensuring the writing is legible before I pocket it.

Emery is sprawled on all fours in the soil, gently touching her throat. Her shoulders rise and fall with panic as she watches the weapon in my hand.

She knows. She knows she's lost this fight and is no longer of use to me.

But before I make another move, another batch of voices rings out from inside the cave.

47

I WATCH in horror as Isaiah and a horde of his own pirates burst through the cave opening with their weapons raised. Everyone shouts in surprise as Chadwick's pirates draw their own weapons, and Chadwick grabs Reese before he can run away, holding his knife against the judge's ribcage. I scramble backwards until my back smacks into a large boulder buried in the sand.

For a heartbeat, no one moves. Chadwick breaks the silence as he rolls his eyes. "Dasher."

The clown chuckles bitterly. "The sailors on my ship noticed you reaching the island, but how did you manage to slip past me?"

"It's not my fault you weren't paying attention."

Isaiah's arm is eerily steady as he points the muzzle of his pistol at Chadwick. "I was attentive enough to catch the boy running out of the cave and figure out how to get back here."

"Where is he?" Reese demands.

Isaiah tilts his head and smiles. "I'm surprised you didn't hear his screaming echo down the cave."

The blood drains from Reese's face, and I press my hand over my mouth.

"I'd love for you to hand the judge over to me, Warren," Isaiah says.

"I want my sailors back first," Chadwick snaps. "I found him first. I have the power. I want Lewis
and Annette back."

Isaiah lifts his eyebrows and sighs. "Is that all?"

Chadwick burrows his heels in the sand and sets his sharp jaw.

Isaiah sends three of his sailors away to find Lucky and Annette. I swallow and scan the crowd, searching for a gap where I can run without anyone noticing. I count more than twenty pirates standing on the beach.

"I don't want this to end in a mess, Warren." Isaiah glares at him. "I don't think you do, either. There are others who are coming here to convene, and you do not want to be in the way."

Chadwick scowls. "Who? And to convene about what, exactly?"

"*You* are not going to be here to hear it." Isaiah's gaze is sharper than broken glass.

Chadwick narrows his eyes and tilts his head.

"I told you I had friends hidden in many places, but you need to stay out of my way." For the first time since I've known him, Isaiah's cold tone is dangerously even and serious. "Do not test me."

I stare at Chadwick, trying to gauge his expression and finding nothing but thinly veiled panic. I think he sees the exact way this is going to play out because his eyes flick to each member of Isaiah's crew, studying their positions, weapons, and their proximity to Chadwick's own crew.

I quickly count the pirates, and it would be twelve of Chadwick's against Isaiah's ten once Lucky and Annette arrive.

Chadwick's eyes flick to me, as if he can sense what I'm thinking. He shakes his head, but I clench my jaw and glare at him. He won't stop me from fighting to escape and for a chance to return to my family and right everything that's gone wrong.

But Reese. Thea. A nagging voice is insisting that, after everything, I can still save them. That I am not a broken husk of the sailor and soldier that I was before.

Reese looks at me, his expression stern and eyes sharp. He glances at the pocket the envelope is in and nods ever so slightly.

My stomach drops as I dig my fingers into the sand and let the fine grains burrow under my nails.

Someone is doomed no matter which way I choose, but I refuse to let it be me again.

I slowly slide my hand into my pocket and curl my fingers around the grainy wood of the pistol handle, waiting for someone to attack first.

Movement near the cave entrance catches my eye as one of Isaiah's pirates leads Annette and Lucky out of the cave. Annette winces as she supports the weight that Lucky's injured knee cannot, and he leans against her as a crutch as they hobble forward. Lucky's face twists with discomfort.

Chadwick stands as still as a statue when Annette looks at him. She glances down, guilt plastered across her face as her cheeks flush.

Lucky tries to limp forward, but Isaiah raises his pistol at him and stares expectantly at Chadwick. "Well?"

Chadwick's jaw tightens. He marches Reese forward and brushes past Mikhail, who's holding his pistol behind his own back. His feet are staggered as if he's ready to run.

I hold my breath as my eyes flick to Isaiah's pirates. One of them takes notice of Mikhail's odd stance and slowly reaches for his own weapon, and others around him do the same.

One of Chadwick's pirates steps forward to bear Lucky's weight as Chadwick begrudgingly pushes Reese forward, and a bullet cracks through the air.

I flinch as Mikhail's shot zips past Reese, and Isaiah shouts in surprise as he hits the sand, clutching the side of his face. More shots and shouting ring in my ears as I leap for Reese, who's crouched and covering his head as the two pirate crews collide, their swords clanging and guns firing right over our heads.

I grab his arm and drag him through the sand as he regains his footing, but we only make it a few yards from the chaos when someone grabs the collar of my shirt. I turn, bracing as the blade of a sword slices toward my body, but the pirate's head snaps to the side as he collapses into the sand.

Standing over him, holding a red-stained rock, is a panting Lucky. We freeze, me from dumbfounded confusion and him from shock. He blinks and drops the rock as he stumbles back, grimacing. "Go," he grunts, turning and hobbling through the uneven sand.

And that's it.

I don't hesitate, pushing through the confusion and ignoring the aching tremble in my shoulder as I grab the fallen pirate's sword. Reese continues to run, but I glance back as the crowd parts, and Chadwick surges through, his pistol raised and eyes fixed on the back of Reese's head—

My body beats my mind and reacts with shrill panic as I lift the weapon Reese gave me at his hut, pull back the hammer with my thumb, take aim, and fire. It should have hit Chadwick between the eyes, but he notices me and flinches back the moment I pull the trigger, and the bullet strikes the gun and sends it flying from his hand. It lands in the sand, smoke curling from its bent barrel.

His attention snaps to me, and he stays frozen as I reach down and snatch the fallen pirate's pistol, pouring sand from the barrel. Chadwick surges forward, drawing his sword with terrifying speed. He's gotten what he's come for, but a sheen of unadulterated hatred burns in his eyes like fire as he storms toward me.

I steal one last glance to ensure Reese is out of the way before Chadwick lifts his sword above his head.

"Go!" I scream at Reese. "Ready a boat!"

I barely have time to parry Chadwick's attack, and the clang of the swords reverberates throughout my entire body. I stumble backward and nearly lose my balance as he forces me back, and my shoulder screams with pain. I use my off, but healthy hand to push against the flat end of the blade to combat the weakness in my injured arm.

Sweat beads on his long nose as he glares at me, and as he surges forward again, I duck, letting our blades slide across each other before pulling mine back and retreating toward the massive ship skeletons.

"Coward!" he shouts at me.

Ordinarily yes, I would be a coward for running, but I need him as far from his crew as possible so this last stand is between just him and me. He is without a pistol. I am not. The further we are from someone learning that fact and jumping to his aid, the better.

As I jump onto the wooden drydocks where the ship skeletons are positioned and reach into the pocket for the second pistol, I feel Chadwick's footsteps creaking on the platform behind me, quick as a whip. I barely have time to duck before his sword cuts through the air in an arc where my neck would have been.

I recover quickly and spin to face him, gripping my sword with two hands as we circle each other like wolves waiting to pounce. Chadwick kicks a wooden crate full of tools out of his path without breaking his intense stare, and his breath whistles through clenched teeth.

My heart pounds as I gingerly step over a mallet. I doubt I could reach the pistol in my pocket and take aim in this position before he'd run his sword through my heart.

"There's nothing waiting for you when you run home," he spits. "You are going to die as the filth everyone sees you as."

Always let your opponent attack first, my father's voice echoes in the back of my mind. *Let them attack first and watch for their weak point.*

I don't need to win. I need two seconds of space.

I purse my lips and swallow my pride despite his comments. My hands begin to tremble as I tighten my grip, lower my arms, and read-just my footing to bait him to move, and he does. His lanky frame allows him to move with the speed of a snake, and as I sidestep to the right and reach into my pocket, he spins with incredible speed and forces me to parry with my injured arm. I cry out as the shock jolts the joint, but I jump back and reposition my footing just in time for another attack.

Most of my sparring partners have been men, but none of them compare to Chadwick and his relentless fury as he swipes at me over, and over, and over, forcing me to dodge and block instead of going on the attack.

"You're a pathetic excuse for a captain!" he snaps as he takes another swing, nearly nicking the side of my head as I duck away. I cut toward his shoulder, which he blocks with ease.

"You should never have been in that position in the first place." He strikes again, and I parry. "After all the lies—" His blade slices through the shoulder seam of my coat. "After all the innocent people you've targeted—"

"That can't be undone!" I gasp, knocking him off balance as I block his attack and shove him backward. Tears well in my eyes from the pain in my shoulder. "I can't fix that!"

"I don't want you to fix anything." He swoops down, grabs a sharp, rusted screwdriver from the deck, and advances on me.

I lunge to attack that hand, but too eagerly. I come too close to him, and he effortlessly strikes me across the jaw with his elbow. My vision blurs, and through the haze, I bring my sword up and catch the fingers of his sword hand. He hisses in pain and drops the weapon in surprise, and I barely have time to catch his wrists and stumble backward until my back smacks into one of the scaffolding support beams. The tool's tip hovers inches from my throat, and I have no choice but to drop my sword and use both hands to keep Chadwick's arms away from my neck.

The air goes still for a moment, save for our heavy breathing. My jaw aches as I stare down at the rusty tool and dig my skull into the beam to keep as far from it as possible. In the darkening sunset, sweat trickles down Chadwick's temples, and his entire body is deathly still as his icy eyes cut into me. His lips curl into a sinister grin. "Justice is cruel, isn't it, Miss Walker?"

I wince from the exertion as he forces the screwdriver closer to my throat, and I clench my jaw.

His voice is cruel as it speaks in the back of my mind. *You are going to die as the filth everyone knows you are.*

I can't. I won't. Even though there might not be anything for me on the other side of this, I will *not* die by his hand.

With what little strength I have left, I thrust his hands to one side and force my body off the beam, spinning away. Residual sand on the pistol handle slips against my fingers as I fumble for the weapon on the deck. I set the hammer just as he turns to face me. His eyes widen as he stares down the barrel with horror, his mouth agape and trying to form a thousand words he'll have no time to say before I—

Click.

The trigger only moves halfway. I pull it a second time, and sand spills from the gap between it and the wooden handle. Terror fills my stomach as I click it again, and again, but nothing happens.

Chadwick stares at the gun as if in a trance, and my focus scrambles across the deck as I search for another weapon, but in my panic, I don't notice the figure coming up behind me until he's kicked my knee in and shoved me to the deck. I cry out in pain.

"Stay down," Isaiah snaps as he kicks my pistol out of reach with the toe of his boot.

My knee and shoulder throb in unison as I curl up on the wood, blinded and disoriented by the pain as it rips through both joints.

"I warned you what would happen, Warren!" Blood trails down the side of Isaiah's face, and a long, red line traces across the left side of his head and ear from where Mikhail's bullet grazed him.

I force my head up just in time to see Isaiah grab Chadwick's collar and punch him in the face. He collapses, and Isaiah kicks Chadwick square in the ribs, drawing a pained gasp from the captain.

I look back toward the mouth of the cave, where bodies lie strewn across the sand. A few that are still standing rush into the cave. Some come toward us, but Lucky and Annette are nowhere to be seen.

But that isn't what terrifies me.

Off in the distance, I count six massive galleons cutting through the haze that's settling over the water. My heart stops as I think back to what Isaiah said about his friends, and it seems they've all come out of hiding.

I look to the small harbor and see Reese standing on another small fishing cutter, and he stares at the scene unfolding with his hands shielding his eyes.

I blink back tears as I try to stand, but my knee, my shoulder—my entire body gives way. I dig my fingertips into the splintered wood and squeeze my eyes shut.

Isaiah retrieves his pistol from the holster at his side.

"Wait!" Pure, unfiltered terror radiates from Chadwick as he screams. He rolls over and holds up a shaky hand. Blood pours from his mouth as he stares at Isaiah with wide eyes. "Stop! Gordon told me! Gordon told me!"

Isaiah stops, though he keeps his weapon leveled between Chadwick's eyes. He raises one blood-stained eyebrow. "Told you what?"

"Look." Chadwick's entire body trembles as he reaches into his pocket and retrieves the piece of paper with the Pereculum coordinates. "I will leave here, and you will never hear from me again. *Please.*"

I frown at his desperation, and apparently so does Isaiah. He scoffs at Chadwick's response. "You won't succeed in that. The sailors who didn't abandon you are dead. You have no way back to your ship."

"Then let me help you." Chadwick's voice is raw and has lost its usual steady composure. "You helped me when I needed it, and now—"

"And now *I* have no use for *you*." Isaiah snatches the paper from Chadwick's hand. "I do not contend with liability, and that is what both of you have become." He turns his attention to me. "It was never personal." He raises his weapon at me and cocks the hammer, glaring at me one final time with his clownish brown eyes as he licks his slimy lips. "I hope you can understand."

A gun fires, but I don't feel the sharp sting of the bullet right away. I've heard from other soldiers who've survived a bullet wound that if shock has set in, you don't feel much. I touch my head, my stomach. There is neither the blood nor the sting of a kill shot, but my attention quickly shifts to the sound of shouting voices. All three of us turn to the source of the shot and see a tan-colored sloop flying under the black and light blue striped Kahuan flag. Soldiers dressed in black and armed with long rifles point at us on the platform, and in the dim light, I can just make out a few of them mounting on the ship's wooden railing and taking aim.

But this is not a fight they are going to win. Isaiah's approaching allies will make sure of that.

Isaiah marvels at the Kahuan soldiers long enough for Chadwick to stretch and grab a nearby hammer, and he smashes the head against the bony knob of Isaiah's ankle. He screams in pain and falls to one knee, and I use the distraction to crawl across the platform. Soldiers in dinghies begin to sail away from the boat and approach the beach at an alarming speed.

Another bullet flies and buries itself in the wood near Chadwick and Isaiah, but each captain is too busy trying to pummel the other. Isaiah ducks and barely dodges another swing of the hammer before noticing my pathetic escape attempt. He throws his elbow against Chadwick's jaw and lunges for his fallen pistol.

"Stop!"

My head whips to the source of the voice and the sound of footsteps crunching through the sand, and I see Reese sprinting toward us with a pistol raised and ready to shoot.

I open my mouth to scream for him to stop, but he fires in Isaiah and Chadwick's direction, and without missing a beat, Isaiah shifts his line of sight away from me and fires at the judge, striking him in the chest.

"No! Reese!" His arms go limp as he falls to his knees. I fight through the pain in my leg and jump off the platform, stumbling and falling in the sand as I rush toward him.

Chaos reigns around us as more soldiers fire from the approaching dinghies.

Reese clutches his chest and falls back into the sand as I scramble to his side, sobbing. "Reese!"

He grabs my shirt as blood trickles from his mouth. "The letter," he gasps, choking on his words as he pulls me closer to him. "Read the letter and d-don't let them . . . win . . ."

"No, no, no, stay awake!" I pat his face to keep his attention, but it's futile. The panicked pain in his expression fades to a sullen calm now. He rests his head in the sand and leaves bloody handprints on my shirt as his grip relaxes. He stares up at the navy, pink, and orange sky, and he doesn't move again.

My red-stained hands tremble as I shake his shoulders, and tears blur my vision. "Reese, please don't. . . "

Desperation edges into my voice as I duck my head and resist the urge to scream.

Nothing. All for nothing.

The gunfire and shouting grow louder as a group of pirates emerges from the cave, firing at the Kahuan soldiers and ducking for cover. Some of the soldiers who have reached the shore stare in my direction and point at the bloody scene while others rush the pirates, though I'm not sure whose they are.

I don't think it matters anymore. We are all monsters.

Air whooshes past my ear as another bullet flies close to my head. I scramble backward in the sand and clamber to my feet before taking off, leaving Reese Gordon behind once and for all.

For once, when I run, nobody is following me and nobody is watching. I don't think a soul on this earth cares where I am or what I'm doing.

I turn my back toward Kahu's soldiers and Isaiah's approaching allies, sobbing as I bound toward the dock and jump into the water near the boat Reese was standing in just moments earlier. The pain in my shoulder is torturous as I untie the boat and push it out into the water with what little strength I have.

Alone.

No Reese. No Thea.

I hope she can at least forgive me.

I turn the sails to catch the wind, letting it carry me away from the chaos of the island and the impending doom of Isaiah's allies.

I sink to the floor of the boat and plug my ears to hide from the gunfire raining down behind me, and the further I drift, the fewer bullets come my way. I dare to steal a glance behind me, and I can still see the carnage of the beach. I can just barely make out Chadwick's icy blond hair glowing in the sunset as he steps off the platform about fifty yards away with a small group of his pirates surrounding him.

He glances back and sees me, and, for a moment, he and I stare at each other. For all the times I've imagined this moment, I expected it to be more triumphant, where the weight of everything that's happened in the last six weeks would lift off my shoulders, and I could finally run away and undo all that's been done.

But somehow, it grows heavier. It sits on my lungs and squeezes my throat until all I can do is collapse onto the floor of the boat again and sob for everything, everyone, that's been lost.

. . .

Warren

Crack.

My body freezes as Isaiah's bullet zips past my head and strikes Gordon square in the chest, and I watch in shock as the judge collapses in the sand.

Isaiah watches with an unhinged look of elation as Emery screams and rushes to Gordon's side. I snap out of my shock and lunge for my fallen sword. Isaiah reacts quickly as well; his hands snatch at my ankle and yank my leg out from under me before I can fully regain my footing. I shout in surprise and recover quickly, clutching my injured ribs and swinging the sword in a wide arc.

But instead of staying to fight, this slimy, dishonorable coward is running away, hobbling through the sand as he retreats to his crew, still clutching the piece of paper with the coordinates to the Pereculum. I now count over twenty of his sailors, and more pour from the cave like rats scurrying out of a sewer.

As Isaiah runs, so seemingly does every goal I've clung to. Rescue Kearon. Jailbreak the Pereculum and let chaos reign in Padstow. My gaze shifts to the beach in front of the cave entrance, where bodies of my crew lie mixed with some of Isaiah's. I can't see their faces, but my stomach wrenches at their loss all the same. I turn to the fighting near the shore, where more of Isaiah's sailors battle with Kahu's approaching navy. Black-clad soldiers fall one by one to the relentless, bloodthirsty attacks of the sailors, all happening with a backdrop of Isaiah's allies and their six massive galleons quickly approaching.

As I watch it all unfold, the pain suddenly catches up to me, and I groan as I fall to one knee. My ribs and the bones in my face ache, and blood trickles from my lip and down my chin.

I crane my neck and stare up at Kahu's massive soon-to-be ships, their curved wooden skeletons becoming nothing more than black shapes against the darkening peach, orange, and cobalt sky.

Is this how it ends? I'm going to die here, having not properly reconciled with Hyde, nor having learned Annette's true intentions in betraying me. I'm going to die having abandoned my mother's words by losing my ambition in twisted hatred, but neither seemed to get me what I wanted.

"Captain!" A voice to my right hisses.

I turn, and I see Gil's head poke over the edge of the platform. He frantically motions for me to come to him, and I force myself out of my trance and hobble in that direction.

I find him, Mikhail, Lewis, Daniel, and Annette crouched below the platform and out of sight. I crouch with them, wincing and holding my ribs. "What are you—"

"We have a boat ready," Gil whispers, pointing to a small thicket concealed behind the massive volcanic rock. "Daniel and I ran during the fighting and readied it so we could get back to the ship."

I frown. "How?"

"It was just tied to the dock over there," Daniel says, tucking his curly hair behind his ears. "No one saw us in the chaos."

I stare at each of them, dumbfounded, but Annette is the only one who returns my gaze with any real emotion. Her eyes shine with tears that she quickly wipes away, and I can tell there are a thousand things she wants to say, but everyone else looks exhausted. Each of them is sprinkled with sand and dirt and is covered in blood that I'm sure isn't their own. Mikhail has a torn, bloodied piece of his shirt tied around a wound on his arm.

Five. Five sailors.

"This . . ." I swallow and force strength into my voice. "This is it?"

None of them meets my eyes.

I force the nausea in my stomach to subside and purposely position myself behind Annette as Daniel leads the group toward the trees. I glance out at the water, and lo and behold, I spot a small cutter floating toward the sunset. I can barely make out a shiny red coat that burns against the falling sun.

I can tell she's staring, and I stare right back. After everything, I couldn't even succeed in the one goal I've had since I first crossed swords with that blasted Walker girl. She was supposed to die today. She was supposed to die standing in the ashes of her ruined life and fade into nothing.

She sinks down to the floor of the boat, and I feel Annette's shaky fingers close around my wrist and pull me forward.

We race away from the drydock, and I climb aboard the small boat as the other three men push the boat out. My ribs scream as I lean over and help Gil aboard, and after, I fall back against the side walls of the boat and sigh.

Annette crouches in front of me with a knit, worried brow.

"You owe me an explanation," I mumble bitterly, refusing to meet her gaze.

She swallows. "I know."

"Annette," Gil grunts as he cranks the windlass to raise the anchor. "We could use your help."

She glances at me and purses her lips before standing up.

My apathy toward her returns, and my thoughts consume me. That's even more sailors weighing on my conscience. More letters I'll have to sit and write to their families, where I'll have to explain how their sons, brothers, cousins, or whoever were brutally murdered at the hands of a sadistic child whom *I* let swindle me into a bad deal.

Perhaps I'll be lucky and find that none of them have a family I can write to. I'll check the log where each of my crewmembers' names is written and pray that I find them all orphans.

Annette suddenly gasps beside me, and I look up. My chest goes numb.

My ship.

My ship has been peppered with holes and its sails are shredded. I do not see a single member of my crew amidst Isaiah's sailors as they patrol the deck. The *South Sun* is positioned on the *Lost Commandeer's* starboard side, and more sailors file across gangplanks situated between the two.

I blink rapidly, as if it will dispel the image from my sight. It can't be right.

Gil freezes at the sight as his oar hovers above the water, drawing an angry grunt from Daniel as the momentum of the boat slows. "What are you . . . ?" He looks up, and his jaw falls.

My mind reels.

Tahj is there.

Alexis.

Hyde.

The princess.

"Go," I blurt, my voice edging with pathetic desperation and ribs hitching with each frantic breath. "Get as far from here as possible!"

Annette rummages through a small compartment at the front of the ship, presumably looking for a map. "If I remember, there's a neighboring island about—"

"I don't care about direction!" I snarl. "Get us away from here!"

My ship grows smaller and smaller as we sail away, and it becomes nothing more than a speck in the distance. Panicked dread rises in my throat as the sky grows darker and darker, and soon the stars begin to grow brighter. The hours drift. The bitter exhaustion festers like disease multiplying in a crowded dormitory.

And it's only then that I touch my chest and take a deep breath.

The night wears. Gil and Daniel lay near the front of the boat, passed out from pure exhaustion, while Mikhail stands at the small helm at the back, hunched over and shivering from the icy sea breeze. Annette hasn't said a word in hours, instead focusing on a loose thread on the sleeve of her blouse.

I have not moved. I have not spoken.

There's nothing to say.

What *would* I say after a loss so massive?

I purchased that ship on my own dime from a retiring merchant when I was nineteen years old. It was my sanctuary on the sea, and every scratch, bullet hole, cannon blast, and chip in the wood had a story that I could recount in full detail. Every drop of ink on the floor of my cabin or pencil shaving under my desk, every tick of the old grandfather clock I insisted on keeping upstairs, and every hushed, late-night conversation with a friend, with a lover—dead. All dead.

My crew, whom I handpicked and befriended to travel the world with me. Dead.

The innocent princess, who was roped into this nightmare against her will. Dead.

Hyde, my confidante and companion since the day we stepped off the sailing school graduation stage.

Dead.

The royal family has lost their darling daughter. Hyde's has lost their son. Their brother.

I choke on air. What am I going to tell them?

I press my hands over my mouth as my lungs burn. Isaiah would never keep liabilities like them alive.

Better dead than a prisoner.

I shudder. What a haunting thought.

I stare at each defeated member of my remaining crew, praying that

Hyde appear next to them, or that he'll tap my shoulder and ask what our next steps are.

Even if he were here, I wouldn't have an answer for him.

I stare up at the stars. I can't see them through the blur in my vision.

Wherever she is now, I could perhaps relate to Emery on at least one more painful experience. We both have seen how quickly we lost the things we've worked so hard for. We have watched it blow away in the wind like it had no worth in the first place.

48

THE BELL TOWER IS RINGING.

The bitter final inklings of the sunset can't be seen through the clouds masking the horizon, which leave a halo of cobalt in the sky. Padstow's harbor, the beautiful, grand, pride and joy of the city, is surprisingly sparse. The few Armada ships present lifelessly sway back and forth in the wind, and there isn't a soldier in sight. I catch myself peering over the edge of the taxi ship, looking for the *Chaplain's Heart,* or someone from my crew or pirate-hunting corps, as I cling to the railing.

But all is still.

My throat knots as we bump into the dock, and I shudder as the breeze rips through my clothes. The one thing I thought would make it home with me was my coat, but pawning it and its last two gold buttons gave me just enough money for a spot on this taxi despite its torn seams and burnholes.

I keep my head down and casually pretend I'm itching my nose or rubbing my eye as my greasy hair curtains my dirty, bruised face. I cross the dock and step onto the cobblestone road, my still-injured knee aching.

The law office looms overhead and casts a shadow over the ground, and just up the road stands the headquarters for The Shining Star and The Messenger. I can't even look at the brick buildings without feeling like there's yet another hole ripping through my chest.

I wonder what they've said.

Padstow chief judge dead, Kailean royal princess still missing. Former Armada Captain alleged to be the culprit?

Tears blur my vision as I wander through the streets, shivering and trembling from the cool breeze and an uncertain fear that seems to hang in the air. I cross to the opposite side of the street to avoid a cluster of Riggs patrolmen and pray they don't stare at me for too long, even though I do the same to them.

The twins' faces seem to reflect in theirs. I hope that justice finds those two cowards and chokes them to death, wherever they ran off to. I hope that if they ever hear someone utter the words *I love you* again, it haunts them like it's haunted me.

I pick up my pace as I pass The Tab, and I can't help but peek inside. The windows and door are propped open, and I see the staff boredly bussing tables for the few melancholy patrons slouched over their drinks. The surrounding streets, which are always bustling and lively, are deserted, with each door shut tight and each curtain drawn over the windows. The throwing range is deserted.

I clench my jaw as I wander up the road toward the rolling green hills. I have dreamed of this moment for two months, yearning for the comfort and relief of wandering through my home once the nightmare was over, but this can't be it. The ache in my chest and nausea in my stomach were supposed to disappear.

A gust of wind picks up, and I shudder and pull the sleeves of my blouse over my hands. My mind is hollow as I wander further and further into the city, trudging up the hill leading to our home.

It looks exactly the same, though the plants around the base of the white stucco look lusher and thicker than they used to. I don't fight the tears as I hike the long, winding walkway that leads to the gate. I run my fingers along the metal bars as I walk along the perimeter to the back of the house, where one of the bars is still loose enough for me to push it out of place and slip through.

When Miles and I were teenagers, we'd sneak back into the house this way if we were out drinking too late. Just past the gate is a back door that leads directly into the kitchen and dining room, though we never use it. The lock is a fixture of the door, and it can be easily jimmied if a small twig is inserted and pressure is applied at the right angle—

Pop.

The door creaks open.

Orchids. The flowery smell hits my nose quickly as I step inside, my throat tight. A vase of them sits in the middle of the granite island, but the petals have wilted, and the stems droop over the edges of the porcelain. The flames in the wall lamps are dim, leaving the kitchen cast in shadows.

I press my hands over my mouth and close my eyes, choking back a sob. I could collapse on the floor here, but I need to see them.

Muffled chatter echoes down the hall, and it grows louder and louder as I approach my father's study. I step lightly and hold my breath.

It was a lifetime ago that the five of us sat in his study after the Sealing, laughing and smiling and joking as if hell wasn't waiting around the corner.

Or was it my mother's?

I don't even remember.

I hug my ribs as I turn the corner to the outlet where my parents' studies are. The hall is dark save for the sliver of light coming from the cracked-open door, and I open my mouth to call out for him.

"—not sure what you're asking, Mr. Nichols," my father says sternly.

My stomach clenches. Has his voice always been so gruff?

"Well, I think it's a clear question, Commander. Are you implying that she was there and had a hand in Gordon's death?"

My father sighs. He sounds exhausted. "No. We're sending another team to Kahu to investigate what happened."

"Just one team?" another nasally voice asks. "It seems like the *death* of the chief judge would warrant more than just a single ship to—"

My mother speaks up next, and it has never sounded so silky in my ears. "We've been understaffed recently with the recent attacks on the other Armada ships, so that's why—"

"Just to confirm," another deeper voice cuts her off. "And please make sure you speak clearly so the horn can pick up the sound—but eight Armada ships haven't returned to port in these last few weeks, is that correct?"

Eight?

I inhale sharply. Who is coming after us in droves like this?

There's a pause before she answers. Her voice is strained. "Yes."

"Have you confirmed who was behind it? Was it Warren Chadwick?"

"What about this 'Dasher' person who's been cycling through the news?" Nichols asks. "Have you heard anything about him? There's been nothing since the attack on the Pere… Priculum. Is that how you say it?"

There is my answer. Every pirate's first move when they're finally free would be to go after the ones who locked them away in the first place.

Even though the nastiest criminals and devils are free, I wonder if Kearon Romney made it out in one piece. Perhaps Chadwick got his wish, even after everything.

"What about Princess Theadora?" the deep voice continues. "Some are saying that Emery had a hand in her disappearance. Have you heard from King Tanuvasa?"

"I want to go back to the attacks," the nasally reporter says. "Has your daughter been tied to any of them? Or has there been any word since the first attack on Fallon Scott's ship?"

"Nothing has been confirmed yet," my father snaps. "Investigations are still ongoing, and that's what we are focused on. I have no idea what the Kaileans are doing about the missing princess."

Missing. Not dead.

I clench my jaw as my chest throbs. Her innocent face flashes through my mind.

"Are there still teams looking for your daughter elsewhere?" the nasally reporter asks.

"Just one," my mother mumbles.

"Please speak clearly enough so the recorder here can hear you, Commander," the deep voice repeats. "Thank you."

"Pick a different story, for the love." My breath catches when I hear Miles's voice, sharp with anger. "We don't know where she is or why she's doing this. That's it. Move on."

"Mr. Walker," Nichols scoffs. "I hope you're aware of the serious ramifications of—"

"Oh, I'm *very* aware," he snaps. "It hasn't reflected well on any of us. I can't go out in public without getting harassed."

"Do you think she was involved in the judge's death?"

He snorts. "Well, she was there when it happened, wasn't she?"

"Miles, that's enough," my mother commands.

My heart clenches.

"Commander, if these ships keep disappearing and the crews are presumed dead, what are your next steps as the Armada's second in command?" the nasally reporter presses. "What are you going to do with all of these pirates running amok?"

"Finally, an intelligent question." Charles's pretentious tone is unmistakable.

"The people want to know anything they can about your daughter's case," the deep-voiced reporter cuts in. "Are you sure there's nothing else to say?"

"Just that . . ." My father sighs. "We do not condone any of it, obviously. She's put the rest of us in a terrible position and will be dealt with swiftly under the full process of law once she's found. She poisoned the title and the position forever."

I step back in shock as gooseflesh ripples up my arms and down my back. They weren't supposed to believe it or cave into the *lies*. This sick, twisted nightmare was supposed to end the second I stepped onto the dock. The second I stepped inside this house and saw them.

"And we still don't know *why* she's doing any of this?" asks Nichols.

"Obiviously not," Charles mutters.

"Mr. Walker," a fourth, shaky voice starts. "Or, the elder Mr. Walker, I should say. What feelings do you have about the matter?"

There's a long, uncomfortable pause. "Disappointment," Charles deadpans. "What else is there?"

"Betrayal," Miles scoffs. "Having your name tied to scum isn't ideal, now is it?"

"Stop it. That's enough for now," my mother snaps. "I will escort all of you out."

"Good riddance," my father mutters. I recognize the familiar creak of his chair, and I quickly scramble backward and crouch behind the massive potted plant sitting next to the door. He flings it open and storms down the hall.

My mother leads three of the reporters out behind him.

"The public is going to eat them alive once they hear this tomorrow," one of the reporters whispers.

Panic fills my chest so quickly that I nearly lose my balance and fall against the wall. I have to get out. I have to get out and run and hide before any of them see me because . . .

Because they will arrest me. Because they will put me on a pedestal and use my name to show others what happens to traitors.

Where could I even go? There isn't a city in the East that wouldn't hesitate to turn me in. Nobody would believe my side of the story.

I touch the envelope in my pocket. The only one who would believe me is dead.

I press both hands over my mouth and fight back the scream rising in my throat. I could handle losing my title and my name and every friend I've ever known, but not this. Not them.

Anyone but them.

"One last question, please, gentlemen."

"Fine," Miles snaps. "What is it?"

I squeeze my eyes shut as the fourth and final reporter takes a deep breath. "If your sister is indeed involved in these attacks on your ships, what would that mean for the two of you?"

There's another pause, and Charles clears his throat.

"I have no sister."

49

The Reporter

Nine thousand nine hundred ninety-nine; **ten thousand.**

Ten thousand silver coins sit in stacks on the floor of my house.

Warren Chadwick, the strange man dressed in black, kept his word. I did not expect much honesty from the smuggler, but here we are.

He was too prideful to deliver it himself, as I met a man with greasy black hair and tattoos who dumped it on my doorstep and left without saying more than a single sentence to me, but I digress. Money is money. A promise is a promise.

The kettle on the stove begins to hiss, and I quickly jump up to silence it. I grab the last teabag in the tin, which should have been thrown out two days ago, and let it rest in the mug as I retake my seat at my writing desk crammed against the wall. I flip through the leather-bound pocketbook I keep on the corner of my desk and adjust the mug so the handle aligns perfectly parallel to the table's edge.

I hold the book so as not to crease the spine or the binding and carefully look over my notes.

Former Padstow Armada Captain Walker seen fleeing scene of Kahu warzone.

Warzone? Perhaps not.

Kahu Collapse . . . Kahu Catastrophe?

"Catastrophe" was used in the title "Kailean Catastrophe" for the story I wrote about Princess Theadora's disappearance, so perhaps I should try something different.

Missing. Sure. Dead? Almost positively.

Everyone will assume that soon enough.

I twist open the ink capsule on my pen and draw a neat, straight line through the story slug. A handful of others sit on the lines below it.

What stories. What *fun*.

I flick to the next page and scan through the assigned stories for the next two weeks, though none of them are quite as exciting as the mutinous captain from Padstow. Others are taking the stories about how ships from navies across the Eastern Commonwealth are not returning to port, with some reporting smoke plumes rising from the ocean from miles away. Towns are beginning to burn with no soldiers there to protect them. The effects of the Pereculum jailbreak have been devastating. No one knew of its existence until its prisoners began appearing with stories of their time there and chaos elsewhere.

I would kill to speak to the man behind that. I wrote to Chadwick to ask about this strange new member of the crime world responsible for the breakout, but I have not heard from him or seen his bird in weeks.

I stir the teabag and stare at the steam curling from the cup.

Even still, I will always wonder what Captain Walker did to deserve it.

Chadwick was insistent on a story of fraud and exposing the truth, but I believed him. No city with that strong a reputation could stay clean forever, and it felt crass to question it. The money he offered did more than enough talking.

Footsteps crunch on the path just outside my front door, and I pause.

I haven't even risen from my seat when the door flies open, and I am face-to-face with the jailbreaker.

He freezes, and so do I. I blink. He blinks.

The witness sketches of him that came out of Kahu were a poor representation of his age. He's just . . . a *boy*. A boy with symbols inked on his arms and a bone-chilling death count, but a boy nonetheless. Dimples indent his cheeks as he smiles with the charm of a veteran businessman and tilts his head. "Hello."

I stare at the pistol on his left hip and the sword on his right as he steps into my house, favoring his left leg.

"Please pardon my intrusion, but . . . " He notices the stack of coins in the corner. "Oh! That must be Warren's payment."

I blanch. "How do you—"

"He was a colleague of mine until very recently. That is what I came to speak to you about." Dasher crouches in front of the stack and twirls a single coin between his fingers. "I understand you two worked together."

I stutter like a drunk. "Y-yes, that's . . . why do—?"

"Did he happen to tell you if he had a main city of operations?" Dasher puckers his lips like a fish as he studies the coin. "Or perhaps a consistent mailing address?"

"He contacted me out of Midway, initially." I ease back into my chair as my heart pounds like a hammer. "Why do you ask?"

"See, that's the first place I checked for him." Dasher clucks his tongue and flicks the coin in the air, catching and pocketing it. "I fear he may have known I would check there, because I could not find a single trace of him. Nobody has seen him in weeks."

I swallow and dig my nails into my palms. "H-he didn't tell me anything about his whereabouts, and I've only met him in person once. I promise I don't know anything. Please don't hurt—"

"Oh, never!" Dasher spins on the balls of his feet as he stands.

"That isn't why I'm here. I thought I would at least ask about him before proposing my original idea to you."

I watch him nervously as he closes the distance between us with light, deliberate steps. He seems awfully personable for a pirate. For a *killer*.

"I am looking for him so I can cover my bases." His chapped lips curl into a kiddish smile. "He is not a man you want to be enemies with, and I have leverage to draw him out into the open."

"Leverage?"

"Such a powerful tool, don't you think?" His chuckle is light and high-pitched like a bird's call. "This leverage is something—or *someone*, I should say—whom I know he'd come running for in an instant. I also have someone else I'll use to draw Captain Walker out of hiding."

"Captain… *Padstow's* Captain Walker?" I frown. "Why? Why do you care?"

"I won't be specific, but I need a way to send the message to the two of them." His eyes widen as he positions his first two fingers like the barrel of a pistol and presses them against his temple. "I suppose you don't know the true story of what's happened with them over the last two months, but I cannot have them compromising what I've worked to build."

The pieces fall together in my mind. "Well, I don't know where either of them is. The only way to send them both a message is to send random capsules out into the world for them to hear."

"Exactly. I could easily double your pile for helping me with that." He gestures to the stacks of

coins. "If that will sway your decision."

He won't have to tell me twice. I readjust my footing. "Well, logistically—"

"It is all figured out." He tilts his head and stares at my cup of tea and the weak tendrils of steam

curling from the liquid's surface. "I have friends on all corners of the map."

"Do you?"

"I am not a fool. I came prepared."

I stare at the novas, flickering under the lantern light. I lick my lips and nod at Dasher. "What are you planning?"

"A story so powerful that people will talk about it for centuries." He flashes his crooked teeth at me and grips my shoulders. "Because, my reporter friend, what good is a story if no one will read it?"

acknowledgments

I would not have been able to do this without my family. Thank you Mom, for keeping me grounded when I would overthink and overanalyze everything to death. I would have fallen off the boat long ago if it weren't for you. Thank you Dad, for making me smile when I needed it. Your funny messages and memes always seemed to come at just the right time. Emmitt and Noah, I love you guys so much.

I need to give a big shoutout to my aunts and other friends who beta-read this for me. Your feedback truly helped, and I'm grateful for you.

Major, major, MAJOR thanks to my awesome editor Lia, who stuck with me through a long, laborious editing process. It was really tough for us both, but I'm forever grateful for your help and patience.

A big thanks to my little indie author group: Kynsie, Kay, Marthe, Janal, and Sofia. Thank you for your support and for listening to me complain about marketing and other things. I can't wait to read your books.

Another huge thanks needs to go to Lindy, my awesome cover designer who listened to me ramble about cover ideas that absolutely made no sense. Your friendship means so much to me.

My final thank you must go to you for reading this book. I cannot tell you how much it means that you're holding it. I wrote this during my time in college, and I may as well have been raising a baby for how much time, effort, energy, tears, and love that went into it. Thank you for giving it a chance.

about the author

Rylee Stagg is a self-certified English nerd who has two degrees in creative writing and professional and technical writing. She has also dabbled in media writing and served as her college's copyeditor for two semesters. She grew up just outside of Las Vegas and loves basketball, which she insists she could have gone pro in if it weren't for her bum knee. She loves spending time with her family, reading, and discussing books. She has plans for a sequel to Gold Coast, and there are many more stories to come. You can keep up with what she's doing on Instagram: @staggwriter

Stagg also encourages you to leave a review on Amazon and Goodreads if you enjoyed reading. She promises to thank you personally with a handwritten note (not really, but it would mean the world to her).

www.ingramcontent.com/pod-product-compliance
Lightning Source LLC
Chambersburg PA
CBHW051256130726
47987CB00004B/1545